Geoff Ryman

HIM

**ANGRY
ROBOT**

ANGRY ROBOT
An imprint of Watkins Media Ltd

Unit 11, Shepperton House
89-93 Shepperton Road
London N1 3DF
UK

angryrobotbooks.com
twitter.com/angryrobotbooks
A Virgin Birth Can Only Mean One Thing

An Angry Robot paperback original, 2023

Cover by Francesca Corsini
Edited by Simon Spanton Walker and Andrew Hook
Set in Meridien

ISBN 978 1 91520 267 3
Ebook ISBN 978 1 91520 275 8

Printed and bound in the United Kingdom by TJ Books Limited

9 8 7 6 5 4 3 2 1

PRAISE FOR GEOFF RYMAN

"Geoff Ryman has long been one of our finest writers, with no two books the same (or even similar). With *Him*, Ryman rewrites the Greatest Story Ever Told, using all the tools he has developed from his fantasy, science fiction, and historical fiction to craft something new from material so familiar, giving an immediacy and a reality and a shocking sense that we have never encountered this story before, nor this prophet nor his teaching. It's the kind of novel that will win awards and reach hearts and minds and be burnt on bonfires too. A profoundly religious book, in such unexpected ways."

Neil Gaiman

"*Him* feels like the real story at last. Ryman's uncanny ability to get inside people makes this one of the greatest versions of the old story. The family drama, Yeshua's parents and siblings—all the key moments seen as if by lightening—it comes alive in a supremely vivid way. This time for real. It's unforgettable."

Kim Stanley Robinson, award winning author of The Mars Trilogy

"Ryman offers an exceptional journey into the heart of human experience with this profoundly affecting story. Beautifully imagined. It has a transformative, compassionate power. I loved it."

Justina Robson, award nominated author of Silver Screen

"Ryman challenges his readers as he always has, with an enormous, defiant, heart. *Him* is exhilarating and liberating to believer and non-believer alike."

Paul Cornell, author and screenwriter

"Here is the Son of God you never knew. *Him* is shocking, moving, profound and reverent. Only Geoff Ryman could have written this book. It is a masterpiece."

Michael Swanwick, Nebula award-winning author of Stations of the Tide

"Potentially blasphemous, definitely thought-provoking. Ryman asks a simple question and supplies a complex, multifaceted answer that stays with you long after you finish reading."

Antony Johnston, creator of Atomic Blonde

"History is what a living society makes of the past."
Andrea M Berlin

PART 1
HOME

CHAPTER 1
MOTHER

Maryam laboured up the Mount of Olives, wondering how this morning could be so like any other.

From over the walls that lined the road came the sound of mothers calling and children squealing. A gateway groaned open and a woman in an apron threw dirty water onto the street. The servant apologized and was startled when Maryam snarled, "Pour blood on me!"

A human beast of burden struggled down the hill, holding back a cart full of firewood. A sweat-stained rag was wrapped around his head; his face was creased down the middle of his cheeks. His eyes caught hers as he passed: *you think I endure?* Despair in those grey eyes, as if he knew who she was and what had happened. Despair that his own life would only be work, pain, and early death.

Over the flat roofs, the Temple rose like a snowy mountain in sunset, marble and gold. Looking so proud – but it couldn't stop the Romans. What it had was beauty, and what use was beauty? What use was any of it?

* * *

The gate to the house hung open so she slipped in sideways. Their host was waiting in the shade and jumped forward as soon as he saw her.

"What has happened, what has happened?" he demanded.

Maryam felt like a seed popped from an apple, tiny and hard. "Where's the babe?"

The old uncle said, "I didn't wake her. What's going to happen?"

Maryam looked at his anxious, kindly face and found that all of her sympathy had been burned through. "They're going to kill him," she said, and went round the side of the house to mount the steps to the upper floor.

The child Rutit was not asleep but lazed under a blanket, singing to herself. Maryam leant over her and kissed her and said, "Come, Baby, we're going back to be with your mother."

Maryam took the child's blanket, found her tiny sandals, and bundled her up. The uncle was leaning against the doorpost.

"What's this?"

"Don't make me say it," she said.

The host was outraged. "They can't be that stupid. What did the Kohen Gadol do? He's supposed to defend us. Will they stone him?"

Maryam couldn't remember the fancy Greek word. "Some horrible Roman thing."

She pushed past him, but the household had lined the steps and crowded the courtyard. She would have to squeeze past them on the open staircase near the edge. They shouted questions. *You left him alone, cowards, why should you know anything?*

The householder told them, "They're executing him."

The useless cries of dismay or shock. Maryam looked at their faces, round-eyed and undone. They had expected exile, at worst prison. But this? This was without precedent, bad beyond imagining.

She began to walk down the outside of the steps, turning the infant away from the edge.

Someone took her arm and shouted, "Make way! She has a child with her."

Down the steps, across the crammed courtyard, each person touched her or bowed or said, "Mother we are so sorry." Or "Mother be at peace." She realized someone had knelt to kiss her feet. "Pray for us, Mother."

Tears came. "Pray for him!"

CHAPTER 2

THE LIONS OF EDEN

Years before, Yoazar barBeothus rose from cushions and gestured for his niece to sit.

Maryam was still standing, uncertain of how to accomplish that. She was used to dining couches, not cushions on a courtyard pavement.

Yoazar began to roll up his scroll. Maryam plonked herself down like a mattress. Her dress – it looked like Yoazar's tablecloth, all red and blue stripes with tassels. She liked to dress, poor thing.

Yoazar forgot himself in appraisal of his niece. From the front, the girl could be beautiful – those glittering eyes, the long front teeth that made her smile bright and distinctive. From the side she looked like a pigeon – plump cheeks and a beak.

"Uncle." She hauled in a breath, and her smile faltered. "Rabuli. I have some news."

Had she found a husband? Yoazar moved the mountains of his face into something like a smile. "I pray it is good news, Maryam."

"Yes. I suppose." Her eyes flickered downward then back up. "I am with child."

6

Yoazar sagged inwardly. *Oh God. Poor stupid girl – all that learning, see what it does for you? Ah well, it is God's way.*

Her hands twisted the tassels of her tablecloth dress. Maybe she had indeed made it herself from a tablecloth – her father was dead and the family was not prosperous.

Hesitant – normally his niece was too confident. "The… the pregnancy came about in an unusual way."

There is only one way of getting pregnant, and there's nothing unusual about it. A handsome young scribe? Her cousin? Sex with another woman who'd just had sex with her husband? In his years in the courts, Yoazar had heard all of that, and more. He indicated she should help herself to figs and bread. "Unusual how, cousin?" He hoped his voice was sympathetic.

"Well. I didn't do anything." Her hands, her cheeks, all quivering.

What did that mean? Yoazar reached for her hand, but stopped before taking it. "You were forced?"

She shook her head, but she was smiling, almost swollen with joy, her eyes closed as if in prayer.

Then she told him. Angels, annunciations.

Yoazar's hand jerked back. *First her cousin Elisheba with her miracle birth and now this. A fashion for religious mania.*

Women who are unfulfilled, they flap like doves without realizing it. A friend of his mother's would sit in the market, legs apart, skirts hoisted high. A poor pigeon seller finally did what any man would do. Yoazar had helped the simple fellow escape the usual punishment. It was so unfair, given the provocation.

"No point then asking who is the father." Yoazar realized that he'd said that out loud – but perhaps it was just as well. "Can you find a man to support you?"

She looked surprised, then smiled. "It could be that God will protect me."

Sometimes women only thought they were pregnant. *Poor Maryam. The glittery eyes.*

Yoazar rumbled. "Well. There will always be a place for you to live here. What has your mother said?"

She looked downcast then. "I haven't told her yet. I was hoping you would explain to her the wonderful thing that's happened."

Yoazar had worked his way up the priestly hierarchy by taking on difficult instances and helping. (A donation from his supporters to Herod the Great had not gone amiss either). He was shocked by nothing. Human folly, anger, weakness, all of these made him sad and slow, but never angry. He'd long ago realized that God rarely granted miracles to individual people. Religious authority had to be used sparingly. "Maryam. I will do everything I can."

Her hand was on her belly and her face was cocked to one side. "I felt it. There was a strange sensation – a kind of cramp and a warmth. I could tell something – unusual? – had happened. To be honest, I thought it was sickness."

Perhaps it is. Women get growths and die. Yoazar found he had nothing further to say. His servant girl flapped out of the kitchen with some mint water. This time of year, after the rains, delicious spring water trickled through the Kohen Gadol's fountain.

The Kohen Gadol and his niece talked for a while about Maryam's mother Avigayil; about how after all these years she still mourned her Damascene husband.

"If you or your mother ever need anything," Yoazar began.

Maryam held up a hand against the offer. She's tough,

Yoazar thought, and that comes neither from her father nor her mother.

Finally the priest apologized but he had work to do. "Peace be to you, Maryam."

The overdressed, haughty little thing marched out of his house bunched like a fist. *She knows I won't tell her mother about the angel. She knows what I think of her.*

Yoazar's wife Tara stood waiting, half hidden behind the pillars. He saw his wife's anxious face and flicked her forward with a wave of his hand. "So she's told you this nonsense as well."

Tara nodded once, hugging herself; she was the twin of Maryam's mother. "She believes it."

They were members of the Kohanim. There was no question of someone in the family or their class being held up to public shame.

Tara sighed. "She really is the most moral woman."

"She's mad. I don't suppose you know of any man mad enough to marry her?"

Something about his wife's bunched cheeks. *Ah. The seriousness, the shaking, the sideways approach.*

"There's Yosef," she said.

My goodness. The cleverness of women. Yoazar blurted out a laugh. "He's crazy enough."

Tara seemed to melt with relief. She laughed too. "He'll believe her."

They both laughed. Yoazar loved his wife.

Yosef had gone about proclaiming that Adam and Hawa were not a man and a woman.

Plainly a man could not give birth to Hawa as Adam did

(so Yosef said). Hawa was called helper, companion, servant, even soldier – "ezer" – the male form of the word, and thus neutral of course. But for a woman?

Yosef had said in public in the Place of Gentiles, (and here Yoazar had felt faint and faltered) that Adam had not been a man and Hawa had not been a woman.

Yosef was like an ever-blooming flower of foolishness. He was a Levite, with a role to play in the temple, but he had no authority. He had said in public, declaiming not one hundred steps from the Beth Yahu, that Adam and Hawa had the sex – or sexlessness – of angels. They were neither or both, and since they were immortal, plainly they had no need to reproduce.

The audience were devout people waiting to enter the Court of Women. Yoazar had heard them growl, so forced himself to laugh and airily say, "Oh, Yosef, that is so clever, you keep us so amused."

Yosef held a finger to the sky. "Amusing? Kohen Gadol, for me, it is a catastrophe." You could see in the man's swimming eyes that he meant it. "The loss of half our selves is a separation as devastating as Babel."

In the crowd, smiling grimly was Eyanaphon, Eyanaphon the Sadduci, so young and small, beautiful like a woman, with dark gazelle's eyes and something eager in his face. He was already leading young fierce men in immaculate white. Yoazar had known then: *there will be trouble.*

Yosef came back the next day to say the same thing. Eyanaphon was not there, but his party were. And they said, "You talk of such things in public?"

Before Yosef could answer they said, "And how would we have children? You are counselling the end of the Yehudai?" Followed by: "You think God wants his sons to perish from the Earth?"

The term "Son of God" – barYahu in the Common Tongue – simply meant you worshipped the God of Yisrael and to do that (unless you were one of those Shomeronai who worshipped at that mountain) you had to live in Yehud. You had to be near the Temple or at least make pilgrimages to it.

Women, of course, could not be Sons of God.

Yosef looked miffed. "It is not for all. But. If a man were to take a knife to his private parts, he would be moving closer to Godliness."

Some people laughed. Some shook their heads. Yosef was a Levite; a member of a tribe with complex relations with the priestly clans. He had gone beyond bounds.

One of Yoazar's innumerable cousins nodded knowingly and muttered to him sideways. "They say he tried to do it to himself. Uh! That unspeakable thing, when he was younger."

Yoazar loomed over Yosef and said, in a low voice. "You are coming with me now before you get yourself killed." That was only a slight exaggeration.

A day later, a story started to spread that a boy of thirteen, at that crucial age, inspired by Yosef's lunacy had done this dreadful thing, emasculated himself. It couldn't be true. The Kohen Gadol would have been told at once. But people love stories that give them a chance to be outraged.

Yosef was in danger of being stoned. Yoazar had attendants arrest Yosef and hold him in rooms in his own house. Yoazar then went to the Sanhedrin in their circular room at the east end of the Stoa, and asked: can anyone name this thirteen-year-old? Could anyone take Yoazar to him? Yoazar had only recently ascended and was still in a period when everyone wanted him to do well. So they talked to him, and asked questions for him. He visited the most sensible of the families.

No name. No boy. In each house he said, "I am beginning to think this is just a story."

Yosef barLevi was to be sent into exile.

Dangerous religious radicals were sent in exile out of Yehud, north even beyond Shomeron, to the Galil. The people there were crude, rough, not really Beni Yisrael at all. The land had been forcibly converted to belief in the God of Yisrael by the Hasmonean kings only ninety years before. And the way the Galilai spoke! Blurring consonants and vowels.

There had even been a suggestion that the Galilai be barred from the Temple lest they mispronounce a word in the liturgical tongue and offend God.

God moves through talk.

That's what the Perisayya said, at least those who lived among the elite of Yerusalam.

Most of them spoke Greek too. The word hairesis simply meant school of thought, not something to be punished. And how many schools of thought flourished: the Perisayya who argued that the spoken word had the value of the written, the Sadducai who ran things, and of course the saintly Essenai who now mostly lived in the wild (who just to add to the richness also called themselves Zadokites, basically the same word as Sadducai).

Yosef was given the freedom of Yoazar's courtyard.

Yosef's breath smelled of the meat that was caught between his teeth, and of a dental abscess. On days when he didn't ritually bathe for the Temple, a stink as sharp as a dagger thrust itself out of his armpits.

Holding his breath, Yoazar said, "We are deeply saddened by your troubles."

Yosef was silent, cradling his belly as if proud of it. Two miracle births, thought Yoazar.

Yosef rejected wine, even much watered. Yoazar made a point of filling a pitcher of water from his little fountain. "As fresh as the rain. It is such a luxury when someone doesn't have to go fetch it. And it means this house has living water for the miq'va."

Yoazar hoped for a good response – Yosef was famously exact on purification for priests in the Temple.

But Yosef's lips turned inward and his beard bristled. He was a smart man, and no smart man should ever be utterly discarded. Yoazar looked in the man's black eyes and saw loneliness. Swallows screeched at each other over the water.

Yoazar poured him a cup. "A very interesting point you raised. You point out that in Eden, the animals are paired, but Adam not, and that what he envies is the companionship."

Yosef's pudding face was unmoved.

So Yoazar kept talking. "The point being that marriage was created for companionship. Not reproduction."

"Exactly so. Creatures without death, why would they need to reproduce? How would they reproduce? Do you think angels copulate?" Yosef's lip curled.

He hates sex, Yoazar thought. *Some men are not male.* "So. Marriage existed before Hawa disobeyed. It existed for companionship. Have I understood, Yosef?"

The man eyed him suspiciously. "If you understood, you would agree with me."

"Maybe I do. At least in part. Yosef, I can't do anything about the exile. It could have been worse, but Nazareth – there's nothing there. Though there are worse things than living among simple people in the hills."

Yosef chin was tilted upwards, as if to pour tears back into his eyes. "There's nothing worse than being in exile from the Temple. Though of course if God was in Eden it is clear He cannot be only in the Temple. He is a God who covers the whole world."

The man is a quagmire of original ideas.

"I will do what I can to make your life easier there. I will send you food, things to read. But you must help me out. Maryam, my wife's niece, she's confused, she's with child. Would you marry her? For companionship?"

Like the lions of Eden.

"You want her in exile too," said Yosef.

"I want her protected." *Though I can't see you protecting anyone.* "To be fair, a man of God should know how she says the child came about."

There the Kohen Gadol paused. He could not bring himself to state such an offensive thing. "You know the heathen Egyptians, their goddess Isis? A god whispers in her ear and she magically conceives a child. Without a father."

Something happened in Yosef's face, a wide-eyed settling that Yoazar recognized as sympathy.

"You are a learned man, Yosef, a kind one. Maryam needs that. And, as I say, we will make sure that you both are comfortable. We'll ease the exile in any way we can. There would be no question of your having to labour in the fields. You'll have food. We will send scriptures and tracts. Sadly, of course, we cannot exchange letters or visit. It is exile. It will be hard. I'm sorry."

On balance Yoazar thought that Yosef had been won over by the promise of not having to work. And the reading.

* * *

Maryam's mother Avigayil was packing.

The forecourt was laid out with wooden ladles, sandals and two dusty pots. On the stones, Avigayil folded clothes and tablecloths, shaking her head. Throughout the packing she had hardly blinked, but stared as if her very eyes had gone pale from shock.

Maryam was counting plates – some of their fine Greek tableware – and knives.

"Oh, Maryam, Maryam."

Maryam gave her a quick hug. "Ami. Everything comes with a cost. Feel the child, Ami. No. Feel my stomach. This child comes from God. This child will be something – it is not for me to say. This exile is welcome to me, Ami. It will give me a chance to pray, to contemplate, to study."

"You talk like a man," said her mother.

Maryam's face wobbled as if shaking off a fly. "Tuh. Married to Yosef, I will have to BE a man. Oh, Ami! Come, come. For me that's good."

"You'll have no friends. No one to talk to. No family nearby. And Yerusalam, Yerusalam will be forbidden to you. How can you get close to God when you can't visit the Temple?"

This was getting repetitive. "God is everywhere, Ami."

Avigayil's cheeks wattled back and forth. "No, no, no Maryam, God rests only in the Temple. When the Temple of Solomon was destroyed the glory of God was seen moving towards the Mount of Olives."

Maryam stopped folding floor cloths. "Ami. Why would God need to go to the Mount of Olives?"

"It's obvious. It's the second highest mountain and so is closer to Heaven."

It was all Maryam could do to stop rolling her eyes. "Ami, could you go through my dresses for me? You know I have no taste. You pick those that you want me to wear. And whenever I wear them I can think – Ami picked these for me. After all, I no longer have to dress to get a husband."

"Oh, Maryam!"

"And practical things too for a rural life. Ropes, towels, hammers, lamps. I rely on you, Ami." Maryam gave her mother another hug that steered her towards the staircase. "You are my good practical mother. Give the rest of my things to Rut and Eenie, or to the poor."

"You won't be allowed to write to me!" Maryam's mother had clenched her two shaking hands together and had begun to cry.

"Ami. I have nothing to say!" Maryam's smile felt like the wings of a dove ascending. Her mother laboured her way up the external staircase, hand on the wall.

A cart rumbled into the courtyard, bearing Yosef and his goods. The cart had been loaned by Yoazar who had also sent his servant Mikael to drive it. It was nearly empty, except for the scrolls of The Miq'ra.

Maryam shook her head. "Ah, Yosef, Yosef."

He'd brought no furniture. Not one table, no dining couches. Did he eat on the floor?

"I'm not one of these women who care about such things. But…" Maryam had to laugh. "We have been told the house is empty. We'll need something on which to serve food, something to sit on, and something to cook with. Bedding. And it's all got to get into that cart."

But Maryam admired him – Yosef added up. He was whole – lazy, obsessive, observant of the Temple purity laws and otherwise unwashed, but he cared about scripture. Only scripture maybe. There were worse things.

Yoazar's servant spoke with a voice like boulders rolling down a hill. "My master has furniture. What do you need?"

Everything.

Maryam had to list them. "Dining couches. A central table. Folding tables. My aunt has already sent us hangings for doorways. Bedding. Amphorae, a cauldron."

Yosef hung his head, nibbling his beard.

They unloaded what little was in the cart; a few cushions and old clothes and Yosef's scrolls. And his Shabbat lamp, in the old style made of fine black clay. His fingers trembled with worry over the delicacy of the parchment and papyrus. Then the cart thundered its way back out of the gate.

Avigayil came back with the dresses. "Good day to you, Yosef barLevi." She sounded as if she had a toothache.

It's what you said to strangers. It was funny how much Yosef dismayed Maryam's mother. The reverse of the desirable son-in-law: poor, smelly, ugly, no prospects and in exile for being too wrong-headed to be tolerated.

"Ami! These are beautiful! My blue embroidery on blue. I don't suppose we have any smocks and aprons to spare? I will be making my own bread."

"You'll dress like a servant."

"There, there, Ami. Aprons and work clothes, please."

"Not even a dowry. With child. No one knowing who the father is." Avigayil start to sob. "Marrying him." Her mother waved a horrified hand in Yosef's direction.

It was such an insulting way to talk about your son-in-law that Maryam could not stop herself chuckling. "Ami-dear. Your mouth! Work clothes, Ami. Something that I can stain with soup."

Off went Avigayil heaving with sobs. She had to lean on the door lintel to keep herself upright.

Then Yosef began to sob too.

Perfect. There was perfection in how far this was from anything those two wanted.

Maryam had kept talking to Aunt Tara for weeks about how clever and original Yosef's teaching was. An intelligent woman would have understood after three sentences beginning with the word "Yosef". Yoazar thought it was his idea too. They all felt brilliantly clever. She patted her tablecloths flat as if they were her family's heads.

The only person who was getting what she wanted was Maryam.

On the road, Yosef walked stoutly beside the mule.

His chest was puffed out as if he was guiding the cart and protecting Maryam. Mikael was actually guarding them – a big, broad-shouldered brute whom her uncle trusted.

Within a league, Yosef's soft feet were blistered. Maryam got down from the cart to let him ride.

"Just. Just for a while. We'll keep swapping," he said, ashamed. "How can your feet stand it?"

"I had to walk to market every day." Maryam sauntered. As a young female person, Maryam had scandalized her family by insisting on walking over the hills unattended.

Yoazar's man halted the mule and glared at Yosef. "The lady is with child." Mikael looked ready to throw Yosef down.

Maryam's laughter was bird-like. "Let him be, poor man." She held Mikael with her eyes. "He's not up to any of this." The servant shook his head. Maryam clucked at the mule. "Come on. Sooner we get going, the sooner we arrive." Maryam began to lead them. "Nothing will hurt this child."

CHAPTER 3

PARTHENOGENESIS

It wasn't as if Nazareth was on top of a mountain range.

Just a hill, quite hot when they arrived. The village was a day's walk from the lake – the ocean itself was almost as close. Trees survived only near houses or along the terraces where people watered them. Tamarisk, olives, a few dusty palms looking like brokeback old men.

Other than that, white dust and white stones with sharp edges. The track wound its zigzag way up through terraces growing mostly barley. The walled steps looked like a staircase for a god.

Their house of exile, owned by another cousin who rented out the land, had been abandoned for a few years. There was no courtyard or outer wall, and most of the lower floor was a kind of byre with only three walls, entirely open on one side. It was a barn.

"All this light," said Maryam and gestured to the missing wall. "In summer you'll be able to read until sunset."

The floor was exposed bedrock, bare but for the floury dust and grey straw. The stove was good, enclosed in a cone of fieldstone. No chimney, but the cone merged with the wall and belched the smoke outside the house. Instead of an external staircase only an internal ladder led to the two upstairs rooms. There was no cistern and the village well was many houses away. If there had ever been a store of firewood or charcoal, it had all been taken.

Mikael helped them clear the old hay and sweep the floors. Rats scurried out of the straw. Only when it was clean did Maryam begin to unpack the food.

"We have the cheese. We have the olives. We have the bread." Tara had also packed limestone jars of flour, salted meat, salted fish and an amphora of oil. "Tonight we can eat cold."

In winter, they would have to abandon the byre except for cooking. It was too open to the hillside wind. The upstairs rooms were small enough to be lined with the tapestries that Tara had given them. Those rooms would be warm.

That night Mikael ate with them, and then unbidden unrolled his blanket onto the floor of the byre.

Maryam and Yosef went to bed as the last of the sun sank. They had some oil for lamps, but they didn't want to waste it. They fumbled up the ladder in the very last of the light. Yosef paused half in and half out of the upper story.

"I'll be a very good father," he said. "I like children."

"I'm sure you will be."

"I would be happy if we had more children."

"Oh. Well, we'll have to have sex to do that."

He looked agonized, glanced downstairs, whispered. "We could do something else."

"Could we. What would that be?"

He squirmed, pulled himself up, spoke in a voice like the wind. "I could give you the seed."

Maryam burst out laughing. "Oh, Yosef."

"I mean not that. I make it and then. Hand it to you."

That just made Maryam laugh more. The series of images it presented to her. "Well, that's a possibility, yes."

"I will take very good care of the baby."

She believed that – he sounded so solemn. And she mustn't be cruel or hard. She looked at his poor round perplexed face, as boggled-eyed as a frog and found that she was fond of it.

"I know you will," she said. "Thank you." She cupped his hairy chin in her hand and pointed to his room and then to hers. He looked relieved, which made her laugh more. Yosef made her laugh.

There was another exile living within walking distance.

He insisted on being called Raba, Great One. Like Yosef, he was famous for his learning, wild ideas and a tendency to indignation. Unlike Yosef, he actually had followers, other Perisayya from places south of Yerusalam. It was a long way for them to travel.

A village boy was sent to call on Yosef, a skinny lad of about twelve years. He gawped at the exiles, couldn't speak, and finally gabbled out, "Rabuli says come visit him." Then he turned to run.

Though pregnant, Maryam lunged after him and seized his arm. "Where does your master live, boy? What's your name? Speak up. Your name?"

He stammered it out.

Maryam said, "Yehushua. Fine." God preserves. "Yehushua. Sit, have some water and some bread. Then go calmly and tell the teacher that we will be happy to pay respects."

No time of invitation – this teacher she suspected, simply

wanted someone to attend upon him. "Tell him we will visit tomorrow morning."

After the boy left, she muttered: "I wonder if anyone else calls him Rabuli?"

The next morning, Maryam and Yosef visited.

They found the gate to the Raba's house open and walked into his courtyard and waited. This house did have all of its walls and the courtyard was walled too, shutting out any breeze. The sun rose until it was too hot to wait any longer, and they went home.

They went back in the evening of the same day and waited outside the house, looking at its closed doors and its two narrow windows. No one moved past them to see if they were there.

"It's getting dark," murmured Yosef. They got back home with no food and went straight to bed.

Yosef said, "I think I remember who he is now. Achaikos the Perisa. I don't understand how they can be the ones to argue for more flexible interpretation and then be the ones who never stop quoting rules. Ones that, frankly, they've made up."

"How strange to invite us and just leave us standing there."

"Oh, we will have done something wrong when we arrived. What we wore, the hour, the day. I have no patience."

A flash of steel. Maryam liked that.

The boy Yehushua came again. This time Yosef strode out to meet him. "Please tell this teacher that my wife is expecting a child. It is difficult, even dangerous, for her to visit. Especially to stand waiting in the hot sun. We look forward to meeting. But perhaps after the birth of the child."

The boy looked down, embarrassed perhaps at talk of pregnancy. Maryam found herself stroking his head.

They had to live here, find a way. Maryam asked, "Who is your father, child?"

"His name's Platon." A Greek name. "He's a tekton." Greek word. A builder.

"There's work here?"

The boy shook his head. "In Sepphoris. Or there was. He got in a fight." The boy sighed. Maybe fights were a problem.

Sepphoris, the new town only an hour's walk away. About six years before it had been burnt in the revolt. Now, lots of rebuilding to be done. Herod had moved in a new population, Greek-speakers but devout. Their new houses were all said to have ritual baths. Maryam was relieved – the boy's family would be prosperous.

"How do people worship here?"

"My father built a meeting house. It's stone. He made a carving of the Ark of the Covenant."

"He's a talented man," said Maryam.

The boy almost sniggered. "He calls himself a Naggar." In the Common Tongue Naggar meant Learned Man, or a skilled man so it was used for craftsman as well.

The boy nodded at the scrolls. "You're a Naggar too. A real one."

The Nazaredai only knew that Maryam and Yosef were some kind of criminals who had displeased the powerful.

The couple had no money to buy firewood, olives or smiles. There was no reason to interact with them.

Maryam felt mean but she couldn't help but think that these people were not really Beni Yisrael.

At the well, she would greet them in a way that she was sure would have got at least a polite response back home. These women pulled their headscarves across their faces, as if she were a man behaving improperly. They would fall silent when she approached. Or, worse, sometimes they started to run all at once, sandals flapping, sounding like startled birds taking wing. Yehudai women would have been ashamed to be both so timid and so rude.

The food here was different. Tiny black fish were bent into a circle and stuck on frameworks of twigs to bake in the sun. Covered with flies. It would be like eating smelly shoes held together by bones.

Their bread was unleavened, flat, translucent. They left it to dry on the same bare rock that their animals walked over.

The faces. The faces were strange, high cheeked, raw. The woman stared as if in horror. It wasn't Maryam who horrified them, or not only Maryam. She saw them from a distance – they looked at life with that same unblinking stare.

Perhaps they were cowed by their men – bearded, potbellied, scowling, strutting. The males all looked like thieves to Maryam, untutored and aggressive.

She once saw a group of them, evidently thinking this was fun, holding a man by his wrists who was trying to laugh as they smacked his face. Their tight smiles and narrow eyes were shared sideways among them.

The villagers dried little cakes of shit in aerated cones for their musty fires. Maryam had to hope it was animal dung only.

She quietly decided that they would not eat village food.

Praise God that Yoazar's cart arrived at least once a week with flour, oil, bread, and olives.

Mikael would always stay the night. He asked if they were well, fixed holes in the roof, or shook his head at the location of the house right on bare rock. He burned refuse and piled up small stones into a cone around an olive sapling that Maryam planted in a cleft in the ground. Mikael was huge, tall, silent, and he seemed to care for them both, asking slow questions in sonorous voice. "You have made arrangements for the birth? We can send a woman to help." Otherwise they were alone, but left alone.

A family without land and without walls. The Nazaredai walked to their distant terraces with shovels or hoes over their shoulders and eyed Yosef in his byre, reading scrolls. "Naggar Naggar," they said and laughed.

Maryam had to be her own midwife.

It was an easy pregnancy and a swift birth, the blessing of living an active life even though the aging mother was in her late twenties.

Maryam was balancing a jug full of water on her head, carrying it from the distant public well, when a sudden folding, unfolding and a cramp told her that the time had come. She drank much of the water in the jar, went back for more. There was a woman at the well ahead of her. Maryam said she was about to give birth and needed to get home quickly. Could she draw water first?

The woman didn't reply except to lower her own bucket into the well, and before hauling it up she gave Maryam a mean little smile of victory. *You wait your turn.*

The baby got revenge by bursting the waters.

The woman stared appalled as the dust under Maryam

went grey in a spreading sheet. "God forgive me," said the woman in a hobbling version of the Common Tongue.

"Pray. He might," said Maryam.

The woman helped her home, and carried her jug, but once inside she snooped. She looked at the scrolls, the ink stains, the piled oily dishes, the imported plates and the dust: criminals.

"Ah! You're here to help us," Yosef exclaimed, which was cunning. The woman started as if caught out, and scampered away.

Maryam climbed up the ladder, singing to herself. She felt a kind of cushioned certainty that God would make all things well. She spoke to the unborn as if on a ladder into heaven. "Come Little One come, come." *The one who was prophesied.*

Yosef helped her lie down. He shook with a kind of panic.

"Calm, Yosef. Think. Whatever happens is God's will, and you of all people should be reconciled."

"I don't know what to do." He looked so helpless. Maryam wasn't sure what he knew about pregnancy, or what he would do if she died. He looked so forlorn that Maryam stroked his cheek. "It will be fine, Yosef. No harm can come." He fled down the ladder.

One wrench forced a howl of agony from Maryam's lips. She prayed that God would understand it was her animal spirits that had cried out but not her mind. Her head was reconciled. With clenching and what felt like tearing, the newborn almost shot out of her, landing halfway down the bed, still tied to her.

Yosef came back in but now calm and slow. He had a knife, cherry red and hot – how had he built a fire, why did he think a blazing knife was necessary? – and sliced through the cord. It sizzled. He cradled the infant onto her, lowered it onto her covered breast, and then left her alone as if he really didn't want to glimpse any part of her naked. Maryam looked down, her face feeling twisted and lumpy from pain.

The child was a girl – well the baby had no father, so what else could she possibly be? Pink, soft, rumpled, smooth. Enough of a miracle, enough of a miracle for anyone.

"You are Avigayil," Maryam said. "Yes, you are. You are my little Avigayil." She had the thought: *you look so much like me.*

In the Kodesh haKadashim only a swelling in the rock showed where the Aron should have been.

Yoazar entered alone, slipping sideways through the rough, thick hanging. The room was almost empty, its walls as bare and dark as the unknown itself.

He put the shabbat lamp on the table made of brass that was polished until it looked like gold. He was about to turn to bring in the clay vessels, blood of the lamb and the blood of the bull, to atone for sin.

And then stood stock still because the room was not empty.

No one ever dared ask HaKohen haGadol what he saw in the Holy of Holies and he would not have answered them if they did. But if his mirror had asked him, he might have said. "I have seen nothing. That is not how the Lord works."

Through the smoke from the lamp, something moved. The scriptures spoke of a cloud of God.

It was as if the whole room was breathing. The breath trembled. Sighing. Then Yoazar began to hear, or rather almost hear, a creaking sound, a bit like new leather. As if someone was trying not to cry.

The room was full of grief, grief in the air, in the stone, grief that sunk deep into Yoazar's bones, grief he felt not for one tragedy, but hundreds, thousands, millions, an avalanche of loss.

Yoazar's mind was not adequate to hold it. He turned away – was this his task and was he failing? It was said false priests died in the Kodesh haKadashim. Was this what killed them?

The grief clarified into the sound of one child wailing, a child who had lost its parents, lost its home. Without thinking Yoazar reached out towards it and heard himself say, "Poor thing. Poor little thing."

Not long after, Yoazar was removed from office.

CHAPTER 4

WHY BOY? WHY GIRL?

Even from earliest days, the babe would eye Maryam steadily.

The child Avigayil seemed to be counting the parts – hands, legs, face – that had joined to make her, as if the infant knew that Maryam had produced this child entirely out of herself.

Maryam began to feel in the weight of that calm stare something she could only call God. God, Maryam was certain, looked out through those infant eyes. The child didn't cry ever. She signalled for food by smacking her lips. She indicated with a sniff that she needed to wee – it sounded a bit dismissive as if Maryam were a servant. Avigayil did not like messes.

By the child's first birthday, Maryam had begun to talk to the infant as if she were an adult.

"So what do we do with Yosef, Avigayil? Do we reward him? That idea of his. To have another child. Would that that bother you?"

The infant looked like an old man, fat and sleepy. *What's that got to do with me? For you to decide. I will be in charge no matter what happens.* Or something like, from the infant's solemnity.

"Well, if you have a little brother or sister you'll have to be nice to them."

The babe turned her head towards her slowly and blew a bubble of thick resistant spit. *Nice? Oh for God's sake, this has nothing to do with niceness.*

The child was right. Maryam had meant something else. "You mustn't overpower them."

Perhaps, just perhaps one deep breath like a sigh meant: *That's their problem, not mine.*

Yosef didn't talk to Avigayil at all. Indeed, he hardly looked at her. He would slide around her like oil on water.

One night in summer, on the roof next to Yosef looking at stars, Maryam said to him, taking his hand, "You must talk to Avigayil more. Hold her a bit. You're the closest thing she's got to a father."

He seemed to shrink. "I should. I must." He was prone to guilts; ridden by internal demands; quibbling with himself over points of behaviour; as distanced from himself as he was from sex.

Grimly determined to do the right thing.

So Yosef started to read the Torah to Avigayil, though she could not yet speak. Perhaps he saw the adult lurking behind her eyes as well.

He slumped onto the floor, scroll on his lap and read aloud to the crib. He didn't have anything else to say. So the language that the infant Avigayil most heard was liturgy.

Yosef began with the book of Bereshit, and he would explain as he went, explain how everyone else had got it wrong.

It! Was! So! Important!

That people understood that sweeping a house clean of crumbs from leavened bread was designed to make people think about the long months of starvation that the children of Yisrael endured, endured for freedom, for righteousness. That could only come from the heart.

Yosef drove his finger into the floor like a nail.

The child appraised him. *Don't get so excited. You're right, of course.* Her eyes moved back and forth to the empty hearth. *We have no firewood.*

Avigayil seldom wetted herself or cried in the night.

She regarded her own faeces first with what appeared to be astonishment and then lip-curling fastidiousness. The only time she howled was when she was left dirty. The first time Maryam used the pot in front of her in the byre by candlelit, the child eyed her steadily.

Immediately after that, Avigayil began to crawl, and in a matter of days was able to stomp by herself to behind the stove where the pot was hidden. Maryam was sure that the child had learned to walk so that she could use the potty.

As Yosef read to her great rolling waves of scripture the child would sigh, or incline her head, or sit forward, one ear turned towards him. Watching her, Maryam would feel a settling, a bit like trickling sweat. Was the child understanding what Yosef read, understanding the Torah? Maryam had no way of knowing if that was usual.

When the child was eighteen months old, the boy Yehushua came again.

He announced that his teacher congratulated them on the birth of their daughter, and would be pleased to see them. Maryam thought to herself: *After a year? Many thanks for your kindness.*

Yosef barked without looking at the boy. "Tell him that my wife is with child again, so we'll have the same problem as two years ago. Tell your master that we will be very pleased to see him any time he wishes to visit."

The boy looked at Avigayil; Avigayil looked at the boy.

Her sleepy eyes went wide, she leaned forward and her jaw dropped, as if she had never seen such a thing. The boy was tall for his age, his torn tunic scarcely covering his thighs. His long arms, already gnarled from work, dangled from shoulders that were both bony and unnaturally wide. From the side he was a twig; from the front, he was a door.

When he left; the infant wailed and reached out with her hand.

"Avigayil?" Maryam was surprised and worried, then picked her up. The infant howled. "She wants a suitor," said Maryam, trying to be amused.

Yosef bristled, his face puffed up. "She wants other children."

The next day Yehushua came back and said the teacher had invited them to come late afternoon before sunset, evidently determined that they visit him. Yosef thanked him without looking up from his reading. Avigayil's eyes opened wide then rumpled shut. She screamed when the boy left. Something else she had never done before.

Yosef's shoulders sagged and he looked up from his scroll. "We are too alone. She is too alone."

Maryam gave birth to a son, Yakob.

It was a difficult, thrashing birth that lasted long into the night and made Maryam feel that she was trapped in a place where time had stopped.

For months afterwards, the newborn screamed all night. Yakob pissed, shat, vomited and came out in seeping rashes. He was an unintelligent little thing, almost uninhabited. Maryam felt as if the soul had gotten lost, missed the road into his eyes.

"Oh, Avigayil, what we going to do with your brother?"

Avigayil moved nothing – no breathing, no blinking, and no nodding. *You will endure. Most infancies are like that.*

"He's Yosef's son."

Avigayil looked away. And then she said in a tiny, piping serious voice, "And yours."

Only later did Maryam realize the infant had spoken aloud.

Maryam kept talking to herself. "You spoilt us. You were too easy."

Was the infant nursing a half-smile? *I am about to get very difficult indeed.*

Only later, lying next to Yosef, did Maryam say. "I think Avigayil spoke today. I think she corrected me."

Yosef grunted. "You always think Avigayil talks to you."

"Then why do I know what her voice sounds like?" Maryam began to feel a sensation of life itself trickling.

Avigayil would lean on the crib, made clumsily of sticks. She would twist the bark in her pudgy hands and begin with furious baby strength, to strip it. She would peer and peer at her baby brother, saying nothing, peer all day sometimes, not smiling, not scowling; not playing or being cruel when Maryam's back was turned. Avigayil was pondering Yakob, especially when Maryam changed or bathed him.

Maryam did notice when Avigayil began to use, over and

over, the liturgical word for "Why?" The child asked why, even if she could not understand the answer.

"Why boy? Why girl?"

"Because God made us like that." Maryam was folding clothes, thinking quickly – *isn't Avigayil young to be talking?* "Well. Not actually. When God first created us there were no women. No men." The truth according to Yosef.

Then Maryam added the truth according to Maryam, "But I didn't need a man to make you." Should she say: *You are special. You were sent by God?*

"That," said Avigayil, and pointed to Yakob's penis.

Something unhealthy. After that Maryam covered up the infant boy. But whenever she tried to bathe the baby, Avigayil was suddenly at her elbow.

By age three, Avigayil was joining in the boy's games.

Yehushua was by then fifteen years old, far too old to play with a little girl, but for Avigayil he seemed to be a cross between Moses and Samson – strength, power. She gaped at him as if he were a hero, watched him run, play, or fight. She learned that he was not awkward and shy with other boys. His discomfort around adults was a sign of that strength.

Avigayil tried to join in their games. Was rebuffed. Tried again. Ran back and forth shadowing players, as if she had the wheel to be rolled.

Finally they allowed her to pitch sandals. She had no shoes, except the ones she'd grown on the soles of feet, the thick hard skin. Yehushua loaned her one of his sandals to throw – a misshapen platter with straps.

The trick was to toss the sandal and spin it at the same

time so it skidded farthest across the stone. She had to use both hands and swing from the hips to toss it. The sandal would arch high and land flat. She always lost; the boys would laugh. Once Yehushua had to tell them not to pick on her. That, strangely, earned him a baleful glare from her. But it had effect – after that the boys would urge her on. "That's it, Avigayil. Throw hard, not high. Throw low." They let her play with them. She walked as if trying to break the bedrock with her heels. She grew plump and dogged.

None of that was remotely like Maryam had been as a child. Maryam hadn't liked boys – they'd seemed stupid, unnecessary, abrupt, even bullying. Maryam had avoided them and sought out other girls to play with. There were girls in the village but, for Avigayil, it was as if girls did not exist. She ran with the boys.

Yosef finished performing the whole of The Miq'ra.

And since he did not know how to talk to Avigayil or now to Yakob, Yosef started to read aloud all over again. This second performance was a continual battle.

"I don't believe Abraham was that old," said Avigayil.

"Why did he want a baby?" she asked.

"Why didn't he just stay with Sarah?"

Maryam had loved scripture from earliest childhood, but she had always accepted it. It had seemed so obvious to her that it would be sad if Sarah could not bear Abraham's children.

Later:

"Why would anyone kill someone because they wanted his coat? The Beni Yisrael are no more righteous than anyone else."

There was something inhuman about the infant's incomprehension of human feelings. Avigayil had indeed been alone too much, Maryam decided. But surely her new brother was now company?

Yosef: "Perhaps that's part of the story. That God choses Yisrael not because we are better, but because he had to choose someone to make an example of."

"Why?"

"Well, maybe God loves all people the same."

"He doesn't love the Beni Yisrael?"

"He loves the Beni – by that you mean both Northerners and Southerners – but maybe not more than anyone else."

"That explains it."

"Explains what?"

The child's gaze was utterly steady. "The terrible things that keep happening to the Beni Yisrael." She smacked her hands together as if knocking off dust from them.

Yosef puffed up, but now with a kind of humour. He looked up at Maryam and said, "It's good we are in exile. That child would get us all killed. How old is she? Four?"

She was three.

Whenever Mikael's cart arrived the Raba would show up at their gate twiddling his beard while the food was still being unloaded.

Once, Mikael was shouldering up bags of flour and Yosef was cradling two already baked loaves of bread. The teacher moved out of his way and grinned sheepishly. Mikael bore down on him with heavy, meaningful looks, but for the Raba, Mikael was just a servant while he was a guest. Guests didn't work.

Little Avigayil came out and tried to shoulder a bag of flour and failed. Then she tried to lift up a linen roll that would be full of dried dates and somehow managed to get it over her shoulders like a yoke. Mikael stared open mouthed as the tiny child managed to stagger into the house with it. Yosef came out and started to recite. "You shall earn your bread by the sweat of your brow." He was not in a good mood.

Mikael helped move the dining couches to make room for the Raba, to share the bread and dates. The teacher began to question Mikael about his master, his household. Did Yoazar prosper?

"I wouldn't know," replied the big man. "It's not my place to ask such questions."

"Ah I enquire merely as a well-wisher. How is he faring?"

"Better than you," replied the servant. "His household grows more every day."

"Really. How is it filled, with whom?"

Little Avigayil folded her arms and leaned her head sideways, and pushed her lips over to one side of her face. Maryam recognized the gesture at once – the child was deliberately overstating her confusion, miming to make it apparent.

Mikael answered, "With praise and respect."

"How wonderful. Whose? The Romans I expect. They are preparing for a takeover."

Avigayil sighed and moved her head all the way over to the other side.

Mikael answered him. "People who know how to behave."

Avigayil was pretending to be confused by the contradiction between what the teacher professed and how he was acting. The babe was criticising an adult in mime.

Maryam understood. It was what she would have done, had done. But at about age thirteen. Maryam looked at Avigayil's face and realization gathered.

Exactly what Maryam would have done. Adults had always seemed wrong to Maryam. She would mime that wrongness, and no one looked at her and certainly no one would have understood, but that did not matter. It was a silent criticism of someone else's behaviour.

Maryam beamed a smile at her daughter, a slight knowing smile, and when Avigayil looked at her, Maryam flicked her eyes.

And the baby caught it, and fought down a smile. Something was plucked in Maryam's chest. *She knows I understood.* Maryam beamed inwardly at herself. *Imagine how I would have felt if anyone had seen me or understood me.* Maryam knew exactly how good that would have felt, and appreciated all over again what a treasure she had found in her daughter.

Maryam looked at the child's extraordinary face, the sharp nose, and the plump cheeks. In her days of vanity, Maryam had spent hours looking at silver hand mirrors or the polished bottoms of metal vessels hoping to discover a beauty that would silence the arrogant girls around her. She knew her own face. This was no mere family resemblance. She and Avigayil were as identical as twins.

A child from an egg, an egg that starts to grow. Without a father – it is just a repetition. The same body gives birth to the same body. There was something to learn there about how all children were made. A heart of mystery.

She is me. Me over again, to live again in a place where I am understood. She is me sent again from God by miracle.

Avigayil was Maryam, born again, same body, different life.

The teacher turned to Yosef, prodding him with theological questions to see if he could get him to say something objectionable about rituals or divinity. Yosef was now bouncy for him, in a good mood. He'd enjoyed how Mikael had humiliated the Perisa. Having eaten, the teacher excused himself, throwing down his cloth.

After he was gone, after the servant had been bedded down in his cart, Maryam said. "Avigayil looks exactly like me, doesn't she?"

"You've only just noticed? She is you." Yosef looked into Maryam's eyes. "I believe you. That child is something different." His round-eyed gaze was not entirely without fear.

That night on the roof, Maryam slept on her back, hands folded on her breast as if she rested on a barque that at night floated on a sea of stars.

She gave a prayer of thanks for their exile. She understood it now. The exile protected Avigayil.

God, Maryam was convinced, had sent some kind of messenger to earth in the form of her child. In the form of a girl, not a king or a conqueror, but a daughter of the highest religious class. And what, what would be the unfolding meaning of that?

A prophet in the form of a woman? God spoke through women too; there had been female prophets.

This one would be in the form of Maryam, herself. Blessed among women indeed.

CHAPTER 5

DEATH IS PART OF THE LESSON

The tekton's boy Yehushua died.

He was fine in the morning, had a headache at noon, a fever at night, and was mottled and still the next day. Nobody would go near the body.

"Your friend is gone," Maryam told Avigayil, stroking her soft brown hair. Avigayil made a squeak, like a mouse. The squeak erupted into great raw wail. The child understood death.

There was one cure for grief. You see the body; you mourn. That's what her own mother had done for her when their songbird had died. Maryam balanced Avigayil on her hip and carried her though she was getting heavy, as if she had bones of lead. The child wailed the whole way.

The gates to the courtyard hung open as if someone had fled the house. On the steps to the roof a woman was sweeping.

"He's in the barn," the mother said, face closed and angry. Her daughters sat on the steps, dust ringed round their mouths.

Maryam went to the lopsided building they called a barn. From somewhere came the sound of male weeping; a man mourning the loss of his only son. She tripped into the byre expecting to see the father – but he was not there. Only workbenches, tools and the body of the boy, dusty, cold and covered in red dots, with his feet turned inward. Avigayil swallowed her wailing with a sound like a hiccough and went still.

Well, thought Maryam, *Avigayil is from God and can't be harmed. Perhaps even I am beloved by God.* She said loudly, addressing the people in the house, "Has no one washed the body? Is this the house that has a well?"

Maryam took off her own headscarf, flapped to the well, hoisted up the bucket, and soaked the cloth.

The tekton's wife ran down the staircase towards the well. "Madam. Madam what are you doing?"

"I'm going to wash the body."

"God bless you for that, but lady, we know this sickness. It spreads. Where is your little girl?"

"Mourning her friend."

"You must get her away from him. You must." The woman clutched at her with wiry arms, imploring eyes.

"Thank you, Sister, but nothing can harm me or my child."

The hand was snatched back. The wife had seen whatever it was that had sent this highborn woman into exile. Madness! The woman's face went slack.

Think what you will said Maryam's tight smile. She turned and trotted back to the byre.

Avigayil was sitting next to the body quite calmly, stroking the arm that was already puckering in the heat. She was whispering. "Come back. Come back."

"We can pray. And if we can't bring him back, at least we can help him rest."

"He's not asleep," said the little girl, accusingly.

Maryam started to pray for the peace of the departed. The child did not join in. Out of the silence or the dust, an answer seemed to come.

God's messenger was sent to Earth to learn. Death is part of the lesson.

Very well, Maryam said to God, and knelt on the straw and began to wash away the dust. *Maybe, then, just take away these sores, so his mother can come and hold him, weep for him. Not leave him out here alone.* She washed his twisted face. The lips had pulled back over uneven teeth. She tried to push them shut with the cloth, and succeeded in giving him a nasty sneer, like he had contempt for her efforts.

"Come now, Avigayil. Say goodbye. Let his family mourn him. Now."

Her little girl no longer wailed – she was ruminating, scowling slightly. She let herself be picked up. Maryam went back to the mother. "Do you have a sheet to wind him in?"

The mother, dazed, wobbled her head. The woman smelled of loss.

"I'll get one of ours," Maryam said.

The woman's eyes were out of control, veering off in different directions as if they couldn't quite find Maryam's face. "Thank you. Thank you so much." Then weeping.

They went back for the sheet. Maryam was expecting questions. *Why does God let people die? What is death for?* Maryam was prepared to answer *–it is punishment for Hawa disobeying God.* But what would she say if Avigayil asked why Yehushua had to pay for Hawa's transgression? Maryam was prepared to go further. *Since Eden, death is the price we all pay for the joy of having children.*

Instead the child said. "My name now is Yehushua."

"That's a boy's name, Avigayil."

"I'm a boy."

"No you're not, Avigayil. You're a girl. YOU... are more of a girl than anyone who ever lived." She pressed her face against the child's cheek. *You are a prophet come to Earth in a woman's form.*

"I'm... a ... boy," Avigayil insisted, her chin thrusting out.

Maryam localised the source of her own dismay. It flowered into this thought: You came as a woman.

"Oh, Avigayil, my honey bee! I know you are upset that your friend has gone, but don't let it make you so unhappy."

"I am a boy," Avigayil said again.

Let it rest, Maryam advised herself. Evidently allowing Avigayil to see the body had not been a good idea. She had washed the whole body, and she'd forgotten about the effect that seeing male parts – even those of another child – had on her daughter.

"You stay here now and keep your father company," Maryam said, finding the sheet. She stopped and asked Yosef if he could mix some ash with water and bathe Avigayil – it was a traditional way to deal with corpse impurity. She left Avigayil at home, and went back to the carpenter's house. Yehushua's mother, ashamed, came out to help her dress the body.

The mother got ill and died three days later, but Maryam of course did not. Maryam washed the mother's body as well. It could be that one by one the entire family would now die.

She washed herself and all her clothes – she and Avigayil would be protected, but not Yosef, nor anyone else. And she was already enough of a pariah in the village – she couldn't risk being a bearer of disease as well.

* * *

The day after the death, Avigayil went out to the boys.

She told them firmly to call her Yehushua. One of the older boys sneered back at her. She hit him. She insisted on being on the team and one of her little buddies said, "Yesh always said to let her play."

"Him. I'm a him."

Maryam overheard her. *No, no, no, no, no* – grief was one thing, but this was getting odd. She was concerned for her baby's safety. The boys might turn on her. They didn't. They let Avigayil play with them.

In the evening, Yosef laid down a tin tray bearing bowls of porridge and cheese and olives. The family sat down to eat, Avigayil still shiny with sweat and Yakob, sitting next to his father, yearning towards the food.

"Well, Avigayil, do you still think that you are a boy?" Maryam tried to make her smile kindly and indulgent.

"My name is Yehushua," the child said.

For a few days longer. While she mourns, Maryam thought.

But it went on.

CHAPTER 6

SPLITTING GOD

One night when the child was finally asleep, Maryam, alone in the darkness, realized the enormity of what had happened.

Somehow God's prophet on earth had gone astray.

Five years before, fire in the shape of something like a person had spoken not in words but in her mind. Told her. A child would be born made only out of her, and it would be special to God, and it would be in her care.

Distraught, Maryam now went up onto the roof. A truth as stygian as the moonless night opened up around her. Whether it was the influence of Yosef – she permitted herself a tremor of rage at him and his teaching – or some failing in herself, some weakness she had not challenged, God had been poisoned.

The error comes from me. She has my body, my face; not my mind mayhap, but whatever God intended for her, this flaw came through me. Well, then it is up to me to fight it.

The next day, Avigayil went back out again with the boys.

Maryam stalked out of the house. She grabbed Avigayil

by the arm and shook her. "This unclean nonsense stops now! Come inside."

"I'm playing!"

"You are not playing with these boys any longer. There is work to be done about the house, and you will come inside with me! Now."

"No!" The tiny face was furious. Maryam's hand was thrown off.

The Adversary often came from God to test mankind. It was clear at once that this was a trial sent to test Maryam's mettle. *You will find me worthy, Lord.*

Maryam seized again the child's wrist and began to pull. The child tried to hit her, but Maryam was stronger. The child leaned back, to resist.

I see, Lord, how easy my life has been, how smooth my way has been made. Now I must fight.

Maryam dragged her across the stones towards the house. Avigayil's heels started to bleed. Maryam shouted, "You see what this foolishness does? Do you see?"

Avigayil started to wail.

Maryam persisted. "I'm sorry that you are cut, but I cannot allow this. I won't allow it."

"You will," the child whined and coughed herself back into weeping.

"Oh-ho. No I won't!" Maryam knelt in front of her. "Do you want to be dragged? Dragged more? Have your feet cut more?"

"No."

"Then come inside." Maryam jerked her arm and started to haul her. "What does the second commandment say? It says honour your father and mother! That means obeying them."

"You're only my mother."

"No. I'm both your father and your mother."

"So you are a man as well. Like me!"

In the byre, Yosef looked up, his eyes boggling. He had never seen disagreement between Maryam and Avigayil – had never seen Maryam so much as admonish her. "Woe, woe, woe," he said, standing up. "What's all this?"

Avigayil flung herself against Yosef. "She hurt me!"

Yosef looked up, baffled.

"The child is continuing to say she is a boy. She won't stop. She's a girl!"

Yosef seemed to swell. "What difference does it make?"

"Difference? Difference?" Maryam found herself reluctant to explain what she thought the child was. "The will of God is the difference. She, most especially this child, will not be allowed to go astray!"

Yosef blew out and shook his head. "Who do you think you gave birth to? God?"

Maryam didn't answer that question.

She stormed up the ladder and found one of her old, fancy dresses, all red and blue and gold. She could sew it later. What was important now was that the child would not be indulged in this evil one moment longer. Maryam slid down the ladder, dress in hand, landing awkwardly, almost spraining her ankle. She found a knife and cut a strip from it, stormed back and pulled Avigayil's tiny tunic off her. She began to wrap the cloth around her.

"From now on, you wear dresses. Do you understand me?"

The child protested, hugged herself to stop the dress going on, tried to hit her mother (which made even Yosef howl), rubbed her eyes with her fist, stood weeping and half naked in a lopsided dress. She snarled, then flung it away and glared at Maryam.

Yosef knelt down. "Come come, Avigayil, you can't go about naked, and you are old enough to wear a dress. See? Mummy has taken her most beautiful dress and is using it to make something beautiful for you."

"No!" Avigayil shouted.

"See? So pretty." Yosef gave it to her again.

She flung it away.

Yosef picked it up. "No. Such a pretty dress. See."

"You wear it!"

Yosef began to smile. "But I am a fat ugly old Daddy, and it would not look good on me."

"I'm a boy. My name is Yehushua!"

The sun was sinking and they still fought.

Maryam began to worry that perhaps the boy's spirit had somehow lodged in Avigayil after death. Could it be driven out? Was there a witch in the village? Could she ask her uncle to pray for them?

Yosef still tried to placate them both. Maryam became wild at being disobeyed. She tried to tie Avigayil up, to hold her still, while the dress was stitched around her. Avigayil kicked, screamed, roared and finally butted her mother on the lip with her head.

"That's it!" said Maryam. She rolled the child over and slapped her buttocks again and again. "I see that I will have to beat this demon out of you. God of Yisrael come to my aid, come I beg you and drive out this contrary spirit, drive it out and down the hill to the city of the Greeks."

The prayer was given rhythm by the sound of blows.

"In the name of heaven…" Yosef held up his hands, couldn't cope, and fled the house.

And Avigayil recited over and over, her voice bleary, lips swollen. "I am a boy. I am a boy."

Yakob sat staring mournfully, his porridge uneaten. Maryam grabbed her son, raised him up and pulled up his skirt. "You don't have this! See? See? You can never be a boy. Not ever."

"I will pray to God!" the child wailed.

"What? For that?" The idea of praying for such an unheard of thing made Maryam go still inside. Where would such ideas come from?

What if the Adversary was more than just a servant of God? What if it had burst its bonds, preyed now on human wickedness, to undermine God here on Earth? Adversary no longer, what if it had rebelled?

What if the coming of the child had caused the Adversary to rise up, and turn on its master? Jealous of the child now come to Earth? This could be a battle of universal import.

The battle went on for weeks.

Yosef, beside himself and weeping, made them eat. He thrust Maryam aside to give the child some bread.

"You'll kill her. You'll kill us. You're insane!"

"Me? Me insane. Am I the one who says I am a man? Am I the one possessed by the spirit of a dead child? It's better if she dies."

Yosef went still. "What?"

"It's better that she dies than this evil be allowed loose in the world." She didn't say a new prophet sent by God had been undone by disobedience and the shadow of the world.

"She's a child!" Yosef begged.

The child had rope-burn marks. Her ribs were showing. She had bruises. Something had gone wild in Maryam's eyes.

So Yosef rose from his bed in the deepest night.

He climbed down the ladder with Yakob over his shoulder. He crept to Avigayil's corner where she had been trussed like a lamb. Weeping for himself, for their life, for everything, he untied her wrists and ankles, and then he slipped out of the house, carrying nothing but the two children and began to walk in the dark towards Yerusalam.

"I'm a boy," the child whimpered. "My name is Yehushua."

"Yes," whispered Yosef and kissed her. "Yes, you are Yehushua. You are a boy. Yes."

In his wide cool bedroom, Yoazar barBoethus realized that he was being shaken.

Gently, but continually in the dark. "What the…" Yoazar threw off the hand and sat up. A small guttering lamp showed Mikael's anxious face.

"Sir, oh Sir. It's Yosef barLevi. Here, Sir, at the gate."

"Oh for God's sake!" Yoazar threw off the covers. *Can't a man rest?* Presumably he couldn't stand Maryam a moment longer. Coming here! Prison for sure if he's caught.

Yoazar's bad knee gave way as he stood up, and that made him angry again. He threw on his mantle, hobbled across the courtyard and flung open the gate. Before Yosef could say anything, Yoazar grabbed him by the wrist and swung him into the courtyard.

"Are you mad? You are in exile. They will throw you in prison."

His eyes held wide open like his hands, Yosef said, "Maryam has turned on the children. She's like a demon." Exhaustion and despair shook him; his chin wobbled, his eyes shook out tears. His clothes and face were one even coating of dust, except where tears had streaked his cheeks.

Yoazar's mind lumbered forward. "What?"

"I've come to hide the children. Maryam has gone mad. Look at them!"

The little girl's face showed plain signs of a beating. Her wrists had scabs from what looked like rope burns.

Yosef tried to explain, gabbling. A childish thing was at the bottom of it. Avigayil's friend Yehushua had died, and she says she's to be called Yehushua, that she is now a boy. It's not a good thing, but Maryam will kill her, has said she was rather she was dead.

Yoazar slumped. Yosef looked yellow and swollen. "I'm sorry, Yosef." The poor fellow was a woe-begotten creature and part of this woe was Yoazar's fault. Yoazar rubbed his face. "I always knew she was mad." He grabbed hold of Yosef's shoulder and guided him a few steps towards the house.

"How long have you been walking?"

"Two days."

"I'll get you food and water."

There was a thump on the gate. Then another and another and woman's voice bellowed "Yosef! Yosef!"

Yosef waved his hands for silence, pleading.

Yoazar's heart shrivelled in something like terror. It was Maryam. Maryam here and as Yosef had said, she sounded like a madwoman.

"Yosef!"

Yoazar waved at Yosef. *Get them away, hide them!*

The older child put its hands over its brother Yakob's mouth. Yosef pulled them both back, Yoazar waving towards the wine cellar door.

Yoazar waited for a while, as if he had to be awoken, then had thrown on a robe, and come out of his rooms. He called back. "Who is it shouts at this hour?"

"Don't pretend. He's there!"

Yoazar trudged in place as loudly as he could, sandals flapping, before pulling open the door.

Maryam's hair was loose, wild in the moonlight. "Where are they? Where are my children?"

"Maryam? What are you doing here?"

"You have them."

"I don't know–"

"Don't lie to me. Everybody saw him, a man carrying two babes right up to this gate!"

"Your feet! Have you been running all night and all day?"

"Where are they?"

God, to face Maryam in a rage – Yoazar had no idea she could be like this. "Now now now, don't get violent. It just lends credence to the stories."

"What stories? Whose?"

A mistake. Who was there to tell Yoazar any stories except Yosef? Yoazar heard a creaking door, and saw to his horror, one of the children walking towards them.

It was the little girl, her face like a fist. Her hands were in fists. And she was marching. She said in a gravelly voice, not at all childlike: "I am the one who was born. Not you!"

Yosef slunk out of the cellar carrying the youngest. Maryam's lip curled at him.

The little girl shouted at her. "I am the one who knows what I am. Not you. You will call me Yehushua, and I am a boy."

That calmed Maryam. She slumped back, looked satisfied. "You see the demon that afflicts her." She knelt and took the child's shoulders. "Your name is Avigayil, after my own mother."

"Call me Yehushua or you will never see me again."

"I am your mother. Your mother and your father." Maryam's voice was as even as paving. Dust coated her as if she'd been salted for preserving; her sandals were pink; her face looked fat and starved.

The child said, "You are nothing more to me than anyone else. I am here for everyone."

The child is crazy too, Yoazar realized. *They both think they are God.* Just a small part of Yoazar's coiled heart liked that. Maryam was up against Maryam, and she could lose.

Maryam held out a demanding hand. "You will come with me now. Yosef. Where is my son? I want my son."

The older child said, "I am your son."

"Yakob! Now."

Yoazar coughed gently. "Go home with your husband, Maryam. Call the child what it wants to be called, and get going before the sun rises. Otherwise Yosef will be sent to prison."

"Good!" she snarled.

Yoazar felt a growing calm. "If that happens, Maryam, I will make sure you never see these children again. I will not leave them to your mercy. You will have no husband, no children. And I will cease to send the cart. You can run wild in the desert like the madwoman you are."

He gave her a push and she stumbled backwards. He seized the child's hand and pulled. "Yosef. Bring the other child." He moved all of them outside his gate, and then stood across it, barring it. "I am the head of this family. If Yosef is sent to prison, I cannot allow these children to remain in your care. I will take them from you and have you declared insane and sent to that place where the insane go. It will not be a house in Nazareth."

"You heard the abomination that child has become."

"What did you expect with the nonsense you've been telling her about a virgin birth and not needing a father? And you, Yosef, with your wild thinking. You are both to blame. I am close to removing both these children from you now, in any case. Go, before I do so. And if I hear that Yehushua has come to harm or died, then I will have you stoned in public for killing your own child. Get out. You disgrace my doorway. Mikael! See they get home swiftly in one piece!"

The child had a strange small tight smile. "For the child is father to the man."

Maryam slumped into the cart and was still.

She looked pallid, staring ahead, and said in a tiny, bereft voice. "It's all undone."

"Call me Yehushua," the child demanded.

"I can't."

"That is my name. Call me Yehushua."

Maryam's feet were bruised and bloody, and she looked chastened. She had come close to losing the child.

"Call me Yehushua." The child said in a singsong, voice. Then sharp, succinct. "Call me Yehushua." Then demanding. "Call me Yehushua."

Over and over, lurching over the broken roadway, all the way from Yerusalam, hour on hour, even after Maryam had fallen asleep, bent forward, her head hanging. Even when she woke again at Gappiah. "I am a boy. Call me by my name."

The day grew long and hot. They had some bread, which they broke. Their jug of water emptied but there were wells on the road. All through the day, the child did not let up. He sounded so pleased with himself, so insolent. Even Yosef wanted to clout him.

"Leave your poor mother alone," Yosef said.

The child said, "I can walk back and live with Yoazar." The child's face was still and the obsidian eyes bore down on Yosef. This child would do that, no doubt about it.

Maryam was right; it was indeed as if the child was possessed by something. Yosef had not been close to the child but he had felt pity for it being trapped with Maryam's all-conquering love and being seen as part of her.

Now the babe was getting older and children could be cruel, as Yosef so well remembered. This little one had hard eyes. Both of them were mad, both of them could be dangerous. The fondness Yosef had felt for this little creature began to shrivel.

You are not quite human.

They stopped beside the springs at Yenin so that the mule could rest, and they could take water, cheese and bread.

Cold water welled up in an ancient stone basin carved with flowers. The water ran off into a trough for asses or cattle. Local women were chatting beside it; other travellers led their animals to drink. One toothless man flung up an arm and cried "Ho!" to Maryam and Yosef, but he faltered when he got a good look at their faces. Yosef supposed the misery and exhaustion showed.

The child ate bread with merry smiles, smacking its lips as if making fun of them. Yosef cradled Yakob who was thankfully fast asleep. Maryam chewed her bread in heavy-lidded misery.

There was only a hint of orange in the sky, but Mikael announced "We'll drop here for the night."

Normally the child would have run up the rocks or tried to sneak round the back of villages to see what the people were doing. Instead he sat across from Maryam saying over and over in a chant. "I am Yehushua."

"You will stop now," said Yosef. "We need to rest."

Maryam lay down on a cloth over the scrub and dust, and the child leaned forward and began to whisper in her ear.

Yosef did not know what to do. He covered his eyes and wept. He felt that he was not a real man to be so out of control of his family. He'd always been weak. All the reading and arguing, it had all been a cover for his timidity. He had hoped that marrying would at least give him a home, a place of safety, but he couldn't even keep that secure. He envied Maryam her strength.

He knelt beside the child and pleaded. "Please. Please leave your mother alone."

"I think not," said the child. "Her mind is at its softest while she sleeps. If I whisper over and over, the words will enter her mind with her dreams and soak in."

"Please stop. The rest of us need to sleep too."

The child eyed him coldly, and then smiled. "You want your family to be at peace, don't you, Yosef? This the way to do it."

Little Yakob woke up and started to wail. Yosef knelt to calm the littlest while glancing with misgiving at the child. Yehushua lay down next to Maryam's ear and kept on whispering. Maryam whimpered and kicked her bloodied feet, and turned on her other side.

The child reared up over the exposed ear and kept whispering. Maryam covered that ear and tried to slap him away.

The time had come. Yosef had to act, to get him to behave. Biting the inside of his lip Yosef finally laid hands on the child's shoulders.

Then Mikael loomed suddenly behind them both. He wrapped the child in his arms, stood up, and carried him away from Maryam, and kept on walking until the child fell silent. The child didn't struggle, but stared ahead, letting itself be carried out of sight.

They started out again before the sun rose.

The child did not look tired. Mikael still gripped him, hauling him up into the front of the cart. As Maryam rolled into the back, the child started up again. "Call me Yehushua."

"I told you to stop that," said Yosef.

"I can walk and live with Yoazar."

Mikael rumbled from the front bench. "Maybe he wouldn't have you."

"Then I would find somewhere else." This child would do that, no doubt.

Five years old.

"Call me Yehushua," he said as a playful joke as if pulling petals off a flower, then in an unsettling whisper. "Say it, Ami. Say it." The voice never rose, or raged. Sometimes it chuckled, or wheedled or spoke quite calmly. "Who does God protect? Say it Ami." The child did not even sound anxious. "We'll be friends, as soon as you say it."

He had a strength to crush armies.

"Do want to be a king?" Yosef whispered.

The child pondered for a moment. "I already am one."

Over and over and over as the sun swelled in purple-orange haze. The light was pallid on Maryam's hollowed face. She asked in a small voice, "Why do you want to be a boy?"

"I don't want to be a boy. I am a boy," said Yehushua.

Maryam's lips moved, Yosef could see, she was about to say girls can do things. But she didn't – she was too exhausted.

Girls can't preach thought Yosef. They can only go so far into the Temple. They can't become lawyers or priests. They can bear children, labour in the fields or, if they are very lucky, manage the servants, count sheets and have their hair dressed in the knowledge that their husbands are chasing fresher sheets somewhere else.

Maybe the child doesn't want that? Yosef looked at the rock-hard face of the child and saw something simpler. The body says girl but the spirit says different.

"So what does God tell you?" Yosef asked the child. *The God you know inside you?*

"God has no idea what is going on or why. God is confused." The child's lower lip was pulled back in; the face suddenly looked fearful and alone, bereft. No one understood, certainly not God, who had never been imprisoned in flesh before. "Only I know," said the child.

God, thought Yosef, *has just been split in two.*

Maryam stared, perhaps at the rising sun. Then she glanced down and whispered, "Yehushua."

And Yehushua slid over next to her, and hugged her, and kissed her arm. "We'll be home by sunrise, Ami," he said.

CHAPTER 7

TIMELESS STARLIGHT

By the time the child was six, Avigayil had been forgotten.

Who could remember Avigayil, when Yehushua would race with any caravan that came into the village, or run out to meet lone travellers?

"Welcome to Nazareth. Welcome to Nazareth!" he would shout, waving his pudgy arms. He would offer them water from a sloshing wineskin. The other boys would try to join, but the child could always outrace them.

"It is so beautiful in Nazareth."

A bad-tempered tinker spat. "Ptah. Nazareth is all stones." And it was not the kind of place to have much metal to repair. He was on his way to Sepphoris.

"I will bet you the hole that needs repairing in my mother's bronze cauldron that I can get you to say Nazareth is beautiful."

"Ha, ha. You have seen nothing of the world. What do I get if I win?"

"I will walk all the way to Sepphoris with you and keep you amused." The little boy hopped in place.

"How would your mother have a bronze cauldron?"

The little demon squared up to him. "She's the niece of the Kohen Gadol."

The tinker's eyes widened. He didn't believe this little scrap, but he was charmed. "You are on. We have a bet."

"Our stones are beautiful in sunlight. They glow like pieces of stars. And we have two oxen and many goats and grow fruit."

"So do most places, kid."

"So? I did not say that Nazareth was more beautiful than anywhere else. It is part of the world. And do not the scriptures tell us to rejoice and be grateful for the world that God has made?"

The tinker stammered. "That, that."

"Do you deny that God's world, these olive trees, these stones, the broken eggshell of the raven that got eaten. Do you deny that they are beautiful?"

The tinker blurted out a laugh through brown or missing teeth. "No. No little teacher, I don't."

He repaired their cauldron. Maryam silently flicked her hand towards it and said nothing. She sat and stared, a haggard line down each cheek.

Yakob had not started to talk.

Yosef saw children who had been born after their son already taking unsteady steps and saying, "Daddy big" or "Baby hungry."

Was there something wrong with Yakob? Yosef didn't feel able to say anything to Maryam, who he could see was still in mourning for Avigayil.

Whenever the first-born came home, there seemed to be a burst of noise and light that made Maryam turn slowly away, but it transfixed little Yakob, benumbed him.

An instance: Yosef had told Yehushua that there was soup

on the stove – a mix of herbs, olives and well water heated up with a single egg. The child scraped a dining couch to the stove and hopped onto it. The loud noise made Yakob jump. Yehushua served the soup while talking. "We have a new game. We found some rope and strung it between trees and then we try to send things down it."

Little Yakob was staring round-eyed at Yehushua. Yosef hunched forward and said, "Ya-Ya. Don't worry about your brother. Look at Ami. That's your Ami, there." Yosef's hand capped Yakob's skull and turned it.

Maryam was staring through their missing wall, looking at the afternoon clouds, apricot-coloured against a purple sky. Far over the horizon there was a storm above the lake. As soon as Yosef let go, Yakob's head turned back to look at the eldest.

"Say Ami. Hmm? Say Ami." Yosef kissed the infant's disordered head, already covered in hair but the infant was not yet walking or talking.

Yehushua came closer and leaned on his knees. He beamed, his face polished with sweat, his baby teeth a limestone white. "Yakob! Ya-ya? We'll play wheels soon. You and me. It'll be fun. I promise. Ya-ya? Say Ami." Suddenly the child was not performing baby talk. Serious and not at all childlike, Yehushua gave Yakob an order. "Say Ami."

Maryam was sleeping and all was still but the room seemed to turn upside down and the very walls seemed to blink, collapsing into darkness and then opening out again.

Yosef rocked on his couch. But all seemed as before. Was he himself ill?

The child ruffled Yakob's head. And then with the suddenness of a terrace wall giving way to a flood, Yehushua burst into a run. Ran for no reason, across their unwalled yard.

A few hours later, Yakob said, "Ami."

Maryam was still sitting next to the edge of their invisible wall, still staring.

Yosef thought he had misheard, made it up. "What did you say? Did you say Ami, Yakob?"

Yakob pointed in slightly the wrong direction with a finger that looked like three small chickpeas.

"Maryam? Maryam did you hear?" Yosef scooped up Yakob and put him on Maryam's lap. "Ya-ya. What did you say? Say it again."

The infant rubbed his eyes, and then said, "Ami." Maryam finally gave a tiny smile, with something like wonder in her eyes. Yosef cackled and did a little dance on his frail, bowed shins. Yakob, unused to being the centre of approval, moved his hands, and squealed out a laugh.

And Yosef pondered what he had seen, and how the child had commanded, and began to think things he would not share with Maryam, partly because he didn't want to clarify them into words.

Yehushua ran wild.

He organized stone-throwing competitions, with sweetmeats for prizes. He didn't always win – there were bigger boys. But he was plainly determined to do so.

He collected a gang of lads around himself. They would peer over walls into courtyards. Not to do mischief, more from a desire to know and see. Yehushua had the boys work on a map of Nazareth, building by building. They drew orchards and stables particularly, and mapped out pastures and vegetable gardens. They would show up with feed for animals all around the village.

Or Yehushua led them down to Sepphoris from the rocky hill with grass like sparse baby hair. In Sepphoris, houses joined to form continuous walls. He would go to prosperous households clutching fruit and say, "Hello, we are from Nazareth on the hill where only some things grow. Can we trade?" The surprised locals sometimes said yes.

Most of the boys were one or two years older than the child, and had nicknames like Lem or Smooch. About this time, for short, the boys started to call him Yazz. They nicked things like fruit or barley porridge.

"Save some for home. We will be heroes!" Yazz grinned. "Race you!" And he would run up the hill.

Unlikely as it might be, he would play house with the girls. "When we are older we will marry," he would declare to different ones. The girls would giggle or demand that they should be the mother, and take giggling revenge on each other. "No no Sharon, you can be our baby. Our own dear little one." The children chuckled, like the sound of water slapping down over the rocks to the valley.

At the well the women noticed Maryam's swelling stomach. "Sister," they said. "With child?"

Maryam faced up to them. She had to brave being regarded, as she had to bear sunlight. But something made her cheeks bunch up, when she indicated yes, something that felt like pride.

And the women gave little gladsome cries. This was more like it. No hiding away and being strange with scrolls and scripture; this was what wives were for. And it hadn't been a long time since the last pregnancy. Again, what wives were for? Though honestly her husband was hardly well-favoured.

Maryam was a good woman. That boy of hers is a little demon; they let him run free. Something's happened. I reckon she's fed up with him. Can you imagine how exhausting?

Maryam tugged Yakob forward. He could walk. "I hope it will be a little sister for this one."

Yakob stepped forward on his own feet and said with breathy softness. "Hello."

Hello, hello dear, the Nazaredai chorused and laughed.

"My, he is coming on sudden."

"Yes," Maryam said quietly. The villagers said to themselves, O, she's just shy. Modest. Properly brought up, not like the peasants around here.

"Well, they come up at their own speed, don't they? My cousin's boy didn't say nowt til his third summer."

"They say boys come on later."

"Aye, they do."

"It was a relief," Maryam admitted. Wistful-like.

"Aw," said one of the women, Idra, who understood, and she gripped Maryam's forearm. "It must have been a worry for you, but it's all right now."

"As much as it can be with my first-born in the house."

"Ooh, hard to handle, is he? Send him to me, I'll soon sort him out."

Maryam shook her head and said nothing, but her eyes had that stare and didn't blink.

(Behind her back the other women would say things like "There's something thrown about her eldest, and that's worrying her." And some of them with longer memories had a fair idea of what that thing was. They sometimes said murmuring, together. "That weren't no boy." Another woman might shake her head. "No. T'ant. Can you imagine?")

"Well," the nice one said, still holding Maryam's arm. "Anyway, there'll be another little darling soon."

This third pregnancy, Maryam felt in control.

She knew when she would get sick. She knew what she had to eat. She knew what Yosef could do to take care of her. She had friends now and she called in the nicest of the neighbours, Idra, to give him even more information and advice.

("Such a dear, that Yosef," Idra said to the others. "We should all have one like him about the place.")

Maryam felt so blessed that she had a husband who could give her children without having to do that thing they both so much detested.

Yakob gained confidence just as his mother swelled and found it most difficult to walk. He would yell and rage and sulk and demand and throw things. This time Maryam knew how to float unperturbed through this bad phase.

"You threw your cup. Now you want your cup. Ami can't bend. Pick up the cup, Ya-ya. No, I'm not going to. You pick up the cup. I can't bend, Yakob. You wouldn't want to hurt your baby sister would you?"

Wail.

"Now now. You have to be gentle. Be gentle, to get what you want. If you keep being mean I will have to put you in the mean place so you can be mean alone."

And of course Yosef, bless him, would come in and pick up the cup and carry out the howling furious boy.

When finally her spasms began to come, Yosef was out with Yakob. This time Maryam felt she could control the pain, hold things in place until Yosef came back. She told him without panic or fear that it was time that she got upstairs, out of sight.

"Do you want me to get Idra?" Yosef asked.

"No, no, you'll do," she said. And this Yosef, now so used to walking and moving things, was of great use helping her climb the ladder into their room.

It was not an easy birth.

Labour took most of a day and a night. Maryam entered once again that timeless realm, but she expected it, now, as this new person took over, demanding to enter the world.

From that timelessness as if from a cliff, Maryam felt she could see their lives entire. Their daily progress around the village made a kind of gold-thread pattern. As the family grew in number that embroidery blossomed in size, extending. For some reason, in that realm Nazareth was deep blue-black and the gold thread glistered.

And Yosef was there, reciting the Mizmor. "Behold, children are a heritage from the Lord, the fruit of the womb a reward." He came with his sharp hot knife.

"Why?" she thought she might have asked him, meaning why a knife.

He understood what she meant. "In a dream I was told it would kill disease."

Someone was crying, somewhere.

Yosef was lowering someone towards her. "It is a girl," he said, in a voice as thick as his beard. "A girl for you."

Maryam slept, and woke with dust in sunlight, and sat up. Idra was with her, with something in her lap.

Idra said, "Yosef's sleeping. I hope you don't mind me being here."

"No, no, Sister, it's a kindness. Show me my daughter."

When Idra smiled, her raw-boned face swallowed her eyes. Her caved-in mouth, trapped between cheeks and chin, most naturally took a thin cheerful line.

The newborn's rumpled, red, undistinguished face, was asleep. Maryam took hold of her and held her, exalting, and a ray of sunlight through the broken roof fell on the infant's face and made her burble and turn away.

"Your name is Babatha," Maryam said. "Hello, Babatha."

Babatha was demanding where Yakob had been weepy.

But she was better at sleeping and letting her parents sleep. At times it seemed to Maryam that she could be vindictively messy. "How could so much come out? It's more than we put in."

But, lying clean and washed on the floor, Babatha would smile up at Maryam, grinning toothlessly and pumping out a loud and hearty laugh. *Look to me to be strong. And*, it seemed to say, *look to me to be your friend.*

The first-born showed mild interest in the new sister but less, Maryam felt, than it would have done if Babatha were a boy. There was none of the natural interest a girl should have shown in babies.

Then Maryam would again feel the stab of the loss. The possession of the child, whatever it was, that thing had utterly deprived Maryam of one daughter, had left this rough chortling creature who ran wild all day.

Maryam was devoted to her new daughter. She went to work to feminize the hand-me-down infant clothes. When young, Maryam had made herself fond of embroidery and had congratulated herself on how she made good clothes prettier.

Now Maryam found she could still use a needle, though her fingers had thickened. And it seemed to her she was stitching in not only flowers and leaves and cherubim, but that line of timeless light she saw in childbirth.

When the blossoms came on the village apple trees, Maryam would pick branches for Babatha's hair. Babatha wore flowered gowns. She was told, almost from her first steps. "No, no Atha, no no. Girls must walk with a light step. See? So pretty."

And it seemed to Maryam that Babatha out of her own nature did tread more lightly and throw fewer things than Yakob. Babatha seemed to delight in other girls. When Idra came to call with her youngest, another little girl called Nohra, Babatha would rock back and forth on her fat hips, spewing spittle with eagerness. And how she loved to play games with scraps of cloth or eating pretend meals.

But Babatha seemed to delight in other children, especially other girls. She rocked back and forth on her fat hips, spewing spittle with eagerness. And how she loved to play games with scraps of cloth or eating pretend meals.

"She'll be good about the house, that one," said Idra. Dear Idra, who always seemed to be saying something encouraging.

"Really? I fear she will be a proper little miss. I can't make her do a thing."

And all of them, Maryam and her friends, would beam approval at each other.

When the visitors had gone, lugging their heavy daughters with them, Babatha would still be cheerful, rearranging the spoons she had been allowed to play with, and making experimental noises that sounded like steam or crows. But most of all Maryam loved it when Babatha laughed.

Older children could be horrid. Maryam remembered her own school days. But infants brought such joy. Maryam could not contain herself sometimes, rubbing noses with Babatha or telling her long stories, or tickling her, reducing her to a heap of giggles. For Maryam, infants were a picture of what our unblemished spirits were like. Starlight seemed to waver in their eyes.

Her daughter sat on Maryam's lap as she sewed. There were the stories, the recited Mizmor, the explanations of how to stitch, and the soft easing away of fingers from the needle that could hurt. Perhaps it was this constant attention, but Babatha began to make hard cutting sounds and soft round ones at about a year old and not many months later said her first word: "Baby."

From now on it dims, Maryam thought. The constant starlight in their faces. Oh, there would be plenty of delight left in Babatha still. Teaching her how to cook; making sure she understood her jobs around the house. Babatha would grow into something like a companion. But the timeless starlight in her eyes would fade.

And so by the time Babatha was making simple sentences, Maryam was pregnant again. For a time at roughly two-year intervals, Maryam would have another baby. For whatever reason, Maryam always dated their births by the age the eldest was at the time.

Another son Yoses, was born when the child was eight.

Then yet another son Yudeh when the child was ten.

Boys, but starlight, laughter, sweetness for a time. Maryam yearned for sweetness. She wanted babies.

Baby Yoses might wake and start to howl, and that might set off Babatha, and even Yakob would start to whimper. Maryam could hear the first-born in the children's room say sharply, "Mama's sleeping." And all of them at once fell silent.

In the dark, Maryam shuddered. She felt her way into the room. "Babies have to cry, you mustn't silence them," she told the eldest, and gathered up Yoses to protect him.

Maryam could never place exactly when the distance came between the eldest and Babatha.

Her daughter acted as babies were supposed to act. She giggled, she cooed, she got excited and waved her hands at mealtimes, and she liked being cuddled, tickled, and cleaned. A beautiful baby with eyes like currants in a bun.

The eldest child would drop anything feminine, dresses or flowers, and swagger away from them. The child treated Babatha the same way. It was never unkind to its little sister, just brisk and businesslike. If it picked up Babatha, it was never to cuddle her, but to plonk her down on the floor and say, "Play here, then Atha," and scuttle out through the missing fourth wall into the fields.

It was about then, when the eldest was nine years old that Maryam started to nickname it the Cub, as a way around using a male name.

The nickname amused Yosef. The first time he heard it, he roared with laughter. "Yes, yes, he's like a hedgehog let loose, always snuffling." Dear Yosef. He had no idea how much pain it caused Maryam every time he called the child Yehushua.

The Cub, blunt and beyond shame, rocked with laughter too when it heard it. The eyes glimmered. *I know you don't mean it kindly, but that's nothing to me. It's funny.*

"I'm a Cub. I'm a Cub," it would say stomping like a bear or prowling like a lion. "Grrrrrrrr!"

Babatha squealed in terror. Maryam snatched her up. "You're not to go around terrorizing your little sister. Go on! Get out! Since you prefer the fields to this home! Go!" With a cuff she sent the child scampering and still laughing out of the house.

Maryam thought she detected in the wrinkle of Babatha's nose or in the way she shied away from the child something like repugnance.

So Maryam sat her down to explain. "The Cub is not a boy. She's your sister and her name is really Avigayil. But there's something wrong with her. Something wrong in her head."

She cuddled Babatha, pressed her cheek against the infant forehead. "She thinks she's a boy and she's not."

Babatha said, "I don't like her."

"Like or not like, she's still your sister. But strange." Resting her chin on Babatha's head, Maryam realized she was never going to explain to her other children that Avigayil had been a virgin birth. "You're to treat her kindly. Yes? Pretend there is nothing different about her."

A kiss on Babatha's forehead.

Never say that Avigayil had been a miracle sent from God.

A rocking of Babatha, as if to cling onto her.

Or that something unclean has overcome the Cub and taken Avigayil away.

Unconsciously Maryam began to hum again what sounded like a merry song but was a reiterated prayer. *Send her back to me, send her back to me.* She hummed that tune continuously.

CHAPTER 8

HOME

The child was ten when news spread that the Romans had finally taken over Yehud.

As if to reward Yoazar barBoethus for his reasonableness, the Romans made him the Kohen Gadol for the second time.

Mikael arrived in Nazareth, looking pleased. "He keeps the Romans liking us. They will do a census soon and he will help with that."

Maryam dipped in respect. "Tell your master for us that we are overjoyed for him. If holding this high office pleases him."

Then only a few weeks later, Mikael arrived looking grim.

The cart was fuller than usual. There was a huge clay jar of oil, stacks of firewood, a mass of salted meat and fish. "This may be the last one," he said, grimly. "The master is not well."

Yosef was alarmed. "What? What is the problem?"

"He's in pain. He can't leave his bed."

The other exile, who had come running after the cart, stood on tiptoe, eyes bulging. "Aie! Really? Is there talk of succession?"

"Please," said Yosef. "Some respect. Since you are here to take some of his food."

The teacher could not stop himself. "Changes of Kohen Gadol can lead to amnesty! We might be able to go home."

Yosef turned to Mikael and addressed him. "Mik, my wife would like to be with her uncle now. Can you take her back to him?"

"Yes!" the teacher beamed. "Take us both."

"You can leave me here," said Yosef in a low voice. The wind was louder, but his voice had a rumble to it now. He was very still. "I'm the exile. Take just my wife. And the children."

The teacher was hopping, gleeful. "And whose fault is it that your wife cannot be with her uncle, but her uncle's? He put us all in exile."

"No," said Yosef addressing the teacher without looking at him. "The fault is mine. Just as it is yours and for the same reason. I couldn't keep my mouth shut."

Yosef looked at the servant. "Can you make sure this man gets nothing? No meat or fish or firewood. Not a thing. Since he rejoices in your master's illness."

"I can do that, yes." Mikael looked pleased.

Yosef looked at the Perisa. "Your… big… mouth."

Yehushua leapt up onto the cart. "Let's unload now, Abi." The child was always bright and chirpy around Yosef. When other adults were around he tended to act younger than usual. The smile might have a mocking edge to it, as Yosef was never anything other than taciturn with him. Yosef nodded. Yehushua started to pass down the heavy sacks to him as if it were a game.

Maryam strode out carrying a pitcher. She passed Yosef who was staggering under a sack of barley. He said, "Bad news my dear. Your uncle is not well."

Maryam poured water for Mikael, who drank it all in one

long gurgling draft. She chuckled and poured him another. Yosef came back, smelling of straw and sweat. "I can't go to Yerusalam," she said mildly. "I'm with child again."

Mikael passed her back the cup and his smile was tight, his eyes fond. "Good to see you well."

"We are all well, thanks to you, Mikael. And to the Kohen Gadol. And God, of course." Maryam took back the cup. "You have saved us many times over. Tell my aunt Tara and the man of God the most exalted Yoazar, how much we owe them. How we miss them."

The servant said yes, deep voiced, nodding as if the funeral was already in progress.

The teacher began to dance with frustration. Mikael turned to him. "You heard what these good people bade me. There is nothing here for you." Mikael lumbered towards the teacher, his hands curling. "Now, go on. Get away."

The smile had not quite faded from the teacher's face.

Mikael continued. "There is no one here to protect you. You are an exiled criminal. No one will care if you die." There was fury in the servant's face.

The expression on the teacher's face almost said I'm sorry. He turned to go.

Mikael went back to unpacking and the cart was soon unloaded. Maryam cooked the newly delivered barley with dried herbs. And they ate, and learned that the Kohen Gadol had a fever and that he spoke with a roughened voice.

In the morning, Mikael refused food. "Save your sustenance. You will need it for yourselves." He gathered up the reins of the mule. He paused, and then passed Yosef the reins, mule and cart.

"Keep these," Mikael said, and turned, and walked back to Yerusalam.

* * *

The servant did not come back.

Yoazar must have died, but they could not be sure for there was no news and no food either. No more food would come.

Half a month later, Yosef held his head. "What will we do?"

The Cub produced a chisel that he had found in a corner of the house. Later he passed Yosef a hammer he had made from a rusty head found between houses, joined to a milky branch of cedar.

The Cub said, "We have a cart. We'll collect water and firewood for the village, and then trade. We'll go down to the valley and come back with more firewood."

"We have no skills," said Yosef.

"You must have faith, Abi. We can learn skills."

The next day, the Cub and Yakob were down the slopes with the cart, shouting, "Firewood, firewood for sale or trade." They came home with olives and some cheese.

The two eldest went out every day. Sometimes they snared a pigeon. Though he had caught it, the Cub refused to eat it.

Sometimes they worked in fields or went to ruined barns to salvage stones to repair the terrace walls. The brothers would come home torn, dusty, and exhausted.

The brothers had a great capacity for both play and work. It was fun to climb trees, glean fields, or offer to sweep and clean houses. They were demon gleaners especially of barley or wheat. That sometimes caused anger. The pair of them were so swift and so thorough that folk complained that they left nothing for others in need.

A large woman who hardly left her house lumbered into their byre. "There's others what hunger. They leave nowt!"

"Ask the widow of Talemi," said the Cub, firm faced. "She can't glean. We always give a measure to her." The barley they had gleaned, in old sacks in their little keep, was sometimes all their family had to eat.

Sometimes the house would explode with merriment, Maryam's two eldest children running and chasing each other across its roof, down its ladder.

Maryam would look on in wonder, and try to find in herself any such capacity. Why run, laugh, where did the jokes come from?

Laughter could occupy Yakob's whole face. "So the ladder fell and both of us were still up the tree!"

"I kept shouting, and old Ezra came hobbling by and looked up and said, 'What strange birds in the tree.' And walked on. I'm saying. Sir, sir, please, the ladder!"

Sometimes the boys would wrestle, spurting with laughter, and they'd roll over and lie next to each other, panting, catching their breath, laughing again, and then one of them would suddenly lunge and the tussle would start rolling again. Maryam caught herself musing on the natural violence of boys.

And then remember.

Yosef would sit in the byre with his back to the missing wall so light would fall on his scrolls. But the light was no longer enough for him to read. His eyes were bad. They even looked swollen and sometimes something shivered deep inside them.

The Cub would ask him, "Abi, how are you?"

"Who am I if I cannot read?"

The Cub started coming back while there was enough light and time to read the scriptures aloud for Yosef. Yehushua found himself performing the book of Doniel, included in The Ketuvim, part written in the Common Tongue.

"Multitudes who sleep in the dust of the earth will awake: some to everlasting life, others to shame and everlasting contempt."

The child stopped. His face went still; his smile was small and hard; the sharp little nose looked like it would peck at the text. "So. People rise from death and live forever."

Yosef waved both his hands. "No, no, no, no, we talked about that. It is one of those anomalies. This book, it's a late addition, they almost didn't include it. There is no point getting too precise over this point or that point. The scriptures are," he paused. "Sometimes wrong."

Saying that was one reason Yosef was in exile.

"People die," said Yosef. "Believe it. They stay in the ground, dead. That, that passage. It's something someone put in. Just once. I can't think why. Nowhere else in all of The Miq'ra does it say anything else like that at all. Nowhere else in all of the scriptures."

"Except for Yesha'ayahu." The Cub quoted. "Your dead shall live, their corpses shall rise. O Dwellers in the dust, awake and sing for joy!"

Yosef blinked, face slack. He had just been out-quoted.

The child's eyes were focused somewhere else. "It's a prophecy. It is not true now. But it will be."

Maryam came upon Yosef, hiding on the blind side of the house, hunched and covering his face.

"Are you ill?" she said and he turned his head.

"What is it?" she asked and pulled his hands away and there was a snail-trail of tears down his face.

"I'm useless!" he sputtered.

"No, no," Maryam said, and she meant it in her heart, though her head was thinking *I know what you mean.*

"All I can do is quote or preach and even then no one listens or cares. You'll star-har-ve."

She hugged him.

"Our boys," he said, burying his face in her shoulder. "Our little girl." He made a heaving sound as he surrendered to grief.

"Hush. We'll be fine."

He calmed, straightened up, and wiped his face. "I've got to think of something."

Yosef did. He had the idea of using the cart and the mule to carry people back and forth to Sepphoris.

The men of the village jerked with scorn at first. "We got feet. We can bloody walk," they said with sneering smiles.

"And you carry everything on your backs? You, Platon, you have to wait for them to come to you for your stone. I could take it to them direct for you. And your women would love not to have to carry water or cloth or firewood."

"How much it cost then?"

"Food. Bread if you have it, but onions, dried fruit, a dove's egg. Something."

"How do we get back?"

Yosef glanced at them, batted his eyelids as a way of disguising that he thought they were stupid. "I just drive back and forth all day. You wait and I'll be along."

"It beats walking," one of them said.

And it did. Wives, children, menstruating women wanting a miq'va, deliveries – sometimes they just asked Yosef to collect something for them. He was an errand boy, a child-minder, a man to drive, but a certain light came into his eyes.

It was a soft and sleepy look that Maryam recognized as relief and gratitude – it made Yosef look kindly, rather than puffed out with indignation. He found he could joke with people as he drove them. The sun burned him the honey colour of the inside of pine bark. With little food (sometimes he didn't eat so the children could) and lots of activity all day, he somehow merged with someone else. He went from fat to thin over the course of a year or two.

Yosef thin was a different person. He didn't seem to bristle. He had huge wounded eyes that made him look like a slaughtered animal but when he smiled, those eyes took on the shape of smiles too. How can the slit of the eyes turn upward? But they did, and that alone was enough to make the women, who loved to go to Sepphoris, trust this sweet-faced man to drive them.

But they said to each other with pride, "He's a Levite, you know."

"Yeah. But he's not proud is he?"

And the wives would say. "He's a lovely man, and I won't hear a word against him."

And the men would shake their heads. "No one was saying a word against him. You're bold enough now but you said nowt when he first come here."

"I didn't know him then, did I?"

"His wife's a weird one though."

"Aye. It's what comes of educating women."

"Their lad's a right little bugger."

"Haha! Into everything."

"But work? Tiny little thing, but you see him go repair the terraces. He goes right at it."

"Aye. He's good un."

"But as weird looking as his Mum."

"Leave them alone, them folk in the South, they threw them out without a shekel."

"Just as well they come here then. With us." The villagers were rather proud of their own kindness.

Almost imperceptibly, Nazareth had become home.

Death came to Yoazar in his own bed, next to his wife.

He couldn't breathe. He tried hauling in air but nothing happened. It felt as if his lungs were full of gravel. He kicked and waved and couldn't speak; his wife wouldn't rouse. He realized he had not much time and so much wanted to see her. He whined and kicked and she spun, angry at first, then said his name, and he used the last air in his throat saying, "My God."

Then his life tumbled like a wall, separating into constituents; his youth running in the streets, playing wheel-spin.

His friends Zika and Sayah, then that saucy little thing Elis, always Elis, and his three sons, and the placing of the domed hat on his head, and the sacred, simple mysteries but then slipping back into his own lovely courtyard.

His birds. His fountain. His three lumbering sons.

And then how strange. Walking to him out of the mist of memory as parts of his mind were blown out like lamps, from the light that was left, still alive with light, came Maryam's child, the weird one, glowing, holding out a hand.

CHAPTER 9

OF THE EARTH AS WELL AS THE STARS

At twelve a girl was mature.

A boy had to wait until he was thirteen. At twelve the Cub announced: "I want to go to the Temple."

Maryam paused, and then took the child's chin in her hand. "You want to do that? You know you could not go beyond the Woman's Court."

The child looked away, muttered something. Maryam couldn't quite hear but she was sure the eldest had said. "Men can go there too."

"That's true, both can go, but my child. Eh? Look at me. You – you – will never be able to go into the Temple itself. You know that. Look at me. It would be ritually unclean."

In the dimmest of voices, the child said, "I'm not bleeding yet."

Over her porridge, Babatha looked up, as still as an animal in hiding.

"It's nothing to do with a woman's blood." Maryam took both the child's hands in hers. It was such sadness, having

81

to explain. "You…" her voice broke apart in a mingled chuckle and half sob. "Us. They don't let us in."

Maryam glanced at Babatha. *You too, daughter. You might as well know this now.*

The child's face looked closed as if mouth and eyes were doors. "I need to go."

Maryam relented, and dropped the hands. "Then we will go. At twelve. The age of a girl. That means you go as a girl."

The child whispered. "I need to go to the Temple."

Maryam and Yosef discussed it. The Romans had ruled Yehud for the last two years and the two Herods had no jurisdiction there. Not only had Yoazar died, but also some of the judges who had exiled Yosef.

Yosef stroked his beard. "It's probably safe to go. Nobody remembers us now. Are they going to have records at the gates? Are they going to ask is that Yosef the Levite who was exiled? What will we do with Yakob?"

Maryam shrugged. "Take him too? He's not an infant. The babies we can leave with neighbours."

There was a stirring in the corner.

"The Temple," said Yosef, and his eyes went out of focus, as if he were already seeing it on the hill.

"We'll do it," said Maryam and felt a little tickle start to grow.

They would take the cart and the mule, and if they travelled hard they would only need to spend one night on the road. The more Maryam thought about it, the more joyful she became.

She told the eldest that they were going. She was expecting the child to hop up and down and wave its arms, shout out loud, like she wanted to herself.

The Cub looked calm and solemn. "Good," was all it said.

"I was thinking. It's a longer way around. We'll be coming in on the Caesarea road, but we could go around the Mount and go in from the south, up through the walls, into the Royal Stoa. It's a huge building, built by Herod."

"I know what the Stoa is," the Cub said in a soft voice.

"Where all the commerce happens, all the trade, and many of the scholars too. You could talk to the scholars there. Your father could buy new scrolls." Maryam's eyes tried to push kindness at the child. *You wouldn't have to go to the Court of Women.*

The Cub seemed determined to be unimpressed. "If you like. I thought we could leave the mule by the fountain of Yisrael but it would be good to see a bit more of the city."

Maryam knelt in front of the child took its hands, and stroked them. "Do you know who Huldah was?"

"Oh, Ami," the child pulled back its hands.

"Huldah was a prophet, a woman prophet. You can be a woman and a prophet. There is a gate named after her, her tomb is right there in front of the entrance to the Temple Mount."

The child was disengaging, standing up, moving back. "Yes, yes, and Nodiah, ooh Avigayil and Deborah – there was even a neviah called Maryam! Just for you." And the child pushed Maryam's nose, giggled, and then ran out.

Impudent.

Then from her corner, Babatha said. "I'm going too."

Maryam spun around. "Oh Atha. I wish you could come too."

"I'm going," Babatha announced.

Maryam understood and stroked the child's cheek. "Of

course you want to go, I know that. But what will happen to Yoses and little Yudeh while we are away? You'll be staying with Idra and with Nohra. Won't you like that?"

"I always have to take care of the babies."

This will be a fight. Dear God, please, not another fighting child.

Maryam sighed, stood up, tried to play with Babatha's hair. "That is what us women do."

Babatha tossed her head. "It's not fair. Just because she's older, she gets to go. She says she's a girl when it gets her what she wants."

How old is this child? Six? What will she be like?

Maryam tried to keep her voice sweet. "You'll go when you're twelve."

"No. I won't. I know we won't go. You'll take Yakob and then when it's my turn you won't."

"I am trying…" A tremor of anger that Maryam did not want to show had to be quelled, and she knelt to look into her little girl's eyes. "Babatha. I am hoping by going on this trip as a girl that the Cub will accept she is a girl. I'm hoping this will help."

Babatha pulled in her lips and looked down. "She gets everything she wants by being crazy."

The day of the departure, they found Babatha in the cart, hidden under a blanket next to the breadbasket.

Yosef pulled it back and affected a hearty laugh. "What have I found here? What have I found here?" He picked her up and kissed her cheek. "Ho ho ho. Look Maryam, I have found a little dove in the food. Oh, what a good meal she will make."

Babatha both pushed and stroked Yosef's cheek, and was almost laughing fondly and almost crying as well. "Let me go, Daddy, please let me go."

Maryam's heart was strummed like a lyre. She was denying her daughter something on the grounds that she was a girl. She knew what that would feel like. She closed her eyes, and then half hid them.

Yosef hoisted Babatha up, and she knew what was coming then. Maryam could her hear wailing. "I want to go! Please Daddy let me go. Please! No! No!"

Yosef would be hoisting her over the side of the cart to pass down to Idra. Maryam could hear Idra chuckle. "Come now, babe. Come now, darling."

Babatha's voice broke, screaming. "No-ho-ho." Maryam opened her eyes and saw the Cub looking down at its sister

"You will be blessed, Atha," it said solemnly.

You think that will help?

The eyes had flowered with tears, but the pupils were now steady. Babatha said, looking straight at the Cub. "I hate you."

Yosef said, "Now, now Atha. You don't mean that."

"I truly do," said Babatha.

All along the zigzag road to Yerusalam, Maryam wondered if she had done the right thing.

She talked it back and forth with Yosef. "We could have taken Atha. We could have."

Yosef was her rock. "That would have left Idra to take care of Yoses and Yudeh, and she has enough to do. Babatha will be fine with her brothers. She has already forgotten."

Maryam knew. She will never forget. Maryam eyed the Cub and thought *I hope you are worth it.*

It was first light when they left, and everything was fog-coloured with a hint of gold. Small birds bobbed on the heads of plants, marking territory. Life was beautiful.

They had to go slightly north and east to Sepphoris, then take the road that arched round to Legio, where the great battle had been fought. As their cart bounced and rumbled, Maryam played the numbers game with the child and Yakob, adding and subtracting. It must have bored Avigayil, but she went along with it anyway for the sake of her younger brother.

How Avigayil cared for Yakob, protected him, never fought with him. That alone showed she was a woman inside. Little Yakob got to show off, piping up triumphantly with the answers, and wanted to jump and run. The cart threw him and he cut his forehead, and it was Avigayil who nursed him, kissed him, rocked him, and distracted him.

It was as if Maryam's being were threads that hurt to unwind and re-stitch. Each time she called the child Avigayil, each time she thought of him as her, it pained and stretched and made her smile. *Please God, reconcile her. Please God, give her back to me.*

CHAPTER 10

OLD AT HEART

The sight of Yerusalam sucked all the breath out of her.

The four block towers of the Antonym fortress merged with the great walls of the Mount. In sunrise those walls were as orange as persimmons though pastel with morning smoke. Over the walls, Maryam could glimpse white marble edged with gold – Beth Yahu.

How long since she had stood here and took in all of the city in a single long look? It was as if little Maryam had tripped lightly out of this old carcass to play in the hills again. Home. She was home.

She turned to little Yakob, but his hand was jammed all the way into his mouth and his eyes were round with fear.

She said his name in worry, and cradled him up onto her hip.

Yosef said looking wistful. "It's meant to intimidate, Maryam. We grew up here, made it our friend, to us it is homely. But it is meant to terrify just a bit."

She looked at Avigayil, but the child seemed sullen and unmoved. Maryam wanted her oldest child to be leaping with joy as she herself felt too old and fat to leap.

The bridges tall as aqueducts stretched across the valley, white rough limestone keystoned into arches.

The child said quietly as if in pity. "They try so hard."

The gate was guarded by Roman soldiers.

Maryam and Yosef had never seen that. This was new. Maryam thought of the Herods as Romans, or as good as, friends of emperors and educated in Rome. But Yehud with the Mount of the Temple was now formally a Roman province. Not a protectorate. Not an ally. A province, directly administered.

Two bored soldiers sat warming soup, their helmets off, their armour only leather. These were not Romans; these were Empire Boys, from places like Ephesus or the Nile Delta or Damascus.

It was still early, but it was a working day. Traders pressed against the gateway with their bulky camels, or droves of cattle for the yards, or their cords of wood stacked high on donkeys. Beasts or men snorted, honked or laughed. The traders played games with chips or slept in carts or walked on ahead of their comrades to make sure they had a stall. Maryam and Yosef waited an hour at least as the sun rose and the heat began to bear down.

"The Stoa will be empty by the time we get there." Maryam fretted. They were going to leave the cart and mule at her mother's house, but they had not been able to write a letter to tell her. Maryam had no idea what to expect. What if her mother was sick, or out of the house, and there was no one to stable them?

The soldiers stopped checking any passes, stopped noting down the flow of goods and waved people through. There was a surge of movement; Yosef was ready with the reins; the mule was not accustomed to such crowds. It snorted and stomped in dismay. Yosef had to whisper quietly in its ear. The soldiers kept rolling their hands from the wrists. "Go, go, go."

So much for Yosef's fear of being caught as an exile.

Back as if through time into Yerusalam's noise, the smoke, the smell of cess pits, the bleating of goats, shouts, cries, running boys, men outside doorways talking and nodding, the neighbour women walking and chatting together as they cleaned their ears with knitting needles.

The smells and sounds rolled out and over Maryam as a solid ball of memory. In a gasp she remembered the taste of her mother's cooking, the taunts of other children, the feeling of being different and alone among girls prettier and more powerful than herself, the death of Daddy, the bleak white sunlight through pearly clouds on the day of his funeral, the remaking of dresses in daylight on the roof, the panels that screened from neighbours, the lovely woman (what was her name?) who came to call every day or so, rich and lonely. She had a pet monkey on a leash. Silbo was his name. How could Maryam have forgotten Silbo? She'd loved Silbo. Maryam had a bird in a cage; it sang; one day it escaped and she was heartbroken. Then they found it dead. There was a pageant and she had played Esta and everyone said how well she recited.

But Maryam had forgotten the way to her mother's house.

The narrow streets – stone foundations, mud brick, flat roofs, passageways the width of a single man, blank walls all the same. On the left, there the conical towers of the Hasmonean palace. On the right, higher up the slope, ranged the banks of columns that distinguished Herod's palace, now the Roman Praetorium. Somewhere here in the jumble was her old house.

"It was two corners from the house of the Kohen Gadol," said Yosef. So they asked directions to that complex, now the house of Caiaphas. From its corner they picked their way.

The gate had roses in the shape of wheels moulded into its metal – her heart leapt as soon as she saw them. How could she forget her own gate? She hammered on it and waited, and she couldn't breathe, hopping up and down on one foot. There was a sly touch – Avigayil had taken her hand.

The gate groaned open, swung by Mikael. Mikael, their old friend.

He recognized them at once, cried their names, and pulled them in. And he recognized the mule. "Ah! My old friend." He put his hand to the mule's nose, and the mule snorted as its brain worked its way back to whatever association it had with him.

"Let me tell my lady, she will be overjoyed."

"What are you doing here?" Maryam asked. "Are you working here?"

Mikael spoke walking backwards. "Tara came to live with your mother for a time, but that lady – well, she lives with her son now." Some deep trouble shadowed his face.

He shouted, "My lady. Your daughter is here! My lady!" Then breaking off, lower voiced, waving to them. "Go up go up, she's in the main room, I'll stable. She will be overjoyed."

Maryam's mother came out of her door, unchanged by twelve years living alone. She glided down the steps, smooth hipped, and seized Maryam's hand. "Oh my daughter, my daughter. Oh!" She put her hand over her heart. "Don't stand there, let me hold you!"

Maryam hugged her mother knowing she herself would smell of sweat and dust from the road, and of Nazaredai smoke. Mother Avi pulled back and looked at her daughter, who wondered: had Mama always looked so wise and elegant? Young Maryam had thought her a fool.

"I might not have recognized you," her mother said, swinging Maryam's hand. Her eyes searched Maryam's face. "You looked so dignified."

"We are the same age now," Maryam joked. Her mother's eyes searched her face.

"It's been hard hasn't it?"

Maryam didn't know. Had it? Her mother's smile broadened. "And is this handsome man Yosef?"

As if she had never wept over the marriage, Maryam's mother gave tall skinny Yosef a hug, and laughed heartily. She pulled back, eyes sparkling and Maryam saw: she thinks Nazareth has been good for us.

Maryam stepped back, still on the steps. "And this is Avigayil," she said proudly, her hands twirling the child's hair.

The child said with eyes as black as basalt, "My name is Yehushua."

There was another reason to visit her mother.

For seventy years, the house had had a miq'va. Just the thought of this luxury made Maryam wilt inside. Yosef stopped outside the curtain that screened the basement chamber. The Cub looked at him, questioning.

"No, no, this is right. We are going to the Temple. For this we should purify. Go with your mother."

Maryam scrubbed herself all over before immersing herself, easing herself down the big steps into the water.

"Come, Child, you will feel clean inside and out." But the child fought against disrobing.

"It's the Law," said Maryam wrestling with it.

"Only since Antigonus," said the Child, which was of course true. In dismay Maryam stopped. The child submerged itself, but clothed, and without washing first as women often had to.

Maryam rose out of the water feeling as though she was streaming stars behind her.

Outside Yosef smiled and nodded a bit too much, as he held the curtain up for Yakob, then ducked to enter. He yowled when the water touched him as if its touch was icy and painful. Maryam and her child both laughed. "Ah now you learn Abi. People do more with water than just drink it."

"Only for my God," responded Yosef. They all laughed as a family.

To enter the Temple Mount from the south they had to walk the valley mile along the western wall, under the great bridge.

They passed by the steps and arches that led to the western end of the royal porch, and then though other guarded gates. The great bridge loomed over them; birds flew under it.

Yakob started to grizzle. By the time they stood in the vast southern plaza, he was plainly going to cry. All of it towered – the sweep of steps, the high white wall and all along the southern summit, the Stoa with its giant red pillars meant to balance the fortress of Mark Anthony on the north.

Yakob gave a little wail. The older child knelt. "Hey, Bro," the Cub said. "You have to help me. I can't go in there by myself."

"Come see the tomb of Huldah," said Maryam.

"It's not where she's really buried," said the Cub with thumping certainty. "It's just a box of stone. It's good that she's honoured."

"I used to come here, always, to feel her strength."

The Cub said, "You needed to. I don't."

Ooooh, there were times. Without another word to Maryam, the Cub eased Yakob forward and led him towards the steps. Unwillingly, Maryam followed.

The steps lead to a tunnel, itself a concourse of steps up through the banked wall and the living limestone. There was a cool gasp of shadow. The stone was swept clean but it still smelled a little bit of urine – here of all places. Maryam shook her head as she struggled to catch up to her children. The hollowed-out staircase boomed with the echoes of many voices and the deafening hubbub of the Stoa above. The elder child carried Yakob, who still looked cowed, and kept his solemn eyes fixed on Maryam. At nine years old, Yakob sucked his thumb.

They came up in blinding sunlight, in the wide Concourse of the Gentiles, the hot pavement that separated the Beth Yahu from the Stoa, where Maryam had promised priests would be.

They ducked inside it out of the heat. The Stoa was one huge concourse with four rows of pillars forming three long aisles of stalls. It was the longest building in the world and the middle aisle was particularly tall, with a high vaulted wooden ceiling. Each of the pillars would take three big men to hug.

The Stoa had been the pride of Herod the Great, and was still a primary source of tariffs. The stalls sold rugs, spices, doves, scrolls, gold, and jewels. Nobody remotely thought of it as being part of the Beth Yahu, though it was on the Mount.

The noise, the cool shade, the blasts of warm air, the cries, the talk, and the smells of piled spices and frying breads slammed into them. It finally was all too much for Yakob, who howled and kicked in protest. The eldest put him down and he ran to hide his face in Maryam's skirts.

Maryam said, "Now, now, you are too big a boy to be frightened." Yakob pulled back, mouth pushed sideways out of shame. He both wiped and hid his face with the crook of his elbow.

The older child leaned forward on its knees and said, "Yakob. Go with Aba and look at the scrolls. There are so many wonderful scrolls." Yosef looked a bit relieved – he thought of scrolls as some people thought of sweet honey or wine. Yosef led Yakob away. To Maryam's surprise, the elder child took her hand and began to pull, striding forward with determination.

"Do you know where you are going?"

"To the priests."

Maryam tried to stop. "They used to gather right here on the steps."

The Cub said over its shoulder, "Priests are always where the money is." It stopped, turned and went over what Maryam was to say. "If they ask, you say my name is Yehushua and I am thirteen years old." The sunlight, the stones seemed as white as bone.

* * *

Priests, scribes, scholars, old men – call them what you will – sat at the far eastern end of the market where they were wise for tips.

As an especial service they tested boys who were coming of age and needed to enter religious discussion.

As they approached the men, the Cub began to grin. Its long, slightly buck teeth flashed against the sunburnt skin and there was a shining of something beautiful and daring – and rather merry.

Maryam recognized one of the priests – Eyanaphon. Older now, but still trim, with a firm thin mouth and narrow eyes and the look of something about to pounce. His beauty had become feral. Maryam needed to say, "Not with that one. He knows us." But she couldn't speak.

Some lad was dutifully reciting the Ten Commandments. The Cub turned sideways to get around him. "Such knowledge," it said, a grin in its voice.

The other boy said, "You know more, I suppose?" Maryam knew at once the kind of child this was – plump, shiny-haired, the well-fed child of Kohanim. She'd grown up with boys like this one.

"Yes," said her child and sat down.

"You are out of order, interrupting," said one of those priests as round as the boy. Maryam was sure that scholar and the reciting boy were cousins.

"Come, come," said Eyanaphon, with a smile, looking almost benign – calm but physically uncomfortable. He was leaning backwards while propped up by one elbow. The forearm was held upright and at an awkward angle. He had to jerk his whole body to move, and he winced as he did so. "This is an informal discussion. A celebration, even. All can talk. You ARE of an age?"

"Oh yes," said her child, its smile and eyes unclouded. "Some would say that I am late in coming."

"You look very young," said Eyanaphon.

"So do you," said the Cub.

Eyanaphon said, "You are the first to say that in some time." He laughed, but did not move his head. His other hand was draped, as if broken over one knee. Nothing about him moved, hardly even his lips when he spoke. Maryam had a sudden thought: *is he paralysed?*

"You are old at heart," said the Cub and inclined its head.

Which was rude enough. *This child, this Cub. No one has ever told it to mind its mouth.*

"So," said the younger fatter priest. "What is your favourite part of The Miq'ra?"

The child smiled, enjoying this as if it were the opening play in a game. "It is not for me to pick and choose."

"The Ten Commandments," said the other boy, who wanted to be the centre again.

"You're a good boy," said the young priest. "That is a fine focus for attention and you know it by heart. If you obey those commandments, it will not matter what you can recite."

"Come, come," urged Eyanaphon. "We all have favourite passages." The Cub had already intrigued the Sadduci.

The Cub paused, then said, "And what you hate, do not do to anyone."

Tovi! Maryam's eyes bulged. Tovi was not part of The Miq'ra.

"What do you hate?" asked the other teacher, his mouth still irritated and eyes glimmering.

The Cub's eyes were firm on his. "Valuing what is written above what is lived."

Eyanaphon said quietly. "But what is written IS the Law. Do you value the breaking of the Law?"

The Cub's shoulders rose, the smile widened. For a moment Maryam feared it was going to chuckle. "How could anyone say they value that?" The smile was serene. "The God of Yisrael knows when the Law has been broken, and knows the Law better than any man. And will punish."

Eyanaphon then said. "Tovi is not part of The Miq'ra. Some of the Essenai read him, those in the desert." He leaned forward. "You've been exposed to radical influences. But you don't live in the desert and the Essenai have no sons. You seem to value the folk tradition, what people say over what is written. Are you a Perisa?"

The Cub, still serene, said. "I have no idea what that is."

Maryam was relieved that Yosef had decided to avoid teaching about all controversial sects.

Eyanaphon was absolutely still. It was like watching a statue talk. "They are popular in the North. And there are many here in Yerusalam. They want the Law to change like water, flow downhill. Like the people do."

The other priests chuckled and shifted and scratched and sweated. There was about Eyanaphon something as refined as poison.

The Cub still smiled, but its eyes were hooded. "Could it be – just a question – that God wants the Law to change as times change? Like the seasons. The seasons change but follow God's will."

Eyanaphon and the child had become reflections of each other: the same stillness the same mask of eyes and smile. Maryam found herself afraid and entranced: two cobras face to face.

"Does God forgive murder?" the chief Sadduci asked.

"On the battlefield," replied the child. "As he forgave David the slaughter of Goliath."

"Goliath was our enemy."

"And a neighbour. The Philistines were the neighbours of the Beni Yisrael and are we not commanded to treat our neighbours well?"

"Are we?" Eyanaphon had managed to speak without moving his lips.

"In Vayikra."

The third book of the Torah.

"Child, you have misread. The phrase means fellows among the tribes of Yisrael."

The child recited in perfect liturgical cadences. "'Thou shalt not avenge, nor bear any grudge against the children of thy people, but thou shalt love thy neighbour as thyself: I am the LORD.' Certainly I am sure that neighbours to you means only the Beni Yisrael but where I live my neighbours are Greek, Shomeronai, Sidonai as well as the Beni Yisrael of the North, who are not Yehudai. I think that passage includes them."

"Where do you live?" asked Eyanaphon.

And at that moment, Yosef returned, his eyes still dazzled by all those silver-capped scrolls. But then he saw whom the child was facing. Almost involuntarily, Yosef seized Maryam's hand. They both froze.

The child answered, "In God's Kingdom." That phrase could mean the country of Yehud.

Eyanaphon gave his head the smallest of shakes. "You live outside Yehud. Somewhere in the North. But you've been speaking the liturgical language perfectly. You've been trained. Who is your father?"

"I am a Son of God."

In other words, a Yehudi. Eyanaphon fully closed his eyes, dipped his head, smiled. Acknowledging a point scored.

The Cub hugged itself, but grinned more broadly, and looked down at its feet and then answered again. "My Father is in Heaven."

Maryam could hardly dare breathe. The priest would take the phrase to mean that the child was an orphan.

"Whose family do you live with then?"

"I am the adopted son of a naggar."

Eyanaphon barked out a laugh. "Are you? And how have you acquired this knowledge of scripture?"

"By reading." One of the priests, not a friend perhaps of Eyanaphon, sputtered with laughter and grinned. The Cub talked. "You are a learned man and I do hope that I am not now going to learn that the Beni Yisrael should not read The Miq'ra."

"And your name is…"

"Yehushua. I live in Nazareth. You can find all of this to be true."

Maryam tapped Yosef's hand. *Time for us to* go. Yosef stood transfixed.

Eyanaphon had not moved any part of his body. "Yehushua. So you are a Shomeroni perhaps. Why bother coming to this temple, when you have your Mount Gerizim? Have several temples. God could run among them all. Like an errand boy." Some priests dutifully chuckled.

"The Shomeronai are Beni Yisrael who worship the same God. They simply were not rich enough or powerful enough to be sent into exile by our conquerors."

Maryam knew exactly where this was going. The child was going to say the later Ketuvim were political books, serving the power of the returning exiles. Was there any way they could shut the child up, get it away, without anyone asking who they were?

Coming to Beth Yahu had been a mistake.

The Cub continued, and yes, here it came, as Maryam closed her eyes. "Why do you think the book of Ezra begins with so many genealogies? Because the great families, returning from Babylon, wanted back their position, their wealth. So the new law came that forbade intermarriage. It meant that only the right families could worship God. And that meant forbidding Shomeronai to worship here. They did not forbid themselves. Ezra did, for reasons of power."

Yosef murmured, "The child is a marvel."

Eyanaphon: "You are saying that the scriptures are suspect."

"Doniel and Ezra are not exactly the Torah, are they? So. I simply follow tradition. But Ezra certainly serves the interests of one tribe."

Eyanaphon said: "I really must ask you again who your people are."

"The tribe that Ezra serves."

Eyanaphon leaned back. "Ah! Ah-ha-ha. You are a Levite."

More people had begun to gather. Something about the way everyone on the steps had gone still and hushed, had attracted them. Boys charged with minding pigeons when none were being sold, or parents with children who were also there, all paused to listen. A man sweeping with a broom first slowed, then stopped.

It was as though the air shook with danger, and people eased a step or two closer to hear.

Maryam and Yosef were encircled with people. Traders gave up their trading, and began to crane their necks.

Maryam eased Yosef's hand backwards. *Let them push in front of us.*

"You go," she murmured. Yosef was the one in exile.

Eyanaphon asked again. "Who are your parents?"

"My father is not of this earth. I am now the adopted son of a local man, as I told you."

This child knew perfectly well that Yosef could not be named, must not be known to be in the city.

"Whose son are you?"

Both of them again had the same smile. Both were enjoying this.

"I am…" Pause for effect. "The Son of Man." But "man" in Common was Adam – he was the Son of Adam.

Yakob began to wail, "I want to go home!"

"Me too little one," chuckled one of the priests. There was laughter. Yosef turned his back. And without a glance at Maryam, he began to walk away, holding Yakob's hand.

Maryam could not move. Suddenly there seemed to be something in her eyes. Everything was blurred and dark. As if there were a smokey fire, or thunderclouds. Indeed she seemed to feel a tremor even through the pavements and the mass of stone beneath them.

Then she blinked, and everything seemed to have cleared, the shadow, the sense of overturning.

Eyanaphon had listed sideways, as if about to fall. But then he seemed to bounce and sit up straight. His eyes widened in shock.

Why was he surprised? Had he not expected to be able to sit up straight? He rolled his shoulders, as if they had been suddenly set free. One of the priests near him seemed to ask if he was all right, and he held up a calming hand. And then looked at his own hand.

"It's fine, it's fine," Eyanaphon said quickly and homed in again on the child. Whose smile had grown even wider, and more mischievous, and Maryam knew – it was a face miming innocence. The eyes were sparkling.

Eyanaphon leaned forward, eyes on the child. "You've read the Ketuvim. Does not Doniel write of some mysterious Son of Man? That he shall be given eternal dominion over all peoples and nations?"

"Such a figure is more often called the Son of David."

"You think there is some confusion?"

The child replied, "Doniel says a lot of things that are not said frequently. But then Doniel is a not recognized as a prophet."

"What is your view of that passage?"

"That one day Doniel will be recognized as a prophet. He isn't now because his prophecies have not come true. Not yet. And half the book is written in the Common Tongue."

"You claim to know who will be a prophet."

"Only those already included in The Miq'ra. Unless, of course, The Ketuvim are not in The Miq'ra, in which case I must consider my error."

It was enough to get some of the priests to chuckle again.

"You just said the books were written by men for reasons of state, so are you saying the prophets do not prophesy? Or are they prophets only when you agree with them?"

The Cub paused. "Only when I agree with them." The Cub smiled. "That was a joke."

"You consider The Miq'ra a joking matter?"

"No. Only myself."

Eyanaphon permitted himself something like a smile. The crowd around them waited. White doves cooed and moving air whispered across the pillars of the Stoa.

Then the Cub said. "I have a question for you, Rabuli. If God made the world then God must have been able to see all of it."

A very long pause and Eyanaphon said sounding weary, "Yes."

"Then God can see everything everywhere. Including for example, Mount Gerizim. Or even Rome."

"I can see where this is going." Eyanaphon smile was thinner.

"Are you saying that there are parts of the world God cannot see?"

"No I am not, and you are about to say that that means God can be everywhere and from that you will argue that that means God can reside in Gerizim or Lower Egypt. But God does not. God can see everywhere but he has decided to live with us here. He has a covenant with this place."

"With the place. I'm but a child. Please, explain Great One. Does that mean that if all the Yehudai left this City, God would have a covenant with whoever replaced us in Yerusalam? The Beni Yisrael live in Egypt, Shomeron, and Rome. I thought the covenant was with us."

"God didn't follow us into exile, no."

"You are saying that Ezra's book is wrong when it says God moved the Persians to let us return from Babylon? How could God move the Persians without being with them? In Persia?"

The index finger of Eyanaphon's right hand perfectly masked his grin. Then he noticed it and he snatched it away and regaining poise said, "You have raised an interesting theological question."

There was a rustle of relief from the crowd and the other learned men and priests.

"Does God end?" the child quizzed the chief of the Sadducai

"What? God is without end."

"And therefore God is without beginning, and therefore God lives outside of time. For God, going to the past is like walking downhill. Going into the future is like walking uphill."

"Child. You cannot say what God can do."

The Cub kept on talking. "But only with the mind, because God being everywhere has no one place, and so nothing like a body. God moves by turning his attention to different places. Or to the future, or to the past, to Ephesus and then back to Yerusalam and then perhaps even seeing the Galil. Which is why prophets see the future. God shows it to them."

"How would you know this?"

"Because I think quickly. I have to think quickly, because I am going to die. God does not have to think quickly. God is here, at all times. He thinks at once in all times, in all ages. He thinks with the speed of oceans or rocks or stars. God IS oceans or rocks or stars, all of them, and the spaces between them, fire and light and cold smoke."

Maryam couldn't breathe. She had never heard the Cub talk like this, of eternal things with flat, bright confidence. *You are claiming to know what it is like to be God?*

"They wanted to be conscious – the light, the stones – and so they rose up as animals, and then made men, in order to see and think in time with speed. The dying need speed. Men too will build something that thinks more quickly than they do. Men will make a creature with a consciousness that moves at a higher speed."

And now you are saying that you know the future. That you have climbed uphill.

Eyanaphon said, "I don't understand."

"You will make machines that think faster than you do. Just as dust made flesh, and and and..." The child was starting to stutter and look distracted. "That made animals, and then animals made you – God working through them – all the time wanting the world to perceive. That will allow you to make machines that think."

Maryam thought: *I have no idea what you are. No word for it.*

Eyanaphon was very still but did not look angry. His head was lowered like a bull, his eyes angled upwards, looking almost sad. "Are you a prophet?"

"No," said the Cub.

Eyanaphon leaned back, and seemed to palm smooth the hair on the back of his head, Then, startled, he looked again at the hand. He sounded a bit distracted as he said, "That did not come from reading, child. What you have just now said was outside the Law. It might even be true, or you might be mad. It has never been written, and you are not trained in scripture. Or you couldn't have said it. My advice, young Son of Adam, is to go back to Nazareth and stay a craftsman. Or you will find trouble."

The Cub bowed. "Thank you for the advice, Rabuli."

"Yehushua of Nazareth." said Eyanaphon, clearly stowing the name. He seemed to remember something. "Nazareth. You never met a madman there, in exile, one Yosef barLevi?"

"Nazareth is a small place. Indeed I have, Rabuli. But the man never teaches. He only reads." The child then inclined its head towards Eyanaphon. "With respect, Rabuli. I return."

The Cub made his way out, turning sideways back and forth as though rowing through the crowd. An angry-looking man cuffed the child's head. The Cub kept on walking without glancing once at Maryam. She waited as if listening so that no one would connect them. She gazed at the whiteness of the house of God and knew she would get no closer to it on this trip.

Or perhaps ever.

They did not stay the night at Maryam's old house.

It was too dangerous. She breathlessly told Mikael, "Eyanaphon asked if the child knew Yosef and called him an exile. We have to go."

Mother Avigayil nodded. "Don't think it was unwise of you to come. The child needs to see the Beth Yahu. Only a politician like Eyanaphon would remember the exile or wish you harm. But it probably is wise for you to leave now. If Eyanaphon remembers your marriage, he will come here."

The mother and daughter hugged, and exchanged farewells, but they didn't cry, for that would only increase the unhappiness of the other. "Ami."

Mikael walked with them, leading the mule out towards the city gates.

"There's only me and your mother left in the house, but I will make sure all things are done well," said Mikael.

"What has happened to my Aunt Tara?" Maryam demanded.

Mikael's lips wavered against each other like boulders about to fall. "She knows no one. She remembers no one. Not even her sister or her sons."

"Ah. All gone," said Maryam. She remembered Yoazar, in his garden. The swallows, the wind in their potted olive trees, that fountain. Tara bringing food, giggling, knowing everyone in the city who it was worthwhile to know.

"Everything is worn away," said Mikael, nodding. "It's like sand in the sea, when the tide goes out. Where you stand firm, you can keep the sand still. But all else is dragged out to sea. Around your ankles."

This is a servant?

"Whole worlds go. Everything is washed away. I remember when all the great of the City, Herod the Great himself, would come to my master's house. Now it is as if the master never was."

The servant's vast bulk stirred, and he formed a fist. "That's what God could do for us. Let us walk into the past. That would let us keep things, things that count. Save them. Go back to my master's 35th summer when all the Kohanim gathered for a roast and the Roman legate played dice."

"God promises death," shrugged Yosef.

"Priests do," said Mikael.

The Cub, quiet in the cart, looked down, but his eyes were turned even further inward.

Heat hammered them, and then slowly cooled.

Yakob had been overwhelmed and now slept, exhausted; both Yosef and Maryam had been disturbed by finding her old home so enduring and yet so changed. It was like being a ghost. And the Cub was quiet too.

"What is it?" Maryam asked.

The Cub breathed out through his nose and for just a moment resembled Yosef, not her. "They're so fragile. Doing themselves up as a kind of Greek, hoping not to be noticed while thinking God makes them the secret centre of the universe. And yet. They are so yearning for the world to know that."

Yehushua went still, looking at his knees. "That little pile of limestone. If I took it away from them, what would they have?"

No no no no. Rejection occupied Maryam entirely. She wasn't even sure rejection of what.

"I don't know why I'm here. It hasn't told me. I could so easily destroy them. The Beni Yisrael." The child sighed. "I won't."

For Maryam, darkness fell.

CHAPTER 11

AN ANGEL TO DESPAIR

On the outskirts of Nazareth, Yehushua jumped down from the cart and walked to the tekton's house.

"I know who you are," Platon said, and turned, and went back to hammering wedges into black rock. "You are the witch who stole my son."

"I am no witch," said Yehushua. "I want to be a builder."

The builder spat. "You killed my son, you took his name and now you want his life?"

"I want to work," said Yehushua. "I need a way to earn my bread. My father thinks too much. He's lucky to have the cart, but he has no skills and he can't teach me how to be a Nazaredi. I need to learn how to become a man as well as a tekton. You can teach me both."

"You killed my son."

"At five years old? My mother washed his body and wrapped him. We prayed for him. I am not a witch but I can tell you that the scriptures say the dead will rise and the good dead shall be beloved again. You and your son will be together."

Platon's daughters had married. He'd recently taken a young wife, but it was not a happy marriage, as half the village could hear when he raged at her. Platon had a byre but no animals – there were bow-saws and axes and chisels and wire brushes for polishing. Red welts were open on Platon's hands, fringed with white. It was twelve years since he had attacked a customer in Sepphoris, but still he had no trade there. He made his living dressing stone for other builders. And, of course, the limestone holyware, gifts to the village.

Rage seemed to crackle as red-veined lightning in Platon's eyes. "All my family died. Neither of you got sick, and you changed from a girl into a boy." His eyes were round, ringed with bags, angry and fearful. "What's going on there?"

The Cub's words were slow, low. "I can help you keep your workshop going."

"I can make new sons." The tekton went back to hammering.

"Are they starting work tomorrow?" The hammering got louder. "I can bring in my little brother to help as well. We could use our cart to make deliveries."

The hammer slipped and skittered into Platon's thigh. "Shit!" he shouted. He turned to Yehushua. "You think you can take his place?" He advanced, the hammer in his shaking fist.

Yehushua stayed calm. "I'm saying that God loved your son. God didn't want him dead, and doesn't want you to suffer." Something welled up in him. It forced its way out through the lower edge of his eyes. "God loves you. He wants you and your son to be together."

The builder held him with his gaze. "Did God want him to grow up, to marry, to have sons?"

"Yes."

"Then why didn't he?" A snarl.

"Because that would not be just. No, no, hold, hold." Yehushua held up his hands to ward off the raised hammer. "Other people die of that sickness every day. Yes, God could have come crashing into Nazareth, to save one or two. Would that be just? To do that only for you?"

Platon took one step nearer. Yehushua stepped back, but kept talking. "Do you deny that God is just? How could he save your son from the sickness but not someone else's son? How is God to pick and choose who survives?"

The sinews of the leather face tightened. The sun turned. Swallows darted overhead. There were blocks of stone, gums and resins hardening, nails and saws rusting.

The Cub: "I want to work and learn – nothing else."

The lips went thin, the face clenched, made of stone no longer. "I cannot call you by his name."

"Shorten it. I will change my name, I will tell everyone. Call me Yehush."

Babatha stomped out of Idra's house, hugging her blankets.

Idra followed with the two little boys. Yosef made hearty male sounds at them. Babatha slumped into the cart, fists pushed up into her cheeks. Idra said it had been no trouble, that Norah and Atha had played together. *But?*

"And the boys? Did she help with the boys?" Maryam asked.

Idra looked into her friend's eyes. "She said nowt to them. Didn't hug 'em, nor feed 'em. Acted like they weren't there basically."

Babatha was angry.

Maryam spent that morning trying to make it up to her. She promised Babatha that she would make her a new dress (how and with what?) and the girl just sighed. Babatha liked to help cook, but Maryam realized they had left the city in a hurry and had not bought back with them the delicacies they had promised.

All they had for dinner was stale bread. They could soak it with water and fry it in oil. That was unlikely to cheer up anyone.

Maryam went to Yosef, who was snoring, woke him up, and told him to watch the two babies. Then she took Babatha's hand. "Come on Honey Bee, let's walk." She wanted to take her daughter to the lookout. "I don't want to walk past the well," said Babatha. "I'm tired."

So Maryam picked her up and carried her. For a time Babatha was jiggled like a half empty sack.

They got to the north slope and looked out. Sometimes there was just a hint of ocean to the west, a grey light under the horizon clouds.

Babatha asked almost inaudibly, "What was the Temple like?"

So Maryam described it, the block of white, as white as the sun, with a panel of gold like sunset, the hot square, the hotter people, the vast cool arcade of the Stoa. She said nothing about what the Cub had said, or the way the priests were confounded. She made it sound as if the Cub had said almost nothing at all. They had seen the enemy and he had asked questions, so they had fled.

"You are my only real daughter," Maryam told her.

"It didn't change her, did it?"

It was humiliating that a six year-old understood that Maryam had gone with high and foolish hopes that Avigayil would come back. That Maryam had even left Babatha behind, when she might have gone with them. But Maryam had wanted to get Avi to the Temple; she thought it meant Avi had accepted being a girl.

Maryam finally admitted it. "No. And I don't think she's going to."

"I won't change," said Babatha, and Maryam laughed tremulously, and kissed her.

But it also felt like the angry six-year-old had made some kind of deal.

They got back. Yosef was awake and reading to Yoses and Yudeh, who was elated because Idra had given him a wonderful present – a whole purple onion. They would have bread and fried onion for supper.

Babatha helped cook, acting strangely. She was chirpy, jumpy, talking too loudly. "We're making bread! We're making a banquet for the King. Look, Mummy. I'm making the bread!"

"You are a clever girl."

"The boys are just reading scripture."

To Maryam it felt as if the house had come unanchored and was spinning in a current. Where had the eldest gone? What was it up to? Why did Yosef look so big and sprawled, relieved to be home? Barking out that deep-voiced laugh of his that meant he was happy.

Babatha made a show of serving each of them a spoonful of bread and onion, and still the Cub had not come home. Maryam didn't want Babatha to see that she was worried about it, or was thinking about it. She wanted Babatha to feel that she was important. "Look, Father. The bread will be all crisp."

The onions only slightly burnt were bitter and sweet at the same time. She was able to tell Babatha, "This is delicious, Honey Bee."

"Oh, my little girl, she cooks so beautifully," said Yosef. He so evidently meant it, that Babatha laughed. And Maryam felt anguish that Yosef could make Babatha laugh when she could not.

The Cub came back at sunset, covered in limestone dust.

It dropped down onto a rug with a sigh. Maryam demanded, "Where have you been?" The Cub told the family that it was going to work for the builder, "As an apprentice."

The effect on Maryam was like tearing a ligament. A small sensation, a jink in the flesh, or a light chime of pain that you hope will fade. But the pain settles in and doesn't go.

"You can do it for a while," Maryam said. She dropped a bowl of cold bread in front of it. She didn't want the Cub to be the focus of anything. She just wanted the Cub to be still and silent, and to have done nothing noteworthy.

The Cub appraised her. "Platon will give us food, all of us. And I learn a trade."

The child was going to keep them. Maryam wished she had a stew of wildfowl and a bowl of pomegranates and figs, to show the Cub: See, we can eat without you.

"What kind of work will you do?" Yosef asked him, man to man.

You should be doing the Lord's work.

The Cub enthused; it was learning how to cut stone, they had a saw for stone; it was two ended, and they both could pull and push it. "You can come too, Yakob." The Cub's face was often kind when it looked at Yakob. No wonder – Yakob was nobody's rival. "You can train to be a tekton too."

Yakob, still ashamed of crying in the Temple, smiled briefly, gratefully.

"Both of you can be peasants." Maryam surprised herself. Had she actually said that? "Everyone. Babatha is the person who made the food. Let us all praise Atha. Babatha, yes!"

And Yosef chortled merrily, almost as if he was drunk, which he couldn't be, there was no wine. "Ah! My daughter and my boys. There can be no richer man than me to have such fine children."

He meant it. The children knew he meant it. They knew he thought of the Cub as his son.

She, Maryam didn't think she had fine children. She had children who were poor, malnourished, and looked down on. And one child who ploughed all the rest of them under the soil and would overturn the sky to get its own way.

Babatha sang a little song, rocking her head from side to side. "I'm cleaning plates. I'm cleaning bowls." Her six year-old daughter sang a worksong and that made Maryam want to cry.

Maryam remembered the shadow of fire.

She had been entrusted, and she had failed. *We took you to Yerusalam to show you God, and instead you turn away from God.* There would be no prophecy or miracles or teaching.

That night Maryam kept flinging herself about the bed and or puffing herself up like blankets, and kept commanding herself to sleep. But sleep didn't come.

Yosef turned over. "What is it, Maryam?"

"What are we to do?"

"About what?"

"This idea of working for that ignorant man."

Yosef went very still. She could smell onions, his beard, and his narrow unwashed body. "The boy just wants to help. I think it's a good idea."

"The Cub has turned its back on God."

He stroked her hand. "No, no my dear, not at all. He hasn't, no."

She went into the children's room. There was a lamp burning in case the children cried and she saw the Cub folded on the floor. She bent over it and seized the bare arm. "You," she said. "Up. We have to talk."

The Cub kept its eyes closed. "I have to sleep."

"So do your brothers and sister. I don't want to wake them."

Still unmoving, still eyes closed. "Then go back to bed and talk in the morning."

Maryam felt helpless. "You will get off that floor and we will go down and we will talk."

The Cub said nothing at all. *Very well, we do talk and they all wake up and hear it.* Maryam said, "You are not going to work for that man."

"I am," the Cub said, nestling back into the crook of its arm. Maryam shook the child awake again.

"You'll work with your father if you want to be a peasant."

"There is no other life for me," said the child.

"There is the life of the spirit."

Babatha stirred. "Mommy?"

Maryam said, "Go back to sleep, Honey Bee. Your big sister wants to have a discussion now, here."

The Cub said, "Everyone has a life of the spirit. Especially Platon."

"Him?"

"Have you not even seen the beauty of the things he makes?"

"And what could you make, eh? What were you put in this world to do? Saw stone? I don't know what you were put on Earth to do, but it was not that. It was to do something for God. You said you could destroy the Temple. You are worried about destroying religion as it is." Something welled up in her like magma, something subterranean, so fierce she had to whisper it.

"Break the Temple then." Her words sizzled in the air. "Break it if that was what God put you on this Earth to do. Maybe it needs to be done."

The Cub opened up a snake-like eye. "I see. Destroy the Yehudai so your ambition can thrive."

Maryam was stunned for a moment. "What a horrible thing to say. Your ambitions."

"My ambition is to be a tekton. And to sleep." With that the child appeared to will itself to genuine sleep, a sleep so profound that no words or shaking could rouse it.

But the rest of the household was roused. Babatha started to cry, Yudeh the infant to howl and cough. Yakob was eating his own fist again. Yosef stumbled in looking befuddled. "It's as well, no harm," her husband murmured, patting her arm, thinking her distress was for her other children. "You rest, wife. Please my dear. I'll calm them down." And Maryam knew she was done then, that she'd best leave Yosef to get them all asleep.

The Cub had won, again.

In the morning, Maryam pressed her cheek against Babatha's.

She whispered, "I am so sorry Honey Bee. I'm so sorry I woke you up." She squeezed her tightly, but she knew what she really meant was that she was sorry for what she was going to do now.

"Your sister. The man she is working for is not a good man. I don't think she realizes that. You and me. We have to protect her. I'm sorry it has to be us, you, but I don't want to leave you alone again. So you and I are both going to watch over your sister."

Babatha's eyes were so solemn. Disappointed?

"I know your sister is a problem for you, for all of us. I'm so sorry that we can't just stay here and play and have fun. You deserve fun, Honey Bee." Maryam stroked the hair out of Babatha's eyes.

Then she took her daughter's hand and walked to the house of the tekton.

The Cub had spirited frail Yakob away just at dawn light. Again the thought: The child is possessed.

And so we go, back to the house of Death.

At the man's own gate, Maryam attacked Platon. "What do you want with my child?"

The tekton's lip curled in way that showed broken teeth. "Gah. You're both mad as dogs. Take him back with you."

She held out a hand towards the child, her fingers fanned wide apart. "Come. Come. You heard him. He doesn't want you."

The Cub stood with its arms folded. "I'm staying."

"What do you think you can learn from him? How to be ignorant? How to be cruel?"

The tekton muttered under his breath. "Stuck-up Sadducai bitch."

Maryam turned towards him, chin thrust out. "We're not Sadducai. They are a different school."

"Tuh!" Like a tall building, Platon was rocked by scorn.

She stepped right up in front of him. "This is a little girl. I know what she says she is. She says she's a boy. She's not. A little girl will not be a tekton. She will never be your apprentice." Maryam chuckled in fury. "She's coming home."

Platon looked up suddenly as if struck by a question, his eyebrows raised, "So it's the Law that a builder can't be a girl?" His smile looked like a dagger with two points. "Weren't expecting that, were you?" Then he turned his back to her. "That's cause you think I'm stupid."

Years ago on the road outside Neapolis near an inn Maryam had seen some creature stride out wearing men's clothes, short hair. The creature had made herself enormously fat as a disguise – fatness in men can make breasts.

The miracle birth was going to end up a freak, one of those few poor women in men's dress limping through life and offering male gestures, short hair, pleading eyes and a thin mean mouth.

And no prophecy.

The Cub moved forward to pick up a metal-toothed bow-saw so that both he and little Yakob could use it.

"What are you doing?" The builder said to the Cub, and flicked a finger towards the back wall of his byre and said in a voice full of bile, "Hang that one up. Come back with the shorter saw."

The child, so small for its age, wobbled off carrying the long two-handed saw.

Maryam and Babatha stood to witness. The Cub listened to the tekton tell it how stone could be sawed, and then tried to make a small cut.

"No, send-you-to-the-bottom-of-the-sea-to-be-eaten-by-fish. Shit! You'll wreck the cut. You idiot!" The tekton strode forward, hands raised, then glanced at Maryam.

And stopped.

He would have hit the child. Aha, you see? Maryam knew that this man was dangerous. She was not wrong. Maryam shook Babatha's hand. "I told you, Honey Bee."

The Cub started to saw stone. White dust coated its face, and it pumped back and forth, back and forth. Maryam saw what the Cub wanted. It wanted to be strong like a man though it was not a man, to grow shoulders like a man.

"It's not working," said Babatha. "Can we go? I'm hungry."

"Go home. Get away from my gate," said the tekton.

The Cub walked out to her and said softly, "Ami, we will both be home tonight as always. I'll bring food."

"Do you really think you were born to chip away at stone or grind table legs?" Her smile was grim.

"I think we were meant to eat," said the Cub. "I think we're meant to work. I'm learning how to split stone and make beams of basalt. And the double rows of arches that hold up the beams."

"You're learning how to be beaten by a brute."

The Cub was looking at her very intently. "Maybe I need to learn how that feels. If I am to understand all men."

Maryam leaned forward to look into its face, and she kept her voice low. "You have a birthright beyond the wealth of nations. It is not yours to squander."

The Cub spoke without the lips moving, its eyes sympathetic, and the words precise. "You are right, but it is utterly beyond you and anything you understand." The child turned away.

"You do not turn your back on your mother."

The Cub turned and walked into the courtyard backwards, facing her. "You who know who I am. Do you think I cannot see in both directions at once?"

The child closed the gate so she could not see. Maryam

did not move. Eventually Yosef came with the cart. "Please come, Maryam. The day is nearly done. Our boys will be safe. Please come. Please?"

Maryam had been standing most of the day and was made of frail flesh. Yosef caught her as she sagged and he guided her back to the cart.

"Glad she's not my wife!" The tekton called. "She'd drive an angel to despair."

The cart rocked and wobbled its way home. *I don't know why you would listen to me, God of Yisrael. I don't know why you gave me this burden to bear. But I need you to help me bear it. I need your help just to live and go on.*

It was foolishness, desperation to pray for yourself. You prayed to God for the preservation of his people, to reinforce the covenant, for perhaps a good harvest, or to placate his rage. Why, why would God listen to you?

Then why come crashing into my life, God?

Why send me the child and then leave me unaided? Yes, I am asking your help, God. Help with your child that you planted in me.

The light through her eyelids was red, full of the blood of life. Light filtered through her blood, into her flesh.

And an answer.

This will not pass. It will go on. You must endure.

The cart rocked to a stop. Maryam opened her eyes and there was her life; the house that was missing one wall; the children; the meals to be cooked and the clothes to repair. It would not change, or change only slowly and she would ache for it one day when it was gone.

CHAPTER 12

MALE AND FEMALE SPHERES

Whenever Maryam's life got grim, Yosef gave her another baby.

Another smiling, giggling, beautiful little thing with eyes full of starlight, new-come from God. God was in those eyes.

After Yoses and Yudeh, came a sister for Babatha, a little girl called Tara. Tara was calm and accepting, a placid babe. She would sit, staring, neither crying nor laughing. Maryam was grateful for the peace, but sometimes found Tara dull. For a time Babatha played with her as if she were a doll, and then, in that increasingly male household, became her sister's defender. Tara did not seem to notice.

Two years after Tara came Shemenolo. Though named for the great king, this boy was not at all wise. Shem was always getting into scrapes and contusions.

The women of the house were with the clothes and the food and the cleaning and the healing; the men were with their work or their reading. Little Tara was soon set to helping Babatha clean or peel. The house was divided into male and female spheres.

"As God intended," Yosef told Maryam. He thought to please her. But she wondered where the other Yosef had gone, the one who had said the division of the sexes was a loss as great as Babel.

There was a shadow, a constant shadow.

It. The child. Not so much a child now.

Maryam couldn't call her eldest the Cub once it was adult. Nor bring herself to call it Yehush, which was really no name at all. The gang's nickname Yazz was a hoodlum's name. For her, the child was nameless.

The eldest at nineteen had not grown any taller.

Its jovial friends sometimes called it Zeyr, meaning Titch or Tiny. Zeyr never grew a beard, but then many men went clean-shaven. It was assumed Yazz/Zeyr was just being stylish and Greek.

Maryam's eldest was as handsome as it was ever going to get – brown-faced, button eyes, a huge smile with teeth that were whiter than limestone in sunlight. The legs were massive, stumpy but able to run up the terraces and jump over walls.

Yakob was entranced by his sibling. He worked with the eldest all day. "We'll do it this way," the eldest would say, somehow making any alternative impossible. Yakob would jump to make Yehush happy or agreeable. Yakob tried to be like Yazz and be merry and popular.

But Yakob was growing up tall, pimply, and horse-faced. He looked on his sibling with a goofy wonder, nodding and smiling at everything the little bossyboots said. Babatha teased him. "You're in love with her." Her smile had a curl in it.

The sun came out in Yakob's face whenever the eldest so much as smiled on him or said things like, "That's it.

I told you that you'd get it in the end. No, no, no don't spoil it now just because I told you did it well." A forgiving chuckle.

At home. "Come on Shambleshanks. Let's wash that stinking tunic of yours. Come on. Take it off." Under loincloth Yakob's penis was curving upright without him knowing why.

The eldest would glance it at and say in pity. "You see Shambles? You're a stronger fellow than you thought."

Kindness and patience too for the ordinary brother who, bless him, still could not master any original phrase in the liturgical language. Maryam was not entirely convinced that even now at seventeen Yakob could read.

There were village girls of course, drawn to the eldest by the same thing that held Yakob.

Sometimes the girls and the eldest held hands. Sometimes one of the village girls, plump or buck-toothed, would take brother Yakob's hand in sympathy. And then, out of nowhere, Maryam and Yosef's house would be full of girlish laughter.

Stupid laughter, laughter that if you assembled what had been said, had no trace of wit about it. Just bubbling good spirits. The young people boiled like a pot full of giggles until Maryam would say, "Come now, girls, return to your mothers, return to your fathers. No! Yakob and you, you both stay here. Honestly."

Yakob and the first-born had no real need of Yosef and Maryam – the reverse in fact already was true. Despite what Maryam had said, the boys would escort the girls home, and they held hands, possibly even kissed in moonlight, and Maryam would pray then that none of the girls would lift the first-born's skirts.

But, of course, each time the courtship had to stop. The robes could not be raised. No marriage, no children, but lots of tender smiles and swinging hands and giggles. Or were the girls just playing a game? The eldest's shoulders had broadened and its hands were as rough as pebbles, but even so – to Maryam it was apparent with a glance that her first-born was a girl.

Yet some of the Nazaredai thought of this Yazz as a bit of a demon with the women. Dark chuckles, and groans of, "He's off again, look at him go. Not another one!" And wives nodding, "Watch your daughter around that one. Too sharp a smile, that one."

But then, beside the well, the mothers would seize Maryam's forearm. "I must say that boy of yours, he's a little demon, but you know, they all say, he never goes too far. He never shames us or you or our daughters. This is what it is to be a son of the priests. No misbehaviour."

The mothers of the eldest's girlfriends loved him too, despite the gang of hoodlums who followed him.

Yazz was their ringleader, going off to gamble with them at night and (it was said) to carouse and do daredevil stunts. Fathers sought them out and dragged their daughters home. Sometimes the boys' loud shouts echoed late into the night.

Yakob and the eldest would stumble back into the house red-faced and spurting with laughter. The first-born kept an easy hand on Yakob's shoulder, and Yakob looking almost cross-eyed with glee, boggled by his sibling's daring, wit, wisdom, and kindness.

Maryam wondered if Yakob would ever escape the first-born's stifling wondrousness. What a fate to grow up unknowingly next to a god.

Babatha now had a group of her own. They would stand

by the well and their laughter came to the house like the trickling sounds of a creek.

Left in the house, Maryam could hear Yoses and Yudeh too, the sounds of a race being run or children climbing roofs. There was a craze for mouth-spraying berry juice on the terrace rocks, to silhouette the shape of a hand.

From over Platon's walls came cries and crackling of wood and the smell of fruit roasting over a fire. Maryam could identify Yakob's laugh. Then Esta the wife would join in, sounding both beside herself and melting with gratitude. With a kind of a barking yelp, Platon too would sometimes laugh with them. Platon's laughter sounded like a tortured cow.

Their howls rose up like clouds over Nazareth, as if laughter and fun were part of the campfire sending up sparks, and the sparks rose to become new stars. The screams of laughter always made Maryam jump. She would clutch her heart and only slowly realize it was the sound of people enjoying themselves.

Maryam would catch herself thinking *Why are the old so miserable? Why are we afraid of people having fun?*

Sometimes one of the eldest's girlfriends would visit Platon's house too, and she would join in the laughter, high-pitched and screaming.

And once, only once, the sound of Maryam's first-born raging with anger. The eldest was castigating its master. "Hands off her. Hands off now! In front of your wife? In front of Esta? We're going home. NOW!"

The sparks extinguished. And Maryam would smile to herself – her eldest bossed around even the master builder.

And once, when Esta was laughing, still a child really, over many walls came a lion-like roaring. The sound of a blow travelled across the village. Then sobbing, wailing. The tekton was beating Esta again.

It was too much for Maryam. "I can't stand it," she said and threw down her embroidery, and stormed outside into glowering darkness.

And out of the darkness came the eldest carrying a lamp and talking rapidly to that horrible man. Platon was making noises like a wheel axle. The eldest was cajoling, comforting – Maryam couldn't hear what was said, but she knew her first-born was intervening in another family's life. The tekton sounded miserable for having beaten his wife. Her first-born, that creature, was crafting remorse into something else.

Maryam didn't know this person Yazz. She herself had never taken on anyone else's woes. She certainly wouldn't stride into a marriage and try to change it for the better – that would be foolish, presumptuous. Presumptuous because she, Maryam, had never got to know anyone well enough to help a marriage. The eldest was guiding its master, with Maryam invisible in the dark.

Eldest: "Let's go back. You can talk to her. All will be well."

The firstborn really did have a beautiful voice, deep and high in a sustained note.

Master and apprentice turned, and in the darkness beyond them, between them, was a light, a fluttering inexhaustible glint from the courtyard fire through the tekton's open gate. It really did look, at that moment, as if the light rose out of the space between the two people going back to make amends to the child bride.

* * *

Years before, Platon had built the Nazaredai a meeting house.

The Greek-speakers among them called it a proseuche. A reading room – scripture could be read there but prayers never, let alone sacrifices. The proseuche was tiny, but all its walls were white limestone with a kind of stone table for the scrolls with a bas-relief of the Ark of the Covenant, which Platon imagined had wheels of its own.

Platon had also started to build a miq'va, hewing it out of bedrock. But he had argued with Achaikos over where the water was to come from – it could not be drawn from a well, apparently. In cold fury, Platon had stopped work.

Achaikos still assumed he was the village's religious leader. It was his job to read. Out of humility, respect and a lack of anything better the Nazaredai let him.

But now the eldest even in the middle of the Great One's reading would jump up and start to talk. It was almost as though it was impatient with the scriptures, and thought they needed to be corrected.

The eldest would improvise, start by saying that the mountain of humankind had been viewed the wrong way up. Slaves were the foundation of the world. Secretly they ran it, for they were closer to God. God appointed them while kings only appointed themselves and God cared little for them.

The thing was, when this young tekton spoke, you believed what was said. And Achaikos could hear his own voice trailing away. Achaikos could deepen his own voice, or slow down or speak loudly – it made no difference. His words were less regarded, and he himself seemed fatter, whiter, more collapsed. At those times Achaikos's face would be grey and shadowed with lumps and streaks. Any bruised peasant could see that Achaikos was afraid. Afraid of what this tekton-apprentice might say. For what the tekton's apprentice said could make the whole congregation whoop as if with merriment.

If the Perisa tried to out-quote this workman who sometimes danced and laughed when speaking, if this established man tried to o'er climb the child with liturgical lingo, then this child would slice him like blades of grass with Hebrew, the language of DWD, perfectly enunciated. He'd quote Devarim from memory, rolling waves of it. And grin.

The awful truth was that there wasn't a part of The Miq'ra that the labourer couldn't recite. And if the village drunks and buffoons looked baffled, then he'd simply recite it in the Common Tongue. And it couldn't be from memory. Targum, written translations of The Torah into Aramaic, were not in Yosef's house or any man's house in the village.

The brute was translating The Torah as he spoke, spinning the Common Tongue like flax from the gold of the liturgy, Nazareth's own little meturgeman.

So the story of Shlomo and DWD was told them in the fine filigree of the text, not a summary, but an embroidery in Common. The thing itself was brought home to them. This mason with his chisel-split hands could spin all Shabbat long.

Any peasant could read the old man's bitter, acknowledging twist of a smile. The head shaken up and down in an impatient yah yah yah. The old bore – distinguished gentleman – had been reduced to a childish bitterness.

Sometimes, this child threw even that out, the last semblance of appropriateness.

The eldest would start to sing the Mizmor. And sometimes, he'd just sing comic songs about village events. He would start to dance. He'd hold up his hands, and clap them or grab hands with his dangerous gang of friends and get them all stamping their feet. Peasants, singing liturgy. They would leave the meeting house singing phrases from the Shir Hashirim.

Then he'd lead them all, young boys or bellowing goons or farmhands in a game of sandal-toss – against the walls of the meeting house. As if it were there for that.

Achaikos's eyes burned into him. Fire trying to scorch ice.

This stonemason crowed at him once, as Achaikos was trying to slip past with dignity. "It's not like this in the Temple, old man. Or do you think God wants us to be miserable?"

Flat fact: centuries later the outlines of that stone gathering house would still be found in Nazareth.

After the Temple was destroyed, several priestly families moved there from the ruins of Yerusalam, away from the Romans. The clouds of history washed over Nazareth, terrors and hopes, wars and retributions. Something in the soil drew the small and meek – or merely the sincere. That is the earth they will inherit.

And dust travels round the world.

Maryam fell pregnant yet again.

The village men joked at Yosef's expense, "She's wearing her old man out, that one."

The women didn't joke. "I do hope she's careful. At her age."

Maryam so wanted to see starlight again in infant eyes. The house would be full of laughter. But this time she began to feel frayed. For five months she was exhausted to the point of sitting head in hands for long stretches of the day. She ate little, wanted to eat nothing, and the soles of her feet itched day and into the night.

This time, Maryam knew something was wrong.

She could feel it. The lump lay flat and heavy, and there was no movement. All her other beautiful children had danced in her stomach – but this one was not right.

And when at the end of the fifth month there was vomiting, cramps, and heaving; when Babatha ran to get Idra; when there was a sudden smearing of blood, and then a bone-bending clenching and heaving and rejection, Maryam was grateful. It had been, as she knew, no good. She had been fortunate indeed that the thing had been ejected without killing her. She sweated in bloody sheets, with Idra holding her hand and quietly weeping while Babatha in a desert-storm fury, gathered, wrapped and scrubbed.

"Poor child, poor child, go help her," Maryam croaked to Idra.

"I'm not letting go of you," was all Idra said.

Maryam's brood shuffled in hang-dog to pay respects. The eldest kissed her forehead. The four other boys huddled together. Tara stood forlornly. Yosef stood bowed, hand on Babatha's shoulder, as dignified as the statue of an ancient king.

So that's it. I'm done then, thought Maryam. No more babies.

It took her longer to recover than she thought it would. It was a month before she lowered herself down the ladder. Even then, none of them let her do anything. "Oooh I feel like a queen," she said joking.

"You are one, Ami," said Babatha and gave her the firmest of hugs.

The world was different after that. For some reason, she thought she heard it whispering to her, in the wind. The whispering was a comfort as was the tumbling of doves in the air overhead.

She would be here for a little while yet.

Finally, as if to shut out the world, the boys built the fourth wall.

Yakob and the eldest showed up one day with stone beams and bricks from the local kiln, (mud bricks piled high with arches underneath in which fires were built). They filled in the missing wall, as if to shut out the world. The boys never asked or discussed it with the old couple. They just did it.

"Done now," was all her first-born said, when it was in place, with a beautiful gate, that was only half a gate, hinged on one side in the new wall. It glided open and shut; an insinuation.

"Maybe we liked the sky," said Maryam. There was no light now, but then Yosef didn't read any longer, so why did they need light?

"Not when it blew rain," said her first-born. In storms, one half the room would be soaked. Rain and wind, eternal things.

"Open to God's will," said Maryam.

"God's will runs off you like rain," said the eldest.

Maryam froze. "God's will is between your legs. God's will is there every time you pass water. Or bleed."

The eldest said, glancing up, in a kind of good humour.

"I don't bleed." It was true. Unending work and poor food meant it didn't bleed.

Maryam poised, heavy with some new certainty. "I don't bleed either. At last we have something in common."

"It's God's will." The eldest was still admiring its bowel-market door, swinging it from side to side.

Maryam said, "You know God's will, I suppose."

"Yes," was the only answer she got. Off-hand, simple.

"And what is God's will?"

"That this door works."

That we live for a time, then die. Dust. The eldest was supposed to have come to do God's work. But the teacher had lost its way, was lost to the world and to God. Maryam knew that. How do you even begin to find words for that?

It was too big for words, but that didn't mean it wasn't true. Too big for words was almost a guarantee that it was true.

CHAPTER 13

THE PARTY FROM SEPPHORIS

And suddenly out of nowhere Yoses was thirteen years old, and full of scripture, and it seemed right that of all their children, he should go to the Temple.

And with a snap like a twig breaking, Maryam said, "Babatha should go with him."

There was a hanging moment: eyes stared; mouths hung open.

Maryam pressed on. "My dear." She looked direct at Yosef and made sure she did not glance at Babatha. "I'd love it if we could go again but..."

Old Yosef was already smiling and shaking his head. "My joints. No."

"... we can't go, but Yoses does need to be escorted by someone mature." She finally allowed herself to look at Babatha, who was absolutely still, with that imperturbable smile. "And there is no one more mature than Babatha." Maryam made sure she was not looking then at her eldest. She knew she was insulting it. And then she thought: no, that is not good enough.

"Sorry," she said, without using a name but nodding towards it. "But you've already been."

The eldest's smile was a mirror of Babatha's – as if it were being kindly with a fool.

"So. Babatha is there to go with Yoses, who finally can see what we have cost all our children." Maryam smiled on her daughter.

Babatha looked neither surprised nor delighted. She never moved at anything other than her own pace. She arched a finger and rubbed it under her nose. A curious gesture when told she had been given what Maryam thought she'd been aching for since age six.

Maybe the mistake had been to assume that Babatha would now be childishly happy.

With a gracious smile Babatha stepped forward. "I'll be happy to help. Indeed. My friends tell me that there's a pilgrimage going soon from Sepphoris. The finest people of the first water…" Her voice trailed off, her voice letting them fill in the rest.

The eldest spoke, chuckling. "Skip the bullshit, Atha. You and your fancy friends want to go to the big city."

Babatha turned to comfort Maryam. "She can't help it, Ami. Trying to be male has coarsened her mind. I'm sorry, I'm so sorry you have to put up with this." Babatha shook her head, her eyebrows slanted upwards. Among those in the know in the region, Babatha was regarded as something of a benchmark for beauty and comportment.

The eldest stood up and walked away, chuckling, but as he passed he seized Yoses, and put him in a headlock, laughed again. "They will get you to the city and back, and she will be in the very first water of society." The eldest made a sound like piss hitting a wall.

Maryam realized with a thump that she felt rueful in the same way.

The eldest said, "Come back Yo-yo and tell me all that the priests say, and we'll talk. No one else here will understand any of it."

That must have included Yosef the father. Yoses looked back and forth between them, knowing something had happened and not sure what.

Yosef encircled Yoses with one arm. "This is nothing to do with you, my boy."

The eldest rattled his fingers through his brother's hair and then left.

Babatha strode forward and gave Maryam an embrace. "Thank you, Ami. I don't know. I don't know." Even Babatha's uncertainty was graceful. "She wants to be like that. A ruffian. I think there is some thought there of, of – of course it would be beyond me. Some kind of making-everybody-the-same. But we're not. Thank heavens!" And Babatha laughed.

Maryam was searching Babatha's face. There was still no gratitude. And it had been the eldest whose feelings had throbbed in her bones. It was the eldest who looked like her, who thought like her. Babatha was like the girls back in Yerusalam, people of the first water, the girls who had made young Maryam miserable.

The caravan from Sepphoris came through Nazareth to collect Babatha.

Maryam could see that Babatha was disguising fury. The way her one good bracelet clinked around her wrist as she fussed over Yoses's tunic, slapping away imaginary dust. Her smile was poised, but her eyes were wide and clenched.

Why is she angry? Maryam could not understand.

Then even before they arrived, Maryam could hear the Sepphoridai laughing, she thought, at the village, and its rough, small houses perched on rock. Laughing at us poor folk.

Babatha was embarrassed.

Babatha smoothed down her robe, and then clenched Maryam's hand fiercely. "Dear Ami," she murmured. "Thank you." She straightened all her garments again, held onto Yoses's hand. The boy swallowed hard. He was in his one good robe, which was white and would show the dirt. His lips worked and then swallowed themselves. The three presentable members of the family were lined up.

Fifteen litters trailed towards their house, each with an armed guard. Wagons rumbled behind them, some carrying barrels, presumably of wine. Laughter bubbled out from behind drawn curtains. Lean men, their ligaments and veins sculpted and shining with sweat, bore the litters and then lowered them. A curtain was pulled back.

Inside, in dining-couch posture was a young woman. Yes, she was groomed with kohl around her eyes, yes her hair was trimmed straight and even. Her brow was high and round and smooth, her chin tiny and almost pointed, her eyes wide and expressive. The longer Maryam looked at her, the more beautiful she became.

"Here she is, here she is!" The woman cried holding out a hand towards Babatha.

"Elena! E-he-he-lena!" exclaimed Babatha. She tugged her mother's hand. The family's three presentables – Maryam, Babatha and Yoses – strode forward.

Elena called out to the other biers, "I told you she was gorgeous!"

Babatha smiled, and put her hands on her mother's shoulders. "Elena, this is Ami." She sounded proud.

Elena dipped her head. "The niece of the Kohen Gadol. It is an honour."

There was cawing laughter from behind and above. The village's olive tree by the well contained the eldest perched in its branches, chewing on a leaf.

It mocked them. "Ha ha ha. They have trained their mules to walk upright. With all that booze the biers will be twice as heavy by the time they arrive. They won't be able to walk, but the guards will roll them into the Temple."

Some of Yazz's gang were beginning to gather round. The Nazaredai began to chuckle.

Elena didn't flinch, but held out her hand to Babatha. "Climb in, dear."

Babatha had been practicing. As if she had been carried all her life, she gathered up long her black skirt (with Maryam's white embroidery), approached the bier sideways, then elegantly insinuated her way in by rolling onto her stomach.

The eldest cawed from the tree. "When the mules die of exhaustion, maybe they eat them too. There is nothing in the scriptures about not eating people. Ha ha ha." More Nazaredai laughter.

Babatha was looking strained.

"Yoses, dear, there's no room," she said.

Elena's voice. "Nonsense, nonsense we'll make room. Come here, darling."

Yoses had not been practicing, and tried to kneel inside one leg at a time. His bony knee ground onto his sister with his full weight. She clenched her jaw and made no sound.

From the olive tree: "Yo-yo. If one of them farts, just open the curtain and flap."

By now most of the Nazaredai were gathering or looking

out at the spectacle. Were these people born without legs? To make their fellow men carry them? How utterly and completely Greek of them.

Another Nazaredi voice, "Think of it, all those figs inside them." Maryam looked up. That was the goon called Smooch joining in. Maryam agonized for Babatha. She wanted the caravan gone, to spare them all.

And yet part of her wanted to laugh too. You will see nothing of the road, trapped in your coffins. There'll be no air, and you will sweat, and you will fear thieves every step of the way. And I know you will stay at the inn at Neapolis and that will cost a fortune.

"They will still call you Northerners!" The eldest shouted.

Which of course was why the Sepphoridai spent so much on display. So they would not be snubbed. Maryam's heart went out to them, too. Poor souls. She took Elena's hand. "Thank you for all your kindness to my daughter."

And out of nowhere, suddenly old Yosef stood beside her, with his straggly untended beard, in his long black robe, his head staining upwards. He ignored the Sepphoridai. "Yoses, my son. The priests sit in the Stoa on the outer corridor. Listen to them well and learn. But when asked to speak, speak from the heart."

This was the man who Babatha had not really wanted to display. The curtains on the biers flinched, parted and the Sepphoridai took in the radical exile, the absurd old man who had given up Yerusalam and condemned his family to ignoble poverty.

The caravan had come in laughter but it left in silence.

* * *

On her return, Babatha admitted the Temple and the Stoa were impressive.

She recounted how well Yoses had recited. They only asked him for passages from The Torah, so it was easy for him.

"He did very well," she said, and played with her brother's ringlets. She moved with a new ease, a kind of fulfilled saunter, and her smile looked less posed, as if she were about to laugh with delight. "He really did well. Every inch a Levite and scholar." Yoses smiled shyly, his eyes on the floor.

The eldest strode in sweaty, dusty. "My brother will be a great scholar." It spoke with complete certainty. "A Sadduci."

Babatha leaned forward. "Thankfully my friends didn't guess who the person up in the tree was. Like an ape."

The eldest smiled. "I wanted to humiliate them, Sis. Not you."

Babatha drew in breath. "I have been invited by them to Sepphoris for the Seder feast. May I go, Ami?"

"Ask your father," Maryam whispered.

"Who'll carry you?" asked the eldest. "I'd be your donkey. But of course I'd embarrass you."

Maryam said, hand on brow. "Stop."

Babatha said, composed. "I will walk."

"And go to a feast with dusty feet?"

"Stop," said Maryam.

"It's all right, Ami. I will change my sandals when I arrive. It's not difficult to behave with grace. You just have to think. You should try it some time, Sis."

So Babatha walked to Sepphoris in the declining afternoon. Yosef led their own Seder in a beautiful blue night with moon and stars.

And of course, Babatha had to spend the night in the town.

"I'm going to be married," she announced on her return.

Maryam knew how to behave. She made a gladsome cry, and leaned forward to accept her daughter's kisses, and she thought: *To one of those Sepphoridai.* She saw a lifetime of awkwardness stretching out in front of them. "Who to, Honey Bee?"

Babatha stepped back smartly. "Ami! I'm sorry you don't know him, but I know you will love him like a son. His name is Miltiades and he's Elena's cousin." Her voice broke then in genuine delight. "Oh Ami, he's so tall and handsome."

"I'm sure," said Maryam. *And so it starts. Our household breaks.* "Did, did he go on the pilgrimage with you?"

Babatha looked urgently at her and took her hand. "Ami, Ami. There was no impropriety."

"I know…"

"I promise. The men and the women were all in separate litters. Except of course the married couples. But we did meet – outside the Temple."

Maryam chuckled. "I did wonder why you had so little to say about the Stoa and the Court of Women. You were looking at something else."

Nothing like this ever happened to me. This is how it is supposed to be. Seventeen in the full flower of beauty, so soon taken. Maryam couldn't resist tangling her fingers in her daughter's hair.

Babatha pressed her cheek against Maryam's hand. "I'm so glad you're pleased. They're a very good family, Ami."

"I'm sure they are," said Maryam. *You would accept nothing less.*

Little Tara was standing beside them, looking pudgy and downcast. Babatha saw her and spun and knelt and grabbed her and hugged her. "Oh darling, don't worry. I'll come to see you every day."

"You won't," said the eight year-old, and buried her face against her sister's shoulder.

Maryam stoked the little girl's head. She doesn't want to be left alone with all these boys. Her hand suddenly froze.

She had just thought of the eldest as a boy.

Babatha looked round and up at her mother. "Or. Or maybe, Tara could come and stay with us?" Babatha's eyes were pleading.

Miltiades was not handsome.

He was however big – tall and already pudgy about waist and chin, which he tried to hide with a painstakingly trimmed beard. His face seemed to sink in about the eyes, which were circled with darker skin. But he did have a fine head of thick, wavy and oiled hair, which hung down almost to his shoulders, but not quite or it would stain his white tunic that had gold zigzag trim.

He really did think he was some kind of Greek. Or Roman. Maryam felt a smile somewhere in her upper lip. She found Milt absurd. And he had hairy shoulders.

The conversation was excruciating. Idra showed up and – bless her – flitted about with pitchers of wine or water, pretending to be some kind of household servant. Maryam could say nothing to Idra without embarrassing everyone, but she really wished that none of them honoured this kind of thinking.

That people were better depending on the clothes they wore.

Miltiades addressed all his remarks to Old Yosef. Technically, the marriage should have been arranged between the two fathers. His father was there too, a slimmer, shorter version of his son with weary, watchful eyes. You couldn't actually see the pupils through the folds of flesh, but his skin was reassuringly sunburnt and lined, as if he had done work outside. And it was plain that Miltiades was ashamed of him. They didn't want the old man to speak.

Yosef had nothing to say to Miltiades. So Maryam started to speak. "So, Miltiades. You are Elena's cousin. She's so beautiful."

Miltiades's smile looked carved. "Yes, everybody says that."

Maryam had said the right thing. "We are honoured to have her as Babatha's friend."

The frozen smile did not reply that the family of Miltiades was honoured to know them.

Maryam knew how to take revenge. She looked at his honest old dad and asked him. "And you, Sir, what do you do for a living?"

The son answered for him. "Trading. Land."

Farming, Maryam thought. *Olives and, since you think you are Greek, cheese.* Maryam looked at Milt's broad shoulders. *You must be very handy on the farm. If you can take a moment away from your hair.*

Babatha's eyes widened at her mother in warning. Maryam's looked back at her beautiful daughter. *But who really would be worthy of you?*

Maryam leaned forward, smiling. "Milt. May I call you Milt?"

His smile looked queasy, but he had to be agreeable at this first meeting, so Milt it was.

"Milt, isn't it a wonder how Sepphoris has grown?" They talked about Sepphoris being a boomtown, all that building, and the patronage of the Tetrarch. They did not mention the massacre or the replacement population.

"Lots of work for tektons," said the eldest.

That gave Milt a chance to talk about the house he was building for them both to live in, to raise a family. This was highly unusual – sons usually found a nook in their father's house in which to live. Yes, his family wanted this marriage.

They think they are becoming Kohanim.

Milt and Babatha each leaned in against each other and shared a smile. Babatha at least was genuinely besotted. Good – the alternative was that her daughter was only marrying for position.

Milt kept talking about the courtyard, the two floors, and the rooftop for summer. "We'll plant some trees for shade. Many bedrooms. For the children." In the end, Milt's old father raised a hand for his son to be still.

Yosef bowed to the old gentleman, whose name they had not been told. "You are making handsome provision, Sir." The dignified old farmer leaned forward himself. He had a beautiful husky voice that reminded Maryam of applewood smoke. "We love your daughter, all of us. She's a looker on the outside, but it's the beauty inside we love."

How is it, Maryam wondered, that someone like you raised a fool?

So her daughter's future was settled before it had a chance to be unsettled, children in rooms, a cook to chide and order about, and female friends reclining on couches while being served wine.

And after that realizing that you were fat and sagging and very bored, relieved that in a small town there was little space for adultery.

Looking at this pleased idiot, Maryam saw his middle-aged face, going bald. No. There is always space for adultery.

Not a bad life. Just not one that Maryam would want for herself.

Then little Tara trotted out, dolled up in one of Babatha's most elaborate old dresses with a veil hanging open to show newly ringleted hair, like a proper Sepphoridai social climber.

"Sister. Come and meet my Miltiades."

Tara giggled and was shy. She had Maryam's disappearing chin and beaky nose, but Yosef's melting eyes.

"We're going to have a big lovely house," said Babatha. "You can come and stay! You could have your own room."

"Oh," intervened Maryam. "We're not ready to lose Tara just yet."

But Maryam was sure. That was the plan. It turned out that the old man's name was the same as his son's.

The betrothal ceremony had to be held at Yosef's poor house.

Milt's family paid to have stakes driven into the rock and hangings put up to shade the guests and provide some privacy, since the house lacked a courtyard. They paid to lay out tables with food and some wine, and to have the ketubah, the marriage contract, drawn up. In the modern way the husband's family was not to pay the dowry. Two hundred shekels would be held in trust in case Milt died (or, unsaid, divorced her).

Weeks before, Miltiades barMiltidiades had caused to be delivered bolts of blue and black cloth. The implication was clear: new clothes for the betrothal please. There was not much time, though enough cloth for all nine of them, even Yudeh and Shem.

So Maryam stitched and sewed good new garments for them all. Babatha and Tara sat with her working, and dear Idra too, helping with the embroidery.

But the eldest? What would her eldest even wear – something black like a man? Swathed in veils like a woman with stonecutter's hands? Babatha's eyes swam with remorse, misgiving, and sometimes disgust. What could they all do about the wayward, tree-sitting sister?

Once, the eldest swept back into the house, kicking open the new door then backing in pots of water. It saw them sewing, and mugged a smile at them all especially Idra, who nursed the smile to herself.

"Don't make any clothes for me," the eldest said in a roughened maiden voice. "Don't worry, Sis." It smacked a kiss on the sibling's cheek. "I won't embarrass you by being there."

Babatha's lips worked, shocked and embarrassed, trying to find words. The eldest swept out before words came.

On the day only Milt's immediate family and Elena came.

There was no appetite among the Sepphoridai to climb the hill again to face hoots and catcalls. The family arrived in three litters only. It was Yosef who made sure the bearers all had water and shade and something to eat.

Elena streamed out, taking her friend's arm, and she did look genuinely pleased and delighted. "Oh! I can't wait until we are neighbours. We'll see each other every day!"

Milt's mother came this time, a veil over her head. She had a worn cheerful face and a neck in strands like a turtle's. Around it, a necklace of coins. She bore down on Maryam, her arms outstretched, and hugged her and called her Sister in the Common Tongue. "I'm the mother. I'm Bruria," she said. "We'll leave all the business side of it to the men and have ourselves a sociable time."

Like Idra, Milt's mother hid her toothless smile. Maryam took her arm and agreed that yes they would. The old woman chuckled and darted her head this way and that. "Imagine us, marrying Kohanim."

A daughter of the priestly class meant that the children too would be linked to them, though the titles passed from father to son. That was what everyone was thinking, but the mother was the only person to say it.

Maryam shook her arm to reassure her. "We're nothing special. Just people with big ideas of themselves."

"You're not the only ones," muttered the mother darkly. And they both laughed.

Contracts were signed, and the gifts delivered – two goats, oil, some chickens, four fine silver cups, more bolts of cloth (one with gold embroidery plainly meant for Babatha alone), a jar of honey, and a raft of kitchen implements and pans, some of them not new.

Old Yosef immediately (as was increasingly expected) gave all the gifts to his daughter to take to the new house. Or he would have been thought a retrograde old brute.

Old Miltiades took Yosef's arm. "Hold them for us 'til then. We can't take them back all that way now. Enjoy the milk, eat the eggs." Miltiades Senior did NOT say: your family need the food. The man had known hunger.

The bearers then laid out still warm sections of roasted

calf and apples roasted with mint, dill and cumin. Wine was rolled in barrels. A feast indeed. Yudeh and Shem crammed the food into their mouths in such a way that Idra snatched their hands and wiped their chins. Yoses and Tara, careful of their new clothes, picked delicately.

Yakob dangled uncertainly on the edges, his new tunic too short for him, his long skinny ankles looking twisted and hairy. He kept feeding himself just for something to do. He blinked continually, something he did when nervous. Elena came to him trying to be kindly and friendly, but he didn't know where to look or what to say. Maryam inclined towards him and helped.

"He's very skilled my boy. He makes things in stone, or wood if there is any."

"Wood, in these parts no," agreed Elena. "Much too valuable. Do you make things in wood?"

"Little…" (mouthful shifting to one side) "little folding tables." He'd come out in spots two days before.

Maryam helped again. "That's one of them there."

Elena knelt. "It's beautiful."

"It's not granted to all of our children to be scholars."

"Oh, heavens, I would say your children are blessed with talents." Yakob's eyes were hooded. "But I thought you had another child?" Elena's eyes started to search the small gathering.

Maryam did not quite lie. She put a hand on Yakob's arm and said, "This is our eldest son." Yakob's face went more mask-like.

"He's so like his father," said Elena, trying to be pleasant.

Maryam scooped up a huge dish of food, and after a reasonable time Yakob folded it into a bag and slipped away to wherever the eldest was hiding. Most likely they were drinking wine in the house of Platon. They would be able to hear the clatter and murmur of the betrothal.

The guests left. Night fell. With a hunchback moon curving overhead, the eldest bounced back in looking rather merry, still in a work tunic, streaked with limestone dust. Its sandals had been made supple though constant wear and the tops of its feet were dinged by nails and streaked by the straps. The toenails were broken. "Thanks for the food, Sis. It were delicious." It passed Babatha the greasy bowl. "Not long to wait now 'til you are out of all this."

As expected, the Sepphoridai showed up for the homecoming at Milt's new house.

They reclined under sunscreens of billowing linen. The wine ran out. The house was neither as grand as promised, nor was it quite finished.

Most of Maryam's family came down the hill from Nazareth carried on biers. Yosef gave the children coins to tip the bearers.

The eldest walked, arriving halfway through. It wore man's clothes, dressed for a sister's wedding, down to soft clean sandals. Maryam gaped – the robe was silky, male, black. She learned later that it was one of Platon's old festival robes. Her eldest looked tiny, wiry, weatherbeaten as if it had no beard because it sanded tables with its face. The hair was streaked with honey from constant sunlight.

Babatha froze, turned, did not introduce the late arrival. The person, some nameless Nazaredi, accepted a plate of roast ox and ate standing up.

When plates were cleared this personage jumped up onto a table and began to sing, unasked.

The eldest sang scripture as if this were the proseuche of Nazareth, with a certainty that this would be welcome. The company paused; the keening voice was worth hearing, so clear and cutting, not like a low priestly drone, but with something like a young boy's clarity and purity, seasoned with something huskier.

> The voice of gladness,
> the voice of the bridegroom
> and the voice of the bride,
> the voices of those who sing,
> as they bring thank-offerings
> to the house of the Lord

Babatha's eyes softened. The eldest looked joyful, arms and smile wide. The thick-fingered hands were held aloft.

> Give thanks to the Lord of hosts,
> for the Lord is good,
> for his steadfast love endures for ever!
> For I will restore
> the fortunes of the land as at first, says the Lord.

There was a moment of silence before the applause began. Babatha slumped back, and looked for a moment lost in thought.

And Maryam thought of that voice, that ease with scripture, and felt regret for what might have been.

CHAPTER 14

ENOUGH

Time flows faster as you age.

It seemed no time at all to Maryam that Babatha had given birth to her first child, Theophilus. Greek name. Squalling and fat like his father.

Yoses was rising fifteen. Babatha became all serious, plump and wrapped in scarves. She spoke now with the authority of being the productive adult. Maryam was suddenly a granny.

"You know, Ami, there's a chance Yoses is very talented."

Yoses, slim, browner than the rest of the family though he never left the house, was always reading Yosef's scrolls. Babatha had become his advocate. "He's, well, plainly, he's the most Godly and religious of the family. Excepting you, Abi. Well. Now. Father Miltiades has just sold some land at a handsome profit. And."

She took hold of her parents' hands. "I know how much you care for all of us and how much you wished you could do more for us." She pressed the back of Maryam's hand to her lips, "Father Miltiades will pay for Yoses to study at the Stoa school."

Maryam couldn't stop herself thinking: *they're not your babies*. The vast gift didn't stop her thinking: *that still won't make Miltiades's son into a Kohen.*

But old Yosef's eyes were dim, and he had taken to chewing air with a circular motion when he was moved. "Oh! Oh what kindness. My son! Do you hear? You will study in the Temple school, like I did. I trust you will make better use of it."

The boy stood like a dead tree someone was trying to uproot. Something in the whole situation tried Maryam's patience so she snapped. "For God's sake, Yo-yo, show some gratitude." (Later, she would have no idea why the outburst took that form. She knew it was Babatha and her in-laws who had angered her.)

The young man murmured some kind of inaudible thanks.

Babatha's eyes were swimming again as she looked at her mother, though she was addressing Yoses. "I know you're a bit overwhelmed, Brother."

Maryam had no words for what she felt and was glad that she couldn't find them. The words would have been poison. She kissed her daughter's hand in return.

Old Yosef's hands moved in unison in a praying gesture. "You're going to study in Yerusalam. I have done you no harm." He was rocking slightly and Maryam realized that he was actually thanking God.

"Oh, Abi," said Babatha and started to cry.

"You will be a scholar," said the old man, and hugged his son who still did not move. They knew the years of Herod's reign and of Herod Antipas. So they knew when Old Yosef had been born. He was sixty-one years old.

So came the day, sun and clouds skittering overhead,

when Yoses was to travel by himself in a wagon bearing the barMiltiades harvest of barley to Yerusalam. Yoses at fifteen was even taller, even slimmer, looking nothing like either Yosef or Maryam.

The eldest came striding out to him, and hugged him. Yoses towered over his sibling. The damnable confidence of the eldest had not left it. "Just remember Yo-yo that truth doesn't always rest in scrolls. Just because something is written doesn't mean it's true. You won't remember that. But at least I warned you."

Yoses flinched and his smile took the shape of a bird in flight. Maryam hadn't quite realized until that moment that her shy son was afraid of the eldest. Something in the way the boy pulled back, looked pleased to be escaping, finally escaping this advancing-Roman-cohort of a sibling.

Babatha understood too, and was pleased. Babatha's eyes crinkled up with love, and she kissed Yoses. *She thinks she's saving him. From it, from the eldest.* A feeling like that, Maryam realized, runs very deep.

"Say something to…the eldest," Maryam asked Yoses.

Yoses prevaricated, shuffled. The wagon driver said to Babatha, "Sorry Madam barMiltiades, but…"

"You have to go. Come, come, goodbyes don't get better for being drawn out." Babatha patted Yo-yo, and then swung him up into the cart. She then slapped the buttock of one of the oxen and the cart did indeed jerk forward as she had bidden.

Yoses didn't write.

Yosef fretted and sent long letters of instruction back by travellers, but who knows if the scrolls ever got there.

Out walking, Maryam suddenly realized there were two new houses on the northern reach of Nazareth. When had those been built?

Babatha showed up swollen. And then just weeks later, it seemed, she visited with a new child attached to her breast, a little girl this time. The babe had a Miltiades family name, Seblma.

Yosef caught Shem spying on Tara as she washed. Shem was only ten, and as far as Maryam was concerned, it was natural curiosity. But Yosef erupted into a fountain of grief and recrimination, as if Tara had been mortally wounded. "My little girl!" he mourned, rocking back and forth.

For the first time ever Yosef physically punished one of the children, striking Shem over and over on the soft underside of his wrist. "You never do that again! You take your dirty mind and control it."

Shem, bewildered, ashamed and then horrified stared back and forth and winced in pain and then wailed. He howled for the better part of an afternoon.

Babatha visited and saw how Yosef glowered at the little boy, shaking his head, and rocking back and forth with implied prayer, muttering, "In my house. In my house." The eldest was sitting with Shem, playing cross-match with bits of stone.

Babatha's eyes latched on Maryam's with alarm, and Maryam flicked her hand to come outside: she had to tell her, there was no hiding it.

Babatha whooshed out a blast of air, then took her hand. "Ami, you and Aba have nothing to blame yourselves for. Poor Aba, he so believes in goodness and chastity."

There are things in this marriage I will never tell you, Maryam thought. Yosef hates masculinity – she must have had this thought before, but seeing how shaken Yosef was, how disturbed, it struck her like a fresh revelation.

Babatha hugged her father. "Abi, Abi, it's all right. Nothing too terrible has happened. But this is a household of boys, Abi, men."

"I thought we were better than that. I thought we had raised them to be pure."

"There is another influence in this house than you and Mother. Look, Abi. Tara is a woman now, she's twelve. In a household of boys. Maybe she should now come to live with me and my husband?"

You are taking my babies away from me. Maryam knew as surely as if her foot were caught in a trap that there would be no argument against this.

Babatha looked at the bestilled youngest daughter who was staring at the floor. "Would you like that, Tara?"

Round-faced, round-eyed, Tara wobbled her head from side to side, which may have meant yes. When she cast her eyes down, she nursed a secret smile: she was very pleased indeed.

Yosef quailed, stood taller. "It ought to be him who is cast out, not the girl. It ought to be him."

Babatha took both his hands in hers and shook them. "Abi, Abi, you are not a family of outcasts. You always have us."

"Of course we are not a family of outcasts, that's not what your father meant." Maryam nearly could not move with outrage.

"I've just said that, Ami."

Maryam flicked her wrists for them to talk outside again. In the hot sun, she spun on her heel and looked Babatha in the face. "I want Tara to stay."

"Of course you do, Ami. She's lovely and she balances the house. I know how you love having her here. Tara is comely and graceful, but she's not like you or me. She's a quiet, quiet soul, and she needs to be nurtured." Babatha held up a hand to forestall what Maryam was going to say. "Not! Not that you and Aba haven't provided such a good home for her. But she's like Yoses. She's taken the best of your teaching. Yudeh, Shem. I hate to say it but they're villagers."

Maryam experimented. How far would Babatha go? "Peasants."

Babatha sighed. "Yes. That's not your fault."

"Whose fault is it?" Maryam's voice was small and she waited.

"Ami, we know whose fault it is. It, it can't be healthy living with that thing. God knows what she says to the boys, but she's not a man, so takes being a man too far, takes the worst of being a man, behaving badly, going out at night, swaggering. You know, a real man. Miltiades doesn't have to do that. Poor Aba, he's so upset." Babatha's eyes welled up with tears.

In the end though, it was Tara who decided. The secret firm smile, the glowing eyes. "Please Ami. It's so lovely where Babatha is. Please."

It's the dresses, Maryam decided. The dresses and the cousins and the company, which she is too bestilled to find for herself. And, in time, the marriage. For a girl like Tara, maybe it was best. A local marriage, and it might as well be to someone who could provide.

Only to herself, very quietly, Maryam knew that Tara's quietness was nothing to do with comportment. Tara was slow in spirit. But the poor child so wanted to be with her beautiful, admirable sister. And to be away from both Maryam and her father who were more like grandparents.

Their mule died.

And that changed everything. Yudeh found the beast early one morning, lying on her side next to the house.

It was like losing a family member. The ground was too rocky to bury her, so they sold her to the heathens as meat for the poor. Scavengers dragged away the carcass. The family was left, bereft, in mourning. And they couldn't afford another animal for the cart.

Yosef no longer had a business. He sat in silence not even trying to read, as his eyes were worse. He ate his porridge sitting upright on the ground – dining couches made his spine curve painfully. "What is the point?" he said once and Maryam reached across and took his hand, but she knew what he meant. They both looked at birds in the sky, as if the creatures had flown out of their own chests, escaped but aimless.

Yakob and the eldest worked all hours for the builder. Yudeh and Shem, suddenly sixteen and fourteen were found jobs working on the barMiltiades farms, scything cow feed and binding it, coming back home with black hay dust on their faces. At harvest and ploughing they too stayed in Sepphoris. A great silence descended on the tiny house.

Yosef's smile-shaped eyes with their crinkled lids really did seem to turn up at both corners. He would say things like, "The house is getting quieter, Mother," or "Have we heard from Tara? What news?" or "Yoses hasn't written. I hope he is not being made to feel stupid. He's a quiet boy. He's not stupid."

And her eldest, its tunic fuggy with sweat, would take both the father's hands and say, "He will be taller and broader and more confident. He will be well dressed and washed. And he will no longer really be a member of our family, Abi. He will be accepted as a priest. He will regard us as Yoazar did."

Maryam said, "You're not comforting him."

The eldest said, "Abi doesn't want comforting. He wants the truth. The truth is denied to him by distance. Truly, there is no way for him to know the truth, but you can starve to death for lack of truth."

And the eldest would go outside and look at the stars, his back hunched as if something were swelling inside. Yakob would sit next to the eldest, his whole side nestling against the first-born. They would sit in patient silence.

Like a dunnock fooled by a cuckoo's egg, Yakob loved the eldest. He was now in his twenties and Maryam feared that there could be no other love.

They both lay back together to look at the stars. Like lovers. Yakob even took the eldest's hand. He slept with the eldest at night, heaped over him, in a storm-cloud tussle of blankets.

Well.

She and Yosef had never had sex. And people would say that was unnatural. And who was she to say? Who was she to say what love was, or when it was wrong? And if the world knew, who knows, maybe they'd be stoned. All of them. Yosef for not wanting to be male, the eldest for not wanting to be female, Yakob for wanting only affection. It wasn't healthy like Babatha. It was only that…

Maryam liked her own strange family better than she liked Babatha's.

* * *

Yoses came back for a visit when he was eighteen.

He was tall, still slim across the shoulders. He reminded Maryam of someone but she couldn't quite remember who.

He told his parents he was marrying. Outside the clan. A Zadokite girl, of good family. Very broad-minded people. Lovely. The trip to Nazareth would have been too much for her. You will meet her. One day. He spoke with an accent that struck Maryam as ludicrously over-refined, like a peacock trained to perform stunts.

The eldest crossed its legs, and covered its smile with rough fingers with chipped nails. "I warned you, Bro."

"I'm sorry?" Yoses's lip was actually curled and he regarded the eldest as if it were something unsanctified.

"Truth an't written. It's breathed. Do you have any idea how often you've insulted our parents in just the last five things you said? Oh yes, yes. You don't want your snooty wife to meet us or see us, but she might have a chance to see us at some confirmation of office. Which none of us will be able to get to unless you pay. So. She may not ever see any of us. Which you know perfectly well. You believe truth is written, don't you?"

Yoses looked weary, eyed Maryam, and was surprised by how stony were his mother's eyes.

The eldest was merry. "That's cause you don't speak a word of truth. Naw. For you the truth isn't to be lived. You've got a little list of rules to follow so you don't need to be good-hearted at all."

Yoses looked at no one, not even the walls or the furniture. "We have very different ideas of what goodness is."

"Goodness is in the heart. Not in the wallet or the shoes, or even killing a lamb and saying that you're giving it to God."

Yoses was angry and jerked forward. "The Law…" he was so furious he had to stop and swallow. He'd had years of fury to swallow. "The Law is the Law not by virtue of being written. It is the Law by virtue of authority. It doesn't have to be debated or even thought about. It is the word of God." It was a declaiming voice, loud, something new from Yoses.

The eldest grinned. "Really? Which bits? Ezra? That's by Ezra. The Song of Songs? That's by the king, or so we are taught. So which bits are the word of God?"

Yoses sputtered. "The Ten Commandments."

"Ah! Yes. That's by God. Except I happen to know that Moses on top of that mountain carved them himself, that's why it's so short. But. The rest of the Torah, that's the word of… whom? The rest of the Torah is said to be written by Moses. Except that it isn't." The eldest winked. "Word of God? No. Word of Moses? No. Tradition, yes. Truth? Who knows? Well, I do. But that's not fair for reasons Mum has decided not to tell you."

My God, thought Maryam, if ever anyone decided to let you loose. Or if you let yourself loose. Maybe we should be thankful.

Yoses looked to his mother, shaking his head. *He'll never change. What can you do with that one?*

And again Maryam felt stony, unmoved by her Sadduci son. What the eldest had said felt good to hear, even though it scandalized her. Good to hear such precision, anger, confidence, pushed out of anyone's mouth at high speed. And how sick she was of everything else, and how finally, yes, it was her eldest, her eldest who was… what?

Closest to her.

Yoses sniffed and folded his arms. "You are a Perisa. You have fallen under their influence. Well you would, stuck out here."

The eldest laughed. "The Perisayya want what you want – to say, this is the truth, and only this. The Perisayya are a bit better than you in that at least they allow talk and change. They will replace you. So totally that everyone will think they are you. The Perisayya will become the approved power that you are now."

Yo-yo was determined to show he had grown up. "We shall see."

The eldest yelped with laughter. "No we won't! We won't have time!" The eldest's face had not a trace of anger, was smiling at its brother with an expression that was not unlike love.

"Well, I will have time," said Yoses, and that sounded suddenly true.

Yoses did marry.

In Yerusalam, though he was still studying, so he was a dependent, a favourite of the Kohen Gadol, who sponsored the dowry. The girl's parents provided no money for the exiled family to travel to either the betrothal or the homecoming. Why saddle this promising young acolyte with his exiled parents?

Babatha made no effort to travel either, and Maryam wondered if there had been some kind of falling-out between the barMiltiades and Yoses. Yo-yo would have had no skills in disguising his scorn for the provincial Sepphoridai.

Yosef stopped asking for letters from him, stopped asking for much of anything. Babatha would come every week with the grandchildren who ran around the house and made the old man smile. "It's like warming your hands around the fire," he would say. He would try to recite to the children but they were soon off screaming.

And suddenly Babatha's face was looking both plump and pinched at the same time and you might no longer be struck by her beauty.

And in the cheerful, weather-beaten face of the eldest, lines began to deepen under the eyes, and the mouth so used to hard work and not much food had deep creases either side of the thin lips.

Maryam could no longer pretend that she was referring to a child, even an eldest one, so she really couldn't use that word "it". She was left again with no name for her child.

She toyed with calling the first-born Avi, short for Avigayil. Avi could also be a male name. But then she was still faced with the pronouns. This difficulty really had gone on long enough.

Enough.

Maryam trained herself. Him, him, him, him. He, he, he, he. She rehearsed over and over in her mind. He, he, he, he. Just to ease the house, to ease conversations at the well. And she could bear to use that improvised name Yehush. Maryam gave up hope.

Years passed with a sound like dust in wind.

CHAPTER 15

A HISTORY OF STRANGENESS

Yosef died gently like a passing cloud.

He'd become bone-thin and swollen at the same time, with a ratty grey beard and a cough. Midyear, in the morning, he went to sit outside the house before it got too hot.

Maryam was not sure when the huddled figure had slipped off the cushions and stopped breathing. She went out to collect his bowl and saw that it was still full of porridge. "You haven't eaten," she said. His head had fallen to one side and his mouth drooped dry and open. Maryam knew then that Yosef was no longer there. She stood and stared as the very air around her changed.

Yudeh and Shem were staying in a barMiltiades farm; Yakob and Yehush were working at the tekton's. They could wait; everything could wait. She wanted to stand there, not to move, not to set anything in motion.

But then she imagined how they would feel when they came home at night and found Yosef like that. She felt like a combination of mist and stone; insubstantial and immoveable. When she finally began to walk, it was as though her feet had grown roots to be pulled.

Then Maryam marched with a militant swing to her hips and hands. Yosef's life was over, and what had it been for?

This whole life had been created to protect her eldest. Who had done nothing, nothing with all the reading and scholarship. She was furious with Yakob for being so weak as to be subverted by his brother.

She strode into the tekton's yard and when the man barked something sarcastic, she tossed a hand towards him as if disposing of a pigeon bone. Yehush was turning a stone table leg on a lathe, Yakob pumping it with his foot.

Maryam stood close to them. "Your father is dead."

Yakob, startled, jerked up his head. The table leg stopped turning. Yehush stared at it and said, "I know."

"Oh of course, you know everything, and none of it means anything to you!" Her voice rose, quailed and then broke. Yakob tried to hug her, and she turned her cheek towards his chest and with an opposite impulse pushed him away. "Go back to your furniture. He won't be needing it. I'll go walk to Sepphoris where your sisters at least will put on a show of grief."

Yehush stood, looking rather small, his arms dangling. "What do you want me to do?"

She was already walking away. "I don't know. Preach? Run around with your gang, pretending to be bad boys? I don't know." He started to keep pace with her. Yakob scuttled after them both.

"What do you want me to do, Ami?" Yehush had an infuriating mild smile. "It isn't a surprise. He was old. Everyone dies. And the scripture if it is good for anything should prepare us for death."

"Chooo-oh!" She blasted out a furious breath.

Across the open ground, they saw the body, still slumped outside their door. Yakob broke into a loping run, sandals flapping. When he got to the house, he dropped to his knees and tried to lift Yosef up. "Sit up, Abi," he said. "Abi, sit up!" He began to wail and weep, kneeling on the ground, holding Yosef and rocking him gently.

Yehush crouched beside him gazing at his brother as if curious. Grief took over Yakob in spasms. Snot shot out of his nose. Yehush wiped his brother's face with his sleeve.

"You care about Yakob," said Maryam.

"He's still here," said Yehush, mildly.

"You're not human."

Yehush paused in thought. "I'm learning," he said. He patted Yakob, held up his chin and tried to get him to smile. Of all the things.

They would have to get word to the rest of the family, send Yudeh and Shem abroad with the news. She shouldn't have to do this. She should be left on a stool with cousins and daughters around her to take her hand, and help her mourn. She sat down on the ground suddenly exhausted.

She heard flapping sandals. She turned and saw Idra running in her housedress holding it about herself, wavering in the heated air like a mirage.

"Sister, oh Sister, oh Maryam!" Idra cried out.

And finally Maryam was able to cry. Idra landed in a heap beside her and took her up and held her. Maryam sobbed and Idra kept saying over and over, "He were a good man; a good good man."

Maryam nodded yes. "Too good. Too good for this world."

"He was loved here. You have a fine family."

"Those useless boys." Maryam's voice started out as a snarl and trailed away to thin squeak.

"Ssh ssh," said Idra and kissed her forehead. "They're grieving too."

Yehush was standing and staring at them all, appalled perhaps by all the noise, his head cocked sideways as if someone distant was calling him. Overhead, crows cawed.

Idra sent one of her sons to Sepphoris.

"Tell them all, bring them back. Run! And tell your brothers we need them here. Now. At once."

Her other three sons came. Idra snapped her fingers, and got them to lift up the body, to carry it into the house. "No, no, Maryam, let us do this, Darling. You have enough to bear. Shlomo, help Madam to her feet. Now!"

Her son Shlomo did a reasonable job of helping Maryam to stand, considering she was now half in a faint. Shlomo had a face like rising bread dough, with a concerned light in his eyes.

Hissing strangely through his nostrils Yakob managed to stand, still hugging the corpse, resisting as Idra's sons tried to insert themselves to help lift.

Yehush stared at them, his head tilted sideways. Then he titled it back, and then he followed, walking slowly, unsteadily, as if he was not sure where the ground was. The tekton was suddenly walking beside him.

"They're crying for themselves," said Platon. "That's why it's so loud."

"Hmm." Yehush sounded unconvinced.

Platon explained. "When you're poor, the only joy you got is your family. If you even have that. If you have it and it's taken from you – you never get over it. You can't think on it beforehand. It slams into you, like you dropped a stone beam on yourself."

The wind made even Yehush's hair look baffled – untended pudding-basin disarray. The eyes were slightly crossed with strain.

His expression made the tekton chortle. "You don't know what on earth I'm talking about do you?"

Yosef was nearly through the door. The wind whipped up the streaked garments of the people ahead of them. Idra had thrown on a scarf that had faded to blue grey, but still was decorated with yellow stars. Yosef's hand moved back and forth between them as if beckoning.

The tekton gave a nasty laugh. "You think you know everything. You're more surprised than any of them." The tekton's smile was not kind. "You really are only half from this world, aren't you? I know that. I work with you."

The tekton put a fist onto Yehush's chest and stared into his bewildered eyes. "I hope it hurts."

"Why?" In a tone of genuine enquiry.

"Because I'm hard as my stone inside. I been hammered like my stone."

Yehush blinked. "You're being kind now."

"I am? You're sure of that now, are you?"

"To the limit of your being, yes." It was possible that Yehush thought this was a sympathetic response. Innocence – that was what the tekton saw in this person's eyes. Like a child but not like a child, no fear there or nastiness at all, and no stupidity either, but it was the kind of cleverness that ordinary folks didn't understand, and it riled them.

"I'll leave you to your grief," the tekton growled and shook his head and walked away.

* * *

The family heard Babatha's wailing a village-walk away.

She came running, both hands held aloft. Her headscarf, if she had worn one, must have fallen off in the two-mile run, and the hem of her robe was dusty and torn. "Abi! Ami! Abi! Ami!"

She knelt at Maryam's feet, and then kissed them. She smoothed her mother's hair. She was so distraught one of her filigree earrings had been torn, bloody, out of her ear.

"Ah! The poor soul." Idra held up her hands. "Shlomo. Get your father's wine. Go on. For our friends. Go get them the wine, on the shelf by the hats."

"Oh my daughter. Oh my daughter. Only you understand. Only you. And my friend, my friend Idra!" Maryam held out a hand towards each of them, and the three women all knelt together, wailing.

The doorway darkened. Yudeh, Shem and Tara had come, trailing behind Babatha.

"My fatherless children. My babes!" Maryam held out her arms.

"What took you?" snarled Babatha, furious.

Tara stumbled forward to be hugged, her face looking swollen. Fresh wailing from Maryam and Idra, then Yakob snatched up his brothers and kissed their heads. Surprisingly Yudeh wept the loudest, he who had seemed to be the sturdiest of Maryam's boys, all round like he was made of rocks.

Yehush stared, outside any circle, moving as if on a rocking boat.

What could they do with Yosef's body?

He had to be buried the next day, but his family tomb

was in Yerusalam and it was summer so there was no question of transporting him back, and in any case Yosef only had a few scattered nieces and nephews whom he did not know – would they even welcome the exile back to lie among them?

"He always thought he was going to go home. He always thought he would die in Yerusalam." Maryam mopped her face. "I could never get him to talk about it."

They were poor. Bodies couldn't be buried anywhere near soil that grew food and the only soil in Nazareth grew food. Burials in Nazareth happened in caves or tombs. The poor of the village moved schist aside and tried to pile it up on the newly dead. There had been one disaster, years back, with dogs.

All this was discussed in whispers outside the house, Babatha taking charge. "The sun is starting to set! I have got to get home and look after my own kids. I have an idea, let me see if it will work. I'll try and come back here tonight. Yudeh, I'm relying on you, you're adult now. Make sure your mother drinks water and sleeps. Shem, Tara, you come back home with me."

Babatha glared once at Yehush, and narrowed her eyes at Yakob, who was leaning over his brother, cajoling him.

"Come you two," Babatha said to Shem and Yudeh. "We have much to do." She added in a sing-song voice full of scorn for the two eldest brothers, "And we're the only ones to do it."

Idra sat with Maryam. She lit the Shabbat lamp for her. Villagers came to pay respects, carrying lamps, burning precious oil, to say how much Yosef would be missed. Yosef lay on a blanket on the floor.

Yehush sat in front of him, his legs folded, a finger curled over his mouth as if trying to solve a problem. Yakob sat next to his brother, still holding his father's hand, talking to him. "There, there, Abi. All is well, Abi." Idra brought them both water.

Yehush just stared. Perhaps he is grieving, Maryam thought. Perhaps that is how he grieves. He is part human. Part of him is human, part of him is God. But then, isn't that true of all of us? Would you say that Yosef was not part of God? I know who is the better person.

The tekton's wife Esta came with a pot of stew. Her smile for the two eldest children was flitting, brief but sweet. Maryam glimpsed a different social world in which Yehush was thought of fondly. Esta was now in her thirties, tiny and thin as a cat, still quiet. Maryam found herself stroking Esta's head as if she was a child.

"The food is good. Let others eat. I cannot eat when my husband cannot." Maryam wept again. Esta, this child, leaned forward and kissed the side of her head.

Babatha did come back, walking through the darkness, her sleeves wrapped around her forearms. She lifted the lid off their stew, sniffed the food, and said, "Well done, Yudeh."

Yudeh jerked his head. "That were Esta brought that."

"Oh," said Babatha, surprised. She thanked Esta then leaned over Maryam and said in a low voice, "I've spoken to Miltiades, and his father and uncles, and they agree. We are one family." Babatha extended her hand from her own breast to everyone in the room. "They have a family tomb, and they are happy for Aba to sleep among them."

It's done, thought Maryam, as if a lid had fallen shut and she'd snatched back her fingers just in time. *They've got all my younger children, and now my husband as well.*

Food was laid out on the tables. Yakob and Yehush still sat by the body. Babatha hesitated, then stepped forward and put her hands on each of their heads. "Come you two. You've kept vigil. Come eat something."

Yakob nodded and stood. Yehush didn't move. "I'm trying to read scripture with him, but I can't."

That didn't even make sense. Babatha faltered. "We all loved him. Come. Stand. Eat."

Yehush turned and there was horror in his eyes. "People talk about memory. You have them in memory they say. Memories are less than dreams."

Babatha said, "We make do." She tried to pull him to his feet.

Yehush's eyes grew rounder. "For us he doesn't exist. He's not in the future. And we can only move into the future." Yehush froze, eyes staring as if down into a well. "Ahead, there's nothing."

The next morning Yosef barLevi, wrapped tightly in white windings and covered with an old shawl from his Yerusalam days, was carried down the northern path on a bier by his sons.

Yehush was among those sons. There had been a brief moment outside their house when Babatha objected, but Maryam had insisted. "No. No, let Yehush carry his father." Babatha's eyebrows flicked. Then she genuflected from the head and knees to her mother.

It was still dark enough to need torches and they glinted gold against blue as the sun rose.

The whole village trooped after them. Idra, of course, on whom Maryam rested, supported also by Babatha. They were ganged round by all of Idra's sons and daughters, then the tekton and Esta, and all of Yazz's gang, and the wives at the well, and all their sons and all their husbands. The whole village. There was only the sound of crows, and the sounds of swallows, and of sandals on grit.

Get through this day, Maryam thought. *Get through this day and then the silence comes.*

It was a long walk to Sepphoris. The old and the halt eased themselves with help down the winding track. That track was wider and still defined by two parallel ruts because of Yosef's cart.

So Yosef was interred in the Miltiades family tomb, hollowed out of the softer limestone. Yudeh, Shem, Yakob and Yehush shouldered the bier up onto a raw shelf, and ducked back outside.

Who would speak? Babatha being a woman could not speak. Yoses, the trained scholar, was not there.

Every other funeral any of them had attended, the women wept and wailed. For Yosef, there was silence. Maryam stood as if carved from stone, staring as heat mounted and light reflected from her face as if all her skin were weeping. She'd wept for herself. For Yosef, she felt fury. At his exile; how near he had come to a pauper's grave; how now he was buried among people who in normal life he would never have met. He had lost the barLevi family, they had lost the Temple.

But all the Nazaredai were with them. They respected him. He was not just some strange and disregarded old man, who had been lucky enough to have a beautiful daughter who married well and so was being buried in someone else's tomb. Even the mourners from Sepphoris who did not know him; they could see that this was a man who had mattered to people.

Then, almost unnoticed at first, Yehush began to recite.

Gazelle of Israel
slain on your back!
How the heroes have fallen!

And Maryam thought at once. Yes! This! This is what Yosef was, a thinker, a radical, a scholar. This was his teaching, this was the scripture he loved.

Don't speak of it
in the squares of Gath
Don't spread the news
in the streets of Ashkelon
or the daughters of the Philistines
will rejoice
or the daughters of the ungodly
will gloat

Babatha will recognize snatches of it, but only snatches. Yes, see, she's alarmed, she knows what it says. Now she's slumping because she's realizes that this is deep liturgy and her new family won't understand. It sings of love between two men.

Mountains of Gilboa!
Be there no dew
nor rain on you
And on your slopes
no fertile field!

Yehush recited all of it, making no attempt to adorn it with cadences. He didn't rock with the verse, or speed up and slow down to make it into music. He spoke it in an ordinary voice, like two wives chatting beside the well. Some of the men of Sepphoris grew restive.

But, thought Maryam, these are the words, these are the words. And the way Yehush spoke them, it was as if the grit on the road were speaking, the dust in the air that had once been the flesh of people, as if the baking sun observing another day had paused to remember.

> How the heroes are fallen
> in the thick of battle
> Yehonatan laid low
> slain on your back!
>
> Oh I grieve for you
> Yehonatan, brother
> Dear to me you were,
> and for me
> more wonderful your love
> than the love of women
>
> How the heroes have fallen
> How the arms of war are lost!

Maryam thought. We have a history of strangeness. She looked at the Sepphoridai, bearing this funeral of a stranger as best they could. The two families would separate afterwards with relief, and most of her children would remain here. Strange, and it's best that that's not always understood.

* * *

Decades later, Yosef would be moved into a box of stone, his bones neatly stowed in a beautifully-wrought limestone ossuary. It had reliefs instead of incisions, showing the Covenant on wheels, and cut into the stone, his first name only. The box had been wrought by the tekton.

CHAPTER 16

LIVES LIKE DRAGONFLIES

In the morning Yehush still did not eat.

He sat, his back against the wall, and stared. Yakob leaned over him. "Nowt for it, Bro. The work won't do itself." Yakob glanced at his mother in some distress. "All right then Bro, I'll explain to Platon." Pause at the door. "But see if you can't come later today, yeah?"

Yudeh went back to Sepphoris, with an air that he belonged now to no one. (He would in fact years later move to the lake and become a fisherman.)

Then it was just Maryam and her first-born, like in the oldest days. She put a dipper of water to his lips. "Drink at least." He didn't.

Maryam looked at his faraway face. "I'm sorry what I said. I can see you're grieving." Yehush moved not at all.

The door creaked, sunlight and Idra's lumpy face peeked in. "All right for me?"

"Always." Maryam managed a wan smile but inclined her head towards Yehush.

"Taking it bad is he? You all right, love?" Idra turned and leaned into Yehush's line of sight.

"God is learning about pain," said Yehush with a grim smile.

176

"Should think God knows all about pain." Idra didn't like loose talk about God.

"God's never felt it." Yehush grunted and stood up. "Do stars feel pain?"

Maryam felt a flutter of the old feeling of worry and concern. "Won't you eat?"

Yehush was walking to the ladder, then stopped and turned. "My cousin is a teacher in the South," he said. "I need to hear what he says." Then he climbed the ladder and they heard soft sounds of sorting coming from the upper storey.

"It takes folk different," said Idra. "Some wail and get on with it. Others don't."

Maryam felt the misgiving again. "He said something yesterday, something else odd. Makes me think he's had a change of plans."

"More than likely. He's too smart for this place. He should be the one in the Temple."

Maryam was standing and looking up at the ceiling. "No. He shouldn't. They'd be very bad for each other."

Idra started to laugh, and then realized Maryam was being grave, and put a hand on her shoulder.

Yehush came down the ladder with a shoulder-bag, his thickest work-dress and long heavy cloak on his back. The bag clanked. "I've got to get these tools to Platon," he said. "Then I might go to market." The door creaked open; sunlight flooded again, and Yehush departed.

"He's fine," said Idra, and patted her friend's shoulder. She sat with Maryam for most of the morning then sighed. "Got to stir me bones, things to do."

They kissed and then Maryam was alone. The day wore on. Maryam touched things around the house: Yosef's clothes, his scrolls, his sandals. What would she do with them?

Yehush came back with sacks of flour, dried fish, cured goat, briny olives and new plates. He must have borrowed someone's cart. He shouldered all of the goods into the keep he'd had made now ten years ago, a high shelf over a pan of water. Back upstairs, more sounds of sorting.

Yehush came down the ladder in his best stout sandals, so unworn that the thick straps might cut his feet. He had on a thick cloak, as if it were winter, and from the corner took up one of Yosef's walking sticks. To fend off village dogs?

The first-born pressed his forehead against hers, and said, "Thank you for all you've done."

And started to walk.

"You'll want feeding when you come back, I suppose." Already a trill of panic.

"I'm not coming back," Yehush said, throwing one corner of the cloak over one shoulder. The door swung behind him.

Maryam hauled herself to her feet and caught the door before it slammed. She trotted outside after him onto the bare stone. "What do you mean?"

He kept walking. "I need to do something."

She started to walk with him. "What? What do you need to do?"

He paused. "I need to change God."

Maryam felt a calm, but a calm that restrained something that swelled within her. "God cannot be changed."

"It's people who can't be changed. They live lives like dragonflies, all planned for them and over with before they can think. No. It's God who must change. God must learn."

"God." Maryam was not at all bewildered. She almost felt as though the words had come out of his mouth only moments before they would have come from hers. "God is perfect."

"Seen as a whole, outside of time, yes. But trapped here, God is in time. Do you think a being can be perfect if it cannot learn? Learn how to pity? Learn how to forgive?"

It was happening. Dear God, after all this time, after all that waiting. Thirty years of waiting, and now, now of all times, the child was going to move. Tears welled up, huge tears that advanced down her cheeks in a sheet. She sluiced them away with the edge of her palm.

A voice wailed. "You're going?" It was Yakob in utter despair. He ran across the white bedrock. His long legs seemed to spiral and twist under him. "You're going! Wait!" As he got nearer, he extended his right hand, fingers spatchcocked. "Please take me with you?" A glance, panting towards Maryam, then a glance at what Yehush was wearing. "Wait for me, please, I won't be long."

Yehush smiled, eyes dim, and nodded.

Yakob shambled off towards their house. "I just need to get my cloak."

And following on more slowly like a shadow, came the tekton. He didn't get too close. His smile was awry. "You're breaking your promise. I knew you would."

"I worked for you eighteen years."

"And what am I supposed to do now? You're taking him too." The tekton pointed after Yakob and then spat. "Though he's not much use without you."

"You are no longer young," said Yehush. "The time will come when you will have to stop working."

"Aye! And I could have had me sons working for me." Fury. Disgust. "I thought of you like me sons."

"And you were a second father. But sometimes sons must go."

Yakob had not taken any time at all. Different sandals, the same lanolin-stinking tunic, one of Yosef's old cloaks folded over one arm, and a bag that was limp with all the things that were missing from it.

Yakob was smiling, panting, face changing like water running over rocks, looking at Maryam, wincing, looking at the tekton. "My brother," he said, hands twisting.

Yehush said with his mild smile, "You've brought no food or money. I will not eat. But you'll need to."

"I don't know." Yakob sagged.

"I spent the money buying food for Ami. You can come." Hand on Yakob's shoulder. "But it will be hard, so if you have to go home, do."

The tekton snarled, "Go on. The pair of yous. Go on." He pulled out a soft, tanned leather pouch. It clinked. "Here. You need this. But don't come back. You'll not be welcome." Maryam felt an echo of his rage in herself. She could feel what impelled it.

Yehush did not move to take the purse. It was Yakob glancing back and forth who finally took the money, and said thank you, and then overcome tried to kiss the tekton, who pushed him back.

"You're both of you a pair of pricks. Stay away." The tekton glared at Maryam. "And as for you, I wish you'd never come." Platon stalked back towards his house. "Esta will be heartbroken," he shouted at them, his back turned. "Heartbroken!" His own voice cracked.

"Fare thee well, Ami," said Yehush, and kissed her, and turned and began to walk.

Yakob was pulled this way then that, kissed his Mum,

then was jerked as if on a leash. Yakob said, "We'll be back regular, Ami. You got Shem and Yudeh. You'll not be alone, like. And Babatha. Bye for now. OK Ami? Bye? We will be back regular." Walking backwards, Yakob tripped, fell on his arse, scrambled to his feet.

Poor boy. Go with my blessing.

Loneliness was as wide as the wind.

PART 2
HIM

CHAPTER 17

FREE

"You've heard what she's doing," Babatha said.

It was not really a question. She plonked a covered earthenware dish down onto the table, eyes puffed with exasperation.

"Not really, no." Actually, Maryam had heard, from her sewing group.

"She's preaching." Babatha blurted out a laugh, shook her head, put a finger under her nose. "She's walking around. In public. Teaching scripture. Worse than that, I hear she's gone beyond any of the Perisayya. For changing scripture. Mmm-hmm. Saying that her talking has more authority than the Law or the Temple. And you know how clever she can be, twisting everything around. She's got people following her."

Babatha threw herself down on the dining couch, and blew out. "You don't know this yet but Tara has a suitor. He's Miltiades's cousin. Good boy, a bit stolid, not fiery or intelligent like Milt, but a good match for her. Money, house, sensible lad, good-hearted I would say."

"This is wonderful," said Maryam. *How nice if Tara had told me herself.*

"The point is." Babatha's hands were pressed together and pumping up and down. "Men with prospects don't marry into families that have insanity running in them."

The air about Maryam seemed to prickle.

"It was one thing when you and Aba kept her contained in the house. She could be as crazy as she liked, and it made no difference. But this! It's getting known all over the Galil!" Babatha's arm took in the whole countryside.

"Yehush was very popular here in the village." Maryam felt heavy.

Babatha's fingers became claws. "That name! It's not a real name."

"What else can I call him?"

"Him? It's such a problem." Babatha sighed. "You could call her 'him' here. In the village. But people knew. Don't fool yourself Ami, they knew and some of them sniggered. You know they did."

"If it didn't bother them, why should it bother you?" Maryam asked.

Babatha looked sad and took her hand. "Ami. We have to think about Tara. And Yoses, too. You know he is working with the Kohen Gadol now? The only member of our family to claim our birthright, and what do you think it will do for him to have a crazy sister preaching worse than the Perisayya – pretending to be a man? And Tara? Who will marry her if people think she has a sister who's gone mad?"

Babatha knelt at Maryam's feet and intertwined their fingers. "I'm so sorry Ami. I'm so sorry that this person gives you no peace. And never will. But for the sake of all of us, she must be brought back home."

"Yakob," murmured Maryam.

"Ugh." Babatha seemed to have been thrown backwards.

"Yakob! Has fallen in love with his sister, who thinks she's a boy, and for all I know Yakob is in love with her thinking she is a boy! I mean! Ami! Is this why you raised us? To to to display such – there isn't a word."

"Strangeness," said Maryam.

Babatha's hands offered Maryam the credit as if on a tray. "Strangeness. In public. Before the people, before the men of God." Babatha grunted as she stood up and began to pace again. "As it is, Yoses doesn't want to show his face here again. He's ashamed of us. Don't worry, he's been pretty insulting about Miltiades as well. After we paid for his studies."

Maryam's anger was calm and patient. "Why don't I know any of this? Tara's engagement? Yoses cutting us off. Why am I not told?"

"No one wants to hurt you, Ami."

"Tooh! So they treat me like an idiot, some fool of an old woman who married badly…"

"Ami, I didn't say that."

"Nobody does anything in this family without you, Babatha. So. You can't get the others to help you. Tara just wants to sit and get fat, and now have babies. Yudeh and Shem are now part of your family, the men of your family, and they are too interested in land and trade and position. And Yoses. You're afraid to tell him and all. So. You want me to say yes, let's bring him back because in the end, I am the one with the authority."

Babatha cast her eyes down. "Yes, Ami."

"I don't care if people know Yehush is a woman and is preaching. Good. Let them learn a woman can."

"Oh Mother please." Babatha shook her head as if Maryam had said something predictable and beside the point.

She has not got a particle of Yosef's vision. Well, she is who she is.

Maryam's back seemed to snap into place. "What you say about Yakob is right. He is being made into a public display. And if the teaching is doing harm, by which I mean doing harm to people's minds, not just harm to our family." Maryam covered her mouth with the palm of her hand for a moment then snatched it away. "I need to know. I do need to know what my child is preaching. So we'll go. We will go and listen." Maryam pointed a finger. "That does not mean I want her shut away like someone possessed."

Babatha was still. "You said her."

"Him, her, doesn't matter. Your father called him him for twenty-five years."

But there was no one else now like her Yosef, not anywhere.

Miltiades barMiltiades went with them.

He said because the women needed protection. He carried a long staff that was also a cudgel and he organized the trip like a military campaign. They would be carried in biers; they would take food and wine with them, so they would need protection. He hired armed guards to defend them against thieves and to scout the terrain.

The morning of their departure, Maryam watched him. Chest out, he scowled, looked serious, and nodded to his mercenaries. He folded his arms to make them look bigger and stroked his fine black beard. Maryam found herself smiling. *He really does fancy himself a soldier.*

They could have easily taken the road through Cana to Magdal Nunya, but Tiberias was only two miles further south along the lake. It was a new city, only ten years old, and Herod Antipas's capital. It had a theatre! Miltiades wanted to see the modernity of it.

Since Miltiades was going, Yudeh joined. Shem stayed behind – he had a new girlfriend – and Tara said the travelling would be uncomfortable and that she'd rather stay. Tara was right – it was uncomfortable.

Maryam would have been so much happier walking. Anything, even the hot sun was better than being jostled, cut off from God's clean air by curtains, sweating and cramping on couches, and smelling everybody's sweat including your own, while knowing the bearers could overhear any conversation.

The caravan took a full ten hours of jerks and thumps, with stops for the men to rest and everyone to drink water and ease themselves. It was sunset by the time the biers were lowered in front of the two stone towers of the main gate of Tiberias.

Maryam groaned as she swung her legs out of the bier. One leg had gone to sleep and was weak and numb. One of the porters, thick with sweat, steadied her and helped her stand.

Yudeh flipped himself out of the bier and ran towards the gate. The soldiers looked like piles of melons wearing armour. They glared at Yudeh with flat dead eyes. He was waving his arms and shouting, "Are there games? Will there be games today?" From the way the soldiers growled, the answer was probably no. The bas-reliefs over the gate looked crude and lumpy.

Maryam thought the town looked tiny, not grand at all, raw, new, and stark. Tiberias was jammed against a hillside so that less than half of it needed to be surrounded

by defences. Along that hill ran a long wall of cut stone –
Antipas's palace. It was low and big but not a wonder.

They found their inn, stabled the bearers in a kind of
barracks next to it, and ducked into their tiny rooms that
smelled of sweat and damp stone. They splashed water on
their faces and rubbed off the dust of the road.

The inn's beds doubled as dining couches, and they broke
out their own bread and pickles. The innkeeper kept running
in to ask if they wanted any more food. They had roasted
some fine morsels of lamb, he kept telling them. Wouldn't
they have some? Finally Milt and Yudeh succumbed and
ordered a tray of cutlets. And wine.

"None for me," said Babatha and there was a fight. "You
said we had to be careful with money!" Babatha's eyes were
cold. "You wanted to come here. This town was built on
a cemetery." Her voice went sharp. "Everything here is
impure like in a tomb. Antipas did that deliberately to keep
us out, and reward all of you, you Greeks."

Miltiades called her Woman and drank more wine.

Miltiades was ill the next morning, and lolled in bed until
the sun was high.

Then he wanted to go to the town's famous spas. The
bearers were delighted. They walked to the shoreline and
stretched out on the rocks to sleep some more.

It would not be decent for Maryam and Babatha to go to
the hot baths, so they walked to the jetty. It was a fine jetty,
built of stone, but Tiberias for all its investment by Antipas
was not a major port. Its four boats sloshed and gurgled.

The lake faded into blue-white mist, and the mountains
on the other side were already beige, flat with sunlight, no

shadows to give shape or contour. On the water, triangular sails were everywhere. Crusts of towns glowed white all round the gently curving bays. The wind was behind them now, hot, coming off the land. Some fishermen lounged on the stone dock.

"Have you heard of a new teacher?" Maryam asked them. "The one who talks in Nahum?"

Alarmingly the men laughed. "Do we know him? You wouldn't be meaning Yehush, now would ya?" The man leapt to his feet; his face sunburnt unevenly so that dust outlined the borders of his peeling skin. But he had a cheerful expression.

More laughter. Maryam had to admit that the laughter of strange men alarmed her.

And one of them noticed that. "Now, now, Madam. We knows him you see, that's all."

"He made off with my cousin!" One of them yelped.

"Yer Coz only went because of all those women!" said another.

They really did mean no harm. They really did think they were being friendly and reassuring. An older man spoke, with a disconcertingly deep voice. "You're in luck," he rumbled. "He'll not be in Nahum now. Talk is he's in Migdal Nunya."

The name of the town unleashed a growl of laughter and the mocking high warble that men used when they called after whores or made jokes about them. Babatha took her headscarf and hid the lower half of her face.

"Don't mind them, Missus. It's the next town along. That's it there." The big man pointed. "They've got a meeting ground there for the pious." More hoots. The older man turned, shaking his head. "Stop it, you lot. You're making the ladies uncomfortable."

Maryam and Babatha got back to the inn and were waiting by the biers, which they had packed by the time Milt and Yudeh finally returned from the town.

"You'd be surprised all the dirt that comes out of you, in all that hot water."

"I wouldn't be surprised at all," sniffed Babatha.

Miltiades held out a bolt of blue cloth in front of him. "I bought you this, love." Babatha thanked him in a distant voice that embodied her thought: *We were not supposed to be spending money.*

Maryam unrolled the cloth and napped it out flat. It was a more than enough for a good dress. "Oh! It's a fine weave." She played the peacemaker. "Oh, Babatha I could make you a lovely dress!"

"We're not here for the dresses," said Babatha.

So they went to Migdal Nunya.

Along the dockside, the folded sails of twenty or thirty skiffs lined up like quills. In the old core of the settlement, high stone walls wound along narrow streets as if following the courses of streams.

Out the other side of the town, the family came to some scrubland, rough grazing for goats. Twenty or so sheepskin tents and lean-tos were gathered around one larger tent. Smoke scurried from cooking fires. Women were sitting cross-legged and looked up from their cooking with open smiles as if they expected something good to happen. A skinny man in plainest homespun ducked out of his tent. Miltiades asked him about Yehush of Nazareth.

The man pressed his back from behind with both hands. "Well, you found him then." The man had a sandy-coloured beard, and this close up, looked rather young to be the head of a household. His eyes caught Maryam's and then froze. "I'm sorry. Are you his people?"

They all looked up and blinked. The man chuckled and raised a hand to cover his embarrassment. "Because excuse me, Lady, but you look just like him. You're his Mum, aren't you?"

Maryam said yes. The man chuckled, shuffled. "I hope this'll cheer him up." He called aloud, "Sar! This is his Mum." The young wife stood up, wiped her hands on her dress. "Are ya? Really? Hello, I'm Sarah, this is my husband Thad. Welcome."

The man growled out a laugh. "Come on, I'll take yous to him."

Tents. Goats. Followers. Say forty of them. Something had completely changed.

"Why will it cheer him up?" Maryam asked.

"Oh! We've had a bunch of Sads show up from Yerusalam. You know. Sadducai. First we've had of them. Great grand men they are. You should see him go for them. Well you have I expect."

Thad was gabbling somewhat in excitement. Excited by meeting me?

Maryam began to grin sideways, beginning to feel a little tickle of elation. "He could do that to priests when he was twelve."

"Ha-ha! Really? Oooooh, wish I'd been there!" Thad slapped his thigh. Milt was holding his cudgel ready as if he thought these people were thieves. His eyes looked furtive, moving side to side.

Babatha said, "You call this Yehush him."

Thad chortled. "Yah we do." He put his finger to his lips.

Babatha asked, "No one talks about it?" If you didn't know her, you might think Babatha was amused. A smile, a breaking of a chuckle in her voice – Maryam knew it was anger.

Another finger from Thad. "I think you'll see we don't mind much about any of that here." He smiled. "Maybe that's why he doesn't use a name."

Maryam blinked. "What does he call himself?"

Thad's smile was mild. "The Son of Adam."

He held up the flap of the main tent for them and they ducked into muggy darkness. There were some dining couches pulled lengthwise. Men in white robes were sitting stiff backed, faced by a row of women.

Maryam was struck afresh – really at the very first glance, almost before she recognized the face, Maryam's deep reaction was: why is that woman dressed like a man?

Flanked by women. An older woman sat on proper chair, not a dining couch. She was draped like a Roman in layers of blue and beige, and her hair was high in curls and held in place by a tiara.

And standing over Yehush, another woman glowered at them, rather broad, looking aggressive. Coarse face, ugly curl to her mouth.

Thad shouted. "Rabuli! I found your mum."

And Yehush looked up with an expression Maryam had never seen. The smile was tiny and firm, tight. The eyes were wide, unblinking, somehow clenched, and the eyebrows were wrenched up and to the side. Enraged, amused and in pain.

Thad looked doubtful. "This is your Mum. An't she?"

Yehush stayed seated. "Who is my mother to me, more than any of you?" He looked about his followers.

He knows why we're here. Of course he knows, he knew as soon as I agreed to come here. He knows we want to stop him doing this.

"Who are my brothers and my sisters?" His eyes now were on Milt and Babatha. He suddenly raised his arms, and the smile flashed. He stood up and spun on one heel, his outstretched arms taking in all of the people about him. "Here are MY brothers and sisters. Whoever does God's will is my brother and sister and mother." His face now was almost merry. He turned to Maryam, but his eyes said: *You are not my family.*

The curled-mouth woman shifted, with a kind of jerk, as if she yearned to hit someone but stopped herself. Her cheeks were puffed out with dislike of them and her eyes were watchful.

Yehush slapped his hands together. Enough.

One of the white-robed Sadducai said with a voice like stone rolling away from a tomb, "You drive out demons."

Yehush sat down on a dining couch like it was a bench. "Do I? Is that what I am doing? You're sure, you've seen it?"

"Do you deny it?"

"Deny what?"

"That you drive out demons."

"Yes." The room about him rustled. "I make people feel better by talking to them."

"That is not what we hear."

"If you talked to folk more often. Especially people who are driven out of their homes by their families." And the Son glanced dead at Maryam. "If you talked to people in rags, those wretched who jabber and shiver with grief. If you even perhaps took them into your homes with your kitchen fires and warm soup and talked to them, you know? You might make unhappy people feel better too." The crowd laughed.

From one of the onlookers: "Do a lot more good than incense." Then a roar from the assembly, a roar of rebellion, Northern anger, comeuppance for the Yehudai.

The Sad was unmoved and spoke in a measured voice. "The only thing that can order out a demon is a demon." He had a long lean face expressing disgust.

"So you are saying I'm a demon?"

Then the Sad looked direct at Maryam with a tight smile. "You are possessed by one." Then back to Yehush. "Which is why your family are here."

Maryam felt a stab of panic. She and Babatha looked at each other in alarm. All those preparations, somebody knew and must have talked. But then Maryam looked at the utter calm of this man's face. *No. He knew just from looking at us why we're here.*

"My family are here to drive out demons?" Yehush sounded innocently baffled. His audience laughed.

The Sad smiled thinly. "They have no wish to see you hurt yourself. Or others."

The Son of Adam was having fun. "So. This is news to me, but then I'm not a scholar. Trained. Learned. From writing." His voice sounded so impressed it bordered on mockery. "You are saying that God can't drive out demons?"

"You are not God."

"I am the Son of Adam."

And all the people in the room, in unison chanted. "Let he who has ears, hear."

Adam. It meant human, simply. Adam was made from clay. Yosef said it was pun: humus and human. It was why the Perisayya made such a thing of making dishes and lamps from rough red local clay. *We are of the earth, this red earth. We are of this land.*

The Son of Adam smiled. "So. God CAN drive out demons. If not, your Law would say so. Though I am asking you to think and you don't usually do that. You read instead."

Someone, perhaps Thad, laughed aloud. The Son's smile was steady. "What if it is not me at all who drives demons out, but God? God hasn't done this often. But. Perhaps, now, God is moved by pity?" The Son of Adam smiled and his voice became a rough whisper. "Unlike you. But then, I don't think you can drive out demons."

The man's smile was unchanged. "I was told you talk in circles."

The Son of Adam smiled and gave a series of quick nods, his eyes wide. "And riddles. And stories." And all the people in the tent bellowed. "Let he who has ears hear." They were enjoying themselves.

The Sad's lip curled and he said. "And I was told that there would be all these women around you."

Ooooh, he doesn't like women. If possible the laughter grew even louder.

Maryam knew then – the Son of Adam had accepted his mission. The Son was calling on God to help, and God was listening to him. He was preaching for women, if not as one.

He was not crazy and was doing nothing but good. Babatha would have to be stopped.

They were trapped for hours listening to the Son humiliate his guests.

One Sadduci remained, then finally stood stiffly and left.

"Go with God, Rabuli." Some of the assembly called after him and it sounded like mockery. Then everyone cleared the tent for air and food.

The field smelled of earth, baked grass and a breeze from the lake. The followers of the Son walked through Maryam's family group, ignoring them.

Babatha growled at Maryam, hands pressed to her temple. "How did those men know about us? I promise you Ami, it can't be Yoses telling them anything, I said nothing to him, I couldn't!"

"They knew from our faces."

Yakob came striding toward them, a different man from what he had ever been before. His skin had cleared of pimples. He was thinner than a drawn dagger, and his eyes blazed, and he said, "The Son knows what you're doing."

Babatha looked confused. Yakob was furious at her? This she had never seen.

Yakob: "You've always hated him. Now you're, what? Going to tie him up like a lunatic and drag him home? Shut him up in the house against his will? Did you send those men to torment him, the same kind of men who exiled Aba?" Yakob's voice broke.

Babatha's face moved from shock, to pity and then gathered into anger. "We can't just leave her wandering, saying these unlawful things."

Yakob glared at her, nodding rapidly up and down: *Yes, yes, yes so I was right.* He then looked at Maryam. "You. I thought you understood."

Maryam whispered. "I do."

"Then why are you here?" Yakob demanded.

Truth, Maryam. "I needed to know what Yehush was saying."

Yakob corrected her. "The Son of Adam."

Maryam nodded once in acknowledgement. "The Son of Adam. I needed to know what he's saying in case it harms others."

"You. You will judge. Him." This Yakob had found strength.

Babatha flared. "Talk to your mother with respect."

Maryam did not need defending. "I am the one who gave him birth. I am the only one who really knows what he is." What she said, or how she said it, made Yakob's anger falter.

Maryam turned to Babatha. "This is over."

Babatha fought. She said that they had not begun to deal with this, that they needed to talk to the person, to get her to see how unseemly she was being.

Miltiades undid her. Suddenly he said, "It's too late, Atha. Everybody's seen her. Everybody knows. This is beyond helping." Miltiades turned towards their biers and threw himself into one. But as he had been speaking, the cudgel shook as if his hands were quivering.

He's afraid, Maryam realized. He wasn't expecting so many followers.

Yakob growled at them, saying that there was food in the tents, and waved a hand towards it, before striding away.

Babatha looked glum. "Poor Yoses. Poor Tara. How they will suffer for this."

Then she looked up at Maryam. "You, Mother. This is your fault." Babatha put on a thin nasty voice. "Don't be like your sister Atha, learn your embroidery Atha, your sister betrayed the family. But you like it. Both you and Aba liked what she is. Your teaching." Wiping her cheeks, Babatha stormed away.

Much of what she said is true, thought Maryam in a kind of quietude. *It is my fault. I did help the Son do this.*

I didn't do enough to help.

So what now? she asked the heavens, and the answer was there.

* * *

In the morning, she told Babatha: "I'm staying."

"Why?" Babatha asked.

Maryam might have said: I have so much to learn. She might have said: I'm curious. She might have said: for thirty years my life has been waiting for this – I might as well see it.

What she did say was, mildly, with a smile: "It is the will of God."

Babatha shook her head once. "You're both crazy. Come home when you need to." She started to walk away, thought, turned back and kissed her mother on the cheek. "Love you, Ami." Then she walked back towards the biers. Yudeh bounced in place with a kind of shyness, kissed Maryam and whispered. "This fits. It all fits. I wish I was staying too."

"You can."

Yudeh laughed and shook his head. "Nah. Babatha would kill me." Then he was gone too.

Free, thought Maryam.

CHAPTER 18

THE NEEDLEPOINT OF ARGUMENT

The Miltiades family were soon gone, after more crisp farewells, carried in that clear cool morning on their biers.

Maryam had nothing with her – no clothes, no tent, only one pair of sandals.

A big fellow was walking towards her in the slanted dawn light. He held up a bowl and a spoon. "Brought you some food, Mother."

She thanked him and asked him to call her Maryam, and asked for his name and he said Shemenolo.

Maryam: "Ooh. That's my son's name. Another one of my sons."

Shemenolo had a Shomeroni's face, heavy and huge with tiny eyes. The eyes were too small for the glimmer they were trying to display and his slit of a mouth was so narrow that Maryam half-wondered if he could get a spoon into it. "Yah," he chuckled. "Every other person you meet is called Shem. The Son calls me Kepha."

The name meant Rock.

Maryam smiled – he looked like a rock. The porridge was

made of sorghum with a trace of some sweet spice. Cattle food made rich.

The Rock's tiny eyes and mouth looked merry. "He calls us all sorts. Two twins, he calls them the Thunder Brothers."

"He had a gang back home too." She was indeed very hungry.

The Rock coughed and then said, "Must be hard for you, eh?"

She found she could not answer him, so jammed in another spoonful of porridge.

"It's hard for all of us sometimes. He can say things so cold, they take away your breath. Until you can mull them over for bit."

All she could muster in response was: "Hmmmmmm."

"His love is big. Big enough to take in both you and us. He says that we can't follow him if we don't leave our families. But to me that means we have to love everybody. It don't mean he don't love you."

What Maryam knew closed like a trap, and somehow it was said aloud. "Yes, but he doesn't honour me."

For that truth, not even a saint had an answer. His eyes fell. Hers did not.

Maryam said, "I need to know what the Son is preaching."

The Rock chuckled and rubbed his head. "I wish I could say."

Long exile had taught Maryam to ask the next question. "Who hates him? Who are his enemies?"

Shemenolo's face did an odd sideways shake. "The Perisayya don't like him because they keep adding new laws and he says that's nonsense. They're always here having a go." The Rock imitated a pompous Perisa. "You just broke the Law, and he just says so what?" The Rock chuckled. "Drives em mad."

"There was a Perisa in Nazareth who hated him."

Shemenolo nodded. "The Sadducai took longer to find out about him. But they hate him more cause he never contradicts scripture; he just says the Law doesn't go far enough. Whoo! They quote scripture and he just agrees with them, but then says, God wants more than that. The Essenai…"

She cut him off with a wave of her hand. "They will love that he lives in poverty. But. He's no hermit and he gets drunk at weddings." She shook her head. "The Son is something new."

The Rock sighed. "So I know where he gets it from."

Maryam sniffed. "He gets it from his father – the man who raised him. A kind man, knew more scripture than anyone alive. He died last summer." She held out the empty bowl. "Where do I return this?"

That morning, in a flurry of dust, through scrub, the caravan began to march.

The road north led through vineyards, the plants widely dispersed in the gravel-rich soil. By noon everything was white or grey or virulent blue – sky, lake, soil, shrubs.

Ahead there were clusters of people: joking labourers bearing the tents on their backs, or young children driving goats. A few donkeys bearing loads – the cookware, some bundles of firewood.

But here was a difference: clusters of women, columns of blowing robes, scarves over their heads, walking calmly, chuckling, telling stories, sometimes looking back and calling out children's names. Women walking unescorted as if at home.

Maryam was conscious that she was alone. She increased her pace and caught up with some of the women. "Do you know where we're headed?"

Pause. A plump, weathered face turned to her. "Back to Nahum I expect. We should be there soon. It's not far." She smiled. "Back before the afternoon winds."

Another was peering round in curiosity. "You're his mother."

This was embarrassing. The Son had not greeted her as if she were his mother. By now most of these people would know why his family had come. She had to say yes. She was tempted to say no.

They didn't know what to say either. Why was she walking alone at the back if she was his mother? That's what they wanted to ask. Had his family really come to stop him preaching?

Instead they talked to her about Nazareth, the kind of place it was. "It's like most others," Maryam replied. "Higher, dryer, not so green."

Did he preach there too?

"Yes. Very popular he was."

"Oh I bet."

"Fancy having the Son in your village talking away."

The nearest woman smiled at Maryam. "I think he might have been a handful," she said. Maryam thought she saw a glimmer of sympathy in her eyes. "Not easy."

Maryam felt emboldened. "Do you notice anything odd about him?"

The question was batted back and forth among them by

their eyelids and no answer came. *Yes of course they've noticed* was the answer. The height, the wide hips, the sturdy short legs, the narrow sloping shoulders, and the voice. Above all else the voice.

But it had been the wrong question to ask, at least so soon. Silence fell and the women either increased their pace to escape her, or turned back, saying they wanted to see about their children. The group dispersed, leaving Maryam walking on her own again.

Maybe that's my task here. To ask the wrong questions.

She walked more quickly, unburdened by company, hoping to get to the front. *I might as well hear what he's saying.*

People kept stepping into her path, so she couldn't get close to the Son.

At first she thought it was by accident, just everyone else wanting to be near him. She would try to get through, and there would be a wall of broad male backs interleaved in layers between her and the front of the march.

Then outside of the town of Gennesaret a man jumped down from an olive tree and ran towards the front. Immediately, three men and two women formed a kind of a wall, blocking the man. He jumped up and shouted, "Are you a prophet, Rabuli?"

The voice came high and light, shouted from the midst of people, "No. I am the Son of Adam." A riddle: weren't all men the Son of Adam?

The olive grower blinked. The large woman whom Maryam had seen before, looking even larger in billowing black, thrust herself forward and said in a blistering Migdali accent, "Away wi ya. Goon. Naw. Ya had ya ansa. Move!"

She looked utterly fed up and moved in a series of ugly jerks. *She's led a tough life*, Maryam decided. You could see in the size of her chin, the thick flesh that merged with the neck. You could also see, around the eyes and cheekbones that she had once been pretty with beautiful colouring – even sandstone skin, flushed cheeks, black eyes, black hair.

Maryam watched the Migdali as they walked. She patrolled the area around the Son, less of a companion and more like a bodyguard. Tall, but more importantly broad, with a fearsome glare and a bustling manner, she thrust her way ahead of the Son to clear a path. Yet when he turned to talk to the followers the Migdali would roll backwards behind him, as if time had reversed.

Suddenly Yakob was walking beside Maryam. "You've not gone with Babatha. You're staying?"

She looked at his newly matured face. How to say – I'd been hoping for something like this; I waited three times ten years. Instead, she answered in mild voice, "Yah. Hear what he has to say."

Yakob looked at her suddenly fondly and took her arm. His grip was affectionate. He also was controlling where she walked.

They drew near to Nahum, and more people began to trail along beside them.

Those in the caravan greeted the townsfolk, or even held out their hands to slap in greeting. Some of the caravan stretched out to hand over dried fish or new fishing tackle they had had brought from Migdal Nunya. Maryam realized: *all of these people are followers as well. He's got more than forty then. Many more.*

Nahum had proper buildings more like Tiberias or Sepphoris than a village, with handsome two-storey dwellings, cobbled streets and a jetty out into the lake.

They had only passed four or five houses when the main group in front swerved into a gate. Through it, Maryam glimpsed windowless brick walls, a paved courtyard, and a jumble of flat-roofed extensions. The Rock ducked under the arch. The way he stamped the dust off his sandals made Maryam think this was his home.

The Migdali woman blocked the entrance with outstretched arms. She seemed not to notice Maryam at all, gazing out over the top of her head. "Tha rast a yas – go to the proseuche. It's got space there for yas. Yakob'll show ya the way."

Yakob smiled at his mother, kept hold of her arm and led her past two cross streets out of which blasted hot wind down from the hills. Maryam heard two of the men joking.

"His whore's a fearsome lady," one of them said. "Ha Ha." It was said in such an unusual way, wry and affectionate at the same time. Ha ha.

"Nowt going to cross that one." Ha ha.

When is a whore not a whore? When she's a lieutenant.

The proseuche had a low wall around it.

Yakob helped Maryam step over it into a yard crowded with people sitting outside in the last of the sun, the ground still hot. There was no room for tents.

Yakob introduced her as Maryam to some of the female followers. The women chorused, "Hello, Maryam, hello dear." They sounded like they might be from Cana. Yakob asked them to make space for her to sleep, perhaps find bedding. Then he said to Maryam, "Let's get you some food."

Maryam said, "Let me help." She'd seen women walking back from the hills carrying firewood so she started to walk in that direction. Yakob looked alarmed and insisted on walking with her out to the stonefields. He helped her carry back scrubwood to the rear wall of the proseuche with its makeshift fire. There was nothing to say between Yakob and Maryam, or rather too much.

He stayed to help the women stumble a cauldron full of water over the fire before assuring his mother that she'd be all right, but he had to get back.

"You'll tell the Son that I'm here?" Maryam asked.

"He knows," smiled Yakob, unaware of how deeply disappointing that would sound to her. It meant: *Stay here. Stay away*.

When the women from Cana asked how she knew the brother of the Son, she answered them, "I'm from Nazareth." She waited for them to say Nazareth, but you sound like you're from the South. They didn't; and she realized she'd been flattening her speech. Flattening herself.

That evening in blue light with golden torches the Son came to the proseuche.

He glowed, laughing, smiling, shaking hands, firelight in his eyes, calling everyone by name. The Migdali trawled in advance, allowing or disallowing people to approach.

Maryam backed away, out of the torchlight. Less than a shadow around the Son, Maryam found that the Migdali made her heart ache.

Maryam knew her ache for what it was. She could name it – envy. She was envious of the Migdali and jealous too. Giving the right names to those emotions added shame to them. She hated feeling such things, wrestled with them. This was the loss old people feel around the young who replace them – the young who can achieve what the old now never would.

Could she believe the rough men who had called the Migdali a whore? A whore would have known pleasure. Maryam had not. This Migdali now had the honour of serving and being accepted by the Son of Adam.

What made Maryam crumble was seeing the Migdali with the Son's followers both young and old. They would dip slightly to her, smiling. She had an easy, laughing, forthright relationship with many of them, nodding in agreement, touching their forearms, and making quick joint decisions while tucking her hair back into her head-tie. Giving directions that were accepted and acted on, pushing some people forward to meet the Son, directing others to the Rock, or even to Yakob, who did seem to have authority over practical things like firewood, or spaces to sleep.

The Son was hoisted onto the top of the proseuche's wall by two big men. The crowd began to shush itself, with the swollen-cheeked settling of people expecting to enjoy themselves.

The Son made a sound like thunder by croaking and wobbling his cheeks, and then laughed. He shouted at them like a fisherman on the prow of a boat. "Oi! Oi! You lot!"

There was laughter. The Son acknowledged it. "Well, that went well! We had top men from Yerusalam up here. Did you see? All the way from Beth Yahu. All the way back too (a rattling satirical kind of laugh). Trying to make out I'm a demon. Or possessed. Or mad. Well. I am possessed."

He paused, waited. In the wavering firelight it was as if he came and went in waves.

"I am possessed by the spirit of God. You can keep that to yourselves. You know those people. They'd have my hide. But that's the way it is. You can call me crazy if you like. My family can come across and try to hide me away – most families would. You can do that and be forgiven. Hey, Mum, you're all right, no worries."

Laughter. Eyes searched in the twilight but no one recognized her.

"You can lie, cheat, steal – all of that – and be forgiven. Here's one thing you won't be forgiven... insulting the spirit of God. God is not to be insulted. Especially not when he comes to visit. Nooooooo, I am NOT saying I AM God. But the spirit of God is here with us. And that is something new. What am I?"

And they all chorused "The Son of Adam."

"You're sure now. Is that it?"

The Rock rumbled a laugh and ducked. It was a riddle. Who was the Son of Adam – Hawa, a woman. And who was Adam's father?

You'd probably have to know already the answers – as Maryam did.

The Yehudai called themselves Sons of God. And that just meant a follower of the God of Yisrael, or even more precisely a male Yehudi.

But might mean something beyond imagining.

The Son put a finger to his lips and ssshed for silence. "Don't tell anyone." Then loudly. "All right then!" Clapping his hands once, loudly. Then it was the twins' turn to make a sound of thunder. The Son laughed and pointed at them.

The Thunder Brothers took turns to bellow. "So there were this merchant who had gold to sell. But it was so valuable that he feared for his safety. And so he only sold wooden trinkets. And at the end, he died, and folk found he had all this gold. Why didn't he tell us he had all this gold? they said. Why did he hide it away? He could have used it to build a beautiful house for all of us to share."

The Thunder Brothers paused, waiting, one with an arm across his belly, the other with a finger cocked under his chin, mimicking some grand personages. They'd learned the comic style from watching the Son.

They waited. First silence, then a swelling groan and a kind of chuckle of approval. One of the Thunders pointed to someone. "Get it?" The other Thunder nodded. "You got it. Good. Do you get-get it?" There were more chuckles and both Thunders cupped a hand behind one ear. One of them prompted, "Let..."

And the crowd took up the cry, sounding like the sea. "HE WHO HAS EARS, HEAR." An older woman crowded in between the Thunders, beaming, taking their arms. That'll be their mother, Maryam decided.

A young thin man with spots shouted, "If you've got gold, tell folks, don't be afeard."

And there was a groaning, and people ssshed the young man. You weren't supposed to spoil the story by explaining it.

Then the Son stepped forward holding up his hands. "I'd say that lad there found the gold and didn't hide it." The chuckles then were more forgiving.

And the Son looked direct at Maryam. He was smiling, almost affectionately. Then he turned.

Maryam thought *I'm still not hearing what I need to hear.*
What he was actually doing.

Maryam learned that the Son often crossed the lake, there
and back in a day.

Or he would walk to Beth Saida to speak to people there.
So she took to joining the shiftless young men and the
dazzled young women who loitered around the Rock's front
door.

The Son would emerge, smiling and waving, then stride
forth ignoring her. Maryam would follow, trying to trail after
him. And sure enough some of the men or women would
slip in front of her. A wall would insinuate itself between
her and the Son, and then stop, as if to talk.

Some of the followers might turn to Maryam, and sketch
a smile of greeting or even murmur hello, as you might to
any older woman you did not know.

Once, in a tremor of impatience, Maryam managed to
thrust her way through the cordon. Another cluster of backs
slid in front of her. One half-shaven oik smirked at her over
his shoulder.

Behind him, the Migdali was looking dead at Maryam
with a sideways smile. *You see now do ya? You do owt to harm
him, I'll come for ya.*

Maryam let the Migdali see all the weariness, exhaustion,
heartache, and disappointment that weighed down her face
and eyes. *Is that what you want, woman? Really?*

To her credit, the smile and the gaze of the Migdali looked
confused, and then downcast.

"Maryam?" someone called and both she and the Migdali
turned.

And that meant the Migdali was called Maryam too.

The woman's face jabbed back towards Maryam, her hands in fists. She really had not wanted Maryam to know their names were the same.

The person shouted again. "Maryam! When do we get to hear him?"

"The eklesia. Where else?" she bellowed back, still annoyed. She stormed away, almost seeming to flee.

It was a Greek word. Maryam asked one of the waiting men, "The eklesia, what is that?"

The man was frustrated at being kept waiting. "Bloody Greeks. It's just a fancy-pants way of saying a calling out. They call out, and we're all just supposed to troop out to some field." He made a sound of disgust and walked away.

Maryam knew then she would have to wait. She left and after that did not haunt Shemenolo's door.

Another woman arrived in Nahum.

Maryam recognized her. She was the one who'd been wearing a tiara in the tent at Migdal Nunya. Now the woman was carried into Nahum on a bier, with attendants, and though she wore no jewellery and her dress was plain linen, Maryam knew the kind of face from Yerusalam – wealth and independence and education. This one read and had female friends who read.

An old man sleeping at the proseuche said she was the wife of someone in the court of the Herod Phillipi. She had money that one, and friends at court. The Son and the Rock both came out to greet her, welcome her to the house.

When the Son spoke in the public spaces, this woman would come with a servant carrying a chair for her, and she would sit and look thoughtful, considering, a hand at her throat. And afterwards, the Son would come and dazzle her, with a smile and respectful gestures.

Maryam suddenly saw how he looked to these women – a Greek modernizer, clean-shaven with tonsured hair.

Sometimes the woman would linger after he had spoken, digging her fingers through her hair, scowling slightly. Or she'd lean forward, clasp her hands together and stare at them as if apprising the worth of her rings. Then she'd lean back, cup her chin between her thumb and forefinger and go very still.

Maryam asked folk who that grand lady was.

"Oh, her," a woman replied, and turned. "Tuh," said another. It was as if they didn't want to say her name. Then one said, "Yoanna."

She's fabricating, Maryam thought. But what?

Yoanna would sit alone, for hours, mulling. Finally one of her servants, a black girl, would come and say something, her white teeth flashing against the beautiful curves of her mouth. Yoanna would nod yes, stand, and the servant would pick up the chair. They would stroll back towards the house, chatting as if friends. Yoanna sometimes took the girl's hand.

The Migdali ignored Yoanna. She bustled to organize advance parties to tell the next settlement that the Son was visiting, or she found food and shelter for all those who were crowding into Nahum. Some of her men would eye Yoanna with misgiving.

Sometimes the two women would confer. The Migdali's movements would become edgy, brisk, with lots of nodding, hands on hips, flicking her own nose. The smooth face seemed to swell, and balloon out into frown lines. It would wobble. Around Yoanna, the Migdali seemed less solid.

By contrast, Yoanna would go still, lips pursed and face firm.

They would meet in some form of negotiation, which would end when they both nodded yes. With no gestures of fondness, the two women would part.

We have a rivalry, thought Maryam.

One night, waiting for the Son to come to talk to the eklesia, Maryam saw the Migdali walk towards her, look at her, and hug herself. Here she comes, Maryam thought. She wants allies.

"Mother," the Migdali greeted her.

"Whose?" Maryam asked with rueful twist of a grin.

"His. I know, sorry. An't been hospitable."

"Weren't you? I don't need a welcome. I am here to listen to what the Son says. Even though, yes, he and I don't have an ordinary relationship."

The Migdali settled next to her. "Aw that's not good."

"No. Not at all. I'm used to it. It's interesting to see how the movement grows. And who pays for it."

The Migdali was still for a moment. "It is good that there're generous folk."

"All of them women – well, most of them. I think that's because of the message, don't you?"

No response from the Migdali, so Maryam continued. "This is what I think is different about his teaching. The Son has an idea that goodness comes from the heart. Not from following scripture or ritual, but from that kindness you can see in one person but not in another. Women understand that."

"He says its written down. It's the Law."

"He is showing us that a kind heart will obey the Law as water flows downhill. And that means that the Law itself comes from this idea of goodness. He's saying that God is good or kind."

"I wouldn't know." The Migdali looked away, her mouth sour. Maryam imagined dead babies, drunken men who paid her in copper assarion. The port of Migdal Nunya had a reputation for harbour-front trade and depravity.

Maryam ventured. "I think it means his teaching pulls in kindly folk."

"You're right there." The Migdali tried to smile.

"Like Yoanna," said Maryam, lightly, quickly. "What a good heart she must have."

The other Maryam's smile was odd, hard. "She's still married to a man at court, but they don't get on. She gives us money. We need it."

Maryam's smile mirrored hers. "All of this has got to be paid for. Smiling at the rich is always part of religion. Unless you can force tax out of people."

The Migdali cast down her eyes. "You don't talk like Nazaredi."

"I was sent into exile because of my husband's teaching."

The Migdali began to shift uneasily. *She is not comfortable in the presence of us, the central families*, Maryam decided. The Migdali murmured, "So that's where he learned it. From his Dad."

Maryam felt something in her relent. "I didn't say that. My husband was not his father."

The Migdali could stop her head spinning but couldn't prevent a sideways flick of her eyes.

And for some reason, Maryam was tired of leaving out the truth.

"He's from God," said Maryam. "He embodies God. I

sometimes think God tries to occupy him like a house, but the house is too small and God is too big. God's mind is the universe. That wouldn't fit into a human head or a human language. But the Son of Adam knows something of how God sees. That's why he is able to say that we are all alike, king and slave, in the eyes of God."

The Migdali went very still.

Maryam chuckled. "Are you thinking I'm crazy? I never tell people the story, not even my own children. But I think... People need to know what he is. And I think you know enough about my child's real situation, what the Son is, for me to tell you a bit more. A child made without a man, entirely out of a woman's body is going to be a woman, no?"

Maryam was watching so she saw it. Almost imperceptibly, the other Maryam rocked in place. Maryam's smile settled. This thing she'd been hiding was a dead and withered, useless secret. If this woman and the Son were lovers, then of course she knew.

"When I told my uncle the Kohen Gadol that I had been made pregnant by God – hoo! – you should have seen his face. He went all still and stiff and started talking very carefully." She thought the Migdali might have been snubbed or made to feel awkward herself in her time. Maryam thought she might laugh at a priest going respectable and careful.

Instead, an urgency came into the Migdali's eyes, almost a pleading – a tremulous smile that might have been relief.

"Stay here," said the Migdali, and stood and moved away, surging like a wave.

Left alone, Maryam listened. Standing on a bench in firelight, the Rock was talking to the crowd. He was not talking very well.

The Rock fought for words. "The things I have seen. I can't talk about them. I don't have the words. It's not always big things. It's little things. Like how he talks to everyone or don't let laws get in the way. Not that the laws do. Get in the way. I mean. The laws are good things. He believes in the Laws…"

Maryam thought with a twist: *they should let me preach. I'd give them a lesson in who was among them.*

The Migdali came back with three large, rough-handed men, boatmen.

"Tell them what you just told me," the Migdali said.

"Are you going to drive me out or stone me?" Maryam asked.

To her amazement the Migdali's eyes swelled and went watery. "No, Mother. No! What you said were amazing. I want them to hear it."

So Maryam told them. The virgin birth. The preaching in the Royal Stoa. All of it, except that she didn't say again that the Son of Adam was a woman. The men looked rapt.

"He's said nowt about any of this. Astounded the priests you say?"

"At twelve." Not one of the men said: don't you mean thirteen?

"And you say he sees what God sees?"

Maryam went still, gathering words. "Imagine you live in a land where everyone is blind. You have to explain not only what you see, but what sight and seeing are. Maybe you don't even try to do that. Maybe you just tell stories that teach what you know through sight. God is like a whale that contains all of time in its belly. God can ruminate the past or the future. It's all there. Sometimes, but dimly, the Son can know what God has seen in the future."

They waited, mouths open.

"The past and the future are so different, they almost don't make sense. Almost can't be put into words. All things die, and people don't like to be told that."

"You're saying he's a prophet."

"No. I am not. He is bigger than a prophet. I don't know what to call him."

"Son of Adam," said one of the fisherman. The Migdali caught her eyes, and tried to warn her no.

I am beyond caring. Maryam said, "A son of man is the one thing he most assuredly is not."

Migdali stood straighter, and sniffed, but with her hands on hips. She was being a general again. "Whenever this woman comes, treat her with respect. I know. The Son wants her at a distance. So leave it that way. But you honour her. All of yas. Also. Bring all the women here. So they can hear her."

Most assuredly, thought Maryam, *she's undercutting Yoanna.*

The next day the Migdali called a meeting of women and they all came with questions for the Mother of the Son.

"So you are, like, his Mum." Young girl, washed-out looking, too young to be anything other than unformed but roughened by her work.

"Not like his Mum. I am his Mum."

"You're not what we were expecting. You're all posh." Nervous giggles.

"My aunt was married to the Kohen Gadol." Silence.

"Better watch what we say."

"Why?" Maryam asked.

The Son had once told her that far to the north in unknown lands, there were rivers of ice. These rivers were solid but still flowed a few arm's-lengths a year. Maryam felt like that solid river.

If this meeting were to work, she would have to do the talking. "I've got a question for you all. Let's say for a moment that the Son had been born a woman, was a woman. A woman preaching. How would the lessons be any different?"

No one had ever asked the young escaped servants to think.

"But he's not a woman is he?" A pretty, blank, perplexed face.

"And that's not the question we are answering."

An old granny spoke, her mouth folded in so far it looked as if her face were eating itself. "Nowt different at all. Not one bit!"

Maryam nodded.

"Stopped the stoning of that woman, like, and he said, you men, if you ant sinned or thought about it, or done it with one of these, then go on throw yer bloody stone. Just what I would say." The old whiskery woman sputtered out a giggle, and clapped her gnarled hands. "Not one of them threwd it! Not one of em!"

Later, Maryam asked the Migdali for pens and parchment. "What he says is being lost. We need to keep it. Writing will keep it. Others can read it."

"Aye but we don't have none of that. Don't know how to get that." The Migdali looked bereft and ashamed.

"I'm going to ask Yoanna. She has money. But I want to know if you are happy with that."

"Happy and all. Sure. Sure." The Migdali nodded too much.

* * *

Yoanna had a room of her own in the Rock's house, small but it had a window with shutters, a proper bed and a folding chair in front of a folding desk.

All of which Maryam found surprising for an instant until she remembered that Yoanna was wealthy.

Yoanna bounced to her feet, clasping hands in front of herself. She was draped in Roman dress, folds of gently pistachio cloth with black zigzags along the edge. Alone at home, she had her hair pulled back into a shiny helmet.

"Mother! Thank you for coming to see me. I should have come to see you. Please sit." She had a handsome middle-aged face. High cheeks seemed to pull her mouth up into an airy smile. The way she spoke – it sounded a bit as though she was chewing something delicious. But there was no attempt to disguise the Northern accent. She somehow made the voice of Beth Saida sound patrician.

Right. This one knows the court, knows how to behave. So Maryam behaved, settled elegantly on the only couch.

"So why are you here to see me?" The eyes sparkled with energy.

Maryam explained. No one was writing down what the Son said. She needed scrolls, pens, preferably parchment rather than linen or papyrus. The effect on Yoanna was notable. The smile broadened but hardened. Her eyes widened and sparkled more, and she adjusted the already perfectly placed fold of the pistachio over her forearm. She waited until Maryam was done, but Maryam, seeing she was annoyed, finished early.

"We have those things. You are welcome to them." Yoanna gave her head a toss as if casting off something in her hair. "But we do have a scribe, you might call him, recording what the Son says. You know Mattit-yahu?"

The pretty little tax collector.

"He looks like an intelligent young man."

Yoanna's bright eyes held Maryam. "And you don't sound like a Nazaredi. Did the Migdali send you?"

It was Maryam's turn to smile. *She thinks the Migdali wants to balance her boy. They really don't like each other, those two.*

"I'm not her messenger." Maryam gathered like a fist. "It was my idea but first I told her I was doing it, so she wouldn't feel I was being underhanded."

About halfway through that sentence Yoanna's whole face shifted. The smile became more rueful. "Would you like some wine? I can't stand water, it's boring." She stood up and took out two bowls of cloudy glass.

"I'm too poor. I haven't drunk wine since my daughter's wedding."

Yoanna turned then and looked into Maryam's face with something like sympathy. "We must do something about that." And turned back for two brimming bowls now the colour of blood. "You're a Kohen. You deserve better."

"The Kohanim deserve what everyone else has, not one jot more."

Yoanna settled. "I would rather say that everyone deserves what the Kohanim have." She took a sip of the wine.

So did Maryam. It was horrible, tongue-curling stuff. *Oh God, do I have to drink it all now?*

Yoanna jumped to her feet. "You want water with it. I'm so sorry. Here." She leaned over Maryam. "Please, allow me." She took Maryam's bowl, found another, and re-poured.

This is the wife of the owner of fishing boats from Beth Saida. Her husband is smart enough to make himself a Minister. And she's smart enough to help him do it.

As the wine and water mixed, Yoanna said, "Writing is wonderful. Better than reading."

Brains. It's been so long since I met anyone with brains.

"I've done a lot of reading," admitted Maryam. "Not writing."

Yoanna passed her the bowl and then flung herself back into her chair like a child. "Writing unites people over distance. And over time. It can make small groups of people feel like big ones. It makes empires. It means we have a chance of talking to our great great grandchildren."

Maryam sniffed, saw Yosef reading aloud. "And it can trap us in the past."

Yoanna folded her feet up under herself while still in the chair. She was having fun. "Only if we let it." She played with her hair, as if flirting with Maryam.

She made Maryam feel dumpy and dour. "What if it's God talking on that sheepskin?"

Yoanna smoothed down the back of her neck. "Then. We will save his voice for the ages."

Her whole body snapped around as if this was getting too serious. "And if so it makes sense to have two people writing. Or rather. Two people hearing, because what the Son says is different for everybody. I think you're going to understand what he says better than Mattit-yahu. Are you enjoying the wine?"

"No," said Maryam. And both women began to chuckle.

The next day Yoanna, in billowing blue silk, approached Maryam.

She seemed stretched taller than most women by the way she stood and the vertical folds of her clothing. She clicked her fingers and her servant girl grinned and passed Maryam four silver-capped scrolls, two of papyrus and two of parchment. She stroked the parchment as she passed it. Then a clutch of already cut reeds, and a huge leather bag of powder and a jug to mix and then carry the ink.

Maryam performed gratitude and being overwhelmed at the generosity.

Yoanna shrugged. "It is for the eklesia. What language will you write in?"

"In Common, of course, he preaches in Common."

"Matt is writing it all down in Greek. Turns it into Greek as he goes."

Maryam was shocked. "Whatever for?"

Yoanna twirled a finger next to her temple as if spinning yarn out of her head. "For the world."

Maryam went still. Like gently settling rain came thoughts: a universal God would speak to all peoples. *She plans ahead, this Yoanna.*

Yoanna asked, "What do you think of his name?"

"His name?"

"Son of Adam. I've advised him to use it at all times. And he does. But not on my say-so. The prophecies, you see. This warrior-prince. Uuuuuuhhhh." Yoanna groaned at the tedium of it. "The Prince is called the Son of David. So if anyone asks, we can say, no this is different. This is the Son of Adam."

"Not another David," said Maryam.

"No, Mother. Something much better than that." Yoanna's smile was beautiful, as if there was a joke somewhere and that Maryam would join in the laughter.

* * *

Finally there came a Calling Out.

The Migdali strode up the street shouting, "Eklesia! Eklesia by the jetty."

The Son and his students stood waiting at the dock. The followers crowded into the area around the quay. Really, eklesia meant anyone who believed, or who was just curious and wanted to listen.

The Calling Out was a chance for Maryam to practice writing, and it did not go so well. It took her too long to mix the ink, and then she spilled some, and then she found she could not keep up with what the Son said. She'd get down one phrase and he'd jump to the next. Sometimes she rather thought she got it down right. But usually it would jump from subject to subject never completing a thought.

The papyrus was expensive, and she was wasting it. She gave up and just listened, and was humbled by how bad at listening she was, how little she heard and understood.

But she was struck by the perfection of how he did it.

He spoke with the calm simplicity of the best country people. You could hear the tekton's shop in the vocabulary, in the simple tales. All the embroidery of the scholars was gone, the fine needlepoint of argument.

God would speak like stones.

God would say that neither stones nor people got any closer to heaven by climbing a tree.

People did not get any closer to God by climbing over each other's shoulders, or cutting them down in battle. To God, a king was no better than a slave.

The Son spoke to the crowd with the simplicity and force of the afternoon winds. And, like the winds, those words were being swept away. She mixed a new batch of ink and wrote: Yehush said.

CHAPTER 19

A THUNDER OF WORDS

The next Calling Out made work on the Shabbat.

The little jetty was jammed with boats from across the lake. People had marched in from as far away as Neapolis.

The Son tried to get to the proseuche, but the roadway was jammed. People had come with aged relatives on litters. Others limped with misshapen feet, gnarled and purple. They roared when they saw the Son; reached out to him with greedy hands, plucked at his clothes.

The Rock hoisted the Son up onto his shoulders and began to thrust his way through them. "Make way, make way!"

The crowd surged, pushing the Rock against Maryam. The Son knocked Maryam with his foot. He turned and said, voice low, "They're coming for miracles, not the truth."

"Just say the truth!" She had to raise her voice. He smiled, nodded and pointed at her scrolls. There was a jolt; her body recognized his expression, the same face staring back at the same face.

"Get your ink ready," the Son said over his shoulder. "I feel a thunder of words."

They were near one of the few cross streets. The Son muttered something to the Rock who turned left, pushing his way through. He began to march out of the town, towards the hills, carrying the Son aloft.

This in itself seemed to be a cause for celebration among the crowd. Women ululated in high warbling cries and a skinny-thighed man jumped into the air. The people parted, letting the core group through to follow the Son, Maryam among them.

The eklesia came to a hill, one rising up gently from the lakeside, and the Son hopped from Shemenolo's shoulders onto an exposed rock.

Unusually for him, Shemenolo had become uproarious, laughing and joking with those around him. He then cradled up an old woman, who pretended to protest and hit him, shaking her head and laughing.

Maryam had seen the woman before. She was bone thin and her left eyelid drooped. She walked balanced shakily not on one, but two sticks. What Maryam had first taken to be short hair was in fact baldness.

Shemenolo now swooped the woman up on to the rock next to the Son. Some folk nearby whooped when they saw her. She smiled a thin, sharp smile and waved. She acted like a beauty. She put her hand on her heart, and then held it out to the crowd.

The Son crouched down and laughed with her and rubbed her bald head. The crowd cheered that.

The woman lay back on the outcrop at an awkward angle, and rolled onto her side, resting her head on her arm. It was a gesture of surrender to the Son.

Then the Son stood up, throwing both hands into the air at the same time. And he began to sing.

Back in Nazareth when he read in the proseuche, he sometimes sang, usually a Mizmor, which was meant to be sung. His clear hard voice (rather than melodic or sweet) cut through air and distance. The voice could pass as a boy's. Maryam could not place the words.

He sang, "Happy are."

Maryam fumbled out her bag, the ink was mixed but she still had to uncork it.

The Son sang, "Happy are" again, rolling his hand for the crowd to take up the words and the notes.

The Calling Out roared back HAPPY ARE. He rolled his hand and they sang the words again, the wall of voices without him.

On the rock, the old woman's legs stayed still, dead. She tried to sit up and couldn't. Shemenolo sprang to his feet and lifted her up from the shoulders. She stayed sitting, her legs straight out in front of her. She leaned back onto her palms, and pumped her shoulders back and forth like a naughty child.

Maryam's eyes pulled her in closer and she thought: *I know you.*

You are one of the girls who were too free with her favours. You loved to sing and dance, and you looked everyone in the face and said, no I don't want your life. And there was no good place for you.

"Happy are," and this time the Son sang on, his voice rising up in an unfamiliar tune. "Those who are poor but who live in the Spirit." Maryam fumbled her quill and got most of that written down.

He paused smiled, looked at them all, let his grin spread. He sang the next words. "For yours is the Kingdom of Heaven."

The paralyzed woman mimed holding up something huge and round in her hands. She flung it out over the crowd, then laughed and clapped her hands.

"Hah…" began the Son. "Hah…" The eklesia understood and sang out, HAPPY ARE. He smiled and waited for a beat then sang, "Those who mourn and have reason to grieve."

Some people shouted, leapt to their feet, waved their hands; some of the eklesia ululated. The woman on the rock hid her eyes while smiling, as if overwhelmed by beauty.

The Son sang out in voice yearning for the sky. "For they shall be comforted."

And the paralyzed woman mimed casting what might have been flower petals, from out of her heart over the heads of the assembly.

"Hah," began the Son.

HAPPY ARE the multitude roared.

The Son keened, "The meek! For they shall." And there was a long peroration as his voice spiralled into the air. "… inherit the Earth." The paralyzed woman seemed to hold up flat something large, a chest perhaps. She emptied it over the heads of the crowd.

Maryam had to remind herself to write, to take her eyes off the woman. The words flowed on.

"Happy are…those who hunger for and thirst for righteousness."

The faces in the crowd. Angular, lined faces that never normally showed their broken teeth in smiles or laughter were letting sunlight blaze on them.

"The merciful … for they will be shown mercy."

The paralyzed woman covered her mouth and then pressed her hands together.

"The pure in heart... for they will see God!" The crowd roared again. The paralyzed woman turned her hands somehow into a bird that flapped its wings. Maryam thought: *she's showing people what they are feeling.*

"Happy are... the peacemakers... for they are the children of God."

The woman mimed something round and placed it on her own head.

Maryam thought perhaps the excitement had peaked with the pure in heart. But the Son kept on singing or speaking or getting the crowd to repeat the words. The roar shook the earth. The paralyzed woman beamed in contentment, and held up hands that looked too big for such thin arms.

The Son sang and talked for hours.

Didn't he get tired? Nobody moved. Maryam's hand ached, and she couldn't keep up with his words. She had moved onto the papyrus, now hastily scratched and dribbled on. She used the formula over and over. Yehush said, Yehush said.

That you are commanded not to murder, but now beyond that, to not even be angry.

That you were not only never to swear an oath on God but go beyond that and not even swear an oath on your own head. For your head was made by God.

The Son said that it is not enough to love your neighbour, but you should love your enemy.

If you help the needy, do it in secret, don't make a show of it. He mimed being an ostentatious grand person, sweeping robes and dropping a tiny coin.

If you are fasting, wash your hair and face, look lively, and don't make a show of it. He mimed a long face, slumped shoulder, dragging hands.

So many things, turning everything upside down, and that high voice rolling down the hillside like boulders. That voice demanding to go far beyond the Law, the commandments.

For your Father in heaven will know the truth, will know the truth in your heart.

The sun rose to a zenith, and then it began to sink.

The sun made all the land look hazy, and the light was golden on the surface of the lake. Birds swooped low, scooping fish out of it. Maryam kept trying to rest, but then he would say something that she would have to try to write down, sideways now along an edge of scroll.

He talked about worry, how worried everyone was all the time. The crowd laughed because their life was worry. Their only constant friend was worry.

The Son said: "Look at the birds of the air. They don't sow or reap or stow away in barns and yet your heavenly Father feeds them. Are you not more valuable than birds? Is worrying going to add a single hour to your life?"

He started joking about fashion of high people in robes (he kept his eyes away from Yoanna). Then he sang a beautiful tune that Maryam hoped she would remember. "Look at the flowers in the field. They don't work or spin. But I tell you that even Solomon in his splendour was not dressed as well as these."

Maryam had tears in her eyes as she wrote. It had all been worth it. Everything had been fulfilled.

* * *

Eventually, darkness lowered itself.

The Shabbat had ended and the eklesia began to troop down the hill.

That number of feet moving over rocks in twilight sounded like the running of a stream. The air was cooler now too and mint-blue.

The Migdali stomped up next to Maryam. "Bless ya," she said. "You been at it!"

Maryam held out the scrolls. "All full."

The Migdali uncapped and unrolled one of them. "Scratching away."

The Rock was carrying the paralyzed woman, piggyback this time, and her cheek was pressed against his and she looked as excited as a child. Maryam touched her arm. The woman smiled at her.

"That was beautiful, those things you did, those motions," Maryam said.

It was not clear that the woman had heard her, but she beamed at Maryam with black teeth, the wisps of hair on her head like high clouds.

The Rock said, "Her name is Shushan. She can't hear you all that well, but when she says something, people listen."

With the artlessness of a child, Shushan reached out and stroked Maryam on the cheek. She laughed, pointed at Maryam and then winked. Maryam imagined her in inns, drinking wine.

They were nearing the road, and a man was limping along it to intercept them.

"Oh God, oh no," groaned the Son.

The man's clothes were in rags. As he approached, Maryam caught a whiff of something, the smell of a burn wound.

He was criss-crossed with cuts and there was something wrong with his face. Part of it seemed to be hanging loose as a flap of skin.

The Son kept on walking and the man kept pace. Even in dusk Maryam could see flies on his cut flesh. Her eyes skittered over the rest of him. Fingers were missing and his feet were dark-stained bandages.

"Rabuli, Rabuli, please," the man begged. The Son strode on. "Great One, you could make me clean." The man was angry, crazed with fever, hunger, loneliness. Why should God so afflict him? He said in a voice that sounded like it was sawing stone, "If you wanted to, you could!"

The Son stopped and swayed in place, his eyes, indeed his whole face closed. He had just said to thousands of people, hide your good deeds, don't seek to profit from them. The man, exhausted and starved, sank to his knees and begged in a voice thick with mucous that could no longer form words.

"All right, yes. Be clean." The words were muttered, bitten off, almost covert.

The whole universe blinked.

The stars seemed to go out for a moment, and all the air seemed to be pulled out of their lungs like a tide. The world itself was dizzy. It swayed as if drunk. The honking geese overhead flew backwards. Behind them, there were cries and queries from the multitude.

Then the world shook itself awake.

The man was whole. The skin on his face plastered down and smooth; his bare legs no longer swollen but firm and shapely with muscle. Both feet and all his fingers and toes were in place. He was young, not yet twenty. Maryam had thought him ancient.

"The air. I can feel the air," he said in a young, soft voice full of wonder.

The Son leaned in closer to him. "Don't tell anyone. Please. Don't say anything."

Behind them, still packed full of the Son's spinning, tumbling words, amid the birds of the air, the flowers of the field, all the people began to sing the new tunes. Happy are... Happy are. Shushan waved her arms, like leading a band.

Maryam realized: Shushan had not asked for her illness to be cured.

As they walked down the hill Yoanna and the Migdali had an audible, public fight.

Their voices rose sharply again, and this time Maryam could hear.

"No one is going to come to listen to repent, repent!" Yoanna gave a musical chuckle that Maryam found dismissive.

"That's NOT what he says!" Everything about the Migdali was bunched.

"They are coming because someone they love is dying, and he is the only person in the three kingdoms who can actually cure anyone."

"That's coming for the wrong reason. He asks them to shut up about it and so should we."

This needs to stop, Maryam thought at the precise moment that Yoanna looked at her and said, "Mother, what do you think?"

Maryam had words in place. "You're both right. We need people to come so that they hear. But God hates miracles."

Both women went still. Yoanna queried, "Why?"

"When he was five years old a friend died, and he said then that God didn't want the boy to die. But why save one person and not another? Miracles are not just. Miracles pick and choose."

The Migdali still looked belligerent. "So we shut up about them."

"That is what he tells the people he cures. But." Maryam smiled. "He's good at getting other people to say what he doesn't want to say himself."

Yoanna looked up and away as if amused.

"We do what we're doing now. Let them come to be healed. And stay to listen. Only, we don't fight about it." Maryam linked arms with both of them, and tried to make them march in step and be merry.

But in the dark, they stumbled on rocks.

The next day in the yard of the proseuche, Maryam heard a voice say behind her. "Maryam?"

It was Esta, little Esta, Platon's wife, here from Nazareth, standing next to Yakob. Maryam yelped in surprise and hugged her.

Esta laughed too. "I've come to join you."

She'd been escorted to Maryam by Yakob. Yakob did not look pleased; he was scowling.

Esta looked suddenly solemn. "I've got to give you some news."

"I'm sorry, Ami," said Yakob, looking down.

"Your Babatha. She's back home. She's left her husband. There's been something terrible."

CHAPTER 20

THE CHILDREN'S ROOM

In the dark of the old Nazareth house, Babatha sat slumped on the floor.

She looked up at Maryam but otherwise didn't move. Tara sat on a dining couch, straight and stiff as a broom handle, staring down at her folded hands, half a room and a silence between them. Babatha had two new folds of skin under her mouth.

A third person in the room bounced to her feet and said, "Ah, good you're back." The person lunged forward and kissed Maryam.

It took a moment for sun-dazzled eyes to see who this was: Miltiades' mother, Bruria. "You been told?" the old woman asked.

"Only that something's happened."

"That son of mine. He knows well enough he done wrong. He been at your younger one as well."

Tara almost imperceptibly shrank and lowered her head, like a feather thrown on flame.

The old woman kept on. "Wahl. You know boys. He says to his Dad, she's her sister, like, they're same, you marry one you marry the other, same flesh and blood. So I tells him, so you think you got two wives now do ya? Have you paid two dowries, talked to the parents? You think your cousin will marry Tara now?"

Something pleading in Bruria's eyes. Maryam soured in a moment. *She's acting righteous.* Then immediately following: *but she's taken our side against her own.*

Babatha's jaw clenched like a fist. "I'm not going back." She sniffed, shook her head. "Can't go back there." She turned to her sister. "We have to find a home for her, too."

Maryam waited for Babatha to say something else, something kind or forgiving or angry. Then Maryam turned to Tara, and whispered. "Have you lost your virginity?"

Tara finally spoke. "Yes." Maryam went to hug her. Babatha curled up her knees and hugged them. Tara said in a wan voice. "It's not my fault."

"Nothing's ever your fault," growled Babatha.

The old woman explained. "I thought I'd brung my boys up right. But they hear things, boys, from the men, you know." She did an agonized dance. "I mean he's ruined em both."

No he hasn't. Maryam knelt in front of Tara. "Foolish men, men who marry for show or profit, such men yes, they want a virgin. Only because they are afraid. Of what, I've never understood. It's not like the seed lurks for years inside us."

Babatha couldn't stop herself making a spurting sound of laughter and looking up with surprise and a touch of admiration at her mother. Maryam worked Tara's hands in her own. "But real men, men of heart and blood, know that we have heart and blood. And don't judge."

Babatha's voice was flat. "Tara doesn't want a real man. She wants a house." Babatha made a smacking noise as if moving something stuck between her teeth. "Mine."

God, what a situation. Babatha has a choice of being homeless or accepting what her husband did. She's blaming Tara at least a little bit and I'm not sure I don't as well. And Yosef's body rests in the barMiltiades family tomb.

Wives who left husbands – where could they go? Back home, yes, but no one else lived in this house now.

"What about Theo and Seb?" Maryam asked Babatha, still stroking Tara's head. Babatha's son Theophilus was already ten, his sister Seblma was seven years old. The Law said children over six had to be returned to the husband's house. Babatha had lost at least two of her children.

"He's keeping them. My little boy, my little girl. They wouldn't let me have them. I tried to take my baby Rutit. Milt and his brothers tore her out of my arms." Babatha's face was swollen like a fist.

Bruria looked stricken. "They're part of the family, they were born to us. We'll take proper care of them, we will, all of us." The old woman may have thought she was being reassuring. She glanced at Maryam's house, the bareness of it.

"He's broken the Law," said Maryam.

Bruria reminded her. "So has Tara. A woman taken in adultery."

There was a chance Tara could be stoned. It was so often the women who were stoned. The men, they were allowed to try; it was the woman's job to resist. Tara had never resisted anything in her life. Maryam kissed the top of her head.

"That won't happen." Maryam promised her.

Well Maryam had her daughters back home, now – truly back. And she had lost the eklesia. Maybe only for a while. At least she'd had it for a time. She remembered the sunset light on the lake. The birds, the singing, Shushan's dance of hands.

A mountain had dropped from the sky on her family. There was no walking around it or digging through rubble to rescue things of worth. The shame of it would spread over all of them while Milt would concoct some story that he could tell to his mates in his cups at night. Oh, he might regret; he might feel pain; but he would somehow make himself aggrieved and talk about how Babatha had left him.

Maryam calculated and then said to Bruria. "You're going to keep Theo and Seb, I know. But Rutit. You have no use for the infant. Let us have Rut back."

Bruria began to make a noise, like that might be difficult.

"She's not safe there," said Maryam.

Bruria's shame and empathy turned to anger. "She's a baby."

"She'll grow. Ten years, she'll be twelve with no one there to defend her. I'm sorry, no. If anything happens, people will say look what she comes from, this scandal. There's no chance Rutit will reach marriageable age untouched."

Bruria glared. "Who do you think my family are?"

Maryam spoke carefully. "I think they are of good stock, but wealth came, and the sons are spoiled. The baby girl comes back here."

The old woman shifted. Girls, of course, were no use. They had to be found husbands. A few years from now she might be useful about the place as a kind of servant, but then, Maryam's eyes were bearing down on her.

Bruria seemed to chew on her own cheek. "A baby girl is better off with her Mum. Better do it quick."

Babatha stood up with the slow deliberation of the moon in its course. Her posture was distorted, one shoulder higher than another. It looked like she might hit someone. "Here's what else is going to happen, Bruria. Your son will divorce me and marry Tara."

Both Maryam and Bruria made noises of surprise.

Babatha eyed them, eyed the world. "He has ruined her. Especially the way it all came out." Babatha eyed her mother. "He's been bragging. Talking to the men, how he had both sisters. The young one and the old one. Everybody knows. There's no keeping this quiet." Her mouth wrenched. "He's turned Tara into the village mule. Unless he marries her."

Bruria's chin worked, trying to find words.

Babatha kept advancing. "It's better for Theophilus and Seblma that they have Tara as their stepmum. She'll have more reason to love them than any other second wife would." Babatha's smile was knife-thin. "And I keep the dowry."

Bruria looked affronted.

Babatha stared her down. "That's what it's for. If the marriage fails. It means I can eat. And Milt can marry Tara without a dowry."

They all gaped in silence. "That way," said Babatha managing the most bitter of smiles, "we are still a family."

Bruria nodded once, firmly. She left with Tara, and that night, under darkness, brought the baby back herself. The dowry of course was another matter.

Babatha stayed.

At once she rearranged the pots and stacked the firewood in the children's room of all places. She brushed and swept in a rage even in the middle of the night.

There was a fight. "It's my house," Maryam stormed out of the bedroom. "I want to sleep. Leave things. Or ask me."

"Oh yes, it's always YOUR house." Babatha's eyes swam with water. *She's lost everything*, Maryam reminded herself, and tried to hug her and Babatha pushed her away.

Or she would sit unmoving, all day, staring ahead. "I thought the sun shone out of his arse." She would glower at Maryam. "I must have looked a right idiot." She would get angry again. "Why didn't you stop me? You knew he was an idiot."

Maryam tried to distract them both with Little Rut. Rutit at least they could both agree on and find in her some delight. Rutit would dangle on tiptoe like she was dancing. She would giggle and spurt. She could make them all laugh then, for a moment.

Rut began to talk and that felt like a miracle. Rut could clap her hands and shout out "Ami walk!"

"No," Babatha said. "You are walking. Rutit walking." She pointed to Rut, prodded her, tickled her to make her laugh.

Rut could soothe Babatha, make her look big and competent again, a wry calm smile on her face. "Up we go!" Babatha would lift up Rut over her head and the child lacked all fear with her.

At other times, Maryam worried that the child was sickly sweet. Rut called everyone "Ami", even Idra when she visited. And Rut clung and looked anxious and cried very easily. Maryam would go dark inside then; dark with rage at the Miltiades. Those days they had torn Rut away from her mother had dislocated the child's sense of what a mother was.

They had no news from Sepphoris. Late one afternoon, Shem slipped away from the fields to visit them. No, he had no news of the dowry. But Tara and Milt had married quietly. Everyone was pretending nothing had changed.

"What of Theo, what of Seblma?" Babatha demanded. Were they eating? Was Theo reading anything? Were they unhappy?

Shem shrugged and went awkward. "They won't let them ask after you. They're saying you did things and they kicked you out."

Babatha said quietly, "What about you? What do you say?"

Shem ducked under his elbow. "I can't say nowt."

"Can you tell them about me? Please? Tell them I miss them?"

Shem wobbled his head to mean *possibly not.* "I, I can't really tell them I've been here."

"Are they buying you too?" Babatha's eyes were hard upon him.

Shem shrugged and looked even more embarrassed. "There's nowt else to do around here," he mumbled.

Babatha said it as softly as a falling feather. "You could work for the tekton." Shem acted as if he hadn't heard. Then Babatha said quietly, "If you are any kind of person, you will tell them. At the very least, I should get my dowry."

Shem's mouth angled downwards in an ouch of embarrassment. He would say nothing. When he left, Babatha did not say goodbye.

She stood staring at the wall. "I tried. I tried so hard with everything."

Maryam murmured something meaningless.

"I get Yoses the money for his studies, and he despises us. And the Miltiades. Do you know how they got so rich? By being ruthless. By tricking people, by taking their land, getting them in debt. Making them into slaves. Ruthless people are ruthless at home."

The whole face slumped, as if the flesh were about to tear away from the skull. "I want to kill him." Babatha was running her thumbnail back and forth next to a fingernail, not cleaning in, more like trying to cut the skin. Maryam took Babatha's hand to still it. Babatha looked at her mother, her face hanging heavily. "Where is righteousness?"

Maryam shook that hand and buried her own face against Rut to catch the baby-smell. "Righteousness is with your brother."

Finally, after weeks, Bruria visited them again.

"What a business! What a business. Ooh. You'll be wanting to know, I know. We've got the divorce done…"

"And the marriage," said Babatha.

Bruria paused then nodded. "And the marriage yeah. So. We can't find the two hundred right away."

"You spent it. You don't have it." Babatha was bitter. "So. Basically you got me for free."

"What I've said is that we pay ten a month, regular. Fair enough? We stop after twenty months."

"What choice do we have?" said Maryam, darkly.

"Well," said Bruria, drawing herself up. "Yer women without husbands. And a baby."

A pall of scandal settled over them.

The women of Nazareth called less often. Idra would still come for a natter with her old friend. Just as though

Maryam were fully part of the village, Idra would relay the gossip. Mostly about a marriage, or a land deal, or an infestation of an orchard.

"I hear much of that son of yourn," said Idra. "They say there's a whole town's worth of folk following. Other things too. Other things I find hard to believe. Just knowing him as he was."

Maryam felt a rush of yearning. She was missing this great thing. "He heals the sick."

"Does he?"

Maryam drew herself up. "I saw him cure a leper."

"They say all the sick people crowd round. That'll worry folk."

Babatha tied up her hair, ceased to rub it clean, wore homespun. She took off her gold earrings and necklace and hid them behind a loose stone in the children's room. Sometimes she didn't come down that ladder. "Nowt much of anything, anywhere," she said once, sounding more and more like a Nazaredi.

Maryam would sometimes sit in her yard and look at the clouds to the east. Those clouds would be hanging over Lake Tiberias. And it was like – only like – the clouds were illuminated, reflecting the surface of the water that was flickering green and red from her eldest and the eklesia walking beside it.

And then, out of nowhere, the Son came home.

CHAPTER 21
POSSESSED

Men appeared over the hill and Maryam felt a jink in her heart before she quite recognized them.

Yakob and Yehush. Even she was surprised by the dam-burst of joy she felt. She did a little dance, holding up both of her hands. She called, "Babatha! Babatha, your brothers are home!"

The Son launched himself at her and hugged her. "Ami, Ami," he called her. The Son's smile was knife-edge and his hair was longer, untended and lank; the face was puffy. And his eyes – fixed, gleaming, misdirected.

"What's happened?" she asked, stroking his face. They were exactly the same height.

The Rock was with him, and he stepped forward and called Maryam Mother and put his hand over his heart. Behind him from the core group the men she only slightly knew: Andreas, Philipos, barTalemi...

None of the women.

Babatha came out of the house and the Son flung himself onto her, pulled her to him, buried his head in her shoulder, and began to weep.

Babatha staggered backwards, partly in surprise. She

turned her widened eyes towards Maryam. The Son's shoulders heaved with sobs. Babatha's smile fluttered; she took him fully into her arms. Babatha and the Son had never been close: what was this about?

The Son frantically whispered something to Babatha, and Maryam drew closer to hear. "It's so brave of you. It is so right that you turn your back on him." The Son drew back, and pointed a finger. "He will suffer. God's retribution will come."

This was new. God rebuked whole peoples who displeased him, not individuals.

Then from the direction of the well came a shout. "Oi! Yazz!" His old friend Smooch was waving to him. Behind him Lem and Yob came running.

A voice behind her said, "Good morning, Ami." Maryam spun around. Yakob peered down at her with concern, as if she had grown smaller and was not looking well.

How long had he been standing there? "Yakob, my boy," Maryam said, and hugged him. He looked broader, wiser – *Yosef*, she thought, *he looks like Yosef*. He kissed her and then looked at the old house, his eyes wistful.

Smooch slammed into the Son and tried to wrestle him to the ground. The Son yelped a laugh, and Smooch's pals slapped Yehush about the shoulders. "Too late for that now, Smooch, you're a married man." The Son called their old names, shrugged free from Smooch and kissed his sandal-throwing mates on the lips. The way he laughed made him look angry. "Rabuli! Rabuli!" they shouted almost like it was an insult.

More calmly, the rest of the village, those who were at home, women mostly, sauntered toward them.

Nohra, Babatha's childhood friend, was stout now and

commanding. "Well it's something, tizn't, when a local lad teaches the Sadducai."

"I hope you gives them what for, Yazz." Lemuel was now unhappily married to Nohra. She was plump; he looked like an assemblage of twigs.

They were proud of their Mage, prophesizing and performing wonders. "Do they call ya Yehush of Nazareth then?"

The Son tried to look pleased, nodding yes, but he was shivering at the same time. *He might not be up to this.* Maryam had never once before thought of the Son as being frail.

His old friends, the gleaners or herdsmen or grape thieves bellowed, both sarcastic and overjoyed. "Ah he only talks high talk now. He's forgotten Common."

The Son rollicked back, trying to act like Yazz. "Ah! Nahum. You should hear Nahum! Nahum makes all you Southern Nazaredai sound honey-voiced."

Nazareth was south of the lake. Yes, they lived in the South, like Yehudai. A round of laughter. "Just two days away from Yerusalam!" they roared.

The goodwill spilled over to the Son's followers. Smooch and Lemuel greeted the strangers as friends.

And it was true, as soon as these strangers opened their mouths, you could hear the sound of the Lake, rough like they were covered in fish scales.

"You're a fisherman?" a smallholder bellowed and sniffed as if at the fishiness. It was all in good humour and he meant nothing by it. Much. The smallholder was indeed small, and thin and knotty as a branch, and the fisherman was huge and gentle-faced Shemenolo. His eyes twinkled, and his tiny mouth made a moue that could have meant *so you say* or *I won't get angry.*

His old friends demanded tales of adventure and the Son tried to oblige. "We sail every day to a new port, a new town. One step ahead of Antipas's taxmen. Sometimes we go to the Philippi's lands and camp out there."

"Ah and the women, eh, Yazz?"

"Ah, I'm a man of God now, Smooch." Followed by a groan from the Nazaredai and a roar of laughter.

But the Son's eyes were cast down.

The village women saw that this mob was going to plant itself on Maryam so they turned back to get food.

Their eyes glistened at Maryam again, full of kindness again. "You can't feed alla these, Sister. We'll get it, don't you worry. See to your son."

Which was just as well as all Maryam had for herself and Babatha was some olives, dried goat and rock-hard bread. The Son by now was looking too distracted to even know what this place was. Yakob's face crumpled when he stepped inside the tiny lopsided house. Maryam was afraid he might weep.

He helped the Son sit on the bedrock floor – he wanted the couches to be for the women. It was Yakob who told the next joke. "We never had a courtyard wall. We used to watch what you lot got up to. Smooch and Yal."

A mock-shocked hooting like owls, and Smooch and Yal and Yob, the old gang, pretended to hide their heads.

Nohra held out a bowl of wine and said, "Take, Rabuli."

The Son pulled back from the wine, looking terrified of it. He shook his head, tried to smile, indicated Yakob should have it, and so the second son took the bowl, smiled warmly at their old family friend, Idra's daughter. Then shy Yakob drained the wine in one. Whoa! The old gang hooted and clapped his back.

Babatha came forward with her baby, and lowered it into the Son's arms. "This is your uncle. Your uncle Yehush. Say hello."

The Son sat staring at the babe, holding her awkwardly out from his body. "What a wonder she is. She is a miracle."

"Her name is Rut," Babatha was looking at the Son. She settled on the ground next to him. "So there's been trouble then?" she asked. "With you too?"

"There's always trouble," the Son said, staring.

"What kinda trouble?" Babatha's voice was quiet.

The Son still did not cradle the infant. *Breasts,* Maryam decided. *He's worried the babe will know he has breasts.* Babatha reached and took back Rut from his stiff arms before the child started to cry.

"You been attacked or something?" Babatha asked.

The Son said calmly. "They drove us out. From Nahum. They…" He broke off. "There were too many of us."

Babatha spoke up, addressing the crowd, all listening. "It were quite something. Thousands. That's what Ami says. Thousands of people, all sorts."

Maryam said quietly. "We had to find five thousand blankets."

"The eklesia followed us," said the Son quietly, eyes still closed. "To Beth Saida."

"You could have sent 'em away," said Babatha, eyes boggling.

The Son began to look angry. "They keep wanting me to heal them. Change the universe. In the future they will make pictures that move and they will make those pictures of animals because they love them. But they won't save them." The Son shook a finger. "They will let them die or be eaten. Because. They are not there to change things. God is like that."

Maryam felt the urge to write this down but then thought: *What would I write down? Moving pictures?*

All Babatha had understood was the reference to animals. "What about those pigs? The tinkers say you sent demons into pigs."

The Son nodded enthusiastically. "And they all ran off a cliff and died."

Babatha almost chuckled. "Farmers must have loved you."

Smooch defended him. "What they deserved, them heathen. Bringing their unclean beasts onto our ground."

The Son looked mildly pleased, but he wasn't blinking. "Pigs are unclean. The demons put themselves into the pigs to punish themselves."

Babatha's face went slack.

"And that drove the pigs crazy. Poor, poor pigs." The Son's eyes watered for the hogs and then for the demons. "Demons are incomplete. Like, like people who have parts of their minds missing. But. They are still part of God." An open-handed gesture, as if this were self-evident.

"They're here of course because I'm here. The weight of God." Yehush's middle fingers formed a triangle, which he drove into his palm. "The weight of God in me is so great that it tears other parts of the universe into shreds. Like flickers of fire. That's why they obey me, because they are bits of God, and that's why there are so many of them. Right now." He nodded and smiled. "So we just… clean em all up." He tried to look merry.

Babatha's face darkened. "So… your being here tears God up into little bits of demons."

The Son looked peeved; he was tired of explaining. "It's like what pulls everything down into the Earth."

Babatha's finger traced a circle in the air, her eyes full of misgiving. "So… would you say that… you are possessed?"

"Yes!" he said as if relieved. "That's it exactly. I am possessed – but by God!" His eyes looked at Babatha with love and gratitude.

"How do you know it's God?"

He nodded: *good question*. "The size. It shifts and I see rivers of stars. Because it loves. It it it loves. And it doesn't stop. We can love things, people, and then stop. That's that what baffles God."

Babatha's eyes narrowed. "I don't know about God being baffled, but I am." The crowd laughed.

He talked about bees, how we love them but don't understand them. Can't be them. We may not love spiders but we rescue them when they are caught in an amphorae.

"Myself, I crushes em," Smooch laughed.

Everyone laughed but the Son kept talking. "You don't want the spider to die."

There was something seriously wrong. The Son's voice broke, and a tear escaped down his cheek. He was crying for a spider. "God gets angry!" Tears were flowing. "And that is when God mistakes. God mistakes in a rage…" The Son's voice went thin and trailed away and broke up into sobs, and he covered his eyes. No one moved.

"God makes mistakes?" Babatha's voice was limp.

"Steady on, mate," said Smooch, embarrassed.

The Son covered his eyes with the tips of his fingers as if he were blind. "It it it has to learn. It has to learn by living through what we live through."

As if someone had plucked a string, Maryam realized something. *The Migdali isn't here.*

Dusk came; it was Shabbat; they crowded into the meeting house.

The air was hot, dusty in orange lamp light. From out of nowhere, as if night had materialized, in limped Platon, the tekton. He had a walking stick and used it to tap people out of the way. "A stool for an old man," he growled. "Let's hear from our local Great One."

Smooch shouted out, "Hey, Yazz, you'll read for us?" A general assent. People remembered the old times.

"He read well enough for my Esta," chortled Platon. "Got away with her right smartly. Still with him I reckon."

The Son bounced to his feet and tried to look lively. His forehead glowed with sweat; his hair was pasted flat.

An attendant, a young boy in training whom Maryam did not know, passed the Son a scroll from the meeting house's small collection.

The Son eyed the scroll, paused, and flicked his eyebrows. "This is no accident." He chuckled and looked up at them. "The reading is from the writings of Yeshaayahu."

He started to read, but not in the liturgical language. "Behold my servant." As he read, he effortlessly turned the liturgy into Common Tongue. There was a sigh from the Nazaredai.

"I will support him," the Son seemed to yelp rather than

read the lines. "My Chosen One whom my soul desires. I have placed my spirit upon him. He shall promulgate justice to the nation."

He rolled on like that for enough time to lose everyone but still buoy them up in a mood. "With truth shall he execute justice. Neither shall he weaken nor shall he be broken, until he establishes justice in the land, and for his instruction islands shall long."

The Son interrupted himself. "That doesn't mean what you think. It means I will not break Yerusalam or the reed Rome. Or the flickering candle of Yehud. For they are already broken."

Son of David. This is exactly the sort of thing Yoanna advised him not to say.

The Son started again but in a light throwaway voice as if eager to finish. "So said God the Lord, the Creator of the heavens and the One who stretched them out, who spread out the earth and what springs forth from it, who gave a soul to the people upon it and a spirit to those who walk thereon."

He stopped. "That means you." He rolled up the scroll with a careless rattle, shoved it at the attendant and sat down.

Silence.

Platon coughed out a laugh. "He always were bit of prick. Actually, not so much of prick." The laughter of others scrambled what he may have said next. Did Maryam hear Platon's chuckling growl say, "Not one you can see anyway."

The Nazaredai did not look angry – they looked confused. The reading had been short and not fun. Nobody had sung, nobody had danced, and that is why they had once loved Yehush of Nazareth, their own boy.

The Son leaned back, with a slightly sour, maybe even smug grin, unmoving, waiting for something.

He spoke again. "Today this scripture is fulfilled in your hearing."

The men looked at each other.

"How?" one of them asked.

There was no challenge in the question. Yob was unschooled, had hardly heard scripture that he could understand. Scripture was not for such as him. He'd said so himself frequently, a modest fellow, if anything too humble. He just wanted to see his lad, who had once been kind to him. Yob hadn't heard much of the Son's doings around the lakeside. Curing warts or calming down madmen, or whatever marvels he was supposed to have performed.

Maryam: *He just wants you to remember him, call him by name. And laugh.*

The Son looked irritated, bounced up and down. "You're going to say that I am arrogant and immoral and should not preach. You're going to say to me, 'Physician heal thyself'. And then you're going to want me to do magic in my home town like I did in Nahum."

He paused, waited, and slapped his own shoulder. "I will tell you a truth. No prophet is accepted in his hometown."

And he started to quote all kinds of instances when prophets had ignored the Beni Yisrael and cured other peoples – which was not the same thing at all as being rejected by them. More like the prophets or even God himself rejecting the children of Yisrael.

But the minds of the Nazaredai were untroubled by any of that. They just wanted to know where their friend had gone.

This Yehush looked half starved. The tendons of his neck stood out, his cheeks were raw, and there was a line of muscle encircling his mouth, like a lute string. And he was dirty, wearing the same robe he'd left in. It looked like it hadn't been washed.

"He's gone bonkers," said Lemuel.

Platon rose, lurched and hobbled forward, and finally had his revenge for the killing of his son and the taking of his name. "Naw. He just told you. He's God's Chosen. Tell you something else. He always thought he was. I could tell you more, but won't out of his respect for his mother. Who I would point out, I never married. So he can't be my son. Good evening, Maryam. I see he's treating you with his usual respect."

The old builder thumbed his nose at them all and left, bobbling on his stick.

Yob rubbed his newly bald head and pleaded. "Come on, Yazz. Eh? How you been? Tell us a few, or else just tell us what you been through. You shoulda come home, lad. Before you got into this state."

The Son murmured something like, "I don't have a home."

"Then come back when you feel better," said Smooch, a heavy-boned ploughman with a ready wit. "Or don't come back at all." Only one other of the old gang barked out a laugh. Smooch jammed on his sunhat, quashed it at a comic angle, and launched himself out of the room.

No, no, no, no, Maryam thought. *These people loved you, what have you done?*

* * *

All fifteen of the eklesia unrolled blankets to sleep on the ground by the well.

Fifteen was enough to be threatening. Women would not want to go to the well with fifteen men sleeping next to it. No wonder people in other places had moved them on. "Come inside," Maryam begged.

"Can't fit all fifteen inside," said the Son, rocking from side to side on the stone, trying to get comfortable. The blanket was torn in places.

"Well you two, sleep at home at least."

Yakob squatted down next to him. "Babatha sleeps with her baby in the children's room, yes? Don't worry, Ami. We're used to it." He lay down beside his brother and as if they were lovers, hugged him all the length of his body.

"It's cold," said Maryam. Her heart ached for them both. Sleeping like homeless men on the ground, no food. She also felt anger.

She crouched next to the Son and hissed, "Why did you do that?"

Pause. "Do what?"

"You rejected them. They didn't reject you."

He stirred, but kept his eyes closed. "They will reject me."

Maryam understood something. "We can't see the future, you know. For us to see things, they have to happen first."

The Son sat up. He blinked, staring. Grit clung to one side of his sunburnt face. "God wants me dead," he said simply. Then he rolled to his feet, and snapped his fingers.

One of the fifteen groaned, but only one. They sat up, head on knees or in hands. One snorted himself out of a deep sleep. They began to crawl to their feet and silently roll up their blankets.

"What are you doing?" Maryam asked in something like alarm.

Yakob felt for her in the darkness and took her hand. "He wants to move on."

Maryam trotted back to her house to find them food.

Tears had started in her eyes. *The fool. The idiot. He will die of cold on the road all alone.*

Babatha slumped down the ladder and said in a sleepy voice. "Do we have anything to give them?"

"We've got nothing to give ourselves," said Maryam, feeling suddenly overwhelmed. "They're all going to starve."

Babatha took her hand. "No they won't."

"We've got nothing they can carry." Babatha looked blank, Maryam clarified. "They're going. Now. In the night."

"Ah," said Babatha, and spun away. Her feet clumped back up the ladder. Maryam fought down despair. She found an old rag to make a parcel of bread and olives. Her fingers trembled slightly with impatience. She had to get it to the Son before he left.

She trotted back towards the well. She didn't want to shout, so she said only slightly louder than usual. "Don't go yet. I have some food for you. Don't go yet!"

Someone met her halfway, enfolded her. "It's good, Ami. He's waiting for you. He wouldn't go without saying goodbye."

Yakob guided her forward, one arm over her shoulder. From the house came the sound of a baby crying.

"Where will you go?" she asked Yakob.

"I think, probably back to where all those people are waiting for him. If they're still there."

"How will you find the road in the night?"

The Son spoke out of the darkness, in a light voice like frost. "I could find the road if the sun exploded." Overhead, the stars were so thick it was as if the sky were woven.

Behind them, against the pale rock of Nazareth, a billowing shadow sailed towards them, a child wailing.

It was Babatha. "Ready?" she asked.

"Yes," said the Son, with his back to them.

"I'm. I'm going with them, Ami," Babatha said.

"What?"

"Well there's nothing else here, is there? I've tried everything else." A hiss of air that was partly a chuckle. "And. I believe him."

She took hold of Maryam's hand. "Come on. I know you want to be with him too. Come with us. And you can tell me that thing you've never told me. Whatever it is."

Babatha gave Maryam's hand a tug, and it was as if she'd tugged on all of them. They all began to move, a shuffling of leather on stone.

Maryam had nothing to pack – again no robes or shoes or bed. Babatha settled a blanket around her shoulders.

"I'll hold the baby," Maryam said. Her granddaughter was cradled into her arms.

Here they were, what was left of them, setting sail in the dark. Babatha was beside her now. Babatha had heard the Calling Out, and that was itself a miracle.

CHAPTER 22

THE FRAGILE SKIN OF THINGS

They were tough, this eklesia.

They walked through the night into the dawn, sometimes singing. The Rock would tell jokes about fishing nets or stubborn goats. Dawn kissed their faces, and the caravan stumbled forward, exhausted. Exhaustion made Babatha bitter. "You talk about righteousness," she said to the Son. "There is no such thing."

The Son didn't look at her but did answer. "You're right. There is only love."

Babatha chortled, and drew the word out in scorn. "Love. Well maybe your mother loves you. No one else loves you."

"Your father will love you."

"Yeah, well our Dad was different."

"Your father in heaven."

Babatha snorted. "Just as well."

"Will love you. But not yet." Something in the way the Son said it made Babatha laugh.

They came down from the hills into scrubby pasture. Broken stones were strewn about the ground as if someone hoped they would sprout. A light dew was keeping down the dust. The scrub was thorny and not as tall as a man.

In the distance, sheep were bleating. Shepherds still crouched, sheltering under the thick felt shawls that could stand by themselves like tents. Two of the returning eklesia picked up stones to throw in case the shepherd dogs should attack. Shepherd dogs were huge, with leather collars to protect their throats from wolves.

The Son's voice was mild. "You could of course kill Milt." Babatha breathed out in contempt. "No, really. It's early. Go home, find a knife, kill him, come back here."

He was joking. Somehow smiles merged with the early sunlight.

Babatha said, "I'll see where this gets me."

They joined the road from Ptolomais that ran north through unsettled land.

The eklesia had gathered on the plain of Ker Azim, where no one lived, a stonesfield. The stones were black and sharp-edged and there was no water.

The camp was now vast. Smoke from its fires made the black basalt slopes look russet-coloured. The track between the tents must have run half a league. No wonder Nahum had become terrified.

Gusts of human odours – milk, disease, feet and stale greens being boiled until they were safe to eat. Women were squatting over informal fires in a field, boiling up barley, feeding the embers bundles of grass and scrub. Some of them scowled in the sun. Others had a wild blank stare in their eyes, as if the person had been startled and stayed that way. Maryam knew that look: hardship.

Little children ran half naked. Raw hides were strung across bushes or twigs implanted in the ground, a windbreak only. How would that keep out rain? A baby wailed.

The Son raised his hand to a smiling grandfather, then to a lady who appeared to have set up a cloth-dying factory in large clay pots. The old grandfather coughed out a laugh and pointed. "He's back."

A woman by the fire said shyly, "Bless us, Rabuli." A teenager stood up, hands on hips, smiling. A chorus of greetings. Their tired faces became more lined as they smiled. The smiles looked relieved.

Maryam thought: *They're here for the same reason that I am. There is nothing else for them. The Son ends their despair.*

So they live in the wilderness where they dig a trench and shit bare-bummed in sight of their neighbours, wave away flies, bake in the sun, freeze at night, and get rained on. And it brings them joy.

The Calling Out started to sing. A slow steady building of voices. No one importuned the Son to heal them. There was no mad rush of hands waving to be touched. Just the sound as if the earth itself had begun to sing.

Maryam knew the notes. She'd heard them before. The Son had sung standing on that rock. And because she knew the notes she could remember the words.

"Happy are the humble." The words came in waves.

"Happy are those who mourn."

Maryam thought of Yosef.

Everyone was promised something. All of them were told when no one else would tell them such, that they were precious and that God saw them, knew them.

The Migdali dragged herself up the slope towards them with some of the other leaders. The Migdali's face was cast down, as if the path were muddy. As she drew nearer, the tension increased. Maryam glanced at Shemenolo, who shrugged.

The Migdali inclined her head towards the Son. "Welcome back, Rabuli." Her voice was small and cool.

"Sister," was all the Son said. Then he began to walk again.

The Migdali's face relaxed when she saw Maryam, and swept towards her. "Mother! Course it's you who bring him back to us."

The male students all continued to trudge down the slope. The Migdali took Maryam's hand. "Come, Ami, come eat." She glanced at Babatha.

"This is the Son's sister," Maryam began.

"I know," the Migdali said a bit sharply, then relenting. "I remember." Pause. "So you believe him now, do ya?"

Babatha was wary – and had been walking all night. "Some of the things he says, yeah. I'm here because there's nothing else."

The Migdali seemed to ponder that. "Not a lot else. You're right." Babatha began to stride faster to catch up with the Son.

The lake was not even in sight, nor was there a single tree. Had they all been cut down?

"What do they drink?" Maryam asked the Migdali. "How do they all eat?"

The Migdali looked up and Maryam saw exhaustion in her face too. "Miracles," she said, and after a beat added, "One after another. Someone brings some bread and somehow it feeds them all. Some fish. Everybody gets some. Somehow."

"How many of them?"

The Migdali only gave her head a shake, her eyes hooded. Maryam yearned to ask her, how are things between you and my son? But actually she had seen enough to know.

And this vast plain of people, away from any town to hear them – the Calling Out had stalled.

"He says God wants to kill him," Maryam said.

"Some of the things he says…" the Migdali trod particularly carefully, looking at her feet. "Don't make sense." She looked up and her eyes met Maryam's, and they were bleak.

"Where's Yoanna?" Maryam asked, and regretted it at once.

"Yer-oooo-salam," said Migdali as if stretching sourdough. "We've got a new strategy. Her idea. We'll be announcing it in a day or two." She walked on in abandoned silence.

"Ha ha. She's always fabricating. Can you tell me what it is?" Maryam asked gently.

"Preaching in the Temple. She goes ahead to make the way straight. And we set up little eklesias in the thirty-one biggest towns."

Maryam took her hand.

The Migdali asked, "Can you tell me why it would be thirty-one towns and not plain thirty?"

Maryam whispered. "It's how old he is."

The Migdali mimed shock and disgust but looked hale again. "Wha?"

Maryam smiled. "He's thirty-one years old. He says that things are held together not just because one thing causes another, but because one thing is LIKE another. Something about the smallest part repeats the biggest, smaller and smaller into the heart of the universe."

"Did he always talk like that?"

"It's gotten worse."

"He doesn't love her, Yoanna. He just doesn't love me."

"He loves everybody."

"And that's as good as nobody."

True for us both. They walked on holding hands.

Maryam, Babatha and the infant were ushered into a large tent, sky-blue with embroidery.

Inside there were only women. Had the eklesia split into two camps, male and female? Maryam saw Shushan propped up on a carpet. Maryam grunted stiffly as she knelt to give her a hug.

"Welcome home," Shushan said.

The Thunder woman everybody called Zebedee's Widow brought Maryam and Babatha water in a jug. When asked her name she always said, "Zebedee's Widow". The Migdali came back with bowls of porridge and wine. Babatha looked at all these women and became impatient. "Where did the Son go?" she asked.

The answer was "probably asleep", but the meaning was plain: *we are not to go and see him.*

Babatha's face was like a fist. It said, *I'm not here to talk to a bunch of women*. "I'm his sister," she said, and walked out to find him.

Maryam tried to follow but Shushan eased her back. "Us old uns rest," she said. Maryam nodded yes in relief, and settled onto the carpet despite the sharp stones under it. The old woman folded up next to her and she slept.

Babatha walked in a kind of rage.

Angry still that life had let her down so badly; that she had been so wrong about nearly everything. That she did not know how she felt about her elder sister who was also her elder brother. How her mind kept circling back to him, like a lion who had lost her cub.

"He will answer me," she said aloud.

She found him with no tent to cover his head, seated on bare rock, surrounded by his gang.

"You women ought to know your place," one of them muttered. Same name as one of Babatha's brothers. It could have been one of Miltiades's brothers.

"This IS their place," the Son said and gestured for her to sit. Shem passed her a bowl of water.

"Am I to call you Rabuli?" she asked ruefully.

"Brother will do."

"Brother. If I am not to kill my husband, what should I do?"

"Stay with us and find all the other kinds of love."

"What other kinds of love?"

The Son shrugged as if picking one at random. "The love of righteousness."

"Even when I can't see it anywhere?"

"What did you expect? Righteousness is invisible."

"You're right there. The reward is invisible too."

The Son echoed her. "You're right there."

She looked dead at him. "So what is this invisible reward? Dead in a field from overwork? Dead at fifteen from childbirth? Living on nothing with the taxman wanting your last shekel? What reward did Dad have?"

"You." The Son relented and smiled. "And The Kingdom of Heaven. And yes, that's invisible too."

"Well what is this Kingdom then?"

"You know it when you see it." The Son smiled. "Especially as it's invisible."

Babatha laughed and shook her head.

Shemenolo, the Rock, joined in. "Sister, if this man's family have done you a wrong, God sees, and God will punish them."

Babatha muttered with a smile. "I'll punish him, more like."

The Son said in a calm voice. "I promise retribution. That makes some people like me." Still smiling with small, quick nervous nods. "Wrongdoers will live after they die, but in eternal pain."

Babatha's chuckle was crooked. "Eternal? Bit more'n I'd wish even on Milt."

"I say to you, it's what will come," said the Son. "Before the day of your own dying."

"So you get to do all the forgiving and God does all the damning." Some of the students chuckled. Babatha looked around; she liked an audience too. "I'd rather it was the other way around."

The Son's voice was mild. "You've lived the life of a rich woman, and you are good at dealing with the world. If life had been even crueller to you, perhaps you'd be crueller back. As it is, for righteousness of the heart to be the measure of us rather than wealth or birth or blind obedience to the Law, there will be this thing called Hell. It's new. God just made it out of the dim place Sheol."

Babatha was smiling and shaking her head at the same time. "So I just leave it to God."

"Yes. And that lets you forgive."

"And suffer," said Babatha, her face kindly, her eyes like stone.

"Of course."

"Pain all round."

"There is pain all around already."

Babatha shook her head and put back on her sandals. "I hope I haven't made a mistake coming here."

"You haven't," he said mildly and took her hand. They sat together in silence for a good long time.

Over the next week, Babatha became Maryam's constant companion and friend, as they had been when Babatha was seven years old.

They passed Rutit back and forth between them, sitting her on their laps or carrying her in a sling on their backs as they fetched water or darned clothes or helped cook in big clay pots, or scavenged wood for fires. They talked.

"So what is this Kingdom of God he keeps talking about then?"

"Oh, I don't know!" Maryam pulled back her sleeves so the gnarled twigs they were gathering were better balanced.

"It seems to be the key."

Maryam was getting a stubborn sadness that curled from the corners of her mouth down her chin. It made two squirrel-like pouches of flesh, and when she shook her head, they quivered. "It's a series of riddles. The Kingdom is everywhere. It is invisible. It is coming. It has always been here. It is of this Earth, it is not of this Earth. I sometimes think," Maryam said, standing up straight, an indication that she had gathered enough. "I sometimes think it's just how the world looks when he sees it through God's eyes."

"And this holy spirit…" Babatha jostled the infant to one side so she could take some of the wood.

"Well, when you asked him the other day if he was possessed and he said yes. That I reckon is the Holy Spirit."

Babatha mused. "So the Spirit of God takes you over and then you see it."

Maryam frowned in a kind of acknowledgement. Was she beginning to walk with a limp? Sleeping on rocky ground was hard on a woman of her age. "I hadn't thought of it like that. But it sounds like it might be right. Who knows? The way he's been talking lately who knows anything?" Babatha's Mum grinned with horsey green teeth, her eyes amused and so clear.

But old.

A few days later the Migdali came back to the blue tent from a meeting on the hillside rock.

She looked pleased, even calm. She called out, "Wives and mothers! Listen. Got something for yas."

People were talking or grumbling, and out of character Shushan gave them all an angry hiss to shut them up.

The Migdali smiled. "Things are moving." She made a fist that slammed forward in action. "The Son has decided. All of us, those who can, we'll all walk to Yerusalam. We'll take it slow, talk to folk on the way. Visit all the cities in the Lands."

That sounded exciting, fun, and yes, finally a change.

The Migdali beamed. Smiling and relieved, she was beautiful. "It's not going to be just the twelve students anymore. Half of them will be women. You know he means it cause he's talking Greek again. Apostoli he calls them. Seventy-two of them. SEVENTY-TWO."

"Hah!" Shushan laughed and clapped her hands. "I can't count that high!" She turned to Maryam and collapsed against her in a giggling hug.

"Yeah? Yeah?" The Migdali was pleased, waved her hands, let the excitement build. "Good, an'it? Now what the seventy-two will do is go ahead of the rest of us. They'll go to all these cities, and say The Son of Adam is coming. But. They'll stay behind after the eklesia moves on. They'll be the seed of the tree in every town."

Some of the women laughed and applauded. Others looked confused or hurt – perhaps a long pilgrimage was beyond them. Some of them had only come to be healed and had not yet been healed, or they liked the camp being close to their homes.

The Migdali tried to lead them all in song, but that was never her great talent. Some women did sing, but others began to pack, and pack grimly perhaps because they could no longer follow. When the Migdali was done, some of the sisters flocked up to her. Some of them hoped they would be apostoli too.

Babatha didn't know what she made of it. Would she follow the eklesia? It would be good to see Yerusalam again. And walking the length of the Lands, seeing all those places – it would be better than sitting still and thinking about Milt. "For the rest of us, there's some water to boil," Babatha said ruefully, and stood up.

That night the Holy Spirit came to Babatha.

She woke up, convinced that her father Yosef had called her name, once. "Babatha."

The voice had sounded so much like her father that half asleep, she felt surprise at her own foolishness at thinking him dead. No, no, Abi was still alive and she could talk to him. She was glad of that because lately she had feared she had been dismissive of the old man when she basked in her big house in Sepphoris. Dazzled by the success of the Miltiades, she might even have been a bit full of herself, arrogant, maybe.

And she flung herself to her feet, impatient to make good. "Abi, you were so wise and kind."

But the wilderness, with its low fires and sounds of bleating animals or sleeping men, was empty.

"Oh, Abi," she said. But in a moment, startled like a bird, it seemed something of her father had awoken, was there but in a different form, as mute as dust, wavering, light and small.

And then it hit.

The ground rippled like water; it caught light in shards as if earth were water and night had been day.

Babatha held up her hand against the light, but that did not block out the world. The light shone through her hand. Broke the world. Mosaic.

The baked ground,
the low tents,
the ebb and flow of ember-light
all bloomed continually, opening outwards
without seeming to gain size
as if the world swelled or
her own eyes.
People stooped or carried or shot across the stonesfield;
not the women asleep on the ground.
These others moved in shadow, their edges blurred.
They flickered as rapidly as the blinking of eyes.
When Babatha tried to focus on them,
she felt herself drop down, falling through earth

as if through layers of unleavened bread.
Each layer was contained in the thing before,
smaller while everything
walked backwards.
Each layer was the moment before.
As she fell, the road swelled
overhead like thunderclouds.
The tents scuttled away in a flash.
The world sneezed and
the moving shadows were gone.
The plants shivered and
shook themselves back into the earth
until no plants, just stone.

Babatha was in a land of fire.
Rivers of rock glowed red and spread over the ground.
Steam and sparks spiralled up into the sky.
Somewhere in the north,
fire shot out of the ground like a kind of lightning.
Burning stone rolled towards her.
She was alone, she was afraid.
Fearful she wrenched herself back upwards.
Through many different kinds
of up and down,
she shot away from the world.
The ground dropped away,
fields swallowed by clouds,
mountains shrivelling.

She kicked and wailed,
thinking she could fall.
She had no feet.

The world stared as
round as an eye,
blue and white, mist and water.
She burgeoned outwards in a panic.
Stars fell about her like rain,
then drew together spinning,
in whirlpools of light.
These too coalesced,
began to writhe about themselves like spangled serpents
folding ever inward into themselves.

Terror.

How will I find my way home?
That thought pulled her back towards the ground.
In a direction she had not known existed.
It was as though she had breathed in too far and couldn't stop.
Her chest expanded,
seemed to stretch itself into pinpricks of light,
break apart into stars.
She saw her ghostly hand
the size of a continent.
Everything swelled and she had no sense of scale.
The whole world spun
then bubbled itself still

There was ground, there was sky
But such a ground.
No trees and all laid out like courtyards.
Deep into the sky giant things rose up

of metal and glass
knives and bottles mixed but
full of light,
and moving inside them,
people like aphids.
And she could hear those people
thinking in unknown languages
of things so new
she understood each word but not a single sentence.
This world Babatha knew
was the death of everything
she had known and loved.

She flung herself away from it,
and began to beg whatever held her
Let me go, let me go.
Something gasped
and everything folded in
and then blew out.
All the different ups and downs,
all the folds and blurrings,
she saw them whole for a moment:
mother of pearl
arrested in its opalescence.

Then with a lurch and a sudden dropping down,
A sensation like landing on cats' paws,
and she was back on the field of stone.
An old gentleman limped past her in the moonlit heat
while crickets buzzed.

* * *

Over in an instant and indescribable.

Babatha had had another kind of mind, one that could see so much more of the world, like viewing it through a diamond. Except that now the light still seemed to shine but out of her.

Babatha walked as if the rocks would crumble beneath her feet, or the Earth might pitch and throw her down.

She found she needed to talk to Ami, though she could not remember the word. There was Maryam's face, asleep on the ground. Babatha crumpled at the knees and burbled. She had forgotten how to talk, or rather could not find the pathway back to words. Those stars, that ground, had no words. She was trying to speak like dust would speak, or ash or rainfall. She blurted out something, a plea for help.

Her mother woke. Babatha mewed. Her mother made sounds of alarm, hugged her, tried to get her to her feet.

Maryam was talking to her but Babatha got only the general sense of what her Mother said, everything partial and scrambled. Babatha glimpsed things, sudden stabs of light. She pointed and howled: *There, there, look there*! But her mother had no idea where to look in the world, or that she even could be elsewhere than on the skin of things. The fragile skin of the world.

Babatha began to weep out of fear and exhaustion. Ami seized her hand, made her stand and began to pull her. Babatha had a half-formed thought: *I am a baby again*.

Ami stroked her cheek, calmed her. Maryam was a series of echoes in both light and time, a golden, blurred threading that stretched back over the horizon towards Nazareth, and back and forth from Yerusalam.

Her mother pulled again, insisting. Babatha could do nothing except follow, though she feared she might fall through the ground again, or burgeon upwards into the sky, and that she would be so huge her mother would lose her grip.

Babatha wailed in terror, for she did not know what would be the consequence of each step. She did not know if she would ever talk again or come back to a world she could understand.

Had they been walking hours? It felt like they had, but they had not crossed the tent. Though this tent was blue and might be bigger than the sky.

Something dark seemed to rise up from the ground, awkwardly at first on all fours. Babatha thought that perhaps the boulders were standing up. Then she feared that there was a bear in the tent; or perhaps Night itself had decided to walk.

No, it was a woman, all in black. The woman enveloped Babatha in her arms. Her words echoed meaninglessly, but the tone was comforting. The woman eased Babatha back down onto the ground. Then Babatha heard,

"The sister, of course."

Babatha picked her way back to words as if walking over broken pottery. She had once been a baby being bathed by her mother in a pot and she had understood every word Ami had said, but could not find the right words back. She understood then that she would have to find the right word for each thing, one for each fragment of the world.

Her mother's voice rose and fell on waves of alarm. Babatha wanted to say to her, *You won't understand. It's all all right. All of it.*

What came out was. "Bill coos cross-beaked. All shit. Shit and sand."

The Migdali translated. "Mother, she's means everything is all right. She's just having trouble finding her own words, aren't you, Darling? But she'll find them again. And more than her words. Many people's words."

She shushed Babatha and soothed her again. It was as though Babatha had sunk under the earth. She would rise.

In the morning, the Migdali was still squatting next to her.

"Good morning," the Migdali said brightly. "Do you still see it?"

Babatha looked. The broken basalt, the thorny scrub, the tents – yes. They were still burgeoning outward.

Everything always expanding until she looked harder, and then it seemed that everything was also shrinking backwards. She focussed again and she could see the smallest details of everything, little particles getting so small and fine that it was like the basalt boulders, the tents, the sand were not really there.

They were really something else, something as tiny and fiery as stars. Those flakes themselves were nothingness twisted until it looked like something. Everything was nothing. And everything. At the same time.

Babatha found words, though her mouth still felt numb, and she drooled a bit when she spoke. "It's all changing."

The Migdali looked pleased and took her hand. "Well done. You're talking." Maryam reached forward and wiped Babatha's chin with her sleeve.

There were so many words. So many people. Babatha said the same thing again in the Roman tongue then Greek, then actual Greek as spoken in Greece. Then in the language of the Persians.

The Migdali patted her hand. "Yes dear. They can all do that." Babatha repeated herself in Coptic, Sidoni, and then a language no one yet spoke.

The Migdali patted Babatha again, and then held up a warning finger. "Stop. Don't keep on at it. You'll drive us mad. Just talk Common."

Babatha giggled, and waved both hands up and down in excited unison.

You could say the whole truth. But you'd have to talk for ever in every language. The universe would not last long enough for the whole truth. You would never stop talking. The idea struck Babatha as terribly funny and she began to laugh.

The Migdali leaned forward to Maryam, and said. "They all go through this. Second childhood. They calm down later."

The idea of talking proper, like a fish or an acacia tree, made Babatha laugh all the more. Truly, she felt such glee. She stood up (this time without shooting off into a star cluster or the distant future) and despite all of the new flesh around her hips and thighs began to dance and sing one of the Mizmor.

She sang in it Common mixed with Greek, then mixed with something else that in her addled state she decided was the language of angels, only she repeated it in Coptic. Some of the women in the tent noticed and ululated for her. Some clapped to give her dance rhythm. Babatha called out thanks to God, and called out for mercy and forgiveness. She knew now.

She was in the Kingdom of Heaven.

Later, as Babatha slept again, Maryam thanked the Migdali.

"It was so kind what you did. I had no idea what was happening." Emotion surprised Maryam; tears came; she covered her mouth.

"Glad I was there," said the Migdali, taking her arm.

"Have you..." Maryam stopped. She knew what blocked her throat: a note of envy. "Have you been visited by the Spirit too?"

The Migdali's face turned slightly green and looked weighted down. "Naw. Noooooo. I were possessed by demons." Abruptly, she walked away.

There was a Calling Out, and all of the seventy-two felt it like a tremor in the earth.

They put down their work, or their lack of it, stood up, or wiped their hands, their smiles dim with relief or gratitude, and started to amble towards the hill.

"Babatha?" Maryam asked as her daughter suddenly walked away.

"You come too, Ami," Babatha said over her shoulder. From all over the camp men and women were being drawn to the bedrock on the hill. Maryam scooped up Rut and trotted after her daughter.

These new apostoli seemed to recognize each other. They nodded to one another, acknowledged each other, but were self-contained. They sauntered. As they drew closer to the outcropping, some of them took each other's hands. They knew each other, like birds.

Maryam felt a tremor of sadness. Just when she had regained her daughter, she had lost her again.

The whole eklesia began to realize something was afoot. There had been all this talk of a long walk to Yerusalam, and new emissaries. Some of them sang snatches of Mizmor, but only snatches, as if the words were butterflies landing on branches.

They jumped from "Happy is the man who trusts in Him" to "The young lions lack and suffer hunger. But those who see the Lord shall not lack anything good."

As they drew near, the Son stood up, brushed his buttocks, and threw up his hands.

"You are the sea!" he half sang. "You come in waves! Flow like water down the valleys. You are the river and you baptize! For you bear the Holy Spirit."

He jumped down from his rock to be among them, calm and affable like his old self. "You can do now what I do. I cure the sick. So can you.

"You can drive away the fragmented spirits, blow them gently back into the fold. You will be able to talk to anyone God needs you to talk to."

He held out his hands, dividing them into sets of two. "You are a pair. Bless and watch out for each other. You walk now to Dalmanuthu and spread the word."

Then the next two. "You are a pair. You walk to Tiberias. Prepare the way, make it straight. We will follow. Tell them not to fear us, we will take nothing from them."

"You two, you're a pair. You two to Philoteria. Tell them that we come bringing with us the Kingdom of God. Heal if the Spirit moves you, but it is news you are bringing. Warn them that the eklesia follows."

He came to Babatha, and held out his hands that took in her and Esta, Platon's wife. "You two are a pair. Bless each other, keep each other safe on the road. You go to Scythopolis."

The lips of Babatha's fixed grin didn't move but still she said. "What-polis? Never heard of it, where is it?"

The Son laughed. "Ah, Sister. Do birds know place names? They just fly."

"Give us a hint." Some of the eklesia chuckled, elbowed each other. Babatha was known to be amusing.

The Son's eyes closed. "Atha, your map is your mouth." Hoots of laughter from those who heard. "Just ask. It's south toward Ginae." The Son's voice rose. "After that we go to Shomeron, then back to cross into Perea and beyond."

He walked on creating pairs: Sebastae, Neapolis, Sekem, Aenon all through Perea to Philadelphia. Some he sent very far north, to Ephesus, or Damascus, places the eklesia as a whole could not possibly visit.

"You ask what will you eat? Do birds ask what they will eat when they fly south guided by the Spirit? You will be housed. You will be fed. And you will be rejected." His voice became exaggerated, and he waved from side to side. "Some folk may even be unkind."

"No!" the eklesia chorused back. "Say not so!" Maryam realized it was one of their standard jokes. Some people must have been very unkind to them, flung rocks to chase them away.

"Well for those places that reject you? Just kick the dust from your sandals. That dust is not worthy for you to even walk on." He grew still and serious. "For you know and walk in the Spirit of the Lord."

Little Esta, the beaten wife of that horrible man, little Esta now walked in the Spirit? Something like pride swelled in Maryam.

And the Son began to sing a new Mizmor with the words "Walk in the Spirit, Walk in the Spirit of the Lord."

The pairs began to sing it too. Without any further preparation, wearing what they wore, they began to walk, shoulder to shoulder.

Babatha and Esta, the two Nazaredai, turned towards the south-east. Maryam knew the road, knew the peril. There was something she needed to say, something Babatha had asked of her.

"Babatha. The thing I never said." Maryam walked with them, but hunched and anxious.

"Yes, Ami," Babatha said calmly.

"Your brother was not born the usual way. I never told you. He does not have Yosef for a father."

"I know, Ami. I know," Babatha reached back and took her hand.

"No. You don't understand. There was no father. An angel came to tell me."

Babatha chuckled and kissed her mother on the forehead. Even little Esta chuckled. "Of course it looked like an angel. But everything, everything is angels." Babatha put an arm around her shoulder. "Ami. It would have saved a lot of trouble if you'd told me earlier. I wouldn't have hated her so much. But no matter now. Really. No matter now."

In the Holy Spirit, Babatha knew.

At a crossroad, Babatha stopped and leaned forward in front of Rut. "I've got to go, my darling," she said, as if to an adult. "You'll be with Granny. It would be too hard for you alone with just me and Esta when we have work to do." She hugged her daughter. "But you will see me in Scythopolis. I promise." She kissed her again, stepped away, and walked on. Esta called goodbye to Rut as well, and gave a little wave with the tips of her fingers. The two Nazaredai walked backwards for a little way, then faced forward.

Rutit let out one long wail and held out her hands. Maryam picked her up and sat her on her hip. "Oooh! My, you are getting heavy. You'll see Ami again. You'll see Ami soon."

Babatha, always the strongest in the family, always the solver of problems, always the one who acted. Who would have thought it? You, the female prophet, doing what even the Son would not do – preach as a woman. The things I have seen. The things I will see.

It bothered her that Rut was used to mothers going.

CHAPTER 23

THE CARAVAN MOVES ON

A few days later the camp, all five thousand, broke up.

In the women's blue tent it was as though the ground itself had stood. The sounds rose up like a flock of birds – clothes being folded, bowls being wrapped in blankets, the rolling of carpets, the dousing of fires and the collapsing of the big tent itself.

Suddenly there was only sky overhead. The Rock finished detaching the main pole. The Migdali sprang a big smile at Maryam but was too busy to talk. She was bustling, telling the women not to worry, to take what they could. No one would get lost, how could they lose sight of so many people? The Rock collected Shushan. He shouldered up her carpet and then swung her on top of that.

"My heart is beating," said Shushan in excitement, and gave Maryam a hug. Maryam decided she might as well stick with the Rock and Shushan for the march. The Son had said they were going first to Dalmanuthu, a mile or so south of Migdal Nunya.

Without any signal, the blue-tent women started to walk. The Migdali strode off to catch up with the Son. Maryam was pleased to see that she and the Rock formed a kind of leadership cluster at the head of a troop. Many of the women followed them, herding their goats and children.

At first little Rut played with other children, running in circles with them; but she soon tired, and Maryam had to carry her.

It was still the cool of the morning. There was pressure to be near the Son, who marched in front. Somehow, not thinking they were trying to, the Rock, Shushan and Maryam caught up with the students at the front, and these days the broad backs of the students parted to let them through.

The Migdali looked happier than Maryam had seen her in days. "Making ourselves a new road," the Migdali said. Maryam looked behind at the caravan stretching out behind them and already, winding through the boulders and the scrub, a visible pathway had been beaten.

"We should be singing," said the Migdali and clapped her hands and tried to sing in her weak and breathy voice. She nodded for Maryam to join in and Maryam dutifully did out of friendship. It was the prayer-song that somehow Maryam could never remember. Why would the Lord lead them into temptation?

Somehow the time was not right for singing. Perhaps people didn't want to open their mouths in the hot sun and the drying air. They edged around the side of Mountain Kinrot and the hazy lake slowly came into view, with its yellow shore and Roman road. And here waiting for them was a large flock of goats, guarded by barTalemi and Mattit-yahu, local sheep purchased by Yoanna's money. The flock joined the caravan.

The sun was at its baking zenith when they finally stepped onto the road's beaten crust. There the caravan stalled and bunched, within sight of Nahum.

Some of the old eklesia had farms to go back to or other lives to resume. The followers gathered into knots of people who hugged each other, wished each other well, even wept to say goodbye. Then those knots broke apart.

Perhaps a quarter of the caravan turned north to walk back to Nahum or Beth Saida or even Caesarea Philippi near the sea. These farmers, merchants, and some tax collectors were the ones with mounts and sturdy shoes, and tunics that were not torn. They took much of the eklesia's food and water with them.

The sick, the destitute, the egregious foreigners with darker skins who spoke strange forms of Greek – these followed south. Many of them limped or were carried, looking scalded by life. They hugged their empty bellies. There was no other place in all of the lands of the two Herods for such as these.

It was these hungry people who filled their stomachs with song. Now the song-prayers rose up. Their eyes yearned for the Son of Adam somewhere in front of them.

At Seven Springs the plain widened and there was a burgeoning of green.

Warm springs flowed into the lake. They grew algae and fed fish. It was at Seven Springs that Yehush had first met the sons of Zebedee, Yake and Yehonnan.

The eklesia approached the town, singing. But they noticed men with clubs across the road. Some few of these watchmen turned and ran back into Seven Springs, and they were soon joined by more men – arborists, herdsmen, and fishermen. They scowled, brandishing adzes, or tossing up and catching sharp flints for throwing. Youths held up slingshots and snarled with broken-toothed grins. "You'll not cross!" they shouted. "Go around, go around."

Out into the lake, the village breakwater arched; boats lined it; men were repairing sails; water birds flew. This should have been a place of peace.

Yakob approached them to talk, and a stone was flung at him and struck him on the head. Maryam covered her mouth. Yakob who had once been so timid, touched his bloody forehead, looked at his fingers and kept on walking towards the mob.

Yakob called. "We want nowt from you. We just want to pass through."

"Aye. You'll go through and more, you'll go all the way around."

"We'll make sure of that."

"You ate all our fish the last time."

Yakob shouted, "We have flocks with us now."

"Aye and we'll have them too, if you go through our land!"

"Payment for last time."

Yakob shook his head and turned back, his eyebrow raised at the Son. The Son nodded yes, and flicked his wrist to go around, and the caravan scrambled back up the small rise to do so. The townsmen, now forty or fifty of them, advanced, fanned out, kept pace with them, herding them away from the shore. Dogs barked at them.

"God, you can smell their stink from here!"

"Skin and bones! There'll be nowt to bury!"

"Look at all those women, flapping around loose." A miming of rape from the hips.

One of the lads, wanting fun, shouted, "Get going" and slung a rock high into the air, so it would plummet down on someone's head. It landed but no one cried out.

An older townsman spoke up, a rough man, large with grey beard but even at his age, big shoulders, flat belly. He held up his hands against the boy, against the rest of them. "They're going, they're going. No need to hurt anyone."

An angry shout. "Yeah, and there's thousands of them and fifty of us."

"Look at em. They're all old or daffy!" Catcalls and cheers.

Maryam drew near to the Son. She touched his arm.

He did indeed look sad. "This is where the Calling Out began. I said I will make you fishers of people. The men here are all rocks. You turn them over and they have a wet underside."

Yakob rejoined the troop. His brother glanced at the wound and nodded acknowledgement. "Well. I did say you will all be persecuted in my name." A woman nearby started bellowing out a song and clapping, the crowd all began to sing those words. YOU WILL BE PERSECUTED IN MY NAME. It was a tune made for marching and it sounded militant.

Gennesaret was on the trade route from Syria, and had given Lake Tiberias one of its names.

Along the road people were laid out on pallets to be cured. The Son strode past them – the caravan needed to reach Dalmanuthu, their first prepared place, before nightfall. As usual, some beseeched, holding out hands. Others cursed. "You're nothing. You're a fraud. Told you, told you!"

A leper was hobbling alongside them, banging on a pan. Maryam thought she had seen his face before somewhere on the road. Another leper was coming towards them in a wide arc like a predatory bird. Before she could say anything

Shemenolo had shouted "Awake there!" Shushan still riding on his back, the Rock stepped forward to protect the Son.

Suddenly they were being jostled by lepers, about ten of them. One of them held up his crutch like a club to strike. Missing teeth, fingers, even eyes, they howled or snarled, "Cure us or we'll touch them. Cure us or we'll spit on you."

The widow of Zebedee screamed and pulled back. Her two sons stepped in front of her. A leper went for pretty Mattit-yahu, chased him yapping like a dog, laughing and reaching out with peeling fingers.

Shushan, still riding Shem, grabbed the leper's hand. She smiled. She would not let him go. "We all die," Shushan chuckled from deep within her throat.

The leper yelped, "Get off me, you old bat."

Shushan looked blissful. "Do you want to be cured? Do you? You're sure?"

"Enough!" The Son shouted. Maryam knew what was coming and had time to seize hold of Rut's hand to steady her.

The world rose up in revulsion, churned, rolled over. The very hills seemed to dissolve for a moment and then reform out of vomit. Rut wailed and clung to Maryam. Maryam's sore hip jinked; she nearly fell, and her gorge rose, digestive juices burning her throat.

Then everything settled, the world reformed.

Little Rut wailed. Maryam hugged the child. "There darling, there, there. It's stopped, see?"

The Son seemed to have been thrown off his feet. He lay on the ground, the Migdali and Yakob holding his hand or his head. The leper was trying to jerk his hand free from Shushan. Her stick-thin arms were able to hold him and she was gurgling a chuckle at him.

"What will you do now, eh? You're the same as everyone else now."

Shushan let him go. His face was unlined and whole. He stared at his hands. The tall one still threatened with his crutch. Shushan laughed a high musical laugh and clapped her hands. "Look. They're still angry! They're clean! But they want their anger." She clapped her hands, laughing, and pointed at them.

Their faces hung limp. They looked confused.

"You'll have to work now!" Shushan shouted at them.

Many of the eklesia had been thrown from their feet. These miraculous disruptions were getting worse, as if the world itself strained more with each one. As they stood up, the followers began to roar. The Son sat up, woozily. Yakob and barTalemi helped him to stand. This had cost him dearly, curing so many at once.

The eklesia began to sing a slow respectful song, a Mizmor, about the Lord being a shepherd. The Son wiped his face on his sleeve and gestured for them all to move on.

The cured men had melted away, except for one of them, the one with the pan. Out of habit he walked with a limp, though there was now no need, and he came near to the Son and spoke in a low voice through a thin mouth. The Son put a firm hand on the back of his neck, nodded, and the man put his hand over his heart and walked away backwards.

Shemenolo said gruffly, "Well what do you know. One of them said thanks. They don't, usually."

Yet at Dalmanuthu they were greeted by women with amphorae who called, "Welcome, welcome."

The apostles Xiamara and Marta each took one of the

Son's forearms. "You said, Rabuli, to make the way straight."

The Son looked relieved and flashed a smile. In torchlight, a smiling Dalmanuthi passed Maryam a cup of water.

The Migdali said, "They remember the last miracle here. Hmm. Yah? Loaves and fishes. Also," and here the Migdali yelped out a laugh. "It's not my beloved hometown. That's the best thing about it."

The Migdali caught Maryam's eye, and perhaps saw the question in it. "There's no whores in Dalmanuthu," said the Migdali, with an odd grin and narrowed eyes.

We're all angry thought Maryam.

They had walked ten miles with no food or water. There were no tents but no rain. To sleep, the eklesia seemed to sink into the very ground, the very night.

Maryam cradled Rut. "Sleep well, Princess."

"Yes, Ami," said Rut as if Babatha had never existed.

The second day they walked only to Tiberias.

Silent women met them with bread on trays which they began to cut in slices as neat as the intersecting streets. They were escorted by the advance guard of T'oma and his twin brother. Both men were tiny, but as slow and calm as the Rock. Quietly, using Greek forms of politeness, they formally introduced the Son to the locals.

The Greek women asked questions like, "Does your God contain all the other Gods inside him?" They were questions that pagans would ask. Baffled, unanswerable, from another world. "Don't you feel unanchored without a statue of your God?"

The women led the eklesia to the theatre, where they would sleep. The Son preached there, his voice rolling out over filled seats, speaking to many more folk than had come to meet them.

The Son tried to make sense for them that there were many Gods, but one God overreaching all.

"So. So your God is Jove?" asked a man in a toga who looked like a Roman you might see in a dream.

The Son paused. "Our god is all gods made one. We say that this God has a covenant with our people. But God made all the world and all the people in it. So he is god for all people."

Maryam thought: *He wants the pagans to follow him. That's Yoanna's work.*

They stayed next at Philoteria, the southernmost shore of the lake.

The two women apostles who had gone there in advance came out to meet them alone, looking downcast. "We are sorry Rabuli, but they mocked us even when we spoke Greek." The followers camped near the shore between towns and caught fish by tickling their underbellies and flinging them ashore.

It was hot or cold; sometimes they starved; sometimes it was as though the world would blossom into a place of joy.

At Scythopolis, a Greek town, people ran out to greet them.

They were mostly women. One of them seized the Son's hand and shouted, "Are you Babatha's brother?" When the Son nodded yes, the woman enthused. "She told me all. You cure the sick. Oh yes, she says that you are all possessed by the Spirit of the Lord."

And out strode Babatha like a queen. The Son took both

her hands and shook his head. "I can cure too!" she said. "I could speak to them in Greek." She chuckled. "It's true. It's all true!"

Little Rut hung back. *She doesn't trust her mother*, Maryam realized. She pulled the little girl closer to Babatha, who jumped forward when she saw her. "Rutit!" She knelt and hugged her, and peppered her with kisses. The child began to giggle.

Babatha looked up at Maryam. "Ami!" Maryam bent over to kiss her and Babatha threw her arms around her neck. "Mother. I have seen God. I am sure of it. I'm not crazy."

Maryam ached for Babatha and how beautiful she was, but couldn't speak. Something solid seemed to have settled into her lungs, making it difficult to breathe. It was partly joy, partly misgiving. Maryam heard herself croak, "You didn't forget us."

Babatha faltered. "Forget you? In two weeks? What are you talking about?" The Son stood over them and Babatha took his hand. He reached out to take Esta's hand too. The Son looked overjoyed to see Esta, then gave his old friend's hand a vigorous shake, and all three of them strode into Scythopolis together.

Babatha had done a wonderful job. People actually lined the road into the town and cheered them. Babatha's beautiful smile had returned. Maryam like everyone else crowded in to be next to the Son. Babatha managed to say without disturbing that smile, "It's strange. The pagans welcome us as much as the Beni Yisrael." Her fingers were curled in Rutit's hair.

The Son preached that night in the courtyard of a friendly house, but he was overcome perhaps with fatigue or joy or strain. His voice cracked and Maryam found she could not understand what he was saying as she tried to write it down. What she got was almost nonsense.

"The Kingdom of God is in all of us – in the stones, in the hills, in the gills of the fish." The Son rocked from side to side. "The Kingdom of God is here!" A great roar from the eklesia. "It has always been here." Silence, bafflement. "God is perfect and complete." Another assenting roar. "But only when seen whole outside of time. Here with us, God is trapped in a process of becoming. That is why the Word can change."

Maryam gave up writing. The crowd still cheered, but it was more like they were cheering him whenever he said something they could remotely understand. Mattit-yahu approached her, doe-eyed, embarrassed, holding out his scrolls. She snapped at him. "No, I have nothing either."

When it was done, she approached the Son, took his arm. Some of the original twelve still clung to their position. They eyed her without smiles. *Jostle each other for position if you like, but don't gainsay me.*

"I'm your mother," she told him, pointing. "And I'm telling you. Go back to parables."

The group relaxed and chuckled. That's what they had wanted to say.

In the morning, yet again, the caravan moved on.

The dogs still barked. Babatha glowed in pink dawn light. *How*, wondered Maryam, *did I give birth to someone as beautiful as my Babatha?* The answer of course was: *she's part Yosef.*

"I'm not coming with you, Ami," Babatha said. "The idea is that the seventy-two take root. We stay to call out and make sure the Word is heard. You see here, Ami, I've done well. I've finally done something well."

"Tush," said Maryam. "You always do everything well."

Babatha knelt again in front of Rut, who remained resolutely unfooled. "You do everything your Granny tells you, Rut." She took hold of her daughter's chin and looked into her firm eyes. "You will be three soon. I will think of you and pray for you. Live in the Word of God."

"Goodbye," said Rut, unruffled. She took hold of Maryam's hand.

In Ginae, the widow of Zebedee made her move.

Boldly, she suddenly said that surely the Son saw how invaluable her two sons were to him. She had to keep saying her sons and their names because there were so many other Yakobs and Yohannans in the eklesia. Surely her two sons were his chief assistants? Could they sit on either side of his throne in his kingdom?

"I think the Rock might have something to say about that," rumbled Kephas's brother.

The Son's voice was weary. "What do you mean, Mother?"

There was almost no subject the widow could not get back around to her sons or her husband within the space of a sentence. Nobody even really knew her name. No, she was the Widow of Zebedee. Did we know he'd been a fisherman with boats at Seven Springs and a house in Beth Saida? Hardly a ministerial position. She was foolish: Maryam's view.

"Well," she inclined her head winsomely, evidently thinking that if she found something delightful, everyone else would. "In heaven, they will be sitting next to you? As they do in life?"

The Son's eyes were closed. "You don't know what you are asking. Are they going to drink from the cup I will drink from?"

He had just been telling them all, again, how the Son of Adam was to be condemned to death.

Andreas snarled. "This is what comes of encouraging women." He sprang, jerked, and then spun away.

The widow began to realize that there was something she didn't understand. Her sons leaned forward, and both of them spoke at once. "Yes, Rabuli. Yes, we will."

The Son opened his eyes, as heavy as stones. "You will indeed." There was something dark in his tone that made the sons of Zebedee pause. "But those places you speak of belong to people chosen by the Father. He chooses."

BarTalemi stood up and joined Andreas. Soon only some of the women and the family of Zebedee were left sitting in the group. The Son chuckled, shook his head and joined the boys. "Come back, join us. No, no, join us."

He persuaded them all to return. The Son said as he led them back, "It's the worldly who have kings who lord it over them. Among us, it is the servant who is the greatest. Who wants to be first must first become your slave." He smiled, his dark eyes hard like volcanic glass.

In Shomeron a multitude marched out to greet them, to garland them with flowers, and give them dates and honey.

The Son had never been to the Shomeronai's capital, that Herod had renamed Sebastae.

The Shomeronai had heard that the Son praised them in his preaching, that he regarded them as every bit as worthy as the Yehudai. They were so tired of scorn; so sick of religious politics.

Here was someone who sang and told stories against the Perisayya whose only message seemed to be that no one else other than the Perisayya followed the Law, meaning countless laws, which the Perisayya seemed to be making up for themselves.

The eklesia was happiest in Shomeron. The caravan had gone out of its way both west and south to enter the land. In every village people gave them water, or bread or even dried dates and flowers. They waited around the wells and asked for the Son's now famous story of the Shomeronai who aided a Yehudi when the priests would not.

Another Maryam and Elisheba were the apostoli for the region, and they walked in progress with the Son.

In these friendly villages, the Son relaxed and, as always when he felt at home, his preaching was easily understood parables about sheep or grain or mustard trees. Those, Maryam and Mattit-yahu could note down.

The old Yisraeli town was partly in ruins. Herod had re-named in it honour of Augustus, and rebuilt in a Roman style with a temple to the emperor and a theatre. Many of the townspeople spoke Greek, descendants of a Macedonian garrison. The tradesmen were all Sidonai.

Among this mix of peoples, the Son sang, the Son danced. He turned the story of the Shomeroni who aided the beaten man into a song. He got the eklesia, and all the people lining the streets, to sing and clap along with it.

The Shomeroni
Did not pass by

People threw handfuls of the last of the spring cyclamen, purple, light pink, or white.

The eklesia then headed east to Neapolis, where a great press of the sick and old gathered, then on to the ruins of the temple at Gerizim, and here the Son preached again about the wife at the well and what he had told her. He let the Shomeronai raise up a lament for their Mount Moriah, even when they cursed the Yehudai for destroying it. He did not join in, but let the song pass like the firelight.

They left the land through Shekem on its eastern border. The press of people grew so great – the entire province, it seemed, wanted to say farewell – that the Son began to have that wild look Maryam dreaded.

The Son sat at the well again, and wept. He told another follower that the man would have to give up all his wealth. He told him that he would be blessed if he left his family. The Son's eyes went wide and staring and he started to sing in a tuneless high wavering.

The song prowled around a strange text that announced The Son would soon be revealed, as if he hadn't been revealed.

The dirge warned that on that day no one who is on the rooftop should go down into the house for his possessions. Remember Lot's wife. "Whoever tries to keep their life will lose it," he sang. "On that night two people in one bed. One will be taken and the other left behind."

Maryam put down her quill. There was no point. It was nonsense. Had he been deranged by visions of the destruction of the Shomeronai temple?

They all knew that when the Son wept it might be not be from sadness or weakness but rage. Seeing tears, the Thunder Brothers tried to keep back the crowd; told a group of children to go back.

"Bring the children! Bring the children!" The Son stood

up, fists bunched. "Don't you understand?" The Migdali swiftly gathered the children and urged them to go back. The children had come with flowers for him. He looked at the limp bunches of tiny flowers, and pulled the children to himself and wept, hugging them. He said something that Maryam could not quite hear.

A cheer grew from those around him. Whatever he had said spread; this they understood: the love of children. This they believed. The roar grew, it became a chant. THE FIRST SHALL BE LAST. THE FIRST SHALL BE LAST.

The Son pulled back, looked in a little girl's face and stroked it. His singing voice rose up, cutting through the sound, and the crowd ssshed itself. His hands over his head in the heart-shape, the Son sang, "Look at the face of a child. Be like a child to enter the Kingdom."

The crowd began to sing with him. BE LIKE A CHILD.

Maryam thought: *That light I see in the eyes of babes.*

At the border they were joined by groups of young Yehudai men, with merry eyes and swords. "Fine army this will make," they groaned.

"Kana'im," warned the Migdali. "Rebels."

And so it went.

At Salim, they broke bread with a wizard, who converted and declared that God had come to Earth. He broke his staff.

The eklesia all knew that something extraordinary was happening. At times the joy was contagious, the sense that nothing was worth missing this march for. Even life itself. If anything, that sense of the extraordinary made them all go quiet. A kind of hush fell on them all, as if they were blanketed by fog.

From there it was a short walk to Aenon on the River Yarden. The river was narrow, deep, swift, and tree-lined. The sky flowed on its surface, rippling in reflection as if the flow showed the progress of God in heaven. The Son settled on the bank and would not move.

A whole day passed.

The sky was cloudless, mauve in twilight; and the trees became shadows; and the Son was still folded in on himself. It was as though he was getting weaker, wilder with every step. Maryam ventured to sit next to him and take his hand. He seized it so hard, with a stonecutter's grasp, that she could feel the rods inside the back of her hand bend inwards.

So she sat there and bore the pain, and stared at his face, willing him to speak. The Rock rubbed the Son's shoulders. Gradually the twelve students gathered in a semi-circle, mostly silent, mostly unmoving. The bulbul sang.

Finally the Son sighed, rubbed his face and stood, saying, "We should eat."

The Migdali hugged her. "Thank you, Mother. I was terrified what would happen when we came here."

Rut had come to be cuddled. The march had been good for her, made her stronger and more sociable, sent her scurrying about to play with other children, but now she was tired and wanting hugging. Maryam was distracted enough to say. "I don't know what's special about this place."

Migdali did the eklesia's trick of talking without moving her lips. Her voice was thin and buzzing as a tiny insect's. "This is where he was baptized. By his cousin Yehonnan."

Elisheba's son, whom Maryam had never met. Herod Antipas had killed him.

The bulbul sang but Maryam would not have been surprised to see, in the dusk, that the sweet voice had come from a dove catching the last of the light.

The next day they waded across the Yarden.

Thousands of them washing off the dust and singing that mountain song of daily bread and forgiveness.

They climbed up into the hills of Perea, to the fastness of Pella, its mean streets full of mud, the air chill, with no plains for them to sleep on. But the mountains and the river crossing had eliminated most of the Kana'im. They had followed the Son only to spread revolt against Rome. Mountain frosts saw them off. The Perisayya and Sadducai had not climbed the hills either.

In Perea, people listened quietly. There the Son was not wild, did not bloviate, but told simple stories of how righteousness would be rewarded.

Then south towards the Dead Sea.

At Rammah, rebuilt by Ptolemy and then called Philadelphia, Brotherly Love, the Son of Adam preached that divorce didn't work. God had joined you and that bond could not be broken. He preached again that the Kingdom of God was at hand – and had always been here. And again nobody had any clear idea what the Kingdom of God was. People hoped that it meant God would come to the world and rule it, relieving people of any responsibility.

Then back west across Yarden, to Yeriko. More healings, more celebrations. As soon as the road turned towards Yerusalam, the eklesia began to grow again.

* * *

In Yeriko town, in its narrow streets, a man kept jumping up over the heads of the crowd shouting "Rabuli! Rabuli!"

He was very short, but seemed to be able to jump half his own height, bounding up over the heads of everyone else. "Master," he kept shouting.

Then he was seemingly swallowed by the press of people. Ahead of them a fig tree was boxed in the middle of the cobbled street. This man began to scramble up it like a village boy, only he was dressed in finely woven linen that was dyed blue and red. Light glinted on the tooling cut into his leather sandals. The Son stopped by the fig tree and the man shouted down.

"Great One. I am Zaccheaus and I am a believer in you. I have been to hear you speak before. I came home and gave away half of my wealth."

Someone perhaps primed and rehearsed, perhaps not, yelled. "It's true Rabuli. He gave everything. Well. Half."

The little man swung down from the branches and landed. "I heard you say the rich could not be saved. I gave away my shoes, my clothes, my grain."

"His gold," someone growled. "He's a tax collector."

There was a spreading of laughter. The man seized hold of the Son's hand and pulled. "Please come rest in my house. Come stay with me, Rabuli. Please. Please."

"Yes," said the Son. "I will. With my brother and mother."

"Yes, yes Rabuli of course, of course." The man beamed, looked around him, delighted, sweaty, in need of a shave. He had a boy with him, and told him, "Run to your mistress. Tell her we have guests. Break out the last of the good wine. Leave nothing!"

The man looked at the Son with what could only be called love. "I will lead you, Rabuli."

Someone else growled, "You will sleep with a tax collector?"

The Son laughed. "One who gives you all back what he collects? Sure, yes." The eklesia laughed and most of the Yerikoai too.

As they walked, the Son leaned in to Maryam and said. "I've never slept in a fine bed. Or ate fine food. I'd like to before I die. That's human too, isn't it?"

Human.

The tax collector's house was walled, courtyarded, with flat roofs on multiple levels and lightwells full of olive trees and tamarisk.

The house had its own well but channels from springs meant it had its own miq'va. Across the doorways in the late breeze, tapestries gently breathed.

The tax collector moved ahead of them showing them the house and giving orders. "Bring water! Bring wine. Fill the miq'va with living water."

Then back, "Rabuli, Rabuli, please don't be offended. I'm not sure what we have. I don't know what will offend more. Our poor show, or the great wealth we have left." He jumped up and down in place.

The Son hugged him into stillness. "Any, all, it will be fine." The Son was short, but Zaccheaus only reached his armpits.

"Will it, Rabuli?"

"God rejoices over you," said the Son.

Zaccheaus seized his hand. "This my wife Zofia. Zofia, show our guests to their room."

Zofia was as tiny as he was, round as a berry, her face covered. "This way, this way," she said, and ran ahead of them on slivers of feet. Both of their hosts seemed to buzz like bees. Zofia showed them a chamber on the first storey with windows and hangings and lamps and carpets and two huge beds of strung horsehair with pillows stuffed with shredded rags. The low tables held porcelain basins, and pitchers full of fresh water and one plaster wall had a fresco representing Moses with the tablets.

After she had gone, the family were frozen for a moment, stunned.

Yakob chortled, "If this is what it's like with half his wealth gone!"

Maryam couldn't stop herself talking over him. "What was it like before?"

The Son looked wistful. "Everyone who has, gets more. More will be given. Those who have nothing." He chortled. "The little they have will be taken away." In his eyes, Nazareth was reflected.

Maryam swung her writing bag down on the floor, found her scroll, unrolled it to where the clip stopped it, fumbled the ink jug, tested the quill in her mouth and wrote as best she could.

"Is this what you just said?" she asked. She held up the scroll. "Is it?" It seemed to her that it was different. Tidier perhaps.

The Son smiled, shook his head. Then he sang it. "Those who have, get more; those who lack will lose."

That's what the Bible says and it still is news.

CHAPTER 24

GOD BLESS THE CHILD

On the road from Yeriko, three sisters arrived at their camp outside the town and asked for the Raba to say a prayer for their dead brother.

Three mouths, one grief. The girls said the same things that Maryam had said over Yosef, what people say when loved ones die.

For once, Maryam could not feel that she was special or blessed; simply that she and the millions all repeated patterns as grains of sand repeat patterns of wear.

Our brother is mourned. He left us too soon, he was so young, he led a good life, he deserved better. How can it be that he was laughing in the morning, and cold clay by evening? Who will support us now?

The Son said to them mildly. "Where is your home?"

The House of Tahani, towards Yerusalam. The Son threw on the cloth that was his bed and coat and blanket, and without a further word, began to walk.

"Rabuli? Where are you going?"

"To see your brother."

"Rabuli, he has been buried three days. He is in our family tomb."

"Say a blessing for him here, Rabuli, and that will be enough."

Two sisters knelt but the third was on her feet ready to go with him. The Son flicked his hand for the other two to stand. His face looked heavy – his eyes were half closed, everything around his chin seemed to sag, and almost imperceptibly, his head slowly shook. Then he turned again and walked.

Shemenolo, the Thunder Brothers, Andreas, T'oma all glanced at each other. The Migdali boggled her eyes at Maryam: *What's he about now?* There was a coughing and shuffling of sandals on dirt as the core team realized that the Son was walking to Beth Tahani with or without them.

It was only four hours' walk, on a calm night with a light chill breeze, in starlight with a nearly full moon. The small body of followers began to sing as they walked, HAPPY ARE and OUR FATHER, but the Son did not join in. He walked as if alone. Maryam asked him if he were well. He did not even answer her.

Beth Tahani was a beautiful town near Yerusalam ringed with orchards of figs and olives and vines.

The air still smelled of dark water in ditches and the air thrilled with mosquitoes.

The Son was the first one at the inscribed rock face, white limestone. "This is the place, yes." Not really a question.

The bewildered sisters nodded yes but said, "As you see, Rabuli, he is behind the stone. Thank you Rabuli. Bless his memory, Rabuli. It will help us grieve."

The Son stood absolutely still, eyes closed, and waited. The sisters fell silent. The crickets and even the gathering eklesia paused.

The world was flung forward. Maryam felt a shiver vibrate through her, towards, she thought, the rock face. This disruption was sharper and more focussed than others. It was if a spear had been thrown through her and into the tomb.

The Son sounded impatient. "The stone?" He stood calmly, but his eyes were full of blood, and blood spilled out of them down his cheeks, red tears.

Nobody moved. The Son's tongue clicked. Shemenolo jumped forward then stopped. The Son said, peevishly, as if it were obvious, "Move the stone away."

Some of the villagers approached with lamps. A woman thrust her way through them. "What is going on? Sarah? Sheba?"

"It's the Raba, Mama."

"Ssshoosh! Him." The mother evidently did not share her son's faith. "What is he doing? What have you asked him to do?"

"Just sing praises, Ami."

"They're opening the tomb! Our family tomb. Stop them!"

Shemenolo, Yakob and the other Yakob, barTalemi and Andreas were trying to push the stone, which was cut like a wheel to allow new burials. It rolled, but then wobbled and toppled and fell and broke. The doorway to the tomb was broken. The villagers, even some of the eklesia groaned.

The Son had not moved, as though he were a stake driven into the ground. He said, almost inaudibly. "Elazar. Could you come out, please?"

The sisters turned, clutched themselves, and clutched their mother, whose face in red torchlight was pale with fury.

"Elazar?" A note of impatience. "Please. Your sisters want to see you. They are here. They have called you back."

Even Shemenolo swallowed, looked askance – a face Maryam had never seen from the Rock, twisted sideways: *Is this a trick*? Was Elazar now waiting alive in the tomb?

Someone stumbled into the mouth of the rock-cut cave. He was shrugging, punching, caught up in a shroud. The sisters shrieked; one of them dropped to the ground.

The shrouded man howled, "Why?" He was trapped in a winding cloth as if in a cocoon. A clumsy forearm pulled back on the wrappings. He stepped into moonlight, torchlight, his face unveiled and blank. He looked like an ordinary young man, heavy-cheeked and beginning to go bald. He stared wildly, but his eyes had gone milk-white and slightly shrivelled. He blinked and the eyes cleared, were whole again, and he looked at his hand in horror. "Back! Here!"

Elazar kicked his way out of the shroud and stumbled naked towards the village. As if wasps were swarming, he beat his hands about his head. "I was in light!"

The Son asked. "Do I call you Elazar? Or are you something else?"

"That's my name. I was part of the light!"

A sister came to him, picked up the shroud and covered him. The mother kept her distance, hands clasped in front of her. Her mouth moved, forming sounds which Maryam could not hear: *Abomination*.

The dead man kept looking about him in confusion. The sister had to turn her head, nose wrinkling. The other sister put a headscarf over her face. Elazar stank of mortification and the grave.

The mother finally moved towards him and then stopped. "Go back," she said. "Go back where you belong."

The Son said. "He will, Mother. In time. Elazar. Look at my finger. See my finger? Follow my finger with your eyes. Good. Elazar? Breathe. In and out like this. Do you remember how?"

Elazar said no with his head, and then yes with his head.

"That's it. Keep breathing. Someone, get water and wash him. Someone find his favourite clothes and dress him again. Are your loins warm, Elazar? Can you have children?"

Elazar quivered in panic and looked back and forth. "I don't know."

"Are you hungry?"

"No." A thin little voice like a child's.

"Sing a song," the Son said.

Elazar looked askance.

"Any song. Any song that you remember. One from one childhood."

And so Elazar sang a song of how the fig tree loves the fig, and how the fig must fall. And how the nightingale loves her egg, though it must break. In a high, straining, drunken voice, Elazar sang, still moving in jerks, looking sideways.

The Son nodded, as if something were confirmed. He turned, tossed his shawl over his shoulder and began to walk back towards Yeriko.

Over his shoulder he shouted, "Drain the ditches or more of you will die."

There was no singing as they walked back. Maryam tripped forward trying to keep up with the Son's furious pace. "What was that?"

He didn't answer.

"Why did you do that? It was horrible. What was the point?"

"I needed to see what would happen."

"Well are you pleased?" Abomination, Elazar's mother had said.

The Migdali joined them. Maryam's eyes raked hers: *Well what do you think?*

"It's done," the Son said, not looking at them. His smile looked relieved, but pained. His dark eyes made the face look like a mask.

"Tell her about Nein," said the Migdali, her voice rough but calm.

"Nein? I raised the dead there too. A young girl. She came back empty of soul or memory. I overturned the world a second time for her so that she could speak. She still didn't know her name. She had to relearn how to walk, to wash, to eat."

The followers crowded in all wanting to hear, all wanting to be central, all wanting to understand. Maryam wished them all away.

"God has changed," said the Son. "It now allows your spirit to live after death as you yourself." His feet ground the dust. He sighed. "All that is left is to go to Yerusalam." His eyes still wept blood.

CHAPTER 25

SAVE US PLEASE

They left Yeriko late in the morning, walking back through Beth Tehani, and up onto the Mount of Olives.

The Son had not slept for two days. On the outskirts of the city at Beth Fazhi, there was a fig tree by the road. The Son stood woozily in front of it and stared.

Yakob put a hand on his shoulder. "Brother?"

"I want to taste a fig."

"Season's over, you know that. Wait 'til the month of Elul."

The Son said, "I won't be here in Elul." Then his face curdled and he shouted. "Give me a fig!" At a tree. And then he shouted. "You will never bear fruit again."

The world went dark for a moment. Looming Yerusalam, its towers and valleys, turned upside down, and when the city righted itself, the fig tree had dropped all its leaves. They lay on the ground, black and shiny as if lacquered.

Stiffly, face closed, the Son marched on. Yakob stared at Maryam, and she covered her mouth. Never before had the Son killed anything, not even animals for meat. And always now this talk of death, his own death.

It was the week before Pesach. All along the road people called from doorways, hoping to make extra money renting rooms. The eklesia began to split. Some of the followers peeled away from the group to take up accommodation. They shouted farewells to each other and agreed to meet by the south entrance to the Mount.

Just after Beth Fazhi, Yoanna's men separated their goats and sheep and drove them west towards the Fish Gate, slashing them with sticks. They took their leave of the Son, bowing to him with hands over their hearts. The money from the sale of the livestock would keep the followers fed in the city.

The rest of the eklesia followed the Son, but the crowd was not huge. They started to climb, up the hill and then along it into a string of villages, blank walls lining the road, trees reaching over the brick to cast some shade. Above the line of dwellings, a few of the old orchards whispered on the slopes.

The road turned round an outcropping and gazed across the vale of Kidron. There was the Temple as if it had spread wings of stone.

Maryam had never taken this road or seen this view. The opposite bank was vast and smoky with distance – this time of day, the light was sideways and the steep slopes and the high walls of the Mount were in shadow. In that light the Temple looked rougher, the face of each block in the wall irregularly hewn.

The southeast corner called the Pinnacle really did tower over a large drop – no paths wound up that cliff face. A wooden walkway crossed the valley of Kidron, unsafe, with no railings and supported by high stone pillars. Birds flew under it. The wind whispered. It was a pathway only for priests into Bath Yahu. Maryam knew of this bridge – Yechezkelk had prophesied that the Son of David would cross it to enter the city. Over it all, the Temple looked like a crown of snow and gold.

By silent agreement, they rested. Maryam bundled Rut up on her lap and called her a brave girl, and gave her water. Rut turned her face towards Maryam for a moment, seemed to sleep, and then with the energy of children, sat up and asked if she could go explore.

The Son did not sit. He stared ahead, eyes unblinking, his mouth twisted, almost smiling, showing how brown his teeth were becoming. Maryam stood up to go to him, but the Migdali slipped a hand over her wrist and held firm like cypress pine.

"I know," the Migdali said. "But you'll get nowt out of him now."

Five of their men gathered up everyone's bags to carry them to the houses that Yoanna had prepared. The Widow of Zebedee, better behaved now, offered to take all the children to the house to rest.

Rut's face bunched up. "No," she shouted.

"Don't you want to go with the other kids?" Maryam asked. "It's a long walk all around the city."

"I don't want to!" And Maryam remembered another little girl who had wanted to see the Temple. She leaned forward and kissed Rut and said, "Come on then. But if you get tired, I can't carry you."

The men, the eklesia's bags, and most of the children turned to head for a house higher up the hill. The Son clicked his fingers and what was left of the eklesia stirred itself.

There were no more than twenty people in their train. This looked nothing like the triumphant entry that Yoanna had promised. The Son staggered forward. Perhaps it was simply sleeplessness exhausting him? Or the weight of the world?

"Hail King of the Yehudai!" shouted one of the Kana'im hangers-on. They hoped for the prophesied prince, and knew exactly what not crossing the Eastern Gate meant. The Son had chosen not to fulfill the prophecy – this was not the Son of David.

The Kana'im sounding rather merry, clattered on ahead, swords slung from their shoulders.

At a courtyard gateway, they encircled a countryman unloading edible crocus bulbs. They had wily smiles as they talked to the old man, easing him away from his donkey. When they took its reins, the old man's jaw went slack and he shook his hands at them; one of them offered a sword while another tossed him a few coins.

"For the Great One, a steed for the Son of Adam," they shouted and burst into giggles. They pulled the slow, tiny beast towards the Son. It was old, bald in patches; its knees were in knots.

"Rabuli," the Kana'im said bowing, keeping their smiles mild. "For your entry into Yerusalam."

A donkey? This is an insult.

Nevertheless the Son looked weary, even grateful. He may have been a country boy, but he had great difficulty getting onto the back of the beast. This added to the Kana'im's hilarity. "All hail the King of the Yehudai."

Suddenly his legs seemed short and stumpy, his feet tiny, and he jumped and slipped back. Maryam realized that she had never seen him ride even in Nazareth.

"Oh Great One, let us help," said one of the naughty boys. They joined their hands into a kind of hoist. The Son put one foot into it, and the lads almost threw him over the beast and down the other side of it. The Son had to smile and wave and try to look less than embarrassed.

The Migdali in a rage launched herself at the Kana'im, fists bunched. They roared with laughter. But they also ran away.

By then the exhausted Son was firmly on the beast's back, so the Migdali took hold of the reins and led it, talking to it soothingly. The owner came to protest and she negotiated with him, telling him where they were staying so he could find his mount. She ended up giving the old man a hug.

The small group eased along the Mount of Olives at the donkey's pace. Villagers passed them and gave them disgruntled glances.

The Son looked like a bumpkin curiosity; he had no riding rhythm, slamming down just as the haunches of the donkey jerked up. There was nothing to cushion the blow or keep him from sliding off. Once the donkey seemed to take pity on him, stopped, and turned as if to say: *Are you sure you want to go on like this?*

Hot sun and a long walk. Rut began to hang on to Maryam's arm. Maryam, worried, asked the Migdali what the plan was.

"You ask me. You think Yoanna would tell the likes of me?" Then abruptly the Migdali called to another Shem from Cana and his brother Heart. "Go on ahead; tell Yoanna it's not working; get people up here with us." They stared back at her. "Run!" she told them and gave Heart a slap on his buttocks to speed him up.

The road dropped down into the vale of Kidron. Going downhill was if anything more dispiriting – they had to firmly stop with each step before going on. The street was uneven, ruts in mud or uneven cobbles broken by feet and carts. The road zigzagged back and forth down the slope as if drunk, so that they could not see what lay around each bend.

Ahead of them they heard a roar. At first Maryam thought it was the stream that ran through the bottom of the valley. Did it ever flood? Had there been rains? The corner of a house jutted out and the road turned back on itself. Around the bend, about fifty young men were running towards them as if in a race, laughing, shouting and gleaming with sweat.

"Rabuli! Rabuli!" they called. Rut whimpered and hid behind Maryam; the Rock stood taller and bunched his fists.

In the lead, a huge man pounded up the hill. He was almost fat but with the kind of bulk that embodies strength. He staggered to a halt in front of the Son. "Rabuli," he chuckled gasping, hands on his knees. The rest of the group staggered to a stop around him.

Shem and Heart smiled at Yehush. "We had a Calling Out of our own."

The fat man, some kind of merchant, wore an ivory-coloured tunic with white stitching. He spun it off his shoulders. "Down, down, Rabuli, you will ride in comfort."

The Son hopped down from the donkey more nimbly than he had lifted himself up. He had recovered his Yazz-ness, laughing and clapping the merchant about the shoulders, and shaking the back of the Canali brothers' necks. The Migdali ran her headscarf over her tongue and used it to wipe away the last of the blood on his cheeks.

The merchant's folded cloak went on the donkey's back; some of the boys crowded in – they shouted for the Raba to ride on their cloaks instead, but the merchant whipped off his scarf, long red silk that he nipped round and round the back and belly of the donkey. The saddle would be secure enough. Then he got down on one knee and proffered. The Son stepped onto his raised knee, and like a warrior horseman, mounted his steed. There was a cheer. This business with the donkey was becoming fun.

The Son clicked, the beast advanced. One of the boys took off his cloak and spread it out on the ground. "Ride my cloak, Rabuli!" the boy said. Another one pulled his whole tunic over his head, though it left him naked but for sandals and loin-wrap. "Mine, Rabuli, mine!"

Along the road ahead, even more of the boys were flinging down their coats onto the ground. Others began to run back towards the Gate. "Make way!" they shouted. "Make way for the Son of Adam."

They reached the bottom of the path, where a bridge crossed a creek and there waiting for them was Yoanna, smiling as if she owned the city.

The donkey seemed inspired by the bridge – perhaps it was familiar. Its hooves tripped happily up its arch.

Yoanna wore homespun – tightly woven, and beautifully cut, but un-dyed homespun nevertheless with her hair hidden in a head tie. "Rabuli, welcome." She tried to take the reins of the donkey, but the Migdali scowled and hung onto them. Yoanna gave her a lovely smile.

"You've done everything perfectly, Rabuli. Everyone, everyone is talking about the last miracle. Nobody ever prophesied that the Son of David would raise the Dead." She turned to address them all. "We have such a welcome prepared for you." She saw Maryam and hugged her. "Ami, Ami, such a day!" She grabbed Maryam's hand and pulled her; the donkey, the Son, the caravan followed. Maryam reached back for the Migdali, to include her.

The Migdali's lips thinned into a narrow-eyed smile, and she waved Yoanna away as if to say: *Don't worry, Ami, I know what she's doing.*

Yoanna lowered her head and her voice. "Of course we need death."

It took Maryam a moment to orientate.

"Without death, kings like Herod would live for ever." Maryam pieced it together: Yoanna was talking about the raising of Elazar.

"Death lets the young have their turn," Maryam said.

"Exactly. Death is part of God's Blessing," said Yoanna, but she was eyeing Maryam sideways with a grin. "It just doesn't feel like it."

Yoanna bumped Maryam sideways and said without moving her lips. "I know YOU understand the meaning of not using that bridge."

Maryam indeed had. The Son was rejecting being the Son of David, spurning the Kana'im. There was nothing she could do but feel as though Yoanna had taken her into her confidence, as if she and Maryam had an alliance based on being smart.

"The Kana'im have noticed," Maryam said.

"Them," said Yoanna with real feeling. "If we are not careful, they will end up killing him. I might kill some of them first." Maryam had to assume that this was some kind of a joke. "Well. They want to kill everyone else. Freedom." Yoanna said the word with real scorn.

They had to walk south around the city walls and through the informal settlements.

The poor had constructed shacks, lean-tos, and animal-hide tents that Kidron floods would eventually wash away. These obstructed the vistas of towers and the sweep of the walls.

A merry child, say about ten, hung from a low palm frond on an untended tree. He rocked back and forth until it broke off. He ran back, balancing the torn end on his thigh to keep it steady. "Some shade, Rabuli," he beamed, his sun-scorched face highlighting his smile. Rut tugged and tugged at Maryam and broke free. She picked up a thin strand of a leaf and held it up too.

More children, then some men, ran to get palm leaves. They climbed up the trunks standing on the trimmed frond-ends and snapped off other leaves, letting them fall into the street. Children, women ran to grab them and hold them up. "Some shade, Rabuli." Their faces were all joyous and they were all laughing, and Maryam, who distrusted laughter, felt a stab of misgiving: was this mockery again? But the laughter had a note of triumph too, and she looked up at Yakob, and he was grinning as goofily as he had at fourteen.

It was kingship that was being mocked: satraps with parasols and parades of soldiers and trumpets. Their king came riding out of nowhere on the back of a donkey and was the equal of any of them.

The Water Gate was jammed with people and animals.

Herds of young lambs for Pesach, a caravan of mules, a team of five camels, and pilgrims with families all waited in the heat.

Along the top of the gate, people were waiting for the Son. They saw him, shouted, waved, whirled their scarves over their heads. They turned and shouted back to the other side of the gate. "He's here!" It seemed to Maryam that there was a great answering roar, but she could not be sure amid all the noise of the main gate.

Lying in wait by the arch, people held litters bearing the sick. They saw the Son and launched the biers like barques. The blind were led towards him; others swung from crutches. The soldiers watched dull-eyed, some of them leaning against the wall in the shade.

Yoanna spotted someone, snapped her fingers, and then slipped free from the followers. She streamed up to the soldiers on the gate. A tall man who wore robes edged with gold joined her. She stood tall next to the soldiers, talking to them and rocking with laughter. The Minister, for that was what he looked like, slipped them some coin.

The soldiers pushed themselves away from the wall. "Back away, back away!" they shouted. With a minimum of effort, they raised their spears and held them horizontally and began to push everyone back, out of the path of the Son. Yoanna's smile swelled as she sauntered back towards the family.

"They're clearing a pathway for us. But it's Pesach so we'll only be able to get through the gate two or three at a time."

The Migdali shouted. "Grab hold of each other, don't get split up. Keep together." She shook the reins of the donkey, led it and the Son though the gate. Yoanna held out her arms as if she herself had opened the gates to welcome them. Yakob took hold of Maryam's hand and pulled.

There was a sound like the sea. The underpass seemed to enclose and dim it. But when Maryam stepped through to the other side of the wall a great roar slammed into her. She couldn't see, as if the noise had blinded her, like all that sunlight on white stone.

They were in a gully, the Tyopoean valley. The rough old cobbles wound off into light, the open space in the city.

The gully was crossed by a series of bridges, like ripples in a pond. Overhead on either side, blinding limestone loomed, the fearsome walls of the Ophel, David's city higher up the slope.

"Keep moving Ami," said Yakob. Maryam recognized to their right a great colonnade – the pool of Siloam. To the left were more gentle slopes and amid the roofs, Herod's Palace and the Hasmonean.

The Son raised his hand, and they stopped. "We are going to the Temple," he said. "We should be pure."

There was a moment of uncertainty. Maryam blinked at Yakob. The Son had always said before that purity was within, not without – something both the Perisayya and Sadducai held against him. Now he slid off the donkey, and waved them all forward, beginning to chuckle. "Come on."

He led them up the slope to the baths of Siloam, there for pilgrims. He passed under the colonnade, did not take the steps down, but gave a cry of joy and jumped in. Maryam stopped. Weren't they supposed to wash before entering the ritual bath?

The Rock was carrying Shushan down the steps into the pool, pretending to be careful with her but Maryam saw. He didn't want to get wet.

The Son laughed and scooped up the water into the Rock's face. He blinked, and laughed, but only a bit. So Shushan splashed the Son back.

Others began to jump like children into the pool. Other pilgrims looked on in shock, some in anger. The Migdali helped Maryam down the steps and then, to surprise her, splashed her face, chuckling.

All at once, in the cooling waters, the eklesia began to

sing, but children's songs now, songs Maryam had not heard since her father sang them. Tears sprang up in her eyes. Laughter rose like the cries of seagulls. Even the serious pilgrims began to laugh – for the water was indeed a joyous thing. The Son sprang out of the pool and was surrounded by some of the students – Yake the Lesser and barTalemi.

Waiting beside the pool was a blind man. This old gentleman sat still, his sunhat open on his lap. He did not call out for alms. You had to look at him for a time to notice he was blind, the eyes dim and unfocussed.

Maryam could not see any gesture or movement from the Son. But she did feel the world blink, all the light going out then back on, showing a world put back together in a different shape. She saw the old man jerk forward, gape, stand up, pat himself, look at his hands. He did not cry out. He stood looking at the sky, at tumbling doves that somersaulted in mid-flight. Then he walked down into the living water, washed his face with it, held up his hands.

It was almost as though he always had been able to see; as if his whole past life had been altered.

The eklesia marched on, still streaming water.

The Tyropoean valley was theirs. Once the vanguard of their procession had passed under one bridge, Yoanna's people would desert it, scampering up onto the high road and running ahead onto the the next bridge. The cheering, the waving, the singing never ceased. Yoanna's cheeks seemed to swell, go more plump and red. *You've done this*, Maryam thought, *you planned this all*.

The roaring of the crowd came in waves, and made Maryam feel that it could lift her up off the ground and sweep her off to the highest tower on the Hasmonean palace.

People above them on the main road tapped each other's arms and pointed. *That's him, that's the man who raises the dead.* Some raised eyebrows or thinned their lips in anger. Others shrugged: *he doesn't look much.* People began to keep pace with them to get a better look.

Not all the noises were friendly. On the high road, yobs cupped hands around mouths and shouted insults, their eyes enraged. Men in white linen shook their heads or amused each other making monkey-like gestures. Others scowled, talking with each other earnestly and twiddling their beards. Some stupid kids were bouncing up and down as if crazy, mocking them.

But, around them, Maryam saw either elation bursting out of people's faces or hollowed-eyed awe, perhaps even fear.

The Rock caught up to them, his face split like lightning by a smile, Shushan on his back. Yakob, Maryam, the Migdali clustered around them. The Migdali and Maryam for no other reason than to vent, howled and hugged each other, and all the family began to jump up and down in unison.

From somewhere, those bloody Kana'im began to shout, idiotically, "Hail the King of the Yehudai!" Yakob's face was crossed by worry. A crowd of this size could mean trouble.

The general noise seemed to grow, become almost hysterical, bellowing something almost angrily at them. Perhaps the cry came from opponents?

Maryam couldn't make the chant out at first. Hissssss eee awhah?

Hossshhh nyah?

"It's not Common." Maryam realized. "It's liturgy."

Hosi-ana?

She dug deep trying to remember where it might have come from in scripture. Maryam repeated it, shouting to Yakob, the Migdali leaning in. Yes, in the liturgy, Hosi-ana.

It was as if that focussed the cry. Thousands began to chant clearly over and over Hosi-ana! Hosi-ana! The hills of Yerusalam resounded with it. Maryam looked at Yakob, and her son was nearly in tears. "Hosnee yar?" he said. "What does it mean?" Yoanna joined them, leaning in to hear Maryam.

"It's in one of the Mizmor." She felt a chill run up her arm. "Only one. It means something like 'help us'. It's plural, a request. Please save us?"

Tears of confusion slipped down Yakob's cheeks. "Save them? Save them from what?"

Even Maryam was shaken, partly by Yakob's tears. She remembered him at ten, weeping at the sight of the Temple – perhaps that had not been timidity even then. Maybe Yakob could sense the Spirit move? Or something like?

The sound of the shouting slammed into her like a fist, made her jump, and she herself felt almost afraid. "I don't know. Sickness? Their lives?" She thought of her own life. She blurted out a chuckle. "Everything?"

The Migdali seized Maryam's wrist. "They understand. They just know."

Maryam had to laugh in something like elation as well as terror. "Even we don't understand! How can they?"

The Migdali pulled Maryam to her. "He will save us from God."

* * *

The riverbed ended and opened up at the foot of the Mount.

The eklesia merged with the Pesach crowds – a wall of pilgrims lined up unmoving on the steps of the southern entrance. Some of the Calling Out were waiting for them, a river of them, perhaps originally to make sure the Son had a clear passage. But the press of people was too great and that channel had closed. The rest of the Calling Out surged forward to greet them.

The sheer noise and numbers bewildered Maryam and made her feet uncertain where the ground was. She stumbled, nearly twisting her ankle. The donkey danced backwards in fear, the Migdali wrestling with its reins. The little boy who had first shaded the Son joined them grinning, still balancing his palm frond on his thigh. They edged their way through people.

Old women, dazed young men, flushed girls, and ox-faced peasant men pressed in around them. Their faces looked both surprised and delighted and they reached for them. One woman pressed her face against the Son's left foot, weeping, overcome.

Wild with breathless emotion, the crowd turned and began touching anyone who was with the Son – Maryam, Yakob, or the Rock with Shushan on his back. People shouted, "The Family of the Son!"

A woman with eyes wizened shut as if blasted by sunlight seized Maryam's hand and kissed it. She looked so much like Idra back home that Maryam stroked her face. "That's his Mum," someone said. How did they know that?

Their progress stopped.

The Son stood on the donkey's back. This was a trick for athletes, not someone who had never ridden before. But the beast stayed both firm and placid as he rose to his feet.

The crowd knew or guessed who this was. He emitted a piecing cry that muffled theirs. The eklesia at least fell silent though the roar of the holy day still battered back and forth up the alleyways and hillsides.

The Son gave them a new four-note tune that scanned: Hoseeeee AHHHH na. Hosi, Hosi Ana.

It was a beautiful tune. He sang it again, and rolled his hands, and tried to get them to sing it too. The people made the usual murmured ruffling sound when people are uncertain about notes and words.

"Sing out," he cried. "You know the Lord can hear each one of you. You know the Lord sees you in each and every moment." And he sang again, and added a new phrase.

Save us please, our Father in Heaven.

The song swelled, quoting from a Mizmor. The stone the builder threw away has become the cornerstone.

A lake of people extended placidly all the way to the mouth of the southern entrance, its staircase hewn out of rock. Towering overhead as if threatening to topple, the Royal Stoa occupied the entire Southern end of the Mount.

The Son began to grin. He got the merry, excited look he used to have with his gang back in Nazareth.

"We are going to the Temple. And all of you will get me there." The grin got wider and suddenly he began to chirrup, a silly, loose-shouldered kind of song. "You're going to carry me to the Temple." He sang it several times. It did not catch on but people heard it. "You're going to carry me to the Temple."

And then he stepped off the donkey's back, smiling, pleased, as if anticipating a joke. He stepped onto raised hands.

As if he weighed a whisper, he simply walked across the crowd as if it were the surface of Lake Tiberias. The crowd roared, hooted, ululated. Those on the Temple steps spun around in surprise. He stepped from one upturned palm to the other.

The roar of the crowd focused into the new song, rising and falling. Hosi-ana!

Then as if lightly disembarking from a boat, he stepped onto the first of the tunnel steps. Hand over his heart, he bowed to them all. The eklesia cheered, and the Son turned to climb the southern stairs.

The eklesia followed, one orderly step at a time.

Rut suddenly drooped, hanging from Maryam's hand, a dragging weight. Maryam also felt weighed down. Yakob knelt and scooped up Rut. He began to sing to her the song "I'm going to carry you to the Temple." She giggled and hid her face in his beard. The crowd moved in unison, one slow step at a time.

With Yakob's help, Maryam finally got to the top of the stairs.

By then it was getting late. The Temple shone in the last of the sun, white and gold blazing, as if the spirit of God glowed out of it.

In the blue shadow of the Stoa steps, cast sideways over the Place of Gentiles, the Son was preaching.

Somehow as always his voice carried. Exhausted, Maryam fumbled for her bag, for her reeds, her inks. The Migdali took the tiny glassware out of Maryam's shaking hand and pulled its stopper for her. The Migdali said, "Matt got here ahead of us. He'll be getting this down, too."

Maryam tried to listen and tame the rebellious parchment at the same time.

Someone shouted at the Son asking by whose authority he spoke. "By whose authority did Yehonnan the Anointer speak?" It was a clever answer and people chuckled. Yehonnan had been a Southerner, killed by a Northern king. Who here would dare say the Anointer had no authority? Though he anointed with water and not perfumed oils.

Maryam's cut reed still had not taken the ink. She tapped it again in the glass, and began to write, though the ink had gone somewhat yellow.

Yehush said, "Whoever believes in me does not believe in me only, but the one who sent me. I have come into the world as a light so that no one who believes in me should live in darkness."

The kinship he was claiming with God worried Maryam. Had he been this bold before?

"If someone hears my words, but doesn't keep them, I don't judge that person. I didn't come to judge the world but to save it."

The eklesia roared like one great beast, and began to sing again, those three notes, Hosi-ana.

But Maryam soured. She didn't want a milksop God who didn't judge. She wanted a God who would avenge; who saw what was hidden, what Miltiades had done to her daughters and strike him sterile or blister his balls with cankers.

And along with the very next phrase came that God.

"There is a judge for the one who rejects me and does not accept my words. The very words I have spoken will condemn them at the Last Day."

And the cheers rose up. Yes! People's faces were joyful because the Son promised them that God was always with them, knew them, saw their sufferings. The people yearned for that love, and that vindication.

They wanted revenge.

Maryam corrected herself. Call it justice.

Cold night did not disperse the Calling Out.

Some of the followers took off clothing and piled it in the place of Gentiles to make a fire. They looked as if they had been made anew, in a new Eden. The light from the clothes-fire flickered, red sparks swirled up into the sky. The singing swelled.

Yoanna stood. "I think this is going to go on all night." Rut lay asleep across Maryam's lap. "I'll take her back," said Yakob.

"I'll show you the way," said Yoanna, suddenly gentle and soft. She touched Yakob's arm. "We'll go together." Yakob and Yoanna?

"I'm staying," said Maryam.

"Ah, Ami, of course you are." Yoanna chuckled and hugged her. Yoanna was being someone else again. *People with many selves rule the world.* Yoanna's voice was warm and sleepy. Yakob left carrying Rut, cradling her as if he wished she were his daughter. The three of them were swallowed by the night.

Maryam stayed to join in the singing. Stray priests sucked their teeth with disapproval, but no matter. This was pure goodness. Unclothed, Andreas, BarTalemi, even giant Shemenolo had no fat under their skin. They were as lean as barked twigs. The fire was warm and sent up sparks as if moving stars.

Fully sixty of the eklesia spent all night in the empty Court of Gentiles, singing Hosni Ana or Happy Are or Our Father. Maryam pressed her cheek sleepily into the shoulder of Andreas, whom she did not even particularly like. She rolled to look up at the stars, and rested her head on the thigh of the giant Shem. He snored. The Migdali giggled and Maryam rolled next to her and the two of them sang, the Migdali trying to teach her Our Father. Maryam always got the words wrong.

"This is love," said the Son. But there were no parables or preaching.

The sky greyed, and Shem the Canali volunteered that he knew the way back to the house where they were staying. There were still stars overhead, pale. They walked down the rough way that both was and was not a river, out through the Gate of Water, and all the way up along the Valley of Kidron, listening to the creek laugh. It must have been an hour's walk, but Maryam's mind was dimmed into chuckling forgetfulness.

She found her way to the roof of some house in which they were all staying, and in swelling dawn, she saw her son Yakob, protectively half-mooned in an arch around little Rut. Maryam joined them, sinking into sleep, hearing roosters, and singing a one-note whining song that in her mind was the sound of goodness.

CHAPTER 26

THERE WAS A BOY

The Son of Adam preached on the steps of the Stoa every day for a week.

The crowds were never again as huge but, still, some hundred gathered every day.

They were the old, the destitute, the scholars, and members of the old eklesia, most of them now camped out over the brows of the hills or staying in windowless rooms along the road.

The new songs became popular. The Son evidently loved singing them, swinging his arms with bunched fists, "The stone the Naggar threw away is now the cornerstone." A new version of the tune umpitty-pumped cheerfully.

At night, they returned to the house across Kidron. It was not fashionable, but it was huge and comfortable, multi-roomed and multi-floored. Normally it housed some of Yoanna's household staff and her uncle when he was in the city on business.

Her uncle was an old man but, unburdened by wife, children, or worries he somehow gave a youthful effect – wistful, slightly lost, and kind. "Oh, so many new names." His mouth did a thin sideways downturn when Yoanna wondered aloud if Maryam and her family could sleep in his room. "Maybe that would better with the little one."

"I'd have to move my things," he said blinking. Yoanna laughed. "Don't worry Uncle, you'll keep your room." She adored him. She sat next to him on the same dining couch all through dinner, with an arm through his. "When I was twelve, when I was sixteen, this man saved my life." Even the Migdali looked on her with kind eyes then.

The first few nights in the house had an air of congratulation. The progress had worked – word had spread. The preaching at the Temple was still a success, relatively. The Stoa was for commerce not the spirit, but there was a reasonable attendance. Shem, Shushan, Andreas and many others who were staying elsewhere would crowd into the house for dinner and there were many stories from the road. A sandal stuck in the mud at Yarden that washed up clean on the opposite shore. A pigeon that had plopped on someone's hair. Smoke and laughter and lamplight.

Yoanna lowered herself onto Maryam's couch. "Ami," she said warmly. She asked about the day's teaching.

Maryam was thoughtful. "He keeps saying he's going to die."

Yoanna gave her head a quick shake and swallowed her wine. "That won't happen."

He is God. You are not.

Yoanna held up a hand. "I've talked to the Kohen Gadol. If there is any kind of trouble they'll just exile him for a few years. You've seen what's happening here." Her eyes glowed. "People in all the schools love him. He's uniting the Beni Yisrael, but more than that he's uniting us with all the peoples, the Sidonai, Greeks, Canalai all joining in the worship."

You do not have the Holy Spirit. I don't either. "He raised the dead. That is not of this world."

"The Kingdom of Heaven will be the worship of the true God here."

Maryam was firm. "You haven't heard him. He keeps saying he's going to be killed."

Yoanna's nose went sideways and she sniffed. "He needs to stop saying that." She stood up and went to talk to the Son. The Son turned his face up at her but his smile looked blurred. Then he pressed his hands together and looked at Yoanna earnestly as she spoke.

The Migdali stood next to Maryam, put a hand on her shoulder, and said, "Yoanna's got another plan. That one always does." Maryam had no answer.

The day after that, Maryam woke late.

Her hip hurt. She had not slept during the night and so had drifted off to sleep as dawn rose. She needed help down the external staircase from the upper floor.

It would soon be Seder and she worried about how they would be able to observe it. Today was the day to select the lamb and if Yoanna did not provide, none of them had any money for it. Finally in the afternoon, Maryam swung her bad leg down the valley road and back up – so far, so hot – to get to the Place of Gentiles.

There she found the crowd divided and shouting. Stall-owners from the Stoa were raising their fists, and shaking whips or cudgels at the eklesia.

Maryam recognized Kana'im among them. They bounced up and down into each other's arms, smiles fierce, eyes wild. "He's done it!" one of them shouted.

Mattit-yahu ducked and weaved his way towards Maryam.

"Trouble," she said.

He only nodded, and with his back shielding his scroll, unrolled the clips and indicated she should read it. The Yehush-saids were full of insults, calling people thieves and robbers. The Son had said the Temple itself was infested with snakes.

"He tried to drive them out," Matt murmured.

"Who?"

"The market people selling doves. Or scrolls."

The Son kept getting wilder. "Was he talking about dying again?" Maryam asked. Matt just nodded yes.

Every part of Maryam felt weary, but the ache really did settle in her hands. "I've stopped writing down such things."

Matt continued muttering, "Afterwards – he took a whip to them. A whip! He's never hurt anyone before. He said afterwards. 'They are not here to worship. Why should they live when I will die?'"

"Where is he?"

"I don't know. He said he wanted to be alone."

Maryam scanned the crowd, her heart aching. Her child really did think he was going to be killed. Shemenolo was standing between two merchants and young men she knew to be Kana'im. The Rock was keeping the two sides apart.

She fought her way closer to him and asked where the Son was. The Rock looked utterly weary – creased and baggy, his massive shoulders hunched almost up to his ears. "With Yakob."

"Where?"

He jerked his head in the direction of the hills. "This is no place for you, Mother." The Kana'im spun away from the merchants laughing. "Sell your hides!" they shouted. The Rock shook his head, and took her arm. "Let's get you home."

The house was flooded with afternoon light and that felt wrong.

Maryam had nothing to do, which she hated, and that made her fret more. Where was Yehush? What on earth had gone wrong? Yakob finally brought the Son back at dusk, holding up a hand against any questions. The Son still had a scowling face. He went off into a corner and took up the house's one scroll of scripture and sat reading it. Yakob bowed his forehead to touch Maryam's. It had been a terrible, long day for him. Maryam could smell bitter sweat and exhaustion.

Maryam approached the Son, said something motherly, was not rebuffed, and so took his stiff shoulders in her hands. Still he did not move or speak. She asked him if he was feeling angry; why he had struck people.

What he said then was so far from making any sense. What kind of love was it that loved freedom so much it let all things either burst or freeze? What kind of love would let even itself go dark and cold?

"It will make everything one even temperature," he said, staring ahead, angry and somehow desperate. "No hot, no cold, no difference to do work, just death." He turned to her with agonized eyes. "How could something like that love?" She hugged him, but found no words. His eyes kept staring.

He ate nothing that night. Maryam was on the upper floor and heard footsteps on the roof. She climbed up the ladder. The Son was sitting bolt upright, staring at the stars.

She sat next to him. He said, "It's all so small, really." He looked at her and told her, "Sleep."

And suddenly it was morning and she was folded up on the roof, hips and elbows stiff and splayed.

She drank water, broke bread, and swung her bad leg down and then up the hill, this time with Shem who was carrying Shushan.

Shushan was looking at the hills around them. "This is the best time of year," she said. "Clear skies, but still cool, you can gather in the forecourts and listen all day." She looked up. "You feel your spirit could go up into the clouds. Leave this sick old body." Her teeth were broken and stained, gummed over with something. *Was everyone talking about death all the time?*

A line of scowling merchants stood across the Stoa steps, arms folded. Worse, there were some Empire soldiers, in leather armour with swords, spears, shields, ready for trouble. The Son was not allowed on the steps, so the eklesia – the smallest group yet, no more than thirty – sat in a circle around him.

Mattit-yahu was cross-legged on the pavement, scroll across his lap. Maryam got out her own tiny jar, and the reeds that kept splitting and freckling her hands.

It did not start out as a good day's Calling Out. He talked about stars like dust, how suns thought, how time was a river that flowed in all directions at once. Again, she gave up trying to write.

Then suddenly in that keening voice that drew attention, he started to speak plainly. She had learned to hate the keening – it could break words into rubble. But he told a recognizable story, though partly singing it with sudden elevations into eagle-like notes. He hardly sounded human.

There was a wayward boy
whose mother fought him
out of love
to stop him being hurt.
So is your Father in Heaven
sometimes stern
to help you avoid pain
God knows your pain
that cannot be avoided.
God burned beyond ages until
the universe first opened its mouth to speak.
The Word was fire and light.
The Word was heavy shadow,
denser than rock.
Know your mother loves you.
Your father who is also your mother.
God sees and knows your pain
Your mother's love is your lodestone star.
Always shining,
never leaves you,
always there.

Maryam wrote none of that down out of embarrassment. She was angry, confused; a fly flew into her open mouth, and all the light in her eyes seemed to shine upwards with the solidity of pillars.

"Love," the Son whispered but somehow they all heard. Could there be a miracle of hearing? If words could be heard over the sounds of the market, was that a miracle?

Suddenly the Son's posture and expression had cleared. He looked like a stonecutter.

"Cooking a meal." he said in a normal voice. "This is a parable about cooking a meal. How many of you here have cooked a meal with someone you love?"

A murmur of assent. Most of them had.

"Do you remember the joy you had in the work?"

One woman spoke up, "Not in our house." That got a laugh.

The Son laughed too. "Remember when every task was done in order? All the vegetables peeled, laid out, cooked to time? How the flour and water and sage were kneaded together when there was no meat, and how someone else bought the broth to a boil to cook them? And how the feast was ready for the guests?

"So love brings together the flour, the water, the herbs, and makes the work a delight. When we are angry, we hate the work. The chopping and the kneading and the boiling feel like slavery.

"Love makes all tasks easy. And so this task I am about to undertake will go simply and well."

"What is the task?" someone shouted.

Towards the end of his life, old Yosef would sometimes look at Maryam with such a light in his eyes, which were narrow not wide, as if he were about to cry, except the face overall was joyful. So the Son looked now.

"Saving you," he shrugged, as if it were something small. "All of you."

The cheer spread slowly like ripples across a pond.

And the Son clenched his mouth, pushing up his lower lip. Staggering very slightly, he stepped down.

And somehow Maryam knew: he'd finished speaking. The Calling Out was done.

CHAPTER 27

THE OLIVE PRESS

The first dusk of Pesach came.

Yoanna's uncle felt that he was head of the house. He tussled with the Son as to who would wash the guests' feet.

The Son was immoveable. "You will be here in this house next year," he said, and carried the bowl, and kneeled in front of his students. Then everyone insisted that the Son sit at the head, with all the others fanning out, couching themselves around the table.

The first cup came and the uncle recited the Kuddush. "Blessed are you, O Lord our God, king of the universe." The questions, the first drinking, the singing of the Hallal Tela, all went well.

The Son started to talk. Both Maryam and Matt lunged for their reeds; but it was another stretch of nonsense. Their eyes met; they now both wrote down what they could and compared.

For Maryam, these words were shrouded in fog; she could not even wrench them into grammatical form. Matt shifted closer to Maryam with his scroll. His version of the words were clearer and may even have been what the Son was trying to say – that the lamb they were eating was actually

338

him. He was the sacrifice. The wine was his blood. Then the unleavened bread was his body. And that somehow they would go on eating him?

The Son stared at the walls. Maryam recognized the frozen face, the air of distraction from his return to Nazareth. She knew that he was seething inside. This is how he had looked just before he walked off into the night.

He was going to bolt again. Trying not to alert anyone, Maryam slipped on her sandals.

When he jumped up, she was ready. Without saying anything, the Son strode out of the door with Maryam limping after him. Behind her Yakob was hopping one-footed into his sandals.

The Son marched out of the courtyard, up the road with its high blank walls and bolted gates. With her hip, Maryam could not keep up. As he walked, the Son punched the air.

Amid the sprawl of the city was an old olive press.

It was ruined, but still had a small garden around it. After Seder it was now full of families and children strolling, enjoying the view. Some pilgrims were sleeping rough.

The Son prowled around the park, his hands in fists. A woman's face fell when she saw him, full of fear. The Son growled and suddenly thrust his way through shrubbery to sit folded and hidden in the midst of a thicket. Maryam was able to slip along his trail of broken twigs.

Silently, she took his hand. It was shaped exactly like hers: thick with stubby fingers almost as wide as it was long. The two hands intersected like links in a chain.

They sat in silence as the students called for him. "Rabuli? Rabuli?"

The Son hissed at her not to speak and lifted up the mingled bundle of their hands and kissed them. His face was wet. She made to cup his head, but he fought down her hands and shook her, quite hard: *stay still. Say nothing.*

They waited. Anxious voices asked, "Have you seen a man? Very short. Clean shaven. Walk through here?" or "I know you, you are one of us. Have you seen the Son of Adam?"

They waited motionless in near total darkness. Maryam began to hear the Son breathe – regular and deep. Had he fallen asleep? She nudged him. It seemed to her that he sat up, had indeed slept.

He kissed her hand once more and released it. There were crickets wheedling all around them. The Son coughed and spoke.

"The thing, one thing, that gives me strength. Is. God does not just live in all times at once, but all worlds at once. The world is made of tiny burning stars that do not have a defining shape until they are seen. God sees them and decides, but the other decisions exist as well. World on world on world – all different, branching like a tree, the tree of the Kingdom. God is whole and seen whole only from all those worlds. And at all those times."

"I don't understand," said Maryam. "No one will understand."

"So only God can know God." His voice was breathy, low, like wind. As lonely as wind can sound.

The Son coughed. Or it may have been a sob. In the darkness, Maryam couldn't see, so she gave an extra stroke on top of his hand and then squeezed it, and he squeezed back.

"It means there is a world in which God does not kill me."

"What's different in that world?" Maryam wanted to make this world like that one.

"I can only glimpse it and it's like a fan opening over and over with the same faces only slightly different. Sometimes different stars. Sometimes... sometimes I was born a man."

As he breathed, he creaked like old leather. "There's so much about being human that I will never do. I will never have children, or raise them. I'll never have a wife, someone of my own. God wanted to live all those things too. Here, it wants me to die."

"Why?"

A voice, the Rock's called, "Rabuli, is that you? Rabuli, are you all right?"

Maryam raised her voice. "He's fine Shem, he's OK."

The Migdali's voice. "What's going on? Is there a change of plans? Is he all right?"

"We are talking."

Andreas's voice, barTalemi's, all of them. "Can we see him? Can we get in there? Rabuli, can I help you?"

Something burbled up in Maryam, something she hadn't let herself know was there. "Leave us alone! Let us talk. Please!"

She heard the Migdali herding them. "You heard what Ami said. They're talking. He's good. Come on. We can sit over there. Believe it or not, Andreas, we are not needed right now."

The silence settled.

The Son whispered. "I can't understand it all. But God does not have to do things in order. Here, my dying and its dying with me creates the sympathy. The forgiveness. The understanding that it is horrible to die. And what's horrible about it is. Is that each time someone dies a part of the universe dies too. And so over time, whole peoples go – their songs, stories, wisdoms."

"What does that mean?" Maryam shook their hands hard.

"I must die. So that God lives through the death and so changes. And so God will let you all live in the spirit."

The voice faded. Sounds of night. That bulbul again, and crickets. Maryam waited.

"I've had a glorious life, Ami. Being a kid in Nazareth, running around the place. Aba reading to me over and over until I would never forget a word of scripture. Our mule. Babatha bossing everyone around. Yakob always there, my best friend. And then this. Hosi-ana." He kissed Maryam's hand again.

He's frightened. Maryam took him in her arms and rocked him. Bulbuls and crickets. She said, "You say there is more than one world, this one many times over."

He was almost asleep and murmured. "Dreams are just the lives you live in those other worlds."

"And they are all real."

"All real."

"Then ask God to make it be that you have to die now in just one of those worlds. It can learn from that, can't it?"

In the dark, she could feel his flesh shake no.

But she pressed on. "Then live in just one. Just one world you can die at eighty in your bed. Let this God of yours live through that."

He went still, and everything was held in balance, and then he shivered. "There are too many."

It wasn't rage or anger or even fear she felt, nor boredom when he spoke for hours of incomprehensible things. It was despair that her flesh and blood should know all this and it all be so beyond her.

He slept a little while longer. Then he sat up. "They're coming. It's here."

Then she heard it too, the clatter of leather strips over moving legs and slight metallic noise of swords.

She whispered. "How would they know you are here?"

"They've been searching everywhere."

She shook his hand. *Hide here.*

They heard troops speaking Greek, demanding to know where the one calling himself Yehush of Nazareth was. Was he here? He had been seen coming here. Someone said, "Who? No, no, nothing like that."

Then an anxious female voice. "They're lying. They were all talking to someone hiding. I heard them."

Shouting and threats.

The Son said, "I won't be taken cowering in a bush."

With a crackling of branches the Son stood up. The collar of his tunic caught and tore. The Son pulled himself through the branches and broke free. He said with a calm voice, "Here I am."

Torchlight danced, burning the eyes and making everything dark. Maryam could see almost nothing. She stumbled, limped, and nearly fell.

"That's a woman talking," said one of the soldiers.

"Yeah, they say he's a bit like that, you know, one of them." A soldier mimed effeminacy, and the other soldiers laughed.

"They're all like that, the whole bloody lot of them."

Everyone, the families, the students, some of the eklesia were all standing up now in alarm. In the torchlight that masked all.

"Are you Yehush of Nazareth?"

When the answer was yes, they clustered round, soldiers, rough boys from rural places wearing round leather helmets and sweat-smelling wool. "You've made enough trouble," said one of them, and pushed him. They encircled the Son with spears and then like wind in a bush fire, swept him away.

No, no, thought Maryam. *Not this soon, not this quickly. He's done nothing to hurt you Romans.*

The apostoli and the students looked stunned, skittish. BarTalemi and Yake the Lesser had melted away. Yakob seized Maryam's hand, as did the Migdali. Maryam began to pull them. They resisted. She pulled them harder, straining to march.

"Where are we going?" the Migdali protested.

"To the house of the High Priest," said Maryam. "The soldiers have to take him there. It's our laws that rule in Yehud."

"Do you know where it is?"

"It was once my second home." Maryam could feel the pulse of surprise go through Yakob and the Migdali.

Already across the vale of Kidron, she could see the centre of the city, its palaces and the villas of the priestly class. There was almost no light, no lamps in any windows. There was no singing or sound of prayer. Dogs barked – the darkest and quietest time of the night. Ahead of them and behind them the sound of feet, in darkness on dry soil.

CHAPTER 28

HIM

The Kohen Gadol was seated on a chair in his courtyard.

Caiaphas, that was his name. He looked cold and sleep-befuddled, still in his nightclothes with a shawl thrown over his shoulders. Eyanaphon, that viper, sat next to him, comfortably sprawled.

And next to both of them, Yoses, Maryam's son.

In the white linen of the Sadducai, Yoses had grown into a polished young man. The two authorities were waiting while Yo-yo wrote with a stylus on a wax tablet on his lap. He saw Maryam and wilted, eyes closing briefly then opening again. His shoulders sagged as if under a weight.

The Son stood in his old homespun, mosaicked now with patches of dust and spots of grease. His feet in his sandals were cracked, the toenails broken. Two Temple guards stood either side of him with spears. And next to him, arms folded, at the ready, Yoanna.

Yoses finished writing and Caiaphas flicked a hand towards Maryam and asked the door guards, "Who's this?"

Yoanna started to speak. "This woman is…"

Maryam cut her off, using her clarion voice, mustering her patrician accent. "I am that person's mother."

Caiaphas went very still. "I know you." He peered. "Yes, you're Maryam. Elisheba's cousin. God of my fathers. You were exiled. To Nazareth!"

Caiaphas turned to the Sadduci. "Eyanaphon! This is the son of mad Yosef. We exiled him to Nazareth. Naggar from Nazareth. Well it makes a good story."

They did not know who Yoses's parents were. And so they would not know that this was Yo-yo's brother. Maryam's eyes were hard on Yo-yo. *Are you that ashamed of us?*

Eyanaphon scowled. "I think I met him when he was thirteen. In the Temple. I remember thinking then he was already a great teacher and mad. No wonder. He'd been trained in madness by Yosef."

"And me," said Maryam.

Caiaphas gave her a long, worn look as if to say *I wouldn't take credit for that if I were you.*

Caiaphas resumed talking. "We have to cope with this now, in this house, and keep the Romans out of it. The best and safest thing to do is to say he is in his father's error, and exile him. Back home. To your tender care, Maryam." Caiaphas nodded in her direction in what could have been mistaken for respect.

The Son said his fine, light voice. "I have been in exile all my life."

The old man's bushy eyebrows shot up. "And for the rest of it too, if you want to live. For the Romans, you make trouble. I think your views are ill judged, but please understand. We are trying to save you. Go back to Nazareth. Be a builder. All will be well."

Maryam urged him in her head. *You can preach and prophesy in Nazareth. You can build a new Yerusalam there.*

"You want me in Nazareth, too."

Caiaphas let the hand drop and stood up. "Does that surprise you? You call us snakes, hypocrites, tell us the Temple will fall. You'd have to stay out of Nahum too, everywhere. Stop this... calling out you call it."

The Son smiled, warming to a secret joke of his own. "I could turn the making of a doorway's arch into the telling of truth."

"Good, then go and do that."

Then the Son said. "You are of course right. I am an enemy of Rome."

Caiaphas raised his hands in alarm and let them drop. "No. No-no-no. That is exactly what you do NOT say." He gave his head a quick whisk like he was mixing oil and water.

The Son said: "I won't argue with Rome. I will poison it, so that it will fall from within. To do that I will make it believe in the one true god."

Caiaphas froze. "Convert. Rome."

The Son said very quietly. "That is what I am going to do." With the strangest sideways smile.

"Convert Rome to the worship of the God of Yisrael?"

"To the one true God."

Caiaphas was almost yelping, torn between outrage and hilarity. "Will the Roman Emperor visit the Temple once a week? You think Rome will shift to Yerusalam?"

"More like Yerusalam will shift to Rome."

Maryam realized that she had no idea what the Son was thinking or planning. At that moment, Caiaphas turned to her.

"Mother. Please. Tell your son that he is going back to Nazareth, tonight, under cover of darkness. The Romans have already forgotten him, and all will be well." Caiaphas spun back and covered his forehead with a flat hand.

Maryam stepped up and took the Son's arm. "You can save yourself. Come."

The Son said, "It has to be."

Caiaphas whispered. "If the Romans think you are in revolt against them, you will no longer be protected by our golden laws. You will be a slave who has revolted. Do you know how Romans kill slaves who revolt?"

The Son smiled as if an endearing old aunt had spoken.

"They hammer them to stakes or trees. They call it apotumpanizo or anastauro. They never do it to Roman subjects. To my knowledge not one Yehudi has been subjected to anastauro in living memory. Apart from anything else it's against our own Law, and Rome respects that. That's how the Empire works. Everyone is left with their own gods and their own laws."

Yo-yo was not making notes but sat, cornered, knees together, fiddling with the stylus.

Eyanaphon said, "It would be a humiliation to every Yehudi. It would make us all into slaves."

Caiaphas held up a finger towards heaven. "We are a model for the rest of the Empire – law abiding, tax paying, educated." Caiaphas turned back to the Son, holding out his hands as if to receive water. "Do you have any idea what they do? You are nailed through your forearms. Naked. With your legs spread."

The Son seemed to flicker, and Maryam saw alarm in his eyes.

"You will void your bowels. Sometimes they stick a rod or spear into your genitals. Or they just castrate you in public first. Your feet. Your feet are either side of the stake..." Caiaphas spread his hands wide, and then seemed to hug an invisible cross. "And they nail each foot to the side. Through the heel." His index finger mimed being a nail jammed into the side of the foot. "If they want to be kind, they break both your legs so you suffocate."

The Son's eyes were so sad, like he was saying farewell to a friend. His smile was wide and thin lipped, without humour. Maryam had never seen a face like it – in mourning, full of regret, determined, somehow swollen with reserved power. And something almost vengeful, or perhaps angry. The sad eyes were looking through, out, beyond the walls of Caiaphas's house.

Tears stung Maryam's eyes. Anyone would be afraid. Anyone would be angry – she was. She was angry with God.

Caiaphas had become upset. "No Yehudi could do such a thing!" He threw his hand up with such force it nearly spun around him out of his chair. "The Law allows only four means of execution and anastauro is not one of them!"

Yes, thought Maryam, stoning, burning, strangulation, and decapitation – kindly ways to kill.

Caiaphas leaned forwards, spread his hands and spoke in a low pleading voice. "Please, young fellow. Please. Admit your fault. Say you will stay in Nazareth and cease to teach. At, at, at, at least for a time until they forget. They just want you out of Yerusalam."

"So do you."

"Yes. But we don't want you to die! Are we still snakes?"

"A nest of them."

The listeners groaned.

"There is something I have to do," said the Son in a low voice.

Caiaphas held up pleading hands as if to say: *Do it, but don't say it.*

Someone shouted, "Think." Someone else, a woman said,

"You can still teach us, Rabuli, teach us in Nazareth. We will go there with you!"

Caiaphas turned and looked wide-eyed at Maryam. "Talk to him, Mother. Take him home!" His outstretched, open palm showed the way to Nazareth.

Maryam said to the Son, "Let yourself be advised."

Yehush sounded like a ghost. "I must go to the house of my father." Maryam felt like her bad leg – numb, dead, and alien to itself.

Caiaphas bit his thumbnail, looked distracted, then waved. "Take him then, take him to Pilatus." Then he said, "No. Hold on. I will have to be there." He strode out to get dressed.

The big gate squealed open. Eyanaphon leapt to his feet like a young man and walked backwards toward the gate, eyes fixed on the Son. "Watch what you say. Rome lets us be!" Beyond the gate, the light was greying.

With the two authorities gone, Yoses stood up as if freed and strode directly to the Son. Maryam drew nearer as well. Yoses said briskly, "They are letting you go. Just go home. Yes, they want you gone, but they don't want to see you killed."

The Son looked at his brother with weary misgiving. "Hello, Yo-yo. They reject my teaching."

Yoses gave a quick headshake of impatience. He had become a tall, authoritative, self-contained young man, deep voiced though narrow-shouldered. "Everyone rejects someone's teaching. Sanhedrim, Zadokite, Essenai, Sadducai, Perisayya. We don't go around killing each other over different versions of the Law."

The Son jerked with something like a laugh. "Except when the Temple at Gerizim is destroyed."

"There is no reason for you to die."

Yoanna started to talk, crisply, firmly. "I know it's hard to end the Calling Out here. But go back now. Every general has to know when to retreat." She kept on talking.

Yo-yo turned to Maryam. "Mother," he said bowing slightly. She said nothing but eyed him. *You didn't come to mourn your father*. He held her gaze. "Anastauro is never..." He glanced sideways at the Son, "done to women."

A stirring to her right – Caiaphas had emerged from his house in gold-trimmed robes. Yoses jumped like a startled rabbit and spun back towards his tablet. *Run to your masters.*

Yoanna finished with, "Be advised!"

Briskly, quickly, the guards took each of the Son's elbows. Someone else held the gate against the strong dawn wind and Caiaphas trooped out first. Maryam fought a yearning to take one last look at Yo-yo.

Outside, Shemenolo, the Migdali and Yakob waited anxiously. "What happened? What was said?" They all started to follow the Temple Guard.

"They were trying to save him. Send him into exile."

"So where is he going now?" The Migdali sounded almost angry.

Almost by accident, Maryam said aloud what she was thinking. "He's trying to make it happen." The certainty of it clenched her. "He thinks it has to happen and he's saying things he's never said before."

Yakob said solemnly, quietly. "He said he is here to destroy Rome, didn't he."

"To convert it. To move Yerusalam there."

The Migdali's voice sounded oddly sharp and practical. "It's just as well he talks to one of us, at least."

Maryam took Yakob's hand. "Yo-yo was the scribe." Yakob winced and shook his head and tears started in his eyes. How could this be any worse?

By now, the sky was blue-grey. Already roosters in courtyards were crowing. Goats were bleating, and smoke from wood fires sharpened the air. Not a cloud in the sky, but a strong wind. Maryam had to hold her scarf closed around her head. The narrow streets and the broad squares were empty of people. Overhead doves flew.

The Roman Praetorium was a modest renovation to part of the Hasmonean Palace.

Caiaphas, the guards, and those who followed gathered in front of a small porch, the seat of judgement.

They waited, all of them Yehudai so they would wait on the Praetor's pleasure. The sun rose.

A servant came out with a beautifully carved chair with a back that looked like a lyre. They waited some more, buffeted by the wind. The Son did not move, or speak, or sigh, or shift from one foot to the other. Finally the Praetor emerged from a side door, blinking.

Pontius Pilatus had a creased and puffy face, his lips pressed inward, his eyes half shut. He dropped down onto the chair.

Maryam could see in his face that he'd been drinking late and had a headache, and that he hated this provincial posting among these strange people. *What now*? his face seemed to say. A small scroll was passed to him. He read it almost at a glance.

Without any preliminaries, he said the Son's name in Greek, making it into a question. "Ioachus?"

Caiaphas nodded yes and murmured something lost to the wind and discretion.

The Praetor sighed, looked at the Son and said, with effortless, disinterested clarity, mispronouncing the name in Common. "Yahooch, is that you? Speak up, I can't hear with this wind. You are charged with various offences. Those are religious matters and nothing to me. Public disorder and revolt are serious matters. Did you say that you are the King of the Yehudi?"

"So you say," replied the Son.

"I do not. Not at all," said Pilatus. "You're in trouble. Don't try to be clever." He looked up vaguely in another direction. "Where's he from?"

Caiaphas answered him, a finger across his mouth as if disguising a smile.

"Naza-what?" Pilatus looked disgusted.

Caiaphas murmured something.

Pilatus rose to his feet, and started to walk away. "The Galil? By the lake? That's not IN Yehud. Not my jurisdiction. That's governed by your Herod Antipas. He's here for the holy days. That door there. Go take this to him." Pilatus waved them away.

So Caiaphas, the guards, and the shrinking band of the curious and the heartbroken trooped round to the Eastern door.

Then they waited in the sun and wind until Herod Antipas came out. Antipas looked delighted. He was a slim fifty-year boy with twinkling eyes.

"So you're the Nazaredi! I've heard about you. Show me some magic."

"It would not be God's will."

"Ah. No? All tricks and sleights of hand? I still love magic. I could show you a few tricks, I'm sure. But enough of my hobbies. I'm told that you tell people not to follow the Law." Herod sounded as though he found the idea rather fun.

The priests looked not only sombre but downcast. Herod was utterly Hellenized. He spoke only Greek and Latin, stumbled over the Common Tongue and was positively proud that he understood not a word of liturgical expression. It was said that he had to read the Torah in the Egyptian Greek translation and came to the Temple once a year. He liked raising poultry and studying the stars.

"It's said that you don't sweep your house before Seder. Uh! The foundations of the State rock. You don't ritually cleanse yourself every time a menstruating woman passes by and you'd much prefer to chastise someone for insulting an old woman than for wearing a red dress. And ha ha ha. And a couple of days ago you whipped a money-changer in the Stoa?"

Herod raised up both feet and clapped his hands. "Oooooh! These Southerners won't like that. Cuts into Temple revenues. That kind of thing?" Herod thought he was a real charmer. "We're both from the North," he said. "All this nonsense about Yerusalam is all about their own power isn't it?"

The Migdali seemed to somehow settle like low clouds. "They're going to let him go, Mother. It will be all right!"

The Son said, "You will fall. All these little kingdoms. In a few years, you'll be nothing more than hard-to-translate letters to officials, with titles that mean nothing. You will all be scattered. New little priests will come in with new little books and new liturgical languages, and so it will go on. You will never get closer to God, none of you. Being a king or a priest does not bring you closer to God. Only one thing will bring people closer to God. That they have God in their hearts. And that is as true of slaves and women as it is of kings. I am not overturning the Law. I am overturning everything."

The Migdali, Yakob, the Rock – their eyes boggled with alarm.

"Oh in the name of heaven, he means it." Herod slumped. "Look, it's a holy day. I don't know what the Law says, but I'm not going to be bullied into slamming a madman into a dungeon because his nonsense alarms priests. Even if he has hordes of similarly deluded peasants cheering him on with palm leaves? Well there's a threat to the Empire and the Temple. Palm leaves. The troops will be quivering with fear. Rome itself must be thrilled from the vibration!"

Caiaphas stepped forward looking worried. "My Lord."

Herod waved him away. "He's crazy. Obviously some kind of eunuch. I don't know. He's weird. Amusing in small doses, and I would think mostly harmless. I don't want to have anything to do with this. He hasn't done anything in the Galil that I object to."

Caiaphas stepped forward. "My Lord. Please. Just sentence him to exile. We'll move him on at once."

Herod looked bored. "Right! Madman. You're in exile. Take him away."

The Son said, "Rome will fall too. And it will fall to me."

Herod's smile returned, but it was a chilling smile. He held up a finger. Like it was a needle he stitched the air with it. "Right. This IS the Praetor's problem. Aaaaaaaand. We'll have to go and wake him up!" Caiaphas stepped forward to speak again and Herod cut him off. "No, no. He's plainly speaking sedition against the Empire."

The Son didn't stop. "The Gods of Rome are false. They are not Gods, but superstitions, delusions. Rome is a cesspit of evil. It pollutes the world."

Herod was already up and striding away, gathering his skirts around him. "You've made your point, Madman. No exile." He chuckled. "Maybe they'll wake the Praetor by dousing him in cold water." He giggled.

So they all moved back to Pontius Pilatus's porch.

Exasperation at the back-and-forth turned to a bitter chuckling.

Maryam threw her bad leg like a sack of grain and bobbled up to the Son and said in a low voice. "Are you trying to get yourself killed!"

He looked so far away. Beautiful, really, like a wistful child, in sunrise in pink-gold light. Maryam suddenly stood in a hall of visual echoes – this striking hawk-like, pillow-like face when younger, older, child, and adult.

"God is doing what I asked. The Father agrees. So now I have to do this. It will be good for It. It has no idea what pain is." The Son was looking at his hand as if marvelling at its workmanship. "It's going to be taught very well."

Maryam caught hold of the hand. "Good. Die. You can live to an old age in Nazareth and still die in horrible pain. You can keep explaining things until we understand."

He finally turned to her, and really, the look could be so easily confused with love. "You all already know it." He meant pain.

Maryam began to cry. She shook the hand. "Please. Don't. Please."

The Migdali came up behind her and hugged her. "Listen to her, Rabuli, Yehush, please."

Almost imperceptibly, the Son shook his head. "God has to learn. It must not bully us. We are real. It leaves us free and so blames us for all the carnage. It doesn't understand. Poor, poor God. It doesn't know! That it is not freedom. We don't choose it."

He took both their hands. "Now let me do this."

"Noooooooooo," said Maryam. Her voice had not sounded so stretched and elongated since she was five years old.

"Suns die. All the stars die. But you won't. That's a promise."

Maryam stopped and pointed at herself. "Me. This. Here. Will not die?" It was so absurd it made her angry. Maybe the Son was indeed mad.

"I have undone death," the Son said.

Maryam stamped her foot. "You keep saying that. How?"

"You will all live. In God's Kingdom."

Maryam glared at him. "Does that mean anything?"

"Oh, it will mean. For all eternity."

Maryam, undone herself, let him walk on.

By the time the small group had reached the Praetorium, there were as many guards as people.

A few of the religious class who had been at the High Priest's house looked puffy-eyed but serious. The morning after Seder, everything was quiet, calm, the forecourt empty.

It can't be decided like this, thought Maryam. *Where are the people begging to be saved now? Where are the students, the women, and the five thousand who crowded the shore?*

A trumpet blew flatulently to announce the flatulent king, and suddenly it seemed as if the sound was taking the measure of how empty the pavements were.

The Migdali, huge and soft and smooth, shifted closer to Maryam, and clasped her hand and put an arm around her shoulders. She smelled of spices. Maryam clutched the woman's hand, rings on every finger like armour. Yakob took Maryam's other hand and shook it.

Pilatus emerged, looking more rumpled than the last time, squeezing the corners of his eyes.

"Brother!" said Herod and flung up his hands, strode towards the porch.

The Roman rolled his eyes. "Yes, Brother?"

Herod's middle finger and thumb were pressed together in a circle, the nails of which were pressed just under his lower lip. He looked like a naughty boy. His voice was low, and he looked almost merry. Pilatus smiled. His head gave a little shake and his chest rose and fell.

Maryam stood on tiptoe, almost hopping. She had to hear.

Pilatus's mouth lapped like little lakeside waves. He leaned forward looking bored and amused at the same time.

"It appears that I have to make the decision. This person has been preaching against Rome. He's said that the Gods of Rome are false, that he will convert Rome to the worship of your God. Whose name must not be said." He looked up at Herod and amusement shot back and forth between them, though Herod's smile looked strained. "And there was that ruckus the other day." He turned to the Son. "Do you still say that you will convert Rome?"

The Son said, "Rome will be Yerusalam. And the Temple will fall. And these people be scattered. Everything falls. Even Rome. Everything falls to God."

"Why should it fall to you?" Pilatus's face darkened.

"Because I am God come to Earth."

"I don't see many attendants. Not much glory."

"Gods do not look like kings."

"They don't look like peasants either. This man is mad, but he is also a danger particularly with these Kana'im about the place. And I have a headache. Crucify him, and that will be an end of it."

The Kohen Gadol stepped forward. "Praetor. We have never crucified here. We have no means to do it."

"Find a tree," said Pilatus.

Maryam knew what had to be done. She shouted, "You cannot crucify a woman!" Everything went still. The Praetor was looking at her. Maryam pressed on. "Crucify a man if you will, Lord, but this person is a woman."

Mournfully the Son turned his head. The Migdali gave a squeak and covered her face.

Maryam declaimed. "She calls herself Yehush, but she was born Avigayil."

A titter of amusement. Maryam turned on them. "I'm her mother."

"It's a matter easily resolved," said Caiaphas. He looked at Maryam, nodded and his eyes said: *well done*.

But the Son's face stroked downwards once, diagonally, and then over and over: *no no no no no*.

Pilatus shrugged, pointed, and two soldiers strode forward. They seized the neck of the simple homespun that Maryam herself had woven and stitched together. It was the colour of the dust of Nazareth, and would smell of that dust, and straw and bread and home, and three years on the road, and damp from baptising.

The soldiers grabbed the collar but the homespun wouldn't tear. Then they saw where the bush beside the olive press had torn it.

The Son's eyes were closed, and his lips were rabbiting in prayer, closed but frantic, nibbling as if on grass.

The Roman swords slithered out, as polished as mirrors, looking like they could leave a permanent cut in air. They dug into the cloth of the neck and sawed.

Caiaphas had worked back towards Maryam and took her hand. "This is true, right? You're telling the truth yes?"

Maryam was suddenly bitter and sarcastic. "I was there at the birth."

The swords cut the cloth. The ground rocked. The sky blinked. People cried, seized each other's hands, felt giddy. Then the shadow that had passed over the sky cleared and Maryam felt a gathering sense of dread.

The old robe fell away. The Migdali's hand jerked in Maryam's as if seized by a fit. For Maryam everything – the palace, Antipas, the Praetor – seemed ghostly.

The only solid thing was the Son, a blazing white as if a stronger sun shone upon him, white as if he were made of marble.

Under each nipple was a small pouch of flesh; a man who'd eaten nothing but bread for five years might have that. The pubes were as bald as a child's. There, a scrap of a penis lay dormant, resting on eggs. It was even circumcised.

Herod's face creased with amusement. "Behold the Man," he said.

As if in a nightmare, the Roman guards and even some of the crowd tittered.

Caiaphas dropped Maryam's hand and strode forward, bunching his fists. "Praetor, please! This man is a lunatic, from a family with a history of madness. Please, Lord! Let us deal with him!"

Pilatus looked weary. "The mother said crucify him if he's a man. So be it."

Maryam hissed. "I didn't say that!"

"As for the means, he's a tekton. Have him make it."

"We can contain his crazy teaching!" Caiaphas wailed, but Pilatus had already stood and was walking away. Maryam tried to shout, but her throat was clenched.

Yakob seemed to kneel at the feet of the Son, to pull up the torn robe. The Son did not move.

Pilatus and Herod marched off together, relieved, arms folded, friends it would seem, with Pilatus saying something laconic out of the corner of his mouth. Herod's head rocked back in amusement.

Like that? It was done as easily as that? There was a sound of wind, of cool morning shadow. It was unheard of, a Yehudi in his own city, a Kohen was going to be crucified.

It had taken a miracle to achieve that.

She was finished, everything was finished.

That was it, she was done. Done with God, done with Yerusalam, done with all of this. She turned and marched away, swinging her leg.

So learn, God. I hope being nailed hurts!

Voices behind her wailed. "Mother! Mother, please don't go!"

Maryam staggered on, her bad leg twisting.

The Migdali enveloped her, sheltering her. "Mother please! Please!" She wrenched Maryam round to look at her. "It were a miracle, Ami. Beautiful!" Her face was as smooth as polished limestone, fervent, yearning. "To give him what he wanted all his life."

Maryam might have screamed, screamed to make the Temple fall. Instead she said, "I have to see to Rut."

Maryam wrestled but the Migdali would not let her go. "It was kindness."

"To kill him?"

"Don't leave him alone now!" the Migdali begged her.

"God betrayed me."

Took my body, tore a child out of it without a husband, sent me to Nazareth. God could have made a Queen here on Earth. But THAT was the miracle it sent.

Yoanna was upon them. She reached out, blocked Maryam's path. "You can't go. He needs you."

"He's never needed me." Maryam shrugged her way free from them and stood confronting.

Yoanna's eyes were wide and watery. "We need you! To explain it to us. You understand it. We don't. I don't."

Maryam growled, "Eat your explanations!" Water sputtered out from her eyes, nose, mouth, and she threw off the Migdali's one light hand.

The Migdali was in tears too and turned on Yoanna. "She told ya already, ya stupid woman."

Both of them stalked Maryam, kept pace with her. Maryam stopped, turned and snarled at them. "We don't need an eklesia." She hadn't known that until she said it.

That stopped them. Maryam's hands curled into claws. "Do you think something bigger than all the stars needs us to worship it? What for?"

Yoanna's jaws thrust out. "We need to tell people to be good. His teaching, turn the other cheek."

Maryam laughed in fury. "And love your enemy, and never lust, and give away all your money. He only said all of that to show us that we're not big enough to be good. We can't do it. God needed to understand that too."

Yoanna was fighting, lips pressed thin. "And our Saviour needed to die to redeem us in God's eyes…"

Maryam groaned.

"… and, and if we believe in Him then God saves us for his sake."

The Migdali chuckled. "You're always having IDEAS."

We should have been made free from scripture. All scripture. Maryam fought the writing bag off her shoulder and thrust it at Yoanna. "Take it." She shook it at her. "Take it."

Yoanna did, looking confused.

Maryam was still angry. "I shudder to think what you will make of it."

Yoanna gathered herself. "Please. Be there with us? For him?"

Maryam thought of the horror and faltered. "I can't." The Migdali enveloped her in a final hug, and then Maryam walked away.

CHAPTER 29

MOTHER

Maryam walked towards Babatha through open countryside, carrying Rutit.

The child was wailing so Maryam let her slip out of her arms. The child stopped crying, with a sound like a gulp and toddled ahead. "Careful." Maryam stood up straight to arch her back.

Her feet had taken her down the usual road through Samara. Maryam had no idea if there would be a crossroad to Scythopolis. She yearned to be back with Babatha and be enfolded in her arms. But she dreaded the news she had to tell.

"This way," said Rut happy now, and took hold of her hand and pulled. "Go this way."

Maryam followed. Far away from the road, people were burning stubble, barley probably. Black smoke billowed and there were glimmers of red fire in lines. Rutit pulled her, and it began to seem as if they were racing the fire. Part of it was flowing across the field at an alarming speed.

"See Granny?" Rutit said.

Maryam narrowed her eyes, made them dark, and the fire gained an outline like a silhouette. *Of course it comes now.* She'd seen this thing before.

It both strode and swam over the surface of the ground. It flowed into another field, but passed over the broken stalks and left them unburned. It was like a shadow made of light.

It seemed to have legs but they kicked rather than walked, and the arms paddled, and the shapes from the shoulders were more like fins than wings. The presence stopped and those lacy attachments flowed on across the stony earth, swirled and then settled.

It paused at the edge of the empty ground next to the road. Maryam was sure it meant for her to catch up with it, and prepare herself. Perhaps it didn't want to frighten her.

Rut wanted to be closer and she pulled.

Something spoke – but not the fire or not only the fire or perhaps the fire was only there to be taken as a visible sign.

The voice throbbed out of the ground and through the soles of Maryam's feet.

It shook the edges of the clouds overhead, scattering feathery tops. The air all around her on her hands and cheeks thrilled like a drum skin. The voice came from everywhere, not just the scrap of pleading light.

Fascinated, Rut leant forward towards the light, finger arched, to touch it. Maryam snatched her away, but in so doing touched the light herself. This was a spiritual fire that did not burn. The field behind it was unscathed.

As the thing found words so did the ground and the sky. "Ami," they wailed. "A-meeee."

Maryam had raised seven children and she knew this sound. It was the sound of a child when it learns the world isn't fair, that things hurt, or that it has broken something that it loved.

Maryam sank to her knees in the dust. The fire on the ground thrashed its way toward her. It concentrated itself, folded, and crawled up onto her lap. As it juddered from grief so did the earth around her. The Creator of sand and stars had needed to know what it was like to be created by someone else. Now it needed its mother.

Maryam cradled God.